Linwood Barclay is an international bestselling crime and thriller author with over twenty critically acclaimed novels to his name, including the phenomenal number one bestseller *No Time For Goodbye*, and most recently the *Sunday Times* bestseller *The Lie Maker*. Every Linwood Barclay book is a masterclass in characterisation, plot and the killer twist, and with sales of over 7 million copies globally, his books have been sold in more than 39 countries around the world and he can count Stephen King, Shari Lapena and Peter James among his many fans.

Many of his books have been optioned for film and TV, and Linwood wrote the screenplay for the film based on his bestselling novel *Never Saw It Coming*. Born in the US, his parents moved to Canada just as he was turning four, and he's lived there ever since. He lives in Toronto with his wife, Neetha. They have two grown children. Visit Linwood Barclay at www.linwoodbarclay.com or find him on X at @linwood_barclay.

Also by Linwood Barclay

The Lie Maker
Look Both Ways
Take Your Breath Away
Find You First
Elevator Pitch
A Noise Downstairs
Parting Shot
The Twenty-Three
Far from True
Broken Promise
No Safe House
A Tap on the Window
Never Saw It Coming
Trust Your Eyes
The Accident
Never Look Away
Fear the Worst
Too Close to Home
No Time for Goodbye
Bad Luck
Bad News
Bad Guys
Bad Move

LINWOOD BARCLAY

I WILL RUIN YOU

HQ
An imprint of HarperCollins*Publishers* Ltd
1 London Bridge Street
London SE1 9GF

www.harpercollins.co.uk

HarperCollins*Publishers*
Macken House, 39/40 Mayor Street Upper,
Dublin 1, D01 C9W8, Ireland

This edition 2024

1
First published in Great Britain by
HQ, an imprint of HarperCollins*Publishers* Ltd 2024

ISBN: HB: 9780008555757
TPB: 9780008555733

For Neetha

ONE

Richard

I was steering my students through a discussion on morality and hope in Cormac McCarthy's novel *The Road*, getting bogged down in a debate over whether the reader needed to know what had brought about the apocalyptic conditions depicted in the book, when I happened to glance out the window and see, running across the staff parking lot, a young man wearing a vest that appeared to be loaded with sticks of dynamite.

"I just want to know what caused it," Eldon Delton had said just moments earlier. He was one of the brightest eleventh-grade kids in the entire school, but definitely a literalist. This English class wasn't his favorite—his passions were science and computers, and in all likelihood he'd one day be the next Bill Gates—because it was all subjective. There weren't always right and wrong answers. You couldn't break the story down into zeros and ones. The same book could be fantastic to one person and a pile of crap to another, and that didn't sit well with Eldon. He liked absolutes.

He continued. "Did life on earth end because of an asteroid? Was there a nuclear bomb? Vampires? Zombies? He never says."

"Oh God, Elmo, not zombies," said Olivia Comber, two aisles over, demonstrating what a huge favor Eldon's parents did him giving him a name that could be twisted into a puppet's. "If it was zombies they'd still be running around trying to eat people. They wouldn't just disappear. And not everything has to be *The Walking Dead* or *The Last of Us*."

"I was only saying, as an example," Eldon said.

I stepped in, waving the tattered paperback of the novel in my hand. The book wasn't part of the official curriculum. Most everything board-approved was out-of-date or so stripped of anything contentious that you couldn't engage the kids. If I could get away with the late McCarthy's *The Road*, I'd move on to Toni Morrison. I'd gathered up as many weathered copies from used bookshops as I could find. Some of the kids read online editions they'd either bought, or borrowed through the library.

I said, "I get Eldon's point. When they made this into a movie, they provided an explanation, and we can debate whether that was necessary. But I don't think McCarthy believed it mattered *why* it happened. What mattered was that it *did*. He wanted to explore what happens *after*, to explore what limits people would go to in order to survive when civilization collapses."

"Like eating people," said Andrew, who visibly shuddered. "That part really freaked me out. The cannibals. And that scene with the baby."

"Maybe you shouldn't be such a wuss," Eldon said.

"Hey," I said sharply, giving him a look. Everyone was supposed to be able to express their feelings in this class without being judged. And Andrew Kanin could be a convenient target.

He was on the small side for a fifteen-year-old. I kept hoping he'd hit a growth spurt that would make him less of a potential target for bullies, or even smart-asses like Eldon. He was sensitive, bright, and several years of homeschooling had left him, at least in my judgment, ill-prepared for social interactions with the other kids, but his math and reading skills were top-notch. Full marks to his mom, who had been his teacher until tough economic times sent her back into the workforce.

"The cannibal stuff is no worse than lots of other things in books and TV," Eldon said defensively.

"Should McCarthy have left that out?" I asked Andrew.

He considered the question. "No, I'm not saying that. It made me sick to read it, but it's the thing I most remember, so I guess that means it worked."

"I think it's a love story," said Emma Katzenback, who had, amazingly, decided to look up from her phone for a second. She had it down in her lap where she thought it would somehow escape my notice.

"There's no love story," said Eldon, rolling his eyes.

"Not *that* kind of love story," she shot back. "It's a father-*son* love story."

"Emma's on to something," I said, and it was then that something outside caught my eye.

A man—for a brief moment I thought he was in his mid-teens, but looking at him for a full second persuaded me he was probably as old as twenty—was crossing the parking lot, running between geography teacher Nancy Holcomb's green Hyundai and the three-year-old Lexus SUV that belonged to our principal, Trent Wakely.

He was decked out in camo pants, unlaced combat boots, and an olive-green vest with multiple pockets. Tucked into them, vertically, were items that looked like thick cigars, but cigars weren't generally flat red in color. I was certainly no demolitions expert, but I'd seen enough movies and TV shows to know what dynamite looked like.

The man was striding toward the school's west end, but only one arm was moving back and forth. His right hand was held close to his body, in a fist, as though he had it wrapped around something.

The first thing I thought of was the set of double doors our visitor was probably headed for. They often did not latch properly. Students, and even some staff, were known to prop them open with a brown rubber doorstop or wood shim so they could sneak outside for a smoke and still be able to get back into the building.

None of my students had looked out the window and noticed him. Barely two seconds had gone by since I'd responded to Emma's comment.

"I hadn't thought of that," said Marian Gilchrist, who always took a seat right at the front of the class, not so much because she was particularly studious, but because she wore glasses thicker than hockey rink ice.

I said, as calmly as I could, but unable to keep the edge out of my voice, "I'm going to the office. Eldon, close the shades. Marian, you lock the door behind me, block it with as many desks as you can."

The kids blinked, glanced at each other. A couple of them were forming questions.

"What's going—"

"Why—"

"*Now,*" I said, and because Emma already had a phone secreted in her hand, I pointed and said firmly, "Emma, nine-one-one."

She looked at me blankly, as though asking what it was she was supposed to say when her 911 call was answered.

"Armed intruder," I said. There wasn't time for specifics. And then I bolted from the room, slamming the door shut behind me, trusting the kids would do as I'd said and start building a barricade. Not a bad plan to keep a gunman out of the room, but would it be enough to save them from an explosion?

The west-end doors were at the far end of the corridor, which in the fifteen-plus years I had worked at Lodge High School here in Milford had never looked longer. The hallway was a mile-long tunnel stretching out in front of me. I needed to get to those doors before that man with the explosives strapped to his body.

I ran flat-out, shouting as I went.

"*Lockdown! Lockdown!*"

I sped past classroom doors, open and closed, lessons underway. Jerry Hillier, door open, droning on in front of his calculus class. The students in Rhonda Flynn's chemistry class, visible behind the door window, conducting God knows what kind of experiments. Social studies teacher Preston Hindle, visible for a millisecond through the small pane of glass, no doubt trying his hardest to turn his kids into well-rounded citizens.

I heard doors closing behind me. We'd done the drills. You think it will never happen but know it might. And yet, despite that, no one had fixed that fucking door. Par for the course for our caretaker, Ronny Grant.

Not everyone remembered our emergency procedures. Instead of closing her door, Rhonda stepped out into the hall and called out after me: "Is this for real or just a prac—"

Somewhere, someone wiser shouted: "*Get inside!*"

My route took me past the office. As I flew by I caught a glimpse of our principal, Trent, and shouted, "Lockdown!" one more time.

The double doors, with a steel pillar in the center, were thirty feet away. From this distance, they didn't appear to line up, which told me the door on the right was not securely latched.

Shit.

Twenty feet away.

And then, suddenly, there he was, in the window of the right door. Pulling it open wide with his left hand, his right hand still clenched around something, and stepping into the school.

I hit the brakes. We were practically face-to-face. It's possible I startled him as much as he scared me. He clearly wasn't expecting to encounter anyone, what with classes in session.

I said, "Stop."

He looked at me and blinked a couple of times. And that was when it hit me.

I know you.

I struggled for a second to come up with a name. "Mark," I said.

"Hey, Mr. B.," he said. It was what most of the kids called me. Short for Mr. Boyle.

Mark LeDrew. He'd been in a couple of my classes when he

attended Lodge. First time was way back in ninth grade, an English class, then in senior year, an American literature course he never read a single book for. He was a kind of benign fuckup, the kid who never remembered to bring a pen to an exam, who forgot to double-check that his locker was actually locked.

It had to be three or four years since he'd left. I wasn't even sure he'd earned a diploma, so it was unlikely he'd gone off to UConn or Yale. A tech school, maybe. Or, judging by his garb, he'd been living in the Michigan woods with a survivalist cult intent on overthrowing the government.

Firmly, and calmly, I said, "You have to leave the school, Mark. You can't come in here."

He swallowed. His eyes danced.

"I got something to do," he said.

"No."

The half-open door had come to rest on his back. He'd tucked his free hand into his pocket, an oddly casual gesture considering the circumstances.

I kept looking at his right fist held close to his body. His thumb was holding something down. I could make out the edge of what appeared to be a red button. My guess was, a wire led from that to the four sticks of dynamite tucked into the front of his vest. Two on his right side, two on his left. And if he let up pressure on that button, they would detonate.

"I've got a list," Mark said.

His head bobbed up and down ever so slightly, like his brain was keeping time to some unseen rhythm.

"A list?"

"I know who I have to get." He appeared to be thinking, strategizing. "Need to get them in one room together. I can only do this once."

I understood. You didn't get a second chance to lift your thumb off that button.

"Who do you have to get, Mark?"

"That wicked Willow, fat Sally, and the fucking lawnmower man most of all."

I was guessing he meant Herb Willow and maybe Sally Berwick, a guidance counselor. The "lawnmower man" reference made no sense to me, other than being the title to a horror movie or two.

Herb was a longtime staff member. Taught, among other things, physics and computer science, oversaw the school's chess club, which had been dead for years but came back to life after that Netflix series made chess cool again. I'd seen Herb in the staff room this morning, but tended not to engage. Any conversation with Herb meant listening to his latest list of grievances.

"Mark," I said calmly, "you can't come in here. You're a threat to others, and especially to yourself. It's against the rules." Like you had to tell someone that strapping dynamite to your body was not allowed.

Mark slowly shook his head.

"I don't want to hurt you, Mr. B., or anybody else, but I will if I have to. Maybe you can help. Get everyone together in one room. Then you can leave and evacuate the school. Might get messy."

"What I'll do is arrange a meeting," I said, "but without that." I nodded at his dynamite vest. "Don't want anyone getting hurt, especially you, Mark. What you've got rigged up there, it's kind of game over for everyone, yourself included."

Was I getting through at all? He seemed to be looking right through me.

"We get that shit off you, then we'll have a sit-down. I promise."

It was not a promise I likely could keep. If Mark didn't blow us up, didn't kill Herb or me or any of the other staff or students, he'd be arrested faster than kids fleeing a classroom when the bell rang.

"But first we need to get the right people here, deactivate that."

"They ruined my life," he said. "Mr. Willow, the perv."

Was that one person, or two? What I did know was, Herb Willow was my least favorite colleague. Grumpy, lazy, irritable. Griping endlessly about thick-as-a-brick students, clueless parents, and an out-of-touch administration. One time he wanted an inquiry into who wasn't rinsing out the coffee cups. He should have walked away from the profession years ago but hung on, I believed, out of pure meanness. I could recall Trent, in brief moments of unprofessionalism, expressing a desire to be rid of him.

"Mark," I said gently, "this button you're holding. You let go of that, and the dynamite goes off, right?"

"You catch on fast."

"Is there a delay? If you let go, do we have time to get the vest off you, throw it out into the yard?"

"A couple seconds maybe," he said.

"Can you break the connection? You let go and nothing happens? Is there, like, a wire I can cut or anything?"

"Not really."

I wondered whether I should just run. Try to make it around the corner, down another hall. Get some shielding from the blast.

"So just talk to me. Tell me why you want to do this."

"Mr. Willow said I couldn't find my ass in a dark room."

"Mr. Willow doesn't know shit," I said.

I sensed something going on behind me but was afraid to look over my shoulder for fear Mark would notice. Maybe the cops were here, although I'd heard no sirens, no soft footsteps of a SWAT team coming from some other direction. If there was one, I hoped to God they'd see what we were up against before someone took a shot.

"I got to where I believed him," Mark said. "I've been a fuckup since I left here. So I want to tell him he was right. That he called it. Made it happen. Said I had a head full of porridge. Said he had pieces of wood in his garage smarter than me."

I felt a rage boiling up inside me for Herb Willow.

"Don't let one asshole bring you down," I said, trying not to look at the dynamite but directly into Mark's eyes.

I thought about Bonnie. I wondered how long it would be before word of what was happening here would spread across town to the school where my wife was a principal. I imagined her running out to her car now. I thought about Rachel and how much I loved her. Wondered whether I would ever see my daughter again.

Love.

"There are people who love you, Mark. You might not think so right now, but I'd bet everything I've got on it. Your friends, your parents, your—"

That brought a reaction. A small laugh.

"Yeah, like they give a fuck," he said. " 'Specially my dad."

Then I had a memory about Mark.

"You remember Lydia?" I asked. "Lydia Trimble?"

An oddball, Lodge High's Carrie. An outcast from a poor family. Withdrawn, dressed in hand-me-downs, a target for adolescent tormentors. A couple of tall boys cornered Lydia one day, dangling her backpack in the air where she couldn't reach it, telling her to jump for it.

I was set to intervene when Mark LeDrew beat me to it, grabbing one of Lydia's tormentors by the hair and bashing his head into a locker almost hard enough to knock him out, then turning to the other asshole and telling him to return Lydia's backpack to her.

Eyes wide with fear, he did so.

But Mark wasn't done. "Tell her you're sorry."

"Sorry," the guy had mumbled.

And then, a second demand. "Tell her she looks really nice today."

While his friend was still massaging his head, the kid said, "You look nice today."

"Now fuck off," Mark said, and the two assholes took off.

I related the story. Mark nodded, remembering. "I thought you were going to expel me."

I'd forgotten the part where he realized I'd witnessed the altercation. All I'd done was mouth the word *Go* and let him get away with it.

"That's who you are," I told Mark. "You're that guy who stood up for Lydia. Not some guy ready to blow up the school and himself. Be that other guy."

I don't know that I'd ever seen such sadness in someone's face. If it weren't for his dynamite vest, I would have taken him into my arms, hugged him. His eyes, which only a moment earlier seemed vacant, now glistened, as though he were about to cry.

He took his left hand from his pocket and wiped away a tear from his left cheek. There was a second one trickling down his right cheek. I hoped he didn't reflexively wipe it away with his right hand, taking his thumb off the button in the process.

"Mark."

He looked away.

"Mark, listen to me. *Look* at me."

He did.

"I want you to walk out into the middle of the yard. Away from the building and the cars. And I'm going to call the police and tell them to get their bomb disposal guys here so they can get that thing off you safely. Hear what I'm saying?"

There was something in his eyes. He was really looking at me, for once. His chin started to quiver.

"I don't think I know how to stop it," he said.

"That's why we're going to call in the experts. You're gonna let them do their thing. You're gonna be a hero. You're going to keep anyone from getting hurt. You just keep your thumb on that button, and when the cavalry get here, they'll figure it out. But I need you to start moving away from the school now. Are we good?"

A minor nod.

"Great."

I stepped closer and held the door for him so he didn't have to push it with his body.

"It's gonna be okay," I said.

"I'm sorry," he said, his voice little more than a whisper. "I didn't know what else to do."

He turned around. "That way?" he asked, looking out toward the athletic field and the track that ran around it.

"Yeah. One step at a time. Go right out to the middle."

Mark took one last glance at me over his shoulder and, as he took another step, said, "Okay."

And that was when his right foot landed on the long lace that was dangling from his left boot and he stumbled forward.

As he headed into his trip, he threw out both hands in front of him, instinctively, to break his fall.

I said, "Oh sh—"

I had half a second to turn away and run before the deafening blast.

TWO

illy Finster was kicking back on the turquoise leather couch, legs on the coffee table next to a half-open bag of Cheetos. He had a TV remote in one hand and a can of Sapporo in the other, flipping through the channels so quickly the wide-screen television was a relentless blur.

He put the remote down long enough to reach into the Cheetos bag, stuffed a few in his mouth, wiped his fingers on his threadbare Hartford Whalers sweatshirt to get rid of the orange dust, and saw that he had landed on a station that ran game shows from decades past. It was an episode of *The $100,000 Pyramid*, old enough that Dick Clark was hosting.

Billy stopped flipping.

Some long-forgotten celebrity was rattling off a list of things to her contestant partner. "A frog's skin. A pine tree." The contestant had come up with "things that are shiny" and "things that are smooth" but was missing the obvious "things that are green," so Billy decided to offer some assistance.

"Snot!" he shouted at the screen. "Gangrene!"

"Who the fuck are you shouting at?"

Billy didn't have to turn around to know who it was. His wife, Lucy, halfway down the stairs to the basement rec room. She was lollipop-thin, with streaked blond hair, ripped jeans, and a blue blouse adorned with sparkles, having changed out of her pale green hospital cafeteria uniform.

"*Pyramid*," he said.

"Whoosit's here," she said, making it sound like she'd spotted mouse droppings.

Billy tilted his head back, shouted: "Stuart! Downstairs!"

Stuart Betz waited for her to come back to the top of the stairs before heading down. "Nice to see you, Lucy," he said obsequiously as she passed, barely mumbling a reply.

Stuart beelined it to the bar fridge in the corner of the room, next to the *Fast and Furious* movie poster, and helped himself to a beer. His fashion sense mirrored Billy's. Sweats, oversized sneakers, but instead of a Hartford Whalers shirt he was wearing the Boston Bruins. The two of them, with their similar wardrobes, paunches, and shoulder-length black hair, could have passed for brothers.

Stuart pulled back the tab on the beer and stood in front of Billy. "Do I look funny?"

"You always look funny."

"No, I mean, like I got somethin' on me or bird shit in my hair? 'Cause Lucy gave me a look."

"She just thinks you're an asshole."

He held out the bag of Cheetos to Stuart. But as Stuart reached for some, Billy suddenly pulled the bag back.

"Too slow," he said.

Stuart sat. Billy picked up the remote again, bailed on *Pyramid*, and resumed flipping through channels at light speed. Stuart's eyes widened as he watched the channels flash by.

"You're giving me a seizure," he said, and sniffed.

Billy kept flipping. "Blow your fucking nose. You're like a three-year-old."

Stuart brought out the tattered remains of a tissue from his pocket and asked, "Shipment come in okay today?"

Eyes fixed on the screen, Billy said, "Right where it was supposed to be. They're coming later to pick it up."

"Psycho Bitch and Butthead?"

"Call them that to their faces and they'll stick your dick into a pencil sharpener."

"Hey, they're your nicknames. I never even met them." Stuart sniffed again, wiped his nose, and tucked the tattered tissue back into his pants. "You should introduce me. Cut me in."

"Told you. It's between me and them."

"I could help. Like, stand guard or something. Be part of your security detail. Find other hiding spots." He gave Billy a sad puppy face. "I could use the scratch."

Billy replied with a dismissive grunt.

"Fine. You don't want to mix business with friendship. Whatever." Stuart dug into his pocket and brought out a joint.

Billy shook his head. "Take that outside. Lucy don't want the house smelling like a skunk's ass. Bad enough letting you in. When's the last time you did a wash?"

"Ran out of quarters this week. And why's Lucy all pissy with me?"

"You're creeping her out. Looking her up and down. Starin' at her tits."

"Bullshit," Stuart said defensively. "She's barely got any."

Billy tossed the remote right at Stuart's face, catching him in the eye.

"Fuck!" Stuart said, putting his hand over his eye, rubbing it.

"Not cool," Billy said.

"Sorry. I'm just sayin'. Didn't mean anything by it."

Billy went back to channel surfing, oblivious to the short, hateful glare from his friend. He'd flipped past something that caught his eye, went back a station. It was the Fox affiliate up in Hartford. A woman, mike in hand, was standing out front of an institutional-looking building. Across the bottom, the words SCHOOL BOMBING AVERTED, ONE DEAD.

"Fuck," Billy said, thumbing up the volume. "Some dude just blew himself up."

". . . *could have been much worse*," the woman said. "*The would-be bomber, a former student whose motivations remain unclear at this time, ended up taking his own life, perhaps accidentally, but not before threatening to come into the school and kill an undetermined number of people. Police said . . .*"

"That's my school," Billy said, leaning forward, as though that would give him a better view. "Lodge. That's where I went."

A headshot of Mark LeDrew appeared in the corner of the screen, with his name below.

"You know him?" Stuart asked.

"Shut up. Want to hear this."

Stuart, almost giggling, asked, "They got pictures of him after he was blowed up?"

Billy, shaking his head, raised a silencing palm.

". . . *was met at the door by one or more of the teachers, who engaged Mr. LeDrew in conversation long enough, police say, to somehow talk him out of setting off an explosive device he had strapped to his chest. But when he started walking away from the school, the device detonated, killing the man and injuring . . .*"

"Yeah, don't think I knew that guy. Probably a few years behind me. What's he look like to you? Twenty? Twenty-two?"

"Crawly thing at the bottom said he was twenty-one."

"So, I'm four years older, I'd've just missed him. He'd have been some pimply-faced pipsqueak coming in as I was leaving. Over there? Bottom shelf? My yearbooks. Grab 'em."

Stuart put down his beer, went to the shelf, located the books, and pulled one out. "Which year?"

"Bring them all. He might be—oh shit, whaddya know."

Billy's eyes were back on the TV. It was a long shot of several school staff members milling around near the main doors, talking with police officials. Clearly this was as close as the news crew was allowed to get.

". . . from here we can see teachers and administrators from Lodge High, including some of the staff we believe stood up to the bomber and persuaded him not to come into the school."

There was a close-up shot of a cluster of staff members, one wearing a bloodied sport jacket, bandages applied to his neck and forehead.

"Him," Billy said, pointing at the screen. "That son of a bitch."

Stuart, now sitting cross-legged on the floor, leafing through the pages of one of the yearbooks, hunting for the man who'd blown himself up, said, "What? Who?" He looked at the television.

"Would've thought they'd have gotten rid of him by now. I couldn't have been the only one."

The reporter was on camera again, wrapping up the report, and then the newscast went to weather.

"What are you talking about?"

"The guy. Remember me telling you about when I was on the wrestling team?"

It was no surprise to Stuart that Billy might have some wrestling in his past. How many times had his so-called friend put him in a headlock and driven his knuckles into the top of his skull? That could really fucking hurt.

"Maybe," Stuart said. "Tell me again."

"He's the fucking fondler," he said, pointing at the screen, although the scene of people out front of the school was over.

Stuart started turning the yearbook pages more quickly. "God, everybody looks like a dweeb." He scanned a page, turned it, scanned another. "Okay, sports teams. Football, hockey . . . here we go, wrestling."

"Don't even know if I got my picture took. Wasn't on the team long."

"What was his name?"

"Dick Grabber," Billy said.

"No, seriously, what— Hang on, I found his picture."

Billy was slowly shaking his head from side to side, looking at the television as though the news item were still running, while Stuart studied the yearbook photo.

"So now he's all over the news like a big fucking hero." He looked at Stuart and grinned. "I could sure set them straight on that."

THREE

Richard

It's a bit like a sixth sense, I suppose. Knowing you're being watched without actually seeing who's doing the watching. That was the feeling in the minutes before I woke up on Friday morning. Something was there. Some kind of presence. Taking me in, checking me out.

I opened my eyes. I was right. Only inches from my face was a nose that belonged to my seven-year-old daughter, Rachel. The other half of the bed was empty. Bonnie'd probably already been up an hour, slipped out without waking me. I'd slept in the last three mornings because it had taken me so long to finally nod off, and even when I finally did, I kept waking up after seeing bits and pieces of Mark LeDrew flying through the air.

"Hi, honey," I said.

"It worked," Rachel said, eyeing me through her glasses. "I was sending you a message from my brain to your brain to wake up."

"I'll be darned," I said, raising my head from the pillow. "You have a rare gift."

Her face brightened. "You got me something?"

"Not that kind of gift. A talent."

She looked only mildly disappointed. "I was also reading your dreams."

I had to hope she was not as skilled at that as she was at sending me a wake-up call. No seven-year-old should be able to see what was in my head.

"You were dreaming about cheeseburgers," she said.

"You sure you're not just reading your own dreams?"

She smiled. "I can read minds, too."

"Have you read your mom's this morning?"

Rachel smile cracked. "No."

I shouldn't even have asked. It was an underhanded way to try to find out where I stood this morning, and it wasn't fair to drag Rachel into it.

"But Mom did say you should take the weekend off and not go back to school until Monday, and I concur."

"*Concur?*" I said.

Her parents were both educators, so I shouldn't have been surprised Rachel used, on occasion, a more broad vocabulary.

A glance at the bedside table clock told me it was closing in on eight. "Get ready for school," I said, and Rachel departed. Bonnie and I had kept her out of her second-grade class Tuesday and Wednesday, worried there might be some kind of fallout from the events of Monday, that maybe some reporters would show up at her school, attempt to ask her questions about what her father had been through. Bonnie, an elementary school principal—not at the one Rachel attended—had taken a couple of days herself, but returned to work yesterday, leaving me on my own.

I'd walked Rachel to school yesterday. I didn't want to let her out of my sight right now, and even before Monday's incident we'd been worried about Rachel crossing the street, what with all the truck traffic lately. I think it's fair to say she was almost as reluctant to let me out of her sight. She'd almost lost her father four days ago, and attempts to shield her from what had happened had been fruitless. That first night, she had slept between Bonnie and me, afraid something might happen to either one of us by morning. Trouble was,

I was the one waking up in a cold sweat, startling her and Bonnie, so the next night she went back to her own room.

I'd decided not to wait until Monday to return to Lodge High. I'd tidied up the boat that sat on a trailer in our driveway, searched through some old boxes in the garage and thrown out three bags' worth of stuff, gone through the fridge and pitched anything that was past its expiry date. I needed people to talk to, even if the one thing they were going to want to talk about was the one thing I *didn't* want to talk about.

I went into the bathroom and looked at myself in the mirror. I had small bandages on the left side of my neck and forehead. I'd been hit by shattered glass that had blown out of the double doors when Mark LeDrew's dynamite vest went off. It could have been worse . . . I mean, for me. It couldn't have been worse for Mark. It was a wonder I hadn't ended up dead, or at the very least blind.

When Mark tripped, he was facing away from me, and so was his explosive vest. Investigators determined that only one of the sticks detonated—Mark's reputation as a fuckup extended to his skills at wiring a bomb. But still, one stick packed a punch, blowing him to bits and sending shock waves out in all directions. I had already started to turn away when the glass panels in the door shattered, sending shards my way.

I showered, keeping the water off the bandages as much as possible, shaved and dressed, and threw on a sport jacket, which amounted to my school uniform. It was not, needless to say, the same one I'd been wearing Monday. That bloodied jacket had been taken by the forensic team, and even if they ever offered to return it, I didn't want it. It was not going to the dry cleaner's.

When I got to the kitchen, Bonnie was sitting at the table sipping her coffee and pretending to read the news on her iPad. She would normally have left for work by now, but was clearly waiting to see me before departing. She barely looked up.

"Hey," I said.

"You're really going back today." Not a question. More a statement of disapproval.

I grabbed a cup and went to the coffee maker. "Back on the horse, and all that."

"You don't have to be a hero. You've proved that."

I didn't hear anything praiseworthy in that. More like exasperation. According to Bonnie, this was my failing. A recidivist rescuer. I'm not saying she was wrong. I had a history that predated my encounter with Mark LeDrew.

She continued. "I'm not saying don't go back. I just thought, it's Friday. Go back Monday. Then it's a whole week. You heard what Marta said. It's like when cops are involved in a traumatic incident. They'd take more time before returning to duty, and they're *trained* for this kind of thing. They'd probably go for counseling, too."

Marta Harper, a detective with the Milford police, was Bonnie's sister, and one of the first on the scene after LeDrew died. She'd been to the house a couple of times since the event, once in an official capacity, and once as a concerned sister-in-law.

She'd also been able to tell me a little more about what LeDrew'd been up to since leaving Lodge High. He never did get his diploma despite efforts by our principal, Trent, to steer him into courses he'd be able to, if not ace, pass. His first job was at a fast-food franchise and he was fired from that for being belligerent with customers. He got a job with the city's roads department for six months until he was laid off due to budget cutbacks. After that, he worked for a quarry up around Naugatuck. That would have been where he became familiar with dynamite, and it was believed he'd stolen the four sticks from there at some point—maybe even after he'd left—and studied online videos to figure out how to make his own device.

After he was fired from the quarry for consistent lateness, he had a series of other gigs. Stocking shelves on the midnight shift at a local supermarket, loading and unloading trucks at Home Depot. But Mark didn't follow directions well, didn't anticipate what needed to be done next, lacked an ability to focus on whatever task was at hand.

He lived with his parents and when he was between jobs spent most of his time in the basement watching slasher movies like the *Saw* and *Hostel* franchises. He'd become depressed, by all accounts, and had taken to writing online posts about how the world had screwed him over, how everybody was desperate for him to fail, that perverts and pedophiles were running amok, and one of these days he was going to find a way to settle some scores. He did not, in any of his diatribes, mention by name anyone he sought revenge against.

I hadn't set foot in Lodge High since the police—Marta among them—finished questioning me at the school Monday and the paramedics tended to my injuries. Bonnie feared my return would be traumatic, and there was no reason to doubt that. I sure as hell had been traumatized. I spent the balance of Monday in a state of shock. I had a hard time telling the police exactly what had happened. The blast had jumbled my recollection.

Trent was able to fill in some of the details. I hadn't been wrong when I sensed someone was behind me, watching my interaction with LeDrew. My principal was just inside the school office doors, and while he hadn't heard all of the conversation, he got the general drift.

Maybe the most surprising thing was, Trent had been prepared to take action. And thank Christ he hadn't.

School shootings had become so widespread that Trent, contrary to the board's wishes and without their knowledge, had kept a handgun locked in the bottom drawer of his desk. When many on the far right had suggested arming teachers, Trent, a centrist, had never been one to immediately dismiss the idea. But I'd had no idea he kept a weapon on the premises, or that he had gotten it from his desk and was preparing to use it on Mark LeDrew.

In one of our conversations since the incident—Trent had come by the house to see me on Tuesday—he told me he'd been taking the gun back and forth between home and the school for the better part of two years. He said he'd considered shooting LeDrew, but wasn't sure he could hit him while missing me. Had he managed a clean shot, LeDrew would only have been a few inches from me when his thumb came off the button, instead of several feet.

We came under a nationwide media spotlight.

CNN, NBC—an entire alphabet of networks—had wanted to interview me, but I'd turned down all requests, referring them to Trent.

This is what he'd told Anderson Cooper over a Zoom link:

"It was a horrible, horrible thing, no question. Our hearts go out to that young man's family and what they must be going through now. But it could have been much worse. If it were not for the brave actions of teacher Richard Boyle, for his quick thinking, for the calm manner in which he handled the situation, I just . . . I shudder to think what might have happened. Our school got off lucky that day. God was watching out for us."

I didn't know Trent to be a religious man, and doubted the LeDrew family felt the same way about our heavenly father.

I'd done my best to relate to the police what Mark had said to me about Herb Willow, some unkind words about our guidance counselor, Sally Berwick, and the cryptic reference to a character from a science fiction/horror film, which made no sense to any of us. A lawnmower reference didn't sound all that ominous, although I had a memory of a scene in a Stephen King novel where a policeman got run over by one.

What little Mark had said about Herb sounded credible. I'd heard him bad-mouth kids, to their faces and behind their backs. Were Herb's insults a self-fulfilling prophecy? Even without Herb's negativity, Mark LeDrew wasn't destined to become a rocket scientist. Looking back, it was hard not to think he'd had a learning disability or psychological issue no one bothered to diagnose.

Mark's grudge against Sally was less clear, but from what I'd heard, she'd followed Herb's trail of breadcrumbs, steering the kid down a career path that didn't require a genius-level IQ. But unlike Herb,

Sally was well intentioned. She'd have done what she believed was best for Mark.

Bonnie, bringing me back to the present, said, "I could take today off. They'd understand. Mitch could take the lead." Her vice principal. "We could pull Rachel from school, take the boat up to the lake, find a place to stay, make a long weekend of it."

This was a generous offer, considering how things were between Bonnie and me. It had been building for a while. She blamed my parents, both long gone, whom I never seemed capable of pleasing despite my best efforts. Said I kept looking for approval from others, going beyond what anyone would reasonably expect.

It was pure dime-store psychology, but I was willing to concede there might be something to it. The evidence was overwhelming. Sending money to my down-on-his-luck cousin without talking it over with Bonnie first. Disappearing on a Saturday afternoon to help an inept, handicapped neighbor repair a busted fence when I was supposed to be taking Rachel to the movies. Inviting a troubled student to drop by the house to talk and being unable to find my wallet after she left. I had to cancel all my cards.

"You can't get every kitten out of every tree," Bonnie liked to tell me.

It's not like Bonnie wasn't kind and generous and empathetic. She was all those things, just not to a fault. She wouldn't have been an effective principal without those qualities. But she understood we all have limits, and that we have to tend to our own before overextending ourselves. And she was having a particularly hard time with what I'd done Monday.

"You could have locked your door, called the police, stayed with your kids," she'd said. "But you ran toward the danger. We could have lost you. You're not James Bond. You're not Jason Bourne. You're not even my sister. You're a goddamn high school English teacher."

The best excuse I could come up with? *It seemed like a good idea at the time.* And at some level, she knew, had she been in the same situation, she might have done the same thing. Run to that door and tried to stop a kid with a bomb from getting into the building. But even acknowledging that, she couldn't shake the fact that she had nearly lost me. No matter how much my supposedly selfless actions annoyed her, I know she didn't want that.

Rachel had picked up on the tension between us, and not just in the last few days. She'd overheard the arguments, particularly after I sent three thousand dollars to my cousin Stan when he got fired from his meatpacking job in Duluth. I'd told him it was a onetime thing, and I'd stuck to that, but that hadn't made Bonnie any happier.

So Bonnie coming up with the idea of taking off today for a long weekend was a nice, conciliatory gesture. But I shook my head.

"If I don't walk back into that school today, I don't know whether I'll be able to do it Monday."

She looked at me for a moment, then nodded. "Okay, then," she said.

We usually left for work at the same time. Bonnie would get into her Mitsubishi crossover, usually taking Rachel and dropping her off at her school along the way, and I'd get into my Subaru Forester, which was parked closer to the street because the boat—a sixteen-footer with a fifty-horsepower Merc outboard bolted to the transom—sat on its trailer up close to the garage.

As I was getting into my car, Jack Marshall, our next-door neighbor, was coming out his front door and heading for his van. He'd been to the house after the incident to offer congratulations-slash-condolences-slash-thanks, and his wife, Jill (yes, that's right, Jack and Jill), sent over a cherry pie, because nothing helps you get past witnessing someone blow up like pastry.

Okay, that's dickish. People meant well, and didn't know what to say. I mean, what would I have said to someone in the same situation?

Jack offered a thumbs-up just as a fully-loaded dump truck rumbled down the street and past our houses. Jack gave it a scornful, disapproving shake of the head. There'd been a regular stream of trucks going by lately. The excavation for some new apartment complex a few streets over was underway, and the trucks loaded with fill had been a regular thing of late.

Rachel hopped into Bonnie's car and I got behind the wheel of mine. Once we were both on the street, pointed in different directions, we usually glanced in our rearview mirrors and waved to each other.

Bonnie did not wave this morning.

I had sent a text to Trent the night before to let him know I was coming back today.

Use the main door, he wrote back. West entrance still being repaired. Even if that hadn't been the case, I wouldn't have been entering the school that way. I'd be avoiding that set of doors for as long as possible. Maybe forever.

For more mornings than I could count, I'd pulled into this staff parking lot, but today felt like a first time. This was not the same school I'd entered a thousand times before.

I'd almost died here. I'd *watched* someone die here.

I pulled into my spot, killed the engine, hit the button to retract my seat belt, and went to reach for the door handle.

And I began to shake.

FOUR

"**I** appreciate this is a difficult time for you, but I do have a few more things I need to go over," Detective Marta Harper said, standing at the front door of the LeDrew residence, a modest bungalow in the northeast part of Milford on a tree-lined street.

She had been met at the door by Angus LeDrew, a skinny, pale man in his fifties with thin wisps of hair over a liver-spotted head, and shoulders weighed down by invisible cinder blocks.

"We've told you people everything," he said wearily.

"Is it them?" said a woman's voice from inside the house. "The TV people?"

Over his shoulder, he said, "No, the police."

His wife, Fiona, was as thin as he was, but with features as brittle and delicate as faded, dried flowers. She viewed Marta through dead eyes.

"Oh," she said.

"It's just . . ." Angus said. "We have . . . an appointment shortly." He opened the door wider and allowed the detective to enter the living room.

Everyone took a seat. Marta noticed both of them were unexpectedly dressed up, for how early it was. Angus was in a white shirt and tie, minus a jacket, and Fiona was in a black knee-length dress with a small gold necklace draped around her neck. The detective wondered whether the funeral for their son was this morning.

As if reading her mind, Fiona said, "We buried our boy yesterday."

Angus, grim-faced, added, "What was left of him."

Fiona visibly winced. Marta was well aware that their son's remains had been scattered far and wide by the blast. She didn't have to ask whether they'd opted for a closed casket.

Fiona said, "No one came to the funeral. Not his friends, not his cousins, not one person came."

"My brother," Angus said. "You forgot he was there." He looked at the detective. "He drove all the way down from Syracuse. But his wife, she stayed home." He mouthed the word *Bitch*.

"But no one else," his wife said. "Mark was a good boy. People should have come and paid their respects. My son didn't hurt a soul. He was never really going to hurt anybody. Did anyone at that school die other than my son? Did they?"

Marta sat there, solemnly, and let them talk.

"He just wanted to talk to people," Angus said. "That's what that teacher said. He told you people Mark wanted to set a few things straight, that's all."

"We've had to take the phone off the hook," his wife said. "Hateful calls. Awful people. Saying terrible things about us."

Marta thought it was time for a question. "Did your son discuss problems he had with anyone at Lodge? Students or staff?"

Angus shook his head. "He didn't say anything to me. And it's been a long time since he was there. Don't see what the point was in going back after all this time. You have to move on. If you have a problem, you deal with it. You don't let it fester over time."

Marta looked to Fiona. "He had a hard time there," she said. "He was a very gifted boy, just not in an academic way. The school should have tried harder to understand him. You know? Tried to figure out his needs?"

"Needs," Angus said, coming close to rolling his eyes.

"So he didn't discuss any grievances with specific teachers? Mr. Boyle said he made mention of a couple during their conversation."

Angus shook his head. "That man. I won't say his name."

"Why's that, Mr. LeDrew?"

"He should have done something. All he was worried about was saving his own skin. Making my son walk away first before getting him to blow himself up."

Marta didn't feel disclosing that Richard Boyle was her brother-in-law was the right move at this time, but she couldn't stop herself from saying, "Mr. Boyle worked very hard to deescalate the situation. It's tragic what happened to your son, but it would have been worse had more people been involved."

She decided to move on to something else.

"What do either of you know about how Mark came into possession of dynamite?"

"I had no idea," Angus said.

"He worked for a few months for Jasonland Quarries," Fiona said. "They sometimes used dynamite. I can't think of any other place he got it."

"When did he leave that job?"

Fiona looked to her husband for an answer. "About eight months ago," he said.

"So it's possible he was hiding explosives here, all that time?"

Fiona paled. "I don't know. Out in the garage, maybe."

"You're just assuming he stole that stuff from the quarry," Angus said. "Like he was a thief or something. He might have bought it legit somewhere. You don't know."

"Would that make it better?" Marta couldn't help but ask. "Because the real issue would seem to be what he intended to do with it. We looked at his computer history. He watched a lot of videos on how to build a bomb."

"What do you want from us?" Fiona asked, her voice breaking. "Tell me. What do you want us to do? Admit we're terrible parents? Is that what you'd like? Well, I won't do that. I loved Mark and I did my best by him."

Marta noted that she hadn't said "we."

"It's not all on us. You need to go back to that school. You need to talk to those teachers. Like that Mr. Willow. He was hard on Mark, I know that much."

"He was probably trying to toughen him up," Angus said. "God knows the boy could have benefited from it, needed some direction. That Mr. Wakely, the principal, he was decent enough, trying to steer Mark toward more mechanical things he'd be good at. But you know what it's like these days. The school system's only worried about pushing kids through. Make it the next person's problem."

Trent Wakely had been ready to take their son down if he'd had a clean shot, Marta thought.

Angus's face flushed. "But it's the one who watched him die. He's the one you gotta talk to."

Back to Richard Boyle.

"He was right there. He could have done *something*. Nobody heard the whole conversation. There's only his word about what was said between them. He talked my boy into walking away and blowing himself up to save his own ass."

Detective Marta Harper got to her feet. "Thank you for your time. Again, I'm very sorry for your loss."

On her way back to her car, she saw what the LeDrews' next appointment was. A deep blue Jaguar sedan pulled into the driveway, a silver-haired man behind the wheel. Marta was pretty sure she recognized him. A hotshot lawyer from New York. She'd seen him on the news, usually defending the indefensible.

As he got out of the car, he walked to the end of the driveway, shot one quick look at Marta, then looked down the street, as though waiting for someone else to arrive.

Seconds later, a TV news van turned the corner, drove slowly up the street, and parked across the end of the driveway.

"Oh great," the detective said under her breath.

FIVE

Richard

"**G**et it together," I told myself. "You can do this."

Sitting behind the wheel of my car in the school parking lot, I couldn't move. I'd thought I was ready, that I could come back, but now I was drowning in doubt.

More than once since Monday I'd considered never coming back. Asking for a transfer to another school. Maybe quitting the profession. Even after setting aside fears that someday another nutcase would stroll in—armed, perhaps, with an assault rifle instead of a bomb, as had happened in so many other schools across the nation—teaching for a living had more than its share of drawbacks.

The pay was mediocre, although teachers in Connecticut were compensated better than in some other states. You took work home almost every night. Marking, preparing lessons. Budgets were always being cut back. One day you found you were out of chalk. Or there was no toilet paper in the bathrooms. Textbooks hadn't been updated since the Carter administration. Older schools had no air-conditioning. You sweltered in the months before and after summer.

As supportive as most parents were, it was the hypercritical, impossible-to-please ones that wore you down. Everything you said, everything you taught, your private life, it was all under the microscope like never before. You'd run into a parent at the liquor store, doing something as innocent as buying a bottle of Smirnoff, and suddenly you were an educator who might have a drinking problem. Everyone's phone was a camera, so you never knew when your actions were being captured on video, and when they were, it was often out of context. I'd learned that lesson in a big way a few years ago. And so many issues that today's kids were going to come face-to-face with—racism, diversity, gender identity, sexism—were now third-rail topics. You touched on them at your peril.

Teachers weren't the only ones feeling the stress, either. The kids were dealing with way more than previous generations. Experimenting with drugs and alcohol and sex, sure, that had always been the case. But they were under increasing pressure from home to do well, to make something of themselves. Flunk one exam and you were led to believe you'd thrown away your future. They were being bullied and shamed online. They were sucked into a social media vortex that was leading to depression. They were anorexic, or they ate too much. They were shamed for what they did and didn't do. And they, too, had to wonder whether this was the day someone would want to come into their school and kill them.

Not the sort of shit Beaver and Wally had to deal with when they left home in the morning.

You wanted to help these kids but more often than not couldn't find the support they most needed. Asking the powers that be for a few extra bucks for a kid with emotional problems or a learning disability could be like asking for a ticket to the moon.

And Christ, don't get me started on all the disputes over masks and the horrors of virtual learning during the pandemic. I never wanted to go through anything like that again.

But here was the crazy thing. In spite of all this, or maybe even partly because of it, I loved the job.

I loved the kids, I loved the challenges, I loved that you never went home at the end of the day without a story. A high school was a living, breathing organism where you could never predict what was going to happen. A high school was a small city filled with stories of tragedy and heartbreak, success and inspiration. What kept me going was the possibility that, even if it didn't happen every day—you were lucky if it happened once a month—you might have an actual impact on someone's life. Help them find the thing they loved. Make them look at something in a way they never had before. Maybe, just maybe, you opened their eyes for a moment.

If I walked away, I wouldn't have the opportunity to do that. And, frankly, I didn't know what else I would have done.

I didn't want to walk away. I didn't want what happened to me on Monday to defeat me.

I could do this.

My panic attack in the parking lot shouldn't have surprised me. While I hadn't had any formal counseling or therapy since the incident—not yet, anyway—Marta had had plenty to tell me when we had a private moment.

"You think you're okay, but you're not," she'd said. "Your view of the world will change. Things you could slough off in the past may seem like a big deal. You may have a degree of paranoia. You'll worry all the time about Bonnie and Rachel, more about them than yourself. Don't beat yourself up if you feel overwhelmed, like you can't handle things like you used to. At least for a while. You're fragile, even if you don't want to admit it."

I suspect she'd told Bonnie all of this, too, although Bonnie'd probably already figured it out. Before deciding to go into teaching, and ultimately moving up to running a school, Bonnie had considered following her older sister into law enforcement. She went so far as to attend a police training academy in Bridgeport before deciding it wasn't for her. But she learned a few tricks that had served her well, including, once, breaking up a fight between two students, one of whom had a knife. (This hadn't happened at her elementary school, but at one of her first teaching gigs, in a high school.)

A shot of that kind of courage was what I needed right now.

When I had faced Mark LeDrew, I hadn't had time to think about my actions. Now I had too much time to think.

I took a deep breath and got out of the car. Walked at a steady pace toward the front door. Pulled it open, entered the building.

Holy shit.

There must have been a hundred kids there. Standing in the main hall, applauding and cheering as I entered, a banner strung above them that read WE LOVE YOU MR. B. Among them were various members of the staff, and right up front, Trent, who had a big grin on his face as he brought his hands together.

I stood there dumbfounded, and I'd like to say I was able to hold back the tears, but I couldn't. I was overwhelmed. The stress of the last four days erupted in the form of wracking sobs.

The crowd pushed forward and surrounded me. Everyone offering hugs, patting me on the back, squeezing me, saying things like "You're the best" and "We love you" and "You saved us."

That went on for a couple of minutes. My heart felt like it would burst.

Trent waved a hand in the air and said loudly, "Okay, everybody, if you can give me a moment."

The crowd quieted. When there were only a few murmurs, Trent said: "Mr. Boyle, on behalf of the staff and students of Lodge High School, we want to say a heartfelt thank-you. Without your courage, without your sense of duty and decency, we might be in a very different place today, a place we don't even want to imagine. We thank you from the bottom of our hearts, and to show my own personal appreciation, I'm springing for coffee today."

Laughter. Someone handed him a mug and passed it along to me. I wiped away some tears before taking it in my hand, took a sip, grimaced, and said, "Even worse than usual."

Another wave of laughter. I handed the mug off to someone and Trent gave me a hug and a handshake. His was the first, but not the last. One kid after another came up to put their arms around me, and plenty of them were crying, too. This whole exercise was a tension release for all of us.

One girl, whose dad managed a Home Depot, put a hundred-dollar gift card into my hand.

"I can't take that," I said.

"He said you have to."

A grade nine boy handed me a pastry box tied up with string. "Cupcakes," he said.

A tenth-grade student in a wheelchair rolled herself up to me, took my hand in both of hers, and squeezed it. "My parents love you," she said, her voice breaking.

I leaned over and gave her a hug.

I felt I needed to say something to the assembled crowd. I raised my hands, palms down, signaling everyone to hush.

"Look, um, this is all very kind of you. I think . . ." I stopped, needing another second to pull myself together. I continued, "I think everyone here, all of you, deserve a lot of credit. The love in this school, it . . . it doesn't matter what comes our way . . . the way we feel about each other, that will always get us through the good times and the bad."

One kid shouted, "You're a badass, Mr. B.!"

I smiled, shrugged. "What happened Monday . . . will be with us a long time. Forever, for me, I guess. What I want to say is, I wish things had gone differently. I wish . . . I wish I could have helped Mark LeDrew. I feel like I failed him."

Someone said, "You didn't fail *us*."

"Okay, well," I said, forcing a smile, "we should all get to class. And I need to find a drinkable cup of coffee."

As the kids and most of the teachers drifted away, two staff members stayed. The first was Sally Berwick. She'd no doubt been told that Mark LeDrew had her on his mental list. She put her arms around me and began to weep.

"It's okay," I said, patting her back. "It's okay."

35

Her body trembled. She hung on for about twenty seconds, stepped back, wiped the tears from her eyes, and, looking slightly embarrassed, whispered, "Sorry." With that, she went off to class, leaving just one staff member who wanted to say something.

Herb Willow.

Round-shouldered, balding, a pair of wire-rimmed glasses hanging off the end of his nose, he stepped forward and extended a hand. No hugs from Herb, but that was okay. A handshake would suffice.

I took his clammy hand into mine, and he gripped it hard. Locked onto it so that he could pull me in close to him. He put his mouth close to my ear and whispered.

"I know you told the cops it was all my fault, you motherfucker. Don't think for a minute that I'm going to forget that."

SIX

illy Finster was in the garage out back of his house, tinkering with the blue 1980 Camaro, the front end precariously propped up on jacks so he could work on the engine from the underside if he needed to, not that he would have had a clue what to do once he got down there. The car had been sitting this way, front end up, ass end down, for the better part of two years, ever since he bought it off a guy in Stamford for three grand. Dude had said it needed a "bit of work," which turned out to mean *doesn't run worth a shit*. But Billy'd always loved that vintage of Camaro, and figured, even though he didn't know the first thing about car repair, he could learn a few of the fundamentals and get the thing running one of these days.

And to that end, he had invested a fair chunk of change in recent weeks. A carpenter was only as good as his tools, right? Well, the same maxim surely had to apply to people who refurbished classic vehicles. So Billy had bought a high-torque pneumatic wrench, an air hammer, a wide variety of ratchets and extenders, specialty tools to check a car's suspension and front-end alignment, buffers and polishers, even some new shelving. Lots of stuff. Lucy had said it was like buying a high-end computer for a horse. It could be the best one on the market, but the horse was never, ever going to be able to do so much as check its email.

Pissed Billy off when she talked that way.

She'd popped into the garage to tell him she was going in for an afternoon shift at the Bridgeport hospital cafeteria where she worked. She usually had Friday off but someone had booked off sick and she was going to cover. An entire shift of overtime.

"I'm off," she said.

"Get some beer and some Dorito things."

"I'm not going to the fucking grocery store. I'm going to *work*."

"On your way back," he said. "And not some cheap-ass beer. Good stuff. We've got the money."

"*You've* got the money," she said.

Jesus, this again, he thought. Lucy was as bad as Stuart, wanting him to share the wealth. What did they think this was? Socialism? Billy dug a couple of twenties from his pocket and slapped them into her open palm. She turned and headed for her car.

"You gonna say thank you?"

She shot him a middle finger over her shoulder. Seconds later she was behind the wheel of her Kia and gone.

He had the hood up on the Camaro, looking at the engine like it was the Sphinx. The air cleaner had been removed and was sitting on a nearby bench, exposing the carburetor. Billy, guided by a handbook on this particular model, had taken it apart and cleaned it more than once. He'd installed a new battery, changed the points and plugs, but still hadn't been able to get the damn engine to turn over.

He heard tires crunching on gravel. Maybe Lucy'd come back, wanting more money so she could get some of that soy milk shit she liked or God forbid a pack of cut-up veggie sticks. He hoped it wasn't Stuart. He needed a break from his friend today. Stuart was starting to be like that tiny dog Chester in the Looney Tunes cartoons, the one always running in front of the big dog, Spike, asking: "What do you want to do now, Spike? You wanna play ball? You wanna chase cars?" And Spike takes a swipe at him, knocking him off his paws.

There were times Billy wondered if Stuart's parents dropped him on his head a lot when he was little. He spent half his time laughing at online videos of people walking into poles, stepping out into traffic, getting bit in the nuts by pit bulls.

The side door opened before he could get to it and it wasn't Lucy or Stuart, although it was a man and a woman, standing there, silhouetted in the afternoon sun.

Andrea and Gerhard. Or better known, at least in Billy's head, as Psycho Bitch and Butthead.

Gerhard, thirtyish, short and stocky and bald, looked like he would be the tougher of the two, coming in at two hundred and fifty pounds, with a hint of a snake tattoo coming up from under his shirt collar, big beefy arms under a shirt that was a size too small for him, but it was the woman who always set Billy's teeth on edge.

Thin and wiry, probably close to forty, black eyes set against a dry, wrinkled face, with stringy hair that hung down below her shoulders, she struck Billy as someone who'd spent too much time catching rays on a beach or a prison workout yard. She had a small scar on her right cheek and one eye never seemed to open the whole way, like she was squinting.

This was not a scheduled pickup day. They'd been here this past Monday, so he had nothing for them today. He'd be taking their next shipment off the plane in three days.

"Hey, guys," he said, moving toward them and extending a hand. "Sup? This is kind of unexpected. Want a beer or something?" Billy pointed a thumb over his shoulder at a mini-fridge resting atop the workbench. "Corona?"

"Not a social call, Billy," said Gerhard.

Like it ever was. These two had always been pure business. *Where's our stuff, here's your money, now fuck off.*

Andrea was looking at him with those dead eyes, Billy half expecting them to blink vertically like some half-human, half-reptile thing in a horror movie. She said simply, "Billy."

He nodded.

She asked, "You ever eat Raisin Bran?"

"What?"

"You know. Raisin Bran. Those flakes, they got raisins in them. You ever eat them for breakfast?"

The fuck, he thought. There was a reason he thought of her as Psycho Bitch. Asking shit that made no sense.

"Maybe. I don't know. I guess I've eaten it."

"Remember the song? A jingle, like." She sang it. "*Two scoops of juicy raisins in every box of Kellogg's Raisin Brain.*"

Billy just looked at her. Andrea took a step closer as she continued with her story. Gerhard smiled.

"When I was like fourteen I thought, is there really two scoops in every box? So I buy one, empty it out on the kitchen table, and pick out all the raisins. Every last fucking one." Andrea grinned. "Guess what I found."

Billy shook his head.

"There was like one and three-quarters scoops. What do you think of that?"

Billy shrugged and said, "I guess it would depend on how they define a scoop. Like, what's a scoop? A cup? Half a cup, or—"

"I know what a fucking scoop is," Andrea said. "It's a scoop. Like those little shovel-like things at the bargain-bin store. And this didn't have two of them. So I put all that shit back in the box and take it back the store and tell them I want my money back because they ripped me off and this dipshit store manager basically tells me to fuck off so what did I do?"

She turned her head, posing the question to her partner.

Gerhard put his index finger to his temple. "Tire iron."

"What the fuck are you talking about?" Billy asked.

Gerhard said, "You Raisin-Branned us."

"I what?"

"We did the inventory," Gerhard said. "You came up short."

"I don't understand," Billy said.

"We're short Flizzies," Gerhard said. "Our southern friends, they told us what they sent, we looked at how much we got, and we found what you might call discrepancy."

"Guys, come on," Billy said pleadingly. "You saying I dipped into the shipment? There's no way. You treat me fair and square, pay me good. I'm not gonna mess with that. What's supposedly missing?"

Gerhard said, "It's not *supposedly* missing. Andrea, do we *supposedly* think it's missing, or do we *know* it's missing?"

Andrea said, "We know."

"I've never even peeked inside a shipment. I don't know what's in there and don't want to know what's in there. The fuck are Flizzies?"

Although Billy was playing dumb, a role to which anyone who knew him would say he was well suited, he did know what Flizzies were because on one visit Gerhard had a free pack in his hand, like he'd been sampling his own merchandise. Powerful little pills that *looked* like candy, that were *disguised* as candy, and were often *packaged* to look like candy. But they were *not* candy. They were, in fact, tablets of fentanyl—a wonderfully potent synthetic opioid that could make all your pain go away—that had been manufactured to the highest standards in a Tijuana lab, put in a carry-on bag, flown to a small regional airport south of Hartford that handled international flights, and retrieved discreetly by Billy the baggage handler.

Billy, pointing to a six-foot-wide, floor-to-ceiling set of lockers along the back wall next to the workbench, said, "I bring it back, it goes right in there, and that stays locked all the time."

Andrea asked, "Who else uses this garage?"

"Nobody."

"You've got a wife. You saying she never comes out here?"

"Yeah, sure, sometimes, but Lucy doesn't have the locker key."

"Lucy," Andrea said.

"Yeah, but I got the only key. Lucy's working all the time anyway at the hospital."

"She a nurse or a doctor?" Gerhard asked.

"Cafeteria."

It was true, about Lucy not having her own key. Although there were times, Billy thought but did not say out loud, when he left his full set of keys by the front door or next to his bed or didn't know *where* the fuck they were. He was always calling out to Lucy, asking if she'd seen them. But that didn't mean she'd ever *used* the key.

"Kids?" Andrea asked. "You got kids coming in here, thinking they could eat that shit?"

"No kids around here. All we got is some nosy old lady next door."

Gerhard said, "People snooping around here at night?"

"Why would anyone be snooping? No one knows what's in here. Anyone broke in, they'd steal my tools, and nobody's touched those. I keep the garage doors locked whenever I'm not around."

"The airport, then?" Andrea asked. "You leaving our shit unattended before you bring it back?"

"No way. Never let it out of my sight once I pick it up. When I know it's a flight with your stuff, I'm the first one there to unload."

Andrea looked at the Camaro. "You got friends that help you work on this piece of shit?"

Billy blinked. "Nope, nobody."

Although, he thought, Stuart was often here. But what she'd asked was, was there ever anyone who *helped*, and Stuart was about as helpful as a rash on your nuts. He'd open up a folding lawn chair, the one with the disintegrating webbing, half his butt hanging through the seat, watching Billy work on the Camaro. But did Stuart even know where he stashed the stuff? That it was in the locker? If he did, would Stuart be dumb enough to rip him off if he could somehow get his key when he wasn't looking?

Shit.

Billy, trying not to sound nervous, offered an alternate theory. "Could be someone's dipping into your product before the bag goes on the plane."

Andrea acted as though she hadn't heard, instead focused on

a small box with thick red and black wires leading from it. At the end of each wire was a set of metal alligator clips with rubber-coated handles.

"This some kind of sex thing?" she asked. "Biggest fucking nipple clamps I ever saw."

"That's . . . that's a portable car battery charger. Like jumper cables, but you don't need the other car."

Andrea gazed upon the gadget thoughtfully, picking up the handles and squeezing them so that the clips opened and closed like tiny raptor jaws with jagged teeth. "So I clip these things to a battery and hit this button and it sends a charge?"

Billy nodded.

Andrea looked at Gerhard and gave him a knowing nod. Gerhard came up behind Billy and pinned his arms.

"The fuck, man!"

Andrea moved close to Billy, set the charger and the cables on the trunk of the Camaro, then started to roll up the front of his Whalers sweatshirt until it cleared his nipples. She bunched it at the top so it wouldn't come back down.

"Cut it out!" Billy said. "Fuckin' cut it out!"

Next she picked up the two cables and rubbed the clips over each of his nipples. "So if I hooked these up and hit the switch, what would happen, Billy?"

"It could fuckin' kill me," he said, starting to whimper. "I swear, honest, I didn't take your shit. I didn't."

Andrea opened the clip in her left hand that was attached to the black cable and hooked it onto Billy's right nipple.

Billy screamed as blood trickled down his chest.

She continued to brush his left nipple with the other clip while Gerhard spoke.

"Here's how it is, Billy. You're going to have to compensate us for our loss. Which works out to about what we've paid you so far."

"Please please please," he whispered, looking at the clip in Andrea's hand. "I . . . I don't have that money anymore. I've spent it. On stuff for the shop."

"Is that our problem?" Gerhard asked Andrea.

"That is not our problem," she replied.

"There you have it," Gerhard said. "You pick up the next shipment on Monday. When we come for it, we can settle up."

With that, Andrea dropped the second cable to the floor, leaving the first one still attached, and she and Gerhard exited the garage.

Billy, struggling to catch his breath, tears running down his cheeks, freed himself from the clamp and slowly dropped to the floor.

SEVEN

Richard

My second class back was the same group of kids I'd been with when I saw Mark LeDrew crossing the school parking lot. I knew it was unlikely we'd pick up where we left off, talking about *The Road*.

When I walked in, they were all standing beside their desks and saluting, big grins on their faces. Not all were in attendance, however. Some parents had not sent their kids back yet. I was guessing some never would, that they'd send their kids to different schools, maybe private ones. But you had to wonder whether any school—or mall or church or nightclub or grocery store—was immune when there were so many nutcases out there.

I'd spent so much time telling the police what had happened when I confronted LeDrew that I'd heard very little about what transpired in my classroom after I had run down the hall in a bid to block his entry. I should point out there'd been some whispering that I'd abandoned my kids at the worst possible time, and maybe there was something to that, but in the moment I did what I'd hoped would be in the interests of everyone. We'd never know how things might have played out if I'd stayed put.

Emma Katzenback, the girl with a phone welded to her palm, had done as I'd instructed and immediately called 911. Told the dispatcher a shooter was coming into the school, even though that had been an assumption on her part. An easy one to make, given that I had said "armed intruder." The dispatcher kept her on the line, asking for more details, but not only did Emma not have any, she could barely hear because the other kids had started shoving desks toward the door to barricade it.

The shades had been drawn by Eldon and another student, and then everyone huddled below the window in case there was a shooter and bullets started coming through the glass.

Then they waited. Waited to hear shots. Waited to hear people screaming in the halls. Waited to hear sirens. Most of them started texting or phoning their parents at work or home. Emma hung up on the 911 dispatcher so that she could call her mother.

Finally, there was the sound of Mark LeDrew's bomb going off.

Everyone in the class had screamed. They'd been steeling themselves to hear gunfire, a single shot at least. But the explosion came as a surprise. A bomb? A fucking bomb? Was the entire school going to blow up? Should they clear the door and make a run for it? Pull back the shades, break glass, and escape through the windows?

But within a minute or two of the blast, Trent went on the PA system and told everyone to stay where they were. The situation, he said, appeared to have reached a resolution, but the lockdown would continue until they got an "all-clear" from the police.

"That was the worst time," Eldon said. "Wondering if there was gonna be more bombs, or shooting, or what. The weird thing was, we were all kind of freaking out at first but we were all calm at the same time, you know?"

I nodded.

They had plenty of questions for me, some of them about the most grisly details, but I dodged most of them. "You know the basics," I said. "It's not easy for me to talk about. I hope you get that."

They did.

Eldon said, "They fired Mr. Grant."

The caretaker.

"He's not *fired*," Emma said. "He's on some kind of suspension. That's what my mom said. He kept meaning to fix the latch on that door but never got around to it. I think he *should* be fired. If we'd have been killed it would have been all his fault."

I didn't want to get into it. I made one vain attempt to talk about our current reading project, but the bell was going to ring in two minutes so I don't know why I bothered. I assigned no homework and wished everyone a good weekend. On Monday, I warned them, we were going to get back to work. Tests and essays, I told them. Lots and lots of them. The most homework in the history of homework. No one looked particularly worried.

I noticed there was one student who hadn't said a word the entire period. As he was exiting the class, head down, I called to him.

"Andrew," I said.

Andrew Kanin stopped and turned. "Yes, Mr. B.?" he said.

"Got a second?"

"You want me to close the door?" he asked.

"No, leave it open. You were pretty quiet. You okay?"

"I guess," he said, taking a few steps toward my desk. "This is my first day back, too."

I nodded. "There's quite a few kids still haven't returned."

"My parents didn't want me to come back but neither of them could get off work today and they didn't want me to stay home alone."

At fifteen?

"I promised them I'd text them every hour."

"Okay," I said. "It's going to take a while for everything to feel back to normal."

"When are we going to be reading a different book?"

"You don't like *The Road*?"

He thought for a moment. "I'll finish it, but are there any happy books?"

A wave of guilt washed over me. Maybe, given the current state of things, there were better choices than the apocalypse.

I thought a moment. "How about happy and funny?"

"Sure."

I didn't want to overwhelm him with a list. "Go to the library and find Carl Hiaasen." I spelled the last name for him. "He writes for grown-ups and young adults. See if they have *Hoot*."

Andrew said he would.

I was at my desk, trying to focus on lesson planning for the coming week, when there was a soft rapping at my open door. I looked up and saw Sally Berwick.

"Got a minute?" she asked.

I nodded and waved her in. I got up and the two of us sat sideways in student desks, across from each other, almost knee to knee.

"I just wanted to be sure about something," she said. "He really said my name? You heard him say he was coming for me?"

I wasn't going to tell her LeDrew had referred to her as "Fat Sally," although I had told that to the police. But she was the only Sally on staff, and she tended to fit the description.

"Yes," I said.

She nodded solemnly, as if this confirmation was what she was waiting to hear. "I'm quitting," she said, just like that.

"Maybe that's not something you should decide right now. Give it some time."

"I can't do this anymore. I'm clearly not good at what I do. I thought I was helping that boy."

"You *are* good at what you do. I bet you did everything you could for him."

"No, no, I didn't. I believed what I'd been told by others. That he had intellectual limitations. But I should have judged him on my own, found out what made him tick. I had a sense things at home were not good, that he wasn't close to his father, who was distant, critical.

48

Maybe I could have steered him toward something that would have suited him, but still presented a challenge, instead of underestimating him the way others had. Then maybe he wouldn't have become so . . . so angry about how we failed him. How I failed him."

Sally dug her fingernails into her palms. "It's not that I'm scared some other student is going to come in here and hunt us all down. I don't think lightning will strike twice like that. But I don't want to fail any more kids."

I took her hand in mine, pried open her fingers to get a better grip. "I don't know anyone in this school who cares about kids more than you do."

She smiled sadly at me. "They need someone in the billing department where my husband works. I don't have a lot of experience but they said I'll get the hang of it really fast and the job's there if I want it. I've put in enough years that I'll get a good chunk of my teachers' pension."

"If you think that's what's best."

"Every day now feels like a gift. We have a bit of money set aside, so we think we'll do some traveling, too. I've always wanted to go to London. Have you been to London?"

I nodded. "You'll love it." I let go of her hand.

"I want to see Buckingham Palace." She grinned. "Maybe the king will invite us in for tea."

"I'll call ahead, set something up."

She gave me another smile. "What about you? You staying?"

I shrugged. "I guess. I'm otherwise unemployable."

"Has it . . . changed you?"

I considered the question. "I don't think I know yet. But I'll tell you this. I'm ready for my life to get back to normal." I thought of something I wanted to ask her.

"Did Mark ever mention anything about a lawnmower man?"

Sally pushed her lips out, thinking. "Wasn't that a horror movie? I remember our son watching something like that."

49

"Yeah. But did he ever refer to an actual person that way?"

"Maybe it was something he wanted to be, like getting a job with a landscaping company."

I held her hand again and gave it a brief squeeze. "Enjoy your new life."

EIGHT

erb Willow waited outside the principal's office, wondering why he'd been summoned. The office secretary, Belinda, said Trent had been having private chats with all the staff, that it was no big deal, but Herb was worried it was something more than that. Herb would describe himself as a glass-half-empty kind of person, always expecting the worst, and most of the time life did not disappoint.

The door opened.

"Come in, Herb, have a seat," Trent said, guiding Herb to a chair across from his desk. "How are you doing?"

"I'm fine," he said flatly.

Trent said, "That's good, that's terrific. Just taking some time to talk to everybody, one-to-one, to see how they're doing, if there's anything I can help you with."

"I'm fine."

"And more specifically, to tell you that the board is offering counseling sessions to anyone who feels they would benefit."

"Are they, now."

"Sometimes, in the immediate aftermath of a traumatic incident, people think they can handle it, but then as time sets in they start feeling the effects. Nightmares, flashbacks, stuff like that. PTSD."

"Oh."

"The thing is, I figured what happened might have affected you more than some of the others. Not that we aren't all shook up about it."

"I'm not following."

Trent sighed. "Well, Herb, as you know, you were a likely target."

"You're referring to what Mark LeDrew is alleged to have said before he blew himself up?"

"Alleged?"

Herb nodded. "Yes. Alleged."

"I don't think what Mark said is in dispute."

"Did *you* hear what he said?"

"I was around the corner, not quite close enough to hear the entire conversation between Richard and Mark."

"So you *didn't* hear it," Herb said. "We've only got one person's word."

Trent was quiet for a moment, moving his tongue around the inside of this cheek, before he said, "So what are you saying? That Richard fabricated the conversation?"

"Well, either Mark said those things to try to assassinate my character, or he never said them at all and Richard Boyle made it all up for the same purpose."

Trent said nothing.

"Have you any idea what I've been put through the last few days? Police have *interrogated* me. As if I were a criminal. I have been persecuted. People are whispering behind my back. Did I try to blow up this school? Did I threaten to kill anybody? No. But the way they came at me, you'd think I had."

"So Mark was lying."

"If he said those things, yes."

"Or Richard is lying."

Herb shrugged, as though the answer was obvious.

"Why would Richard do that?"

"He doesn't respect me. Never has. Doesn't value the contribution I make to this school."

Trent said, "So, in the midst of a crisis, in a life-or-death moment, Richard Boyle decided this was his big chance to cast you, of all people, in a negative light."

"He didn't have to come up with it in the moment. He could have thought of it after."

Trent took a moment to collect his thoughts. "Herb, let me lay it out for you. I not only believe Mark said those things, and that Richard retold them accurately, I believe what Mark said was true. I've heard how you talk to your students. You puff yourself up by putting them down. You went too far with Mark LeDrew. Actions have consequences. I'm not saying it's your fault he came here intending to kill us all, but it's possible you lit the match."

Herb stood. "If you speak to me in this manner again, question my professionalism, I'll want my union rep with me. Maybe even a lawyer."

Trent sighed. The meeting was over. Herb turned and walked out of the office.

Herb held himself together until he got back to his classroom. His heart was hammering in his chest, droplets of sweat were beading up on his forehead. Once there, he closed the door, dropped into the chair, and flattened his palms on his desk until he had his breathing under control.

Another panic attack.

God knows, if there was anyone who could have benefited from those counseling sessions it was him. He'd been on an emotional razor's edge since learning what Mark LeDrew had said. Couldn't sleep, couldn't focus, nearly ran a red light the day before. But talking to somebody, spilling his guts to some school board shrink, would amount to an admission of culpability, wouldn't it?

Better to put up a good front that he had nothing to be concerned about. Tough it out.

But Jesus Christ on a cracker, he could have died Monday. If it hadn't been for that son of a bitch Richard, Herb might have finished his day in as many pieces as LeDrew did. Hard to get your head around. *My God*, he thought. *What would have become of Margaret?*

Okay, sure, maybe he'd been a little rough on the kid back in the day. But hadn't his intention always been to make the boy shape up? Make him tougher? Mold him into someone better than he was?

Of course. *That* was why Herb Willow had said those things. That was his story and he was sticking to it. His intention was not to humiliate, but *motivate*. Everyone had their own teaching style. Some coddled. But not Herb. Not a chance. The way you got these dumbass kids to learn things was to badger them, shame them. You were doing them a favor whether they appreciated it or not. Years later, once they'd made something of themselves, they'd thank you.

But he had to tell Trent that Boyle had been lying. The politically correct, touchy-feely admin types would never understand his methods. And let's face it. The LeDrew kid really had been dumber than a bag of hammers.

But it did give Herb pause. How many other current and former students had he spoken to this way? He'd have to modify his approach. If he had to baby them, mollycoddle them, to keep the powers that be happy, well, fine, that's what he would do. Principles be damned.

If Boyle'd had any sense of decency, he would have kept quiet about what LeDrew had said. What was the point? There was nothing any teacher might have done that would justify LeDrew's intentions. Why even bring it up?

What a way to treat a colleague.

Later, on hall patrol—a mundane task that fell to all teachers to make sure there were no strangers in the school, walking around like some beat cop—Herb spotted a student sitting on the floor, back up against the locker, a book propped on his raised knees, a phone on the floor next to him.

"Hey," Herb said. "You can't sit in the hall. Don't you have a class?"

"I've got a free period," the student said.

Herb recognized him. Andrew Keenan, or Kanin, or something. Yeah, Andrew Kanin. Kind of a weird kid. Withdrawn, awkward.

"Go read in the library, or the cafeteria," Herb said. "Someone could trip over you here. You're a hazard."

"I'm sitting here in case someone with a gun or a bomb comes in. I'm close to a door." He pointed to a double set that opened onto the back field. "I'll be able to make a quick getaway."

"What if someone comes in through *that* door? You'll be the first person he sees."

Andrew's face dropped, like he hadn't thought of that. Dumb kid, Herb thought.

Herb asked, "What are you reading?"

"*The Road*," he said.

"That's that one about the dad and his son and the end of the world?"

"Yeah."

He hadn't read the book but was familiar with the late author's reputation. Herb couldn't recall seeing it on any approved reading list.

"Reading it for fun?" It wasn't a sarcastic question. Kids—and plenty of adults—loved apocalyptic storylines. Couldn't get enough of them. Herb could remember, when he was barely ten years old, being transfixed by a TV-movie called *The Day After* that depicted the aftermath of a nuclear explosion. He was unable to stop thinking about it for days and wanted to see it again, but almost no one had a VCR in those days. You couldn't record stuff.

"It's for Mr. Boyle's class," Andrew said.

"Oh," Herb said. "Mr. Boyle. Any good?"

Andrew shrugged. "It's creepy."

"What's so creepy about it?"

"Like, civilization is totally wiped out and it's about how they

survive. People do some really awful things. Like eating each other."
Andrew put the book into his backpack and picked up his phone.
"I have to text my mom every hour."

"Okay," Herb said. He waited while Andrew typed a short note
and hit the send button. "So this book, sounds pretty troubling."

"Yeah."

"Did you ask to be excused from reading it? Because if it's upsetting
to you, if it triggers certain anxieties, you could get an exemption. It's
not right, Mr. Boyle making you read something that upsets you."

The boy considered that. "I didn't know you can get out of stuff
you don't like."

"Well, you can't do it with everything. A lot of us don't like math,
but that doesn't mean we don't have to take it. But if something upsets
you on an . . . I don't know, on an emotional level, something that's
very subjective, then sometimes a case can be made for being excused
from studying it. Like, let's say you had family in your past who were
killed in the Holocaust, you might feel uncomfortable reading Elie
Wiesel's *Night*."

"Who?"

"Doesn't matter. Just making a point." Herb sighed.

"Okay." Andrew tucked his phone into his pocket and turned to
leave.

"Hey," Herb said.

Andrew stopped, waited.

"You might want to talk to your parents about it."

"About what?"

"The book. If it's . . . objectionable in some way, they might want
to know. Just a thought." He smiled and added, "You didn't hear it
from me."

NINE

"Stuart!" Billy shouted. He banged on the door with his fist. "Stuart! Open up!"

Stuart lived in a second-floor unit of a low-rent motel in Milford. Most of the rentals were long-term, with only a few on the first floor available for transients who needed a place to stay for a couple of days, or certain types of businesswomen and their clients who might only need a room for an hour or two.

Billy was hitting the door hard enough that some neighbors had popped their heads out to see what the fuss was about. It wasn't unusual for the police to drop by, always good for breaking the monotony. But this was some regular guy making a racket, looking pretty pissed, and it was better not to get in the way of someone like that, so they closed their doors after taking a quick peek.

Billy heard a chain slide back and then the door opened.

"What the fuck?" Stuart said, a video game controller in his hand. "I had my 'buds in and couldn't hear—"

Billy put a hand on Stuart's chest and shoved him back into the room. He tripped on his own feet and landed on his back on the unmade double bed. The game controller hit the floor.

"Jesus," Stuart said.

"Need a word," Billy said, closing the door behind him and turning off the TV where Stuart had been virtually wandering some dark alley, shooting one person after another.

This was, at least by this motel's standards, one of the nicer units. The bedroom area was up front by the door, while a small nook with a table and four chairs, a small fridge, and a cooktop took up the back. This, plus a bathroom, was home sweet home for Stuart.

He got himself sitting on the end of the bed while Billy paced back and forth, his face flushed.

Stuart said, "You look like you're gonna have a heart attack or something. You got blood on your shirt."

Billy stopped pacing and pointed a finger at him. "You need to be a hundred percent straight with me here."

"'Bout what?"

"Psycho Bitch and Butthead paid me a visit. And not on a pickup day."

"So?"

"They're saying I stole from them."

"Did you?" Stuart asked.

"I look like I got a death wish? Look at this." He lifted up his shirt to reveal a large purple bruise and a bandage taped over the right side of his chest. "Nipple was practically hanging off."

"Fuck," Stuart said. "How did they—"

There wasn't time to finish the question. Billy grabbed him by the shirt, threw him down on the floor, and sat on his stomach, straddling him with his legs, pinning his arms.

"Billy! Get the fuck—"

Billy released one arm and grabbed Stuart's jaw so he could stop his head from moving and fixed his glare on him. "You gotta be straight with me like never before. If you took it, if you admit it, right now, without my having to beat the truth out of you, then okay, we'll figure out how to handle it. Say you didn't know it was theirs. Something. Then you give me the money to pay them back. Make things right."

"Billy, I didn't take—"

"Do not fucking lie to me. This is your one chance, Stuart. Maybe one time, when I was asleep or something, you took my key and opened the locker and helped yourself to just a little of what was in there? Didn't think I'd notice? Didn't think *they'd* notice?"

"You're my fucking *friend*!" Stuart said, taking a swing with his free arm at Billy's face and missing. "Make that *ex*-friend! Jesus!"

And then Stuart started to weep.

"Oh shit," Billy said, getting off his friend and standing. He extended a hand to help him up.

"Fuck you," Stuart said, and found his own way up.

"I'm just—I'm losing my mind here, man. I'm sorry."

Stuart walked to a far corner of the room, and now it was his turn to point.

"Listen, if I *had* taken any of your shit, I'd have been within my rights to do it. You always freeze me out." He sniffed, took a tissue from his pocket, and wiped his nose. "I could have helped you with it, helped you hide stuff, done whatever you needed, but no. That's not how you treat friends."

He opened his arms wide to indicate his residence. "Look at this shithole. How do you sleep at night in your nice house with your nice wife you can fuck whenever you want knowing this is how I live?" He shook his head. "And then accusing me of ripping you off. I didn't do it. I didn't touch your shit."

Billy hung his head. "Okay." He found a chair and sat. "I gotta pay them back. Where do I find that kind of money? I don't make this right, they'll fucking kill me."

"They've got you in place. They *need* you."

Billy shook his head. "They'll find someone else. Another guy at another airport. Bring it in by truck. FedEx it, whatever. I got a good thing going here and I'm gonna lose it if I don't find out what happened to that shipment."

"Maybe somebody dipped into it before it got put on the plane," Stuart said, his voice softening.

"They say no."

"Who else knows what you're holding for them?"

"Nobody."

Stuart gave him a look, like maybe Billy knew but wasn't willing to admit it.

"What?" Billy said.

"It's not for me to say."

"No, no way. No fucking way. Lucy wouldn't do that."

Stuart nodded. "Of course not. You're right. She wouldn't."

Billy bit his lip and looked away.

TEN

Richard

The day was over and I was heading for the parking lot when I ran into Trent in the hall.

"You got five?" he asked.

I followed him to his office. He had his suit jacket off and his sleeves rolled up, not a look he adopted very often but a sign that it had been as long a day for him as it had been for me.

"New watch?" I asked.

It had a blue face with white numbers and a brown leather band. I caught a glimpse of the name TIMEX on the face. He glanced at it, rolled his eyes, and said, "Yeah, the battery on the last one died."

Classic Trent. It was easier to buy a cheap new watch than take a dead one someplace to have a battery replaced. As long as I'd known him, I'd rarely seen him fix anything. He wasn't mechanically minded and, more than that, he couldn't be bothered. Toaster broken? Don't try to determine what's wrong with it. Pitch it and get a new one. Your stick vacuum won't suck because it's clogged? Replace it. It drove his wife, Melanie, crazy. "At least he hasn't replaced me yet," she'd said on more than one occasion.

He'd already told me about the available counseling services, so I didn't know what this meeting was about. He asked Belinda to hold his calls for the next few minutes, then waved me to come around to his side of the desk. I stood at his shoulder as he dropped into this chair and opened a browser on his computer screen.

"Guessing you haven't seen this," he said.

"Seen what?"

"Noon news."

He was on one of the local TV news sites. Trent clicked on an item.

"What is it?" I asked.

"Oh hell," he said. Before he could show me the news item, we had to wait for one ad to finish, and another to start. As soon as he was allowed to skip the rest of the ad, he did so.

I saw a familiar face. It was one of the news reporters who'd been here Monday. She was standing on the street in front of a house I did not recognize.

"Whose house is—"

Trent raised a hand to quiet me.

The reporter said, *"Angus and Fiona LeDrew buried their son yesterday, but their ordeal is far from over. Their boy, Mark, died tragically on Monday at Lodge High School, and his parents want to know why."*

"Boy?" I said.

"While they acknowledge Mark came to the school with an explosive device, which subsequently detonated, no one else was harmed. They believe Mark could have survived if greater care had been taken in dealing with the situation."

Then Mark's parents were on-screen, sitting in their living room, the mother dabbing at tears on her cheek, the husband's head bowed as he spoke.

"We want to know what that teacher who talked to Mark said exactly, whether he told him the best thing to do was take his own life, to go ahead and blow himself up outside the school to save others. Why weren't the police called? Why wasn't there a bomb specialist there? Why aren't teachers trained to deal with these kinds of situations?"

Back out front of the house, the reporter summed up: "*The LeDrews have launched a multimillion-dollar suit against the teacher, Richard Boyle, the school's administration, and the quarry where their son once worked, where it is believed he acquired the dynamite. This is Lorraine Wilders reporting.*"

Trent stopped the video and swiveled around in his chair to look at me. A bird could have flown into my mouth.

"I know," Trent said. "It's nuts."

"I got him to change his mind. He tripped on his goddamn bootlaces and let go of the button. They didn't cover this shit when I went to teachers college."

"That's what you'll tell them. The lawyers. Everyone. I've got a call into the board now. Maybe you sit down for an interview or something, for TV. Make people understand you deserve to have a school named after you, not get sued."

I was numb.

Trent said, "They'll try to make something out of the fact that no one else really saw or heard what happened. There's a couple of cameras, one just above the door that looks out onto the schoolyard, and another at the other end of the hall that looks down toward the west entrance, but none of the surveillance footage really shows that very well, and they don't pick up sound. They can't prove their allegations."

"You were around the corner. You were ready to take a shot. You must have heard something."

Trent shrugged. "Not much, but it's irrelevant. Trust me, this suit isn't going anywhere. You've probably got a case of your own you could file against the LeDrews. You've got to live with that trauma for God knows how many years."

"Why would they do this?"

"Well, money, first of all. And look, they're probably blaming themselves. Not knowing how distressed he was. Not knowing he was making a bomb. They need to find someone else to lay this off on. Putting the blame on you, the school, the quarry, it takes some of the pressure off them." He paused. "I know a little about him, the father. He wasn't much of a presence in Mark's life. Distant, uninvolved. Maybe this is his way of coping with the guilt over that. Going after everyone else."

I had no more words. I turned and walked out of Trent's office and left the building.

Once in the car, I texted Bonnie, asked her to call. But she had the same job Trent did, so she could be in a staff meeting or dealing with a parent or putting out some other kind of fire. There was always something.

I went straight home.

Depending on what after-school activities we might be involved in, Bonnie and I usually weren't back at the house until around five. So when Rachel finished school, she went to Mrs. Tibaldi's place one street over. Mrs. Tibaldi ran a home day care, so she had five kids through the day, then took on another four school-age children once school was out, supervising them until their parents came to fetch them.

It was only four, and I could have picked up Rachel early, but I needed time to think about this latest development.

I was getting out of the car when someone called to me.

"Mr. Boyle?"

I spun around. There was a young man standing there. Mid- to late twenties, I was guessing. Jeans and a sweatshirt, ball cap. As a teacher, you were always a minor celebrity in your own town. Former students spotting you, wanting to say hello after not seeing you for years. Maybe that's what this was. Or just as likely it was someone who recognized me from the news and wanted to offer some words of congratulations or gratitude. If that was the case, he clearly hadn't heard the latest.

"Yes?" I said.

"Mr. Boyle from Lodge High?"

I nodded.

"Remember me?" he asked.

A former student. Sometimes you knew who they were but just as often you couldn't place them. Given this young man's age, he'd probably graduated from Lodge within the last decade. I was struggling to recognize him.

"I'm afraid you have me at a disadvantage," I said, smiling apologetically.

He smiled and said, "Billy Finster."

I was rifling through a mental Rolodex, trying to place the name. *Finster. Finster. Finster.*

The name registered, faintly. I didn't think he'd been a student of mine, but you couldn't remember all of them. Well, Bonnie could. She was amazing that way. Five hundred students in her school, and she could probably name four hundred and fifty of them. For me, it was a little harder.

"Right," I said, nodding slowly. "I remember the name, but you've probably changed a lot since you graduated." I grinned. "You've grown up."

"I guess," he said. "So you're the big hero now. Saw it on the news."

"Yeah, well, it's been quite a week. Listen, it was nice—"

"I need to talk to you about something," he said.

"Maybe another time," I said, glancing at the house and then my watch to suggest I might have some pressing engagement. "But thanks for saying hello."

"I really think you're going to want to hear what I have to say," he said. "It's time to have a talk about what you did to me."

ELEVEN

"How much longer?" the girl asked.

Her name was Allison. She was ten years old and in the fourth grade, and she was sitting in the office of Principal Bonnie Harper, who, instead of being at her desk, was in one of the two other chairs, huddling in close with the young girl so they could talk face-to-face.

"I hope not long," Bonnie said. "Your aunt lives up in Hartford, so it could take a while for her to get here. But I'll stay with you until she does, no matter how long."

Allison nodded. "Do you know why my mom didn't come home last night? I had to get ready for school all by myself today."

Bonnie certainly knew some of it. The details were sketchy, but from what her sister, Marta, who was investigating the case, had told her, Allison's mother, Cherise Fowler, had been found dead in an alley around the corner from the bar where she'd last been seen. The bartender had tried to talk her into taking a cab or an Uber home, as she'd given every indication of being high, in addition to drunk.

She waved him off and departed. Her body had been discovered shortly before noon by a sanitation crew coming through to empty trash bins.

Paramedics and police were called, but there was nothing they could do. The woman had been dead for several hours. And while the results of an autopsy were pending, Marta, who had come to the school when she learned the dead woman's daughter was a pupil here, had said she would not be surprised to learn it was a fentanyl overdose. It was the second such incident they'd seen that week, according to Marta, who told her fentanyl was fifty times stronger than heroin, a hundred times stronger than morphine. Too much of that shit and it was game over.

The only backup contact in the girl's school file was for an aunt named Louise, who lived up in Hartford. Allison's father had vanished from the scene shortly after her birth, and Cherise had been raising the child—if you could call her haphazard parenting that—on her own. Bonnie and Allison's teacher were well aware her home situation was not ideal—perilous, in fact—and they had, as they were obliged to do, notified the authorities on more than one occasion. Allison had been removed from the home a couple of times and placed locally, and last year had spent a month living up in Hartford, attending a different school, while Cherise did a stint in rehab.

Allison frequently came to school without breakfast, wearing clothes that had not been laundered in weeks. She often made her own lunch before leaving home—a peanut butter sandwich—and it had broken Bonnie's heart that she had to ask her if she could make something different in the morning, like a jam sandwich, because two of the kids in Allison's class had peanut allergies and the parents had complained.

Bonnie could remember Allison's cheerful accommodation: "Oh, okay. I can make a sandwich with marshmallow fluff."

Fortunately, the school had a breakfast program in place for less fortunate children, and the child was able to get something to eat even if nothing had been provided for her at home. Bonnie always made sure there was something left for Allison. But this was a girl who needed much more than something in her stomach. She needed a stable home environment, and that was something Bonnie could not provide.

When Allison, sitting there in the office, asked Bonnie whether she knew what had happened, why she was not able to head home like she did every other day, Bonnie was unsure how much to say.

"Your mother had a problem today, so that's why we want you to stay here until your aunt arrives."

"My aunt works till five, I think," Allison said. "It's a long drive to get here. Especially if there's traffic."

"I think maybe she's able to get off early today, so . . ."—Bonnie glanced at her watch—"I'm betting she'll be here within the hour."

Allison nodded thoughtfully. Then, as if asking what the weather would be like tomorrow, she said, "Is my mom dead?"

Bonnie said, "What makes you ask that, Allison?"

The girl looked at her with large, soulful eyes. "She has problems."

"I know, honey."

"I had to go live with Aunt Louise last year while she got better."

"I remember."

"Sometimes she stops taking the drugs," Allison said plainly. "But then she starts doing them again. I tell her not to but she doesn't listen to me."

"That's good advice. But sometimes people won't do what's best for themselves."

"I make dinner for her and do the dishes when she's out of it. I make good hot dogs. They're easy. I just boil them."

"That's good of you, to look after her."

Allison nodded, like you did what you had to do. "I'm scared she won't get better."

"Yeah."

"So is that what happened?"

Bonnie said, "I think that whatever your mother's situation is, it's something your aunt would want to discuss with you."

Allison considered that, then slowly shook her head from side to side. "You're the principal, so it's like you're an official person."

Bonnie leaned in closer. "You're right, Allison. Your mom . . . you asked if she had died. I'm afraid she has. I'm so sorry."

Allison looked away for a moment, unable to meet Bonnie's eyes.

"Even though your mother had a lot of problems, she did something pretty remarkable. She brought up a wonderful, caring young girl. Anyone who could do that is pretty special. Just like you."

Allison went very quiet. They sat there, knees almost touching, neither of them saying a word for several seconds.

"I wish there were something I could say or do to make it better," Bonnie said.

"It's okay," Allison said. "It's okay if you want to cry."

God, this kid, Bonnie thought.

TWELVE

Richard

"What do you mean, Billy? What did I do?"

We were still standing at the end of the driveway. He glanced at the bandages still on my neck and forehead. "Lucky you didn't get your head blown clean off, huh?"

"Billy, what can I help you with?"

He took a few steps over to my car, propped himself up on the back end, and crossed his arms. "You're saying you really don't remember?"

"Sorry, I'm at a loss here. Did you have classes with me? Because, honestly, I don't remember. I'm sorry. I see a lot of students over the years."

And that was the truth. I was as sure as I could be I'd never had Billy Finster in my homeroom or any of my English classes.

"Gym class," he said.

I shook my head, not understanding.

"I didn't teach gym. Never have."

"Oh yeah?" he said. "Then why's your picture in my yearbook, doing just that?"

"What picture? What are you talking about?"

"There's a picture of you and the wrestling team."

I thought back. There was something in what he said that triggered a memory. A teacher had been on leave a while back when his wife became seriously ill. What the hell was his name?

Reynolds.

Right. Anson Reynolds. Taught physical education at Lodge. Was off for the better part of a month. Someone was hired part-time to cover his classes, but his extracurriculars were divvied out among existing staff. I'd been asked to be among those to oversee the wrestling team. I didn't know a damn thing about wrestling, but I gave it my best shot. And I didn't have to be an expert to oversee the team's practices.

"I remember," I said. "I didn't teach phys ed, but yeah, I took on some part-time coaching of the wrestling team, after school, when another teacher was away."

"Yeah, right, bingo," he said, making a gun out of his fingers and firing a shot my way.

More memories started flooding back. I supervised a few matches when other schools came to Lodge for events. And when our team traveled to other schools, I would go along on the bus to keep everybody in line.

He was reading my face. "Coming back to you now, isn't it?"

"What is it you think you remember, Billy?"

"I was on the team," he said. "When we went to another school, you liked to sit right in the back of the bus, like you were supervising, where you could watch everybody, but you really liked it back there because no one could see what *you* were up to. And you liked me to sit back there with you. When we were coming back from a match, when it was dark, that was when you'd really get going. All grabby hands and shit."

"Listen to me, and listen real close," I said, trying to keep my voice under control. "I have no idea what you're talking about, and whatever it is you're implying, it did not happen."

"So I remember it all wrong," he said, smiling.

"Yes, Billy, you do," I said. I was rattled, but I held my anger

71

in check. If Billy had been abused when he was at Lodge, I felt an obligation to get more information.

"Look, I'm not saying it didn't happen to you. I'm saying it wasn't *me*. But if it did happen, it was wrong. Very wrong. You've every right, even after all this time, to have whoever it was held accountable. If you want, I'll look into whatever services are available for someone in your position. Legal, counseling, whatever. I'll speak to my principal. I could set up a meeting between the two of you."

He nodded slowly, but he had this sly grin on his face that wouldn't go away.

If what he was alleging happened, it was most likely Anson Reynolds who did it. Maybe this was something Anson had done before or after his leave. Or maybe it was someone else who'd filled in for him. I hadn't been the only one.

One thing I knew for certain was that Anson, if he was the offender, was never going to answer for this. He was dead. He'd died about four years ago.

But again, how did you get something like this wrong? Even if it was dark coming home on the bus at night. I mean, come on. Somebody puts their hand down your pants, you tend to remember who it was.

And on top of that, I always sat at the front of the bus.

"You make it sound like you really care," he said.

"Believe it or not, Billy, I do. But at the same time, I don't like being accused of something I haven't done. I wish you nothing but the best in dealing with this."

"You're this big hero now, aren't you? Saved everybody from the crazy bomber. What would they think if they knew the truth? Bet they'd forget all that hero shit in a minute if they knew you're a fucking perv. Bet they'd forget *real fast*."

"I don't have any more to say about this, Billy."

"Lots of people coming forward these days," he said. "For a long time, they were too embarrassed, but now they're encouraged to unburden themselves, you know? That it's nothing to be ashamed about. That it's not their fault. That's kind of where I am now. I'm thinking of, you know, unburdening myself."

"All that's true. What you're saying was done to you, it's wrong. Unbelievably wrong. When people in authority abuse the power they hold over others, take advantage—listen, as far as I'm concerned, there's no punishment too harsh for them. The damage they do is incalculable. So I'm prepared, right now, to find you help. A counseling service. I'll call the police, if you want."

"Yeah," he said slowly. "The police. They'd be good to talk to, but the thing is, I wanted to come to you before I went to them because I was thinking maybe we could work something out."

Those last three words hung in the air for a moment. "Work something out," I said.

"That's right. That we could come to some kind of arrangement."

"I see," I said. "So what it comes down to, Billy, is you're a blackmailer."

"Better a blackmailer than a kid diddler," he said. He dug a ratty tissue out of his pocket and wiped his nose. "Ten grand. Ten thousand dollars. You come up with that and it's like I come down with a case of amnesia. I'll forget it ever happened."

"You're crazy," I said.

I was searching for an explanation. Maybe Anson *had* done it, and when this guy decided the time had come to blackmail him, he'd learned Anson was dead. He'd already spent the money in his head and decided to go after someone else.

"I'm cutting you some slack because I know teachers get paid real shitty. If it was anybody else, I'd ask twice that. I'll give you, I don't know, till Tuesday. Because it's almost the weekend and the banks are closed and shit. So, you come up with the money by Tuesday. We can meet at the food court in the Post Mall. Five o'clock. Cash. I don't want a check."

"Billy, you've got the wrong guy."

73

"Tuesday," he said.

That grin still on his face, he gave me a thumbs-up, walked a short ways down the sidewalk, got behind the wheel of a white pickup truck cancered with rust, and drove off.

Jesus Christ, I thought. *I can't go through something like this again.*

THIRTEEN

"**H**ow was your day, sweetie pie?"

God, Herb hated it when she called him that. Thank God no one else ever heard it. What grown man wants his mother calling him *sweetie pie*? But hey, add it to the list of annoying things he had learned to live with, almost didn't even notice anymore. When you've been sharing quarters with your mother for fifty-three years (not counting the time he was away at college) it was a little late in the game to start complaining about pet names. Especially now, what with her in decline and all.

Margaret Willow was where she always was when Herb got home from work, sitting in her recliner with all the buttons—up, down, vibrate—built into the armrest. She still had trouble figuring out the TV remote, usually because she wasn't pressing the buttons hard enough with her feeble fingers, but she'd mastered everything the chair would do. She could tilt it back, lean it forward, even have it massage her legs or back. And when she wanted to get up, the chair would lift her up partway. Herb imagined if it had a faster setting, she'd be shot out of the chair like a Bond villain being ejected through the roof of 007's Aston Martin.

The television, volume high enough to rattle windows, was tuned to a station that ran reruns of crime dramas from the seventies and eighties. Any hour of the day, you could catch a *Murder, She Wrote* or a *Hawaii Five-O* or a *Matlock* or a *Barnaby Jones* and it didn't matter how many times she might have seen an episode, Margaret wouldn't remember it. It had not always been that way. She was losing her memory—short-term and long.

Margaret didn't watch the news anymore, wasn't computer-savvy, and Herb had canceled newspaper delivery to the door more than a year ago. So she was blissfully unaware that four days earlier someone had come to his place of work with plans to blow him up. Martians could have landed in Darien and Margaret wouldn't have known about it, at least not until one of them walked into the living room, took her remote from her, and turned off *Columbo*.

Herb knew she'd have been upset had she known. The real challenge had been acting like nothing had happened. That panic attack at school was not the first. At least he didn't have to fake being happy or cheerful at home, because Herb was never happy or cheerful.

"Fine, Mother," he said, in answer to her question about how his day had been. He came through the front door with a take-out bag in one hand and his school briefcase in the other. "What's new here?"

"McGarrett is chasing this guy who has a rooster and who choked a little girl to death when he stole a fish from a koi pond," she said.

"I brought Chinese."

She smiled. "Oh wonderful. I hadn't quite figured out what to do for dinner tonight." His mother hadn't figured out what to do for dinner since the second Bush was in the White House. "Don't forget extra soy sauce for the rice."

"Okay, Mother."

He set the briefcase on the kitchen table and the take-out bag on the counter. He got out two plates, took out the containers, pried off the lids, and spooned out the food. Take-out was a treat. Most nights he came home and made dinner for the two of them, just as he had for the last twenty-two years, ever since his father came down for

76

breakfast one morning, prepared himself a bowl of Shredded Wheat, and dropped dead.

Herb had never lived on his own. He'd never married, never had a girlfriend, and after his father passed he wasn't about to leave Mother to fend for herself. It was a safe, comfortable existence, living here. His parents had already paid off the mortgage on the house, so it was certainly an economical existence, too. Despite her declining mental faculties, Margaret still did the laundry. She could load a washing machine and put in the right amount of detergent like there was some muscle memory at play. Herb had offered to take on that job but she insisted on doing it. If it made her happy, what the hell, and there wasn't anything laundry-related that might trigger a catastrophe, so long as he remembered to clear the lint filter. But he wanted to keep her away from the stove, didn't want her vacuuming the stairs on unsteady legs.

Herb brought her dinner to her in the recliner, setting it on a board placed across the arms. He took a nearby chair so they could eat together.

"How was school today?" Margaret asked, nearly shouting to be heard over the television.

Herb shrugged. "People don't like me."

Margaret's face fell. "Don't say that. Of course people like you. You're a wonderful boy." She bit into a chicken ball. "I don't understand why you would say a thing like that. You're the nicest boy any mother could have."

She popped the rest of the chicken ball into her mouth, chewed a couple of times, and started to cough. Herb waited to see whether she'd resolve the problem on her own, or if he'd have to jump up and Heimlich her.

She stopped coughing, speared another chicken ball with her fork, and went at it.

The phone rang. It sat on a small table next to Margaret's chair. "I'll get it, Mother," Herb said, but she was already on it. They'd hung on to a landline because Margaret wasn't good with cell phones. She couldn't figure them out, and forgot to charge them. Herb had to remind her constantly to hang up on spam calls. He'd made sure she had no access to credit cards so she wouldn't become a victim.

"Hello?" she said. "I'm sorry, what did you say?"

"Mother?" Herb said, now on his feet, holding his hand out for the phone.

"Oh yes, just a moment." She looked up at Herb and said, "It's for you." She lowered her voice to a whisper. "It's a lady."

Margaret, even at this late stage, never gave up hope that Herb would find someone.

He took the receiver from her, motioning for her to turn down the television volume, and said into the phone, "Yes?"

"Oh hello," said the woman. "I wasn't sure this was the right number, but there's only a couple Willows in the book. Is this the teacher?"

He could barely hear her. Margaret hadn't yet quieted the television. "Yes. Hang on, I'm going to take this on the other line."

He put down the receiver and told his mother he was going to continue the call in the kitchen. When he got there and picked up the receiver on the wall-mounted extension, he shouted, "Hang up now!"

He listened, heard the click, closed the door between the kitchen and the living room, and said, "Sorry."

"Was that Mrs. Willow?"

"That's my mother. Who is this?"

"This is Violet Kanin? Andrew Kanin's mother? He says you and Andrew were talking today?"

Well, well, he thought.

"Yes. Yes, we were."

"I thought, before I take this any further, I would talk to you, since Andrew brought up something I wasn't aware of, and I wanted to confirm it with you before I talked to Mr. Boyle or the principal."

Herb smiled inwardly. "Go ahead."

78

"This book Andrew's been told to read—is it okay if I talk to you about this? Is that appropriate? I didn't want to bother Mr. Boyle, at least not yet, because he's been through quite an ordeal and we're all grateful for what he did."

"He sure is something, isn't he?"

"But this book has made Andrew uncomfortable and I've started reading parts of it and I really don't know how anyone could justify putting it on the curriculum. Not only does it deal with very distressing subject matter, but it's very ungrammatical in places. I suppose the author did that deliberately for some *literary* effect, but if we're trying to teach students proper spelling and sentence structure, this certainly doesn't seem like the way to go about it."

"I hear you," Herb said.

"Andrew said you told him he could opt out of studying it. So if I wrote a note to Mr. Boyle and explained our position, that would take care of it?"

"I think it would," Herb said, and then thought about what he wanted to say next. "Unless you want to take a look at the broader issue."

"The broader issue?"

"Well, let's say you don't want Andrew to read this particular book. What will the next one be? Will it be even more objectionable?"

There was a silence at the other end of the call.

"Hello?" Herb said.

"I hadn't thought about that."

"I guess—and you don't have to do this if you don't want to—but I guess if it were me, I might talk to some of the other parents and see what they think. And when you've formulated your position, as a group, you could decide what to do then. Whether to talk to the teacher in question—I'm speaking generally here, not singling out Mr. Boyle—or whether to take it up with the principal or the school board."

"I see," Violet Kanin said.

"Listen, I'm just tossing out ideas here. It really has to be your decision. And if you don't mind, it's probably best if we keep this conversation between ourselves. The last thing I would want is to be thought of as interfering."

"Oh, I totally understand. Thank you so much."

"Not a problem. Happy to help."

He ended the call and went back into the living room. His mother looked at him expectantly.

"Well?" she asked coyly. "Who was that?"

"Just somebody."

"A friend?"

Herb smiled. "Maybe so, Mother. Maybe so."

FOURTEEN

Richard

This couldn't be happening.

I went into the house in a daze, unable to get my head around the situation I found myself in. On Monday I felt myself perched on the edge of the abyss. Now I felt as though I had fallen in. I felt light-headed, almost dizzy. Like stepping into traffic without looking and having a car whip past you at sixty miles per hour, missing you by inches.

I was shell-shocked.

I wandered into the kitchen, still too fazed to consider my options. I went to the fridge for some vodka and soda and made myself a drink. Downed it and made another. I had to settle my nerves before I began to think about how to handle this.

Ten thousand dollars. By Tuesday. Four days from now.

It was ridiculous. Of course I wasn't going to pay this man off. It was unthinkable.

Right?

I wouldn't do it. Someone I don't remember accuses me of something I didn't do, and I'm supposed to hand over ten thousand dollars to him? Of course not.

And when I refused to comply, what would happen? I call his bluff. Would he really go public? Would he go to Trent? The police? The media? He'd be running an enormous risk if he did. Wouldn't I then tell the world that he was nothing more than a common blackmailer?

Of course I would.

And people would believe me.

Except . . .

What proof did I have? I didn't have our conversation recorded. There were no witnesses. It had just been the two of us. My word against his. Not only the conversation, but what he was alleging had transpired years earlier.

Shit.

None of this was as simple as it looked. When it came to an allegation like this, it didn't matter whether there was any truth to it. Once it was out there, once it was *public*, it could finish you. Even if your accuser could eventually be discredited, charged, tried, and convicted of blackmail, there'd still be those who believed there was something there, some kernel of truth. Just because someone's an extortionist doesn't mean his story is bogus.

I could think of half a dozen celebrity cases to prove the point. That guy who made all the funny movies. That congressman from Florida. Convicted in people's minds, even if never in a court of law. And for a teacher, well, the stakes were even higher. The rumors would be enough to end my career. They'd follow me for the rest of my life.

Again, *Shit.*

This could do more than finish me off. It could destroy Bonnie. It would scar Rachel.

How would Bonnie be able to continue overseeing a school, to hold a position with that level of authority, with her husband accused of molesting a student? I could imagine the attacks on her already.

If you'd cover up for your husband, you'd cover up for your staff.

If you didn't know, you should have. And if you did, you shouldn't be in any job where you're working with kids.

Yeah, she'd be finished.

Rachel would be teased, ridiculed, tormented. We'd have to move her to another school. Or worse. We'd all have to move to another town, start over, find new, different jobs. And what if the accusation prompted an investigation that could remove Rachel from our home?

The potential fallout was immeasurable.

I was giving myself a nervous breakdown, imagining the various possible scenarios.

So then, what if I did pay him?

He'd made it sound like he was looking for a onetime payoff, but what was to stop him from coming back for more? I'd have to find a way to get money I didn't have. If, at some later date, his extortion became known to the police, the big question would be: *Why did you pay him off if you weren't guilty?*

If only he could step in front of a bus between now and Tuesday.

Maybe, just maybe, if I hadn't dodged a similar bullet three years earlier, I'd have told him to fuck off, taken my chances calling his bluff.

But there was the issue of Lyall Temple.

He was a thirteen-year-old kid in my ninth-grade English class. Small for his age, barely five feet tall, freckled, with reddish brown hair. And he was, whatever this word means these days, *gifted*. The only one in the class who'd read *Moby-Dick*, and that included the teacher. He devoured books the way his classmates went through pizza. He took oboe lessons. He collected vintage SF digest magazines like *Analog*, *Galaxy*, and *Asimov's Science Fiction*. He had at least fifty different models of robots from movies and TV shows. He could multiply three figures by two figures in his head. I once saw him solve a jumbled Rubik's Cube in under a minute. He was quiet and hard to read emotionally. Not a demonstrative kid.

Lyall was an original, and I had some familiarity with his sense of being an outsider. When I was his age, I didn't feel that I fit in. Few of my contemporaries shared my obsessive, albeit passing, interests in Ed Wood movies, or the architect Frank Lloyd Wright, or real-life sightings of UFOs.

But my heart really went out to him when his father, coming back from a business trip in Buffalo, was cut off by a tractor-trailer on the New York Thruway and went into a bridge abutment at seventy miles per hour west of Albany. He died instantly. He was forty-nine.

Lyall was off school for more than a week. There was a funeral, of course, which Bonnie and I attended. When he returned, he tried to act as though nothing had happened. He'd never been one to show his feelings. He was quiet before, and he was quiet now.

At the end of one class, he came to me as I sat at my desk and asked what assignments he needed to get caught up on. I told him not to worry about them. But he was insistent. I was going through my lesson planner, looking for a couple of token things he could do that would make him feel better, when he whispered something to me.

"I heard them say his brains were on the windshield."

I put aside my lesson planner and shifted around to face him. He was a dam ready to burst.

"I'm so sorry, Lyall."

Still whispering, he said, "It's in my head."

"It'll take time," I said. "You're a strong kid. But holding it together is hard. You may have to let it out sometime. You can't keep everything bottled up. When you get home—"

His arms went around my neck and he began to sob. Instinctively, I put my arms around him. Held him. Felt his body shake.

My door happened to be open, and it was at that moment that Evan Hayle, an eleventh-grade student and a true shit if there ever was one, caught sight of my attempt to console Lyall, fired off a couple of quick shots with his phone. Within minutes he had shared it online with the comment How to get an A from Mr. Boyle!

My face was clearly visible in the shot, but Lyall, visible only from behind, could have been anyone. It was the next morning when I learned how widely the picture had been distributed. It had gone viral, at least within the Lodge High School community. And as it spread, it garnered more salacious comments. Mr Boyle LOVES his kids and Boyle's Butt Boy and Gives new meaning to sucking up to the teacher were some of the milder ones.

84

It was another student who brought it to my attention the following morning. I was seething with anger, not so much for myself but for Lyall. What a cruel thing to do to someone who'd already been through so much. Trent had me come down to the office, said he was already getting calls from parents wanting to know what the hell was going on.

It got cleared up, eventually. Lyall himself told Trent what had happened. Evan, tracked down as the culprit, said he was only goofing around, that he didn't know it was Lyall, claimed to not even be aware that Lyall's father had died. He was suspended for a week. The dust settled, the truth came out.

That didn't stop people I didn't even know, for some time, from giving me the side-eye. At the grocery store, the gas station. Not everyone got the follow-up memo. Which was why I was struggling with what to do now. I could stand fast. Let this son of a bitch go public. State my denials, fire back with accusations.

But something always sticks. Especially when there's a history.

I needed to talk to somebody. Bonnie would normally have been the most obvious, logical one, but this shit couldn't have come at a worse time.

My personal entanglements, despite the best of intentions, had consistently backfired. That episode with Lyall. That kid who stole my wallet. And most spectacularly, my near-death experience with Mark LeDrew.

Add *Billy the Blackmailer* to the list.

It wouldn't matter that it wasn't my fault. It'd be one more stupid mess I'd gotten myself into, as far as Bonnie was concerned. And what if, somehow, I was to blame? I certainly hadn't abused this guy in the way he'd alleged, but you see a thousand students in your time and make more than your share of mistakes. Had I wrongly accused him of cheating on a test? Given him a D when he'd earned a B in some class I couldn't recall?

There was another reason not to tell Bonnie. The professional one.

Considering her position, was it fair to involve her? Could this blow back on her if this whole mess ever did become public, and she had to admit she'd known about it from the beginning?

And, really, did I want to have to sit Bonnie down and tell her what someone was alleging I'd done?

There was her sister, Marta. A police detective. Could I tell her? Would she believe my side of the story, or be more concerned about how this would affect Bonnie?

A lawyer, maybe. Or Trent. But I'd be putting him in a tough spot, too.

God, what a clusterfuck.

Was paying my blackmailer the worst option, except for *not* paying him? And how would I go about it? Bonnie and I had joint accounts. She kept a close eye on where the money went.

A lot of people might think ten thousand dollars doesn't sound like a lot, at least when it comes to blackmail. If this were a movie, or if I were a politician in the real world, any extortionist worth his salt would ask for a hundred thousand, maybe a million.

But this wasn't the movies, and I wasn't running for office. For regular people, ten grand was a fair chunk of change, no question, even for Bonnie and me, and we both had good jobs and a house and two cars in the driveway. But we'd just paid off the mortgage on that house, scraping together most of our savings to make it happen. We'd had to redo the roof five months earlier when a powerful storm swept through Milford and ripped off half the shingles. And then there was that three grand I gave to my cousin Stan without running it past Bonnie first.

We were not, at this point in time, awash in cash. Banks didn't typically extend loans to blackmail victims.

But I did have one idea.

The boat.

I could sell the boat. I didn't know what it was worth, exactly, but surely it would bring ten grand. I'd kept it in good shape. The fifty-horsepower outboard was well maintained. I had all the service receipts. I could do some quick research on its value, post ads online. But how quickly could I sell it? I had a deadline that was only four days away.

I heard a car pull into the driveway.

Bonnie.

I'd been so preoccupied I'd forgotten to go for Rachel. I came charging out the front door before Bonnie had her seat belt unbuckled. She had the door half open as I raised a hand and walked past.

"Hey, hold up," she said.

"Just going for Rach."

"I'm sorry. I got your text and never got back to you. I had a bitch of a day."

She looked, as she sometimes liked to say of me when I'd had a rough one, like she'd been ridden hard and put away wet. Her face sagged, her eyes were dark. I opened the door the rest of the way for her. Getting out seemed to take every ounce of strength she had.

"What happened?" I asked.

"Allison."

It was all she had to say. I knew the backstory.

"Her mother died. Overdose. Marta came to the school. We had to get the girl's aunt to come down from Hartford."

"Oh honey, I'm so sorry." I took her into my arms.

She shook her head slowly. "What some of these kids have to deal with. Fuck."

"I know," I said.

She gave me an apologetic look. "I'm sorry. Your text. First day back. How'd it go?"

I couldn't, for a moment, recall why I'd texted her. It had been about the LeDrews' decision to sue me. If there was any upside to being blackmailed, it had made me forget Mark LeDrew's parents considered me somehow culpable in the death of their son.

"Great," I said. "Just great. I just wanted to let you know everything went just fine."

FIFTEEN

The bar was called, quite simply, Jim's, and it was the bar where Cherise Fowler was last seen alive.

Marta Harper was attempting to track her movements in the hours, even days, before her death in the hopes of finding out where she bought the fentanyl—and God knows what other drugs in her system—that had killed her.

She went up to the bar, flashed her badge to the portly man behind the counter with the towel thrown over his shoulder, just like a bartender in the movies would do it, and said, "Need to ask you a few questions."

"Sure," he said.

"You here last night?"

"Yeah, I was on. I'm always on. I stand here and serve drinks all day and all night, go home and sleep for five hours, and then come back and do it all over again. Stop me if I'm making you jealous. This about that girl what died in the alley?"

"Yeah. You Jim?"

"I'm Jim."

Marta's eyebrows went up. "*The* Jim?"

The man smiled. "Sorry, I don't do autographs. Bought the place nine years ago. Worked in construction and wrecked my back, so

I decided to try something different. Now, standing all day, my back's worse than ever and I eat Advils like M&M's. ”

“Nice spot,” Marta said.

“What happened to that poor girl, that's not on me.”

“Didn't say it was.”

“She only had four drinks last night, which was probably less than her usual. Can I get you something?”

“How about a Coke?”

“Nothing stronger?”

“I wish.”

Jim got her a drink and placed it in front of her, setting it perfectly on a paper coaster. “How may I be of further assistance to you today, Detective?”

“Cherise Fowler a regular?”

“Off and on. There was a time there, we didn't see her for a few months. She'd gone to dry out or something. Fat lot of good that did. Booze wasn't her biggest problem. Sometimes she was in here she was high, and when she was, I'd politely encourage her to leave. Once, she's sitting over there and this kid walks in and asks her to come home.”

“Her daughter.”

“Yeah, sweet kid. Allison, I think her name was.” Jim frowned. “What's happening to the kid? Didn't get the sense there was a dad in the picture.”

“Gonna live with her aunt, I think.”

“Sad.”

“What time she come in last night?”

“About eight-thirty, I'd say.”

“She sit at the bar or one of the tables?”

“She sat right there.” He pointed to the stool next to Marta.

“Alone?”

“At first. She had a couple vodka shots, then played with her phone for a while. Couple guys came over, checking on her availability.

I couldn't swear to this, but I think she was making some money on the side by providing certain services. I don't encourage that kind of thing. I don't run that kind of place. We get families in here for the food. Chicken wings, pizza, mozzarella sticks. I got a half-decent cook in the back, so long as you like fried and greasy."

"Sure."

"But you know, when it gets a little later and the kids are tucked in their beds counting sheep, you get a different crowd. Some just want to sit and shoot the shit over a beer, and others are here hoping to find some companionship."

"So, those two guys."

"Right, them. She gave them the brush-off. Had the feeling maybe she was waiting for someone else, because she kept looking at the door all the time."

"Someone show?"

"Yeah. Around ten. Woman."

"A woman?" Marta wasn't expecting that, somehow. "White? Black?"

"White, hundred and twenty pounds or so. Skinny, wiry. Forty, maybe. Thing is, she wasn't here all that long. It was kind of busy then, so it wasn't like I had my eye on them all the time."

"She seem like a girlfriend?"

"Like just a friend, or like more than a friend?"

"You tell me."

"Didn't get any kind of sex vibe. We're not exactly that kind of bar, although times have changed. Everybody kind of goes everywhere now."

He had that right, Marta thought. There were very few lesbian bars anymore.

Jim said, "She wasn't even here long. Had a gin and tonic. Cherise left her for a couple of minutes to go to the john, and when she came back the skinny chick was heading out the door. Didn't wave goodbye or nothin'."

"Cherise stayed."

"Yeah."

"Short meeting. You think she went into the bathroom to take something?"

Jim said, "Didn't exactly follow her in. When she came back I asked if she wanted another drink and she just kind of shook her head. She was spacing out, so yeah, maybe she did take something. It was happening pretty fucking fast, pardon my Lithuanian."

"How was she acting?"

"Like a puppet got its strings cut. Lethargic, having a hard time putting a sentence together, all wobbly-like. Finally, she slides off her stool and starts heading for the door, except she's heading in the wrong direction, toward the dartboard, gonna get a dart in her ear if she's not careful. And then she figures out she's going the wrong way, stops for a second like she's thinking about throwing up, and I'm like, shit, if you're going to do that, can you make it to the sidewalk? She finds the door, and out she goes. And I started thinking, I hope she didn't drive, and even if she didn't, I was a little worried about whether she'd be able to get a cab or an Uber or anything and what someone might do to her in that condition, you get me?"

"I get you."

Marta had already been through Cherise Fowler's phone and checked her emails and texts. She hadn't ordered an Uber. There was one call to her earlier in the evening from a number the detective had not been able to identify. Her guess was a burner phone.

"So I left the bar here for a second and went outside, but by the time I got there, there was no sign of her. She must have wandered into the alley soon as she walked out. Maybe she'd gone in there to puke or something and then passed out." He paused. "That's all she wrote."

"Did you actually see this woman give her anything? Did Cherise give her money?"

Jim shrugged. "No idea. Like I said, it was busy around that time."

"Anything else you can remember?"

He shook his head slowly.

"This woman she met with. She ever been in here before? She a regular?"

"Maybe once or twice."

"How'd she pay?" Marta was hoping the woman had used a credit card, that there would be a record of her name.

Jim shook his head. "Cash. You know, I think she was in here one time with some guy."

"You think if you saw her again, you could give me a call?"

"Yeah, sure," he said. "You got a card?"

She did, and she gave him one.

"What about the guy she came in with? Remember anything about him?"

"Like I said, I think it was just once. They sat over at that table, had something to eat. Guy was short, stocky. Bald. Kind of muscular. But there was something about the two of them."

"What was that?"

"Like she was in charge."

"Married?"

"I don't think so. They talked to each other too much. People been married, they come in and look at their phones."

Marta's eyes scanned upward toward the ceiling. "You got cameras?" she asked.

SIXTEEN

Richard

Bonnie would have found out about the LeDrews' intention to sue me soon enough. One of her colleagues would probably text to offer sympathies, or she'd spot an item about it when she went scrolling through news on her phone. But it turned out to be Rachel who broke the news for Bonnie at the dinner table.

"The Drew people are mean," she said.

"I'm sorry, what?" Bonnie said, the words coming out garbled as she chewed a bite of pork chop. "What are drew people?"

"The people whose kid tried to blow up Dad's school," Rachel said, moving some peas around her plate with her fork.

"The LeDrews, you mean," Bonnie said. "Why are they mean?"

"Because they want to take Dad's money."

Bonnie looked at me. "What's she talking about?"

"Where'd you hear about this?" I asked Rachel.

"Mrs. Tibaldi saw it on the news."

Bonnie was still looking at me, awaiting an explanation. "It's nothing," I said. "A frivolous lawsuit."

"*That's* why you texted me," she said, the tumblers falling into place. "Why didn't you tell me when I got home?"

"Your day wasn't much better. I figured it could wait. I'll tell you all about it later."

I didn't want to get into it in front of Rachel, who looked more than a little troubled.

"Everything is sad here," she said, moving a pea around her plate with a fork.

"Sweetheart, what do you mean?" Bonnie asked her.

I should have thought it was obvious.

"Everybody's mad about everything," our daughter said. "Everybody's mad at Dad and trying to blow him up, and you guys are always mad at each other. That's what I mean. Everybody's mad."

"That's not true," Bonnie said, a hint of defensiveness in her voice.

Rachel said, "Remember when I fell on my scooter?"

When she was five we got her a Radio Flyer scooter. A skateboard-like platform with a tall handlebar that she could grip onto as she powered herself along the sidewalk, one leg on the base, the other pumping away. She'd no doubt tumbled off it a number of times, but Bonnie and I both knew the incident she was referring to. She was propelling herself on the sidewalk, on our side of the street, when some jackass more intent at looking at his phone than the road wandered across the street and scraped up against the curb only a few feet from Rachel.

It scared her half to death and she let go of the scooter and tumbled onto the hard cement of the sidewalk, scraping her elbow and knee. The jackass kept on going.

"It wasn't my fault," Rachel recollected, eyeing her mother, "and you didn't get mad and you got me chocolate peanut butter ice cream with pretzels."

Bonnie managed a smile. "I remember."

"But Daddy almost got blown up and you didn't get him ice cream or anything."

Bonnie's face fell. She eyed me for a second, then looked away guiltily. I instantly felt badly for her. She didn't deserve that.

Some wineglasses that sat close together on an upper shelf began tinkling as they jiggled against each other. Another truck rumbling past.

"Those goddamn trucks," Bonnie said, then got up from the table and left the room.

I found her upstairs later, sitting on the edge of our bed, dabbing her eye with a tissue. I sat down next to her. Neither of us spoke for a minute. I finally went first.

"That wasn't fair," I said. "She doesn't understand."

"Maybe she does," Bonnie said. "All too well." A pause, and then, "I'm sorry."

I reached down and took her hand. "Don't apologize. This is what I do. I jump into things I shouldn't, make things more tense around here."

Another period of silence. This time, Bonnie broke it. "Her teacher called me today."

I waited.

"We might have sent her back too soon. She described Rachel as sullen."

"Sullen. Well, this household underwent a traumatic incident this week. Maybe we're getting off lightly with sullen."

"She said it's not new. Rachel is distracted lately, unfocused. Not finishing her exercises. She said she seems . . . kind of flat." Bonnie pressed her lips together, as though debating whether to say what she was really thinking. "I think it's rubbing off from us."

I considered her words. "It's been a little tense lately." I drew in a breath. "I take the blame for that."

"That's not what I'm say—"

I raised a hand. "No, I've tried to be the good guy once too often. Going the extra mile with students and getting bitten in the ass for it. Thinking I can solve everyone's problems. You know how they say the road to hell is paved with good intentions. I've been on that road for a while now, and I need to find an exit ramp."

"Being kind isn't a failing."

"It is when it comes at the expense of those closest to you."

Bonnie said, "We're all products of our upbringing."

A reference, I knew, to my parents, who sought perfection in their kids while rarely achieving it themselves. My elder by eight years sister, Alicia, who left home when I was ten, fled because she'd grown weary of trying, without success, to please them. Wise enough to know it was hopeless, she fled to Europe, met a man, and never came back. She lived in Brussels. The burden to be flawless fell to me when she left, and I wasn't up to it.

All of which made me think we had to be better for Rachel. And that meant I couldn't draw this household into another crisis.

I was going to have to find a way to deal with my blackmailer on my own.

I suggested Bonnie run herself a hot bath and see if a long soak would relieve some of the day's tensions. She didn't need much persuading.

"If I slide under, don't rescue me," she said.

That gave me time to do what I needed to do. Before darkness fell, I wanted to take some pictures of the boat. I would need them for any online ad I would post.

I had decided, somewhere in the back of my mind, that I needed to pull that ten thousand dollars together. Did that mean I was going to pay my blackmailer? It meant that I knew I might have to. But it did not mean that I was prepared for him to get away with it. I was trying to come up with a plan. Maybe I was going to have to find out who might really have abused him. Persuade him he had the wrong guy, but if he'd let me, help him determine the identity of the true culprit.

Fuck, I just didn't know.

There was still enough light to get a few decent snaps. The boat wasn't some fancy cabin cruiser or speedboat, but it still ran me close to seventeen thousand when I bought it more than ten years earlier. An eighteen-footer with a fifty-horsepower Mercury outboard motor strapped to the transom. A fishing boat, primarily, but it was fun to take Bonnie and Rachel cruising around Candlewood Lake, up north of Danbury, when we weren't sitting still trying to hook into some smallmouth bass.

The boat and the trailer it sat on were usually left at a marina on the lake, but I had brought it back home a few weeks ago to give it its annual going-over. Clean it out, change the oil in the Merc, that kind of thing.

I got out my phone and was preparing to take several shots when someone said, "Hey, Richard."

Our neighbor Jack. He'd stepped out front, as he often did just before the sun dropped beyond the horizon, for a smoke. His wife, Jill, didn't like him to smoke in the house. She didn't like him smoking, period, but she'd given up years ago trying to get him to quit.

"Hey, Jack," I said.

"How you doing?"

"Good," I lied as he started walking over. "Good as can be expected, anyway."

I fired off a couple of shots. That caught Jack's attention. He was shrewd enough to put the pieces together.

"Selling the boat?"

"Thinking about it," I said. I decided to try out some of the excuses I'd eventually use on Bonnie when and if the boat disappeared from the driveway. "We don't get up to the lake as often as we used to. And Rachel, she's not all that interested in fishing. Neither is Bonnie, for that matter."

"You've kept it in good shape," he said, taking a walk around it.

He took one last long draw on his cigarette, walked to the street and tossed it into a storm drain, and then came back and surveyed the boat again, hands in his pockets.

"What are you asking for it?"

"I . . . I'm not sure yet. I was going to go online and see what a rig like this with the trailer is going for. I paid around seventeen for everything, but that was ten years ago, so, I'm not sure."

He nodded slowly. "Thing is, as it turns out, I've been thinking about getting something like this. I retire this year, and I'm going to have to find some way to fill the time. I used to go fishing with my dad when I was a kid." He smiled, the memory washing over him. "I'd always wanted to do that with my own boys, but somehow it never happened. It was work, work, work for me. Now maybe I could make it up to my grandkids. Take them fishing the way my dad took me."

"I'm hoping to get ten thou."

Jack turned his head slowly to look at me. "Hmm." A pause. "That seems fair. You sure you couldn't get more for it from someone else?"

"Ten thousand now would be preferable than holding out for, say, twelve thousand two weeks from now."

"Something to think about," he said.

"I'm going to post some ads tonight. See what happens."

Jack was thinking, nodding very slowly. He seemed to be on the edge of a decision.

"I'd have one request, if you didn't find it too out of the ordinary," I said.

"What would that be?"

"Only if you're interested, and no pressure, but if you are, you think you could pay me in cash?"

Jack studied me for a moment, trying to read between the lines. "Cash."

I forced a smile. "I mean, I know a check from you isn't going to bounce or anything." I uttered a short, nervous laugh. "It's just, well, it would be convenient, that's all."

I wasn't good at this.

Jack asked, "Is everything okay?"

I nodded, maybe a little too quickly. "You've got my cell number, right?" I asked. He nodded. "Text me if you decide you want it."

Jack said a goodbye and went back into his house. I was taking a few more shots when a Honda Civic came to a stop at the foot of the driveway. There was a young guy behind the wheel.

"Excuse me," he said. "I'm looking for Randall Street?"

I walked over to him, pointed. "Head that way, take the second right, it's the next left."

"Thanks." He gave me a longer look. "Hey, aren't you that teacher, Mr. Boyle?"

I sighed. "Yeah."

He extended a hand out the window. There was an envelope in it. I took it without thinking.

"You've been served," he said, then powered up the window and drove off.

SEVENTEEN

"**W**hat are you doing in here?" Billy asked, flipping the lights on in his garage.

Lucy spun around. She was standing by the workbench, using the flashlight app on her phone to scan it.

"Hey," she said. "You scared the shit out of me."

"Looking for something?" he asked, stepping through the side access rather than lifting up the broad main door.

"A screwdriver," she said. "One of the cupboard doors is loose. It's a Phillips. Don't you have one of those screwdrivers that has a bunch of different ends?"

"Yeah. But kind of hard to find in the dark, isn't it?"

"I can never find the light switch when I come in here."

It was, to be fair, not close to the door. But still.

"If you wanted a screwdriver you could have asked me to find you one," Billy said.

"I didn't want to bug you," Lucy said. "You were asleep."

And to be fair, again, that was true. He'd nodded off watching television in his basement man cave.

She looked away from him and noisily moved about some tools in a red metal box. "Here we go," she said, holding up a screwdriver for him to see.

"You got my keys?" he asked. He was thinking about that key to the locker that was on the ring with his other keys.

"No," she said. "I got my own."

Again, true. She had a key to the garage, but not one to the locker. He continued to stand by the door, watching her. "You're freaking me out," she said. "There a problem?"

"You been out here before without me?" Billy asked.

"Uh, yeah, like all the time. I *live* here. With *you*. Although there are days sometimes when I wonder why."

"If you need something out here, ask me. Those are the rules."

"Excuse me?" Lucy rolled her eyes. "Are they written down someplace? Is there a form I fill out if I want a fucking screwdriver?"

Billy raised an accusatory finger as he closed the distance between them. She had her back to the workbench. He was half a foot taller and, head bent down, breathed into her face and said, "I keep very important shit in here."

Still gripping the screwdriver, she said, "Well, then you should keep it somewhere else, because if I need a screwdriver or a hammer or some fucking duct tape I'm not going to go looking for it in the bathroom." He stared at her long enough that she had to look away. "You're being paranoid."

"Some shit's missing."

"What shit?"

"The shit I hold for those people." Lucy knew all about his side business, though she stayed well out of it.

"Don't look at me. You think I'm nuts?"

"Well, it was somebody. The last order was short."

"But you keep it locked up." She glanced at the locker. "That look busted into to you?"

"You don't have to bust into it if you have a key. Show me your keys."

"What?"

"Your keys. Show me."

She shook her head, pulled out a set of keys from her front pocket, and tossed them his way. He snatched them out of the air and examined them.

Car key, house key, garage key. And another one.

"What's this one?" he said, holding it up.

"My locker at the hospital."

He still wasn't sure. He moved in closer, his body pressed up against hers. He opened his hand wide and rested it on her shoulder inches from her neck.

"You don't have any other key?"

Her eyes met his defiantly. He felt a sharp, increasing pressure on the left side of his abdomen. The screwdriver.

Her voice was no louder than a whisper. "You get your fucking hand off me."

They both were very still for a moment before Billy brought his hand away from her neck and took a step back. Lucy lowered the screwdriver.

"Suppose you start from the beginning," she said.

"They came to see me. Accused me of skimming some product off the top." He grimaced. "They hurt me."

"Hurt you?"

He lifted up his sweatshirt.

"Jesus," she said. "The guy did that to you?"

Billy's face flushed red. "The woman, actually."

"She *bite* you?"

"No, she—doesn't matter."

"So, like, you're not just trying to fake me out here, are you? I mean, *did* you steal from them?"

"No way."

"It wasn't me, either."

"Then what are you doing in here with the lights off?"

She sighed and held up the screwdriver. "You don't believe me, come inside, I'll show you the loose cupboard door. What about

Stuart? He's always moping around here, hasn't got two cents to rub together. It was probably him."

"Saw him already, says he didn't do it. Said maybe it was somebody closer to home."

That left Lucy momentarily speechless. "That asshole."

"He didn't outright accuse you. He was just saying it wasn't him, so, like, who else is left?"

She shook her head. "I don't want him around here anymore. Accusing me of shit. And he creeps me out. Looking at me like I'm a Popsicle he wants to take a bite of."

There was a moment of quiet between them. Lucy put a hand on Billy's arm. "So what are you gonna do if you can't find who took it?"

"I gotta pay them what the missing shit is worth."

"Which is?"

He shrugged. "A few thousand."

"Jesus. So pay them."

"I don't *have* it, Luce. I've spent everything they've paid me so far. I put it all into the car."

She closed her eyes. "My mother was right."

"What's that supposed to mean?"

Lucy turned away, not wanting to get into it. "So where you going to get the money?"

Billy said, "I'll come up with something."

When he went back into the house, the first thing he did was look for a loose cupboard door that was held on with Phillips screws. He found it. Lucy was telling the truth.

Stuart. It had to be Stuart.

EIGHTEEN

Richard

Bonnie and I went into the weekend pretending everything was fine. She tried to put the death of Allison's mother out of mind. I made no mention of the lawsuit. And I continued to keep Bonnie in the dark about the blackmailer.

Rachel, however, did not pretend to be anything other than what she was, and that teacher had it right: sullen.

I couldn't count on Jack buying the boat so I posted the photos, a detailed description, and an asking price of eleven thousand dollars, on Craigslist. I was finishing up the process on the laptop in the kitchen when Bonnie, wrapped up in a bathrobe after her soak, walked in. Before she could see what was on my screen I hit the yellow dot in the upper left corner and minimized the page.

"What's up?" she asked.

"Just a dumb video."

My phone, which was sitting on the table next to the computer, dinged. A text. I read it quickly. Bonnie wore a who-is-it expression.

"Trent," I said. "Inviting us for dinner tomorrow. Burgers and beer."

While I'd known Trent for several years, we'd socialized little out of school. A few weekday lunches, but we'd never gotten together with our spouses. Bonnie had met Trent a few times through work, what with both of them being principals for the same school board.

"What do you think?" Bonnie asked.

"He's saying it's been a long week for all of us and maybe we need to kick back."

"What's his wife's name again?"

"Melanie. I've met her a couple of times. She's kind of a nervous flibbertigibbet."

"Boy, there's a word I haven't heard since God's bike had training wheels. Might do us some good to go."

I took a moment. I wasn't thinking so much that this was a chance to unwind, as it was an opportunity to pull Trent to one side and tell him about my situation. I had to tell *somebody*, and he might be my best option.

"But only if Rachel can come," Bonnie added. "I want to keep her close right now."

I got that. I tapped out a few quick words in reply and waited while the dancing dots did their thing. "He says sure. They've got a daughter, couple years older."

So it was settled. We were invited to come at five.

When Bonnie went back upstairs, I finished posting the ad. Then I went hunting online for anything I could find on Billy Finster.

There wasn't much, not even when I searched for "William Finster." Combing through social media and other sites, I managed to turn up a real estate agent out in Arizona who also handled time-shares, a special effects expert in Hollywood, an expert in unplugging toilets north of the border in Ottawa, and a Billy Finster on Twitter with two followers whose mug shot didn't look anything like my blackmailer. There was no local phone listing for a B or W Finster, but that wasn't surprising, since most younger people only had cell phones.

When I returned to school Monday, I'd search the office's stockpile of old yearbooks and see what more I could learn about this guy. I was looking for anything that might give me leverage, something that might give me an idea how to handle this.

Because I definitely needed some points on my side of the board.

The next day, Bonnie was behind the wheel, I was up front next to her, and Rachel was in the back, all of us on the way to Trent's house. Rachel was playing some game on her tablet that we had asked her to mute so we wouldn't be driven mad by relentless beeps and explosions. Bonnie glanced my way.

"You're pretty quiet today."

"I'm fine. Wrapped up in my own thoughts, I guess."

"You've been glued to your phone."

I'd been checking to see whether there'd been any nibbles on the boat. None so far.

"Wasting time, is all."

"I get why you're stressed. But is there anything else going on you need to talk about?"

"Not really."

"I've been wondering whether you should go for the counseling."

She was aware the board was offering it for those of us impacted by the LeDrew incident.

"I'm okay."

"You had another nightmare last night. You were kicking your legs, like you were fighting off somebody. Do you even remember?"

I didn't.

"Really, I'm fine."

"Okay, then," Bonnie said, and nothing else was said until we reached our destination.

Rachel and the Wakelys' daughter, Amanda, who was ten, hit it off immediately. Amanda, it turned out, was into bugs. An aspiring entomologist. Amanda asked Rachel whether she wanted to come inside to see her beetle collection, which she kept in the garage because her dad didn't want any bugs—alive or dead—in the actual house. Rachel was uncertain at first. Like, really? Beetles? But once she was gone, we didn't see them again until it was time to eat.

We sat out back on their deck. We'd brought a six-pack of Modelo and some flowers Bonnie spotted at a roadside stand along the way.

Melanie went into something of a tizzy trying to find the perfect vase for them.

"So nice to finally meet you," Melanie commented several times to Bonnie, as if she'd forgotten she'd already expressed the sentiment.

Trent had fired up the barbecue. There was a second one tucked up close to the house, no longer in use. Couldn't control the flame very well, Trent said, so he'd bought another one. While we waited for the new one to get hot enough to start cooking the hamburgers, Melanie invited Bonnie to join her in the kitchen while she pulled together a salad.

"You seem preoccupied," Trent said when we were alone. Bonnie wasn't the only one to notice.

"Kinda," I said.

"What you went through, something like that doesn't fade away in a few days."

"It's not that." Trent waited while I opened a second beer. "Let me bounce something off you. A hypothetical."

His brow furrowed. "Okay."

"This is between us. I haven't discussed this with anyone. Not even Bonnie."

Trent nodded his understanding of the conditions.

"Suppose you had a former student, someone you hadn't come in contact with for several years, actually maybe never taught at all, but you might have had some interactions with at the time. And now this kid—an adult—shows up out of nowhere and makes an accusation against you."

"An accusation."

"Yeah. A serious one. Life-altering. Career-destroying."

"Can you even give me an idea of the nature of the accusation?" A pause. "Hypothetically speaking?"

I hesitated. "Interfering with a student."

Trent raised an eyebrow. "Interfering?"

"Molesting. Sexual abuse. Hypothetically speaking."

Trent went quiet. He looked at the barbecue's temperature gauge. "Almost time to put these on," he said. He opened the lid, a wave of heat hitting him in the face, and took a brush to scrape down the grill while he thought about what to say next.

He put the lid back down and said, "Go on."

"Let's say this person offered to keep quiet in return for a substantial sum of money."

"How much?"

"Ten thousand."

"Not pocket change."

"What do you do?"

Thoughtfully, he said, "Whether there's any truth to the accusation might have some bearing on the issue."

"Does it matter?"

"What do you mean?"

"Even if it's unfounded, if it goes public the person's reputation will be ruined. There will always be people who believe it to be true. And for the record, it's not."

He glanced again at the temperature reading. "Why now? After all this time?"

"Guessing? He saw the news reports about Monday. Memories rekindled. Saw an opportunity." I managed a wry smile. "Who am I kidding? This guy's saying I assaulted him when he was on the Lodge wrestling team."

"The wrestling team," Trent repeated.

"I wasn't the coach, but I filled in some when he was away. Anson Reynolds was on that leave."

Trent did some recollecting. "His wife was ill."

"Right. A few us picked up the slack. This guy, I told him it wasn't me, that maybe it was somebody else. And, Trent, if somebody did do this to that kid, efforts should be made to find out who it was. Not just to save my ass, but to do the right thing."

"Not much can be done if it was Anson. He's dead."

"Still, be worth maybe asking some questions. I don't like smearing a dead guy more than anyone else does, but if that's what happened . . ."

"I don't see how someone could get that wrong," Trent said. "I mean, if it happened when you were, like, five or six or even a little older, you could end up accusing the wrong person. But we're not talking the distant past."

I told him I had thought about that, too. "Maybe it was Anson, and this guy knows it, so he's decided to go after someone else. He wants payback, and doesn't care who he gets it from."

"That's just not right."

I couldn't help but laugh. "No kidding. I didn't know whether to tell you. But I don't know that I can solve this on my own. I haven't told Bonnie for, well, a whole bunch of reasons."

"Can't you just give me a name, Richard?" Trent asked.

I hesitated. "I've already compromised you, telling you this much, that I'm the target. Let's say this kid—this *man*—really is a victim of *someone*. His coming after me could be the product of some very fucked-up thinking."

"You're giving him too much benefit of the doubt."

"Let me think on it. The thing is, like I said, an allegation like this, even baseless, could be devastating. I've already got one strike against me."

Trent cocked his head, like he knew what I was referring to. "The Lyall Temple thing," he said.

"I was vindicated, but you know there are people out there who still think there was something to it. A new allegation comes along, I guarantee that photo will resurface. Those who vouched for me at the time will start wondering, wait a minute, maybe he really *was* a little too friendly with that kid. It'll be two strikes. You'll have people with pitchforks and torches storming the school."

Trent was slowly shaking his head. "I want to say you're wrong, but I don't think you are. You try to control the narrative but you can't, and yet . . ."

"I've thought about talking to Bonnie's sister. But what if she believes the allegation, or at least isn't sure? I'm her sister's husband. Whose interests you really think she's going to care about?"

"Something about this," Trent said, more to himself than to me, "doesn't make any sense."

The glass door to the deck slid open. Bonnie and Melanie, a large salad bowl in her hands, emerged from the house. Melanie smiled and said, "Haven't you got those burgers on the grill yet? What on earth have you been talking about?"

Bonnie gave me a look that suggested she was wondering the same thing.

NINETEEN

Marta had played the security cam video from Jim's bar more times than she could count, trying to get a better look at the woman Cherise Fowler met with, however briefly. Jim had been right about the time Cherise came into the bar, and right again that the woman she'd been waiting for arrived around ten. Five minutes after, to be exact.

Jim's description was pretty on the money, as well. She was white, probably no more than a hundred and twenty pounds. Stringy hair that hung over her face. The camera captured most of the bar's interior, and the fish-eye effect, along with grainy resolution, meant that any distinguishing physical features Cherise's friend might have were difficult to assess.

If there was even a remote chance this woman might return to the bar Saturday night to make another sale, Marta wanted to be there. She believed she would recognize her, even from that shitty video, and presumably Jim would give her a nod if she was the one.

When Marta told her wife, Ginny, she would have to duck out early from the function they were attending that evening, Ginny was neither pleased nor surprised. It was a retirement dinner for one of Ginny's coworkers at the insurance company where she worked. The event was to start after six.

"I can hang in until eight-thirty," Marta said. "The thing might even be over by then."

"That's when the coffee gets served and the speeches begin," Ginny said.

Marta smiled. "Then maybe you'd like to sneak out *with* me."

"I'm *giving* one of the speeches."

"Oh, well, that does make it awkward."

"You go. I'll Uber home. Pretend you got a text or something."

It wasn't as though Marta hadn't done this kind of thing before. Last year she postponed their fifth anniversary dinner because there was a tip a gang of smash-and-grab thieves was going to hit a mall jewelry store. Three of them, all wearing black balaclavas, would rush in, take hammers to the glass cases, scoop up as many goods as they could in fifteen seconds, then go tearing back out of the mall, where the fourth member of the team was sitting behind the wheel of their nondescript, but turbocharged, getaway car.

Marta was sorry they wore those balaclavas, because she couldn't see the look on their faces when they came running out and their getaway car had nobody behind the wheel, their driver sitting hand-cuffed in the back of a cruiser.

What was different about that takedown from what Marta planned for this evening was that the former had been a well-executed team effort, and tonight was something she was doing on her own time. A small reconnaissance that, if she spotted the person she was looking for, might lead to the bigger fish who were bringing this stuff into the country.

The fentanyl boom had been out of control for a long time, and more recently there'd been reports some dealers were lacing the opioid with animal sedative. From what Marta'd learned, you'd be better off dead than taking this shit. Fentanyl laced with xylazine was turning addicts' skin into dead, scaly tissue. Some people were actually losing limbs. The stuff was a fucking horror show. And if you took too much of it at once, you wouldn't have to wait for those ghastly side effects to kick in. Your life would be over before you knew it.

As promised, Marta pretended to sense a buzzing from her purse as dessert—some kind of blueberry crumble thing that looked like it had been made with a cement mixer—arrived at the table. Marta pulled out her phone, shielding it with her hand so no one would notice that it was blank, and shook her head with feigned regret. She made whispered apologies to the rest of the table, pushed her chair back, stood up, and slipped away, but not before catching a look from Ginny that said something along the lines of *You'll pay for this later*.

She had dressed smartly but simply for the evening. Nothing too glitzy glam. Black silk pants and a matching top, simple string of pearls for her neck, strappy shoes with three-inch heels. She'd have gladly gone face-to-face with a serial killer if it meant she could get out of those shoes, which she did the moment she reached the car. She had packed a comfortable pair of sneakers that she laced up sitting on the driver's seat with the door open. The string of pearls she removed and tucked into the glove compartment. Finally, she pulled a plain dark blue sweater over her head that covered the silk top.

Marta keyed the ignition and drove to Jim's.

She found a spot at the curb across from the bar a few minutes after nine. Her hope was that, if her alleged fentanyl dealer did return, she'd come around the same time as she had the other night. She got out of her car, locked it, and went inside, sidling past a couple of young men who'd stepped out of the bar to smoke.

Once inside, she discreetly scanned the room. So far, the woman was a no-show. Marta took a seat at the bar.

Jim approached, gave her a sly smile, and said quietly, "Back again?"

She smiled. "Seen our friend?"

He shook his head. "Have not. Usual?"

Marta nodded, and moments later Jim returned with a Coke over ice, and then proceeded to serve other customers.

The bar was about half full. There were a few couples, mostly in their twenties, and a group of four men in one booth were having a discussion, loud enough to be heard from where Marta sat, about whether Marvel superheroes were better than DC. Three stools down from Marta sat a thin man in his sixties slowly ripping apart a paper napkin, his beer glass nearly empty.

Marta gave him a nod. "Evening," she said.

"It is that," he replied.

Marta had a feeling she'd seen him before. She struggled to place him, then realized she'd encountered him a few days earlier at Lodge High School. He was the caretaker, the one who hadn't fixed the defective latch on the door Mark LeDrew used to enter the building. She couldn't recall the caretaker's name. She was worried he'd recognize her, say something like *Hey, aren't you that cop?* But, evidently more interested in shredding his napkin, he hadn't given her a second glance.

Jim checked in on him. "You want to settle up, Ronny?"

That's it, Marta thought. *Ronny Grant.* She'd heard he'd been fired, or suspended pending a hearing.

"Think I'll have another," Ronny said.

"Sure about that?" Jim asked.

"Never been more sure about anything," he said.

"Because if you drove, I'm gonna want your keys."

Marta wondered whether Jim was always this mindful of his customers' fitness to get behind the wheel, or if this was for her benefit.

"I walked, not that it's any of your fucking business," Ronny said, forming his words carefully, figuring it would make him sound less under the influence, but having the opposite effect. "I'm only a couple of blocks away."

"Okey dokey," Jim said. "You need anything, just holler."

"How about a job?" Ronny asked, snorting a laugh, before he drained his glass and set it down hard on the counter.

Jim fetched him another beer, then turned his attention to Marta. "Let me ask you this," he said.

"What?" she said.

He tapped her ring finger. "How's your husband feel about you hanging out alone in bar on Saturday night, even if it's for work?"

"I don't have a husband."

He glanced down at the ring again. "This for show? Keep guys from bothering you?"

"No," she said, waiting to see how long it took him.

"Oh, sorry," Jim said. "Your husband passed away." Didn't even make it a question, he was so sure he'd figured it out.

Marta didn't want to play with him any longer. "My wife's very much alive, thanks," she said.

A slow, self-deprecating smile crossed his lips. "Do I look as dumb as I feel?"

"Pretty much," she said.

His eyes moved but his head remained fixed. "Don't look now, but your girl has arrived."

Marta took a sip of her Coke. "Alone?"

He hummed an affirmative. "Scoping the place out."

The newcomer took a seat next to Grant, two over from Marta, who continued to nurse her Coke.

All she wanted was a really good look at her. Then she'd depart, get in her unmarked cruiser, wait for her to leave, and see where she went. If she got into a vehicle, Marta would run the plate.

Jim approached the woman. "What's your pleasure?"

"Gin and tonic," she said.

Marta turned slightly on her stool so she could see her better out of the corner of her eye.

When Jim brought her drink, the woman asked, "That girl that was here the other night around?"

"Cherise?"

"Yeah."

Jim snatched up the bills she'd tossed onto the bar. "Not so far."

Clearly she hadn't gotten the memo about what had happened to Cherise, Marta thought.

If she hadn't come to see anyone else, she probably wasn't staying long. Marta figured she would cut out now, wait outside. She threw a five and a couple of singles onto the bar and was about to slip off the stool.

"Hey," said the woman.

Marta turned. "You talking to me?"

"Yeah." The woman was looking at her feet. "What kind of runners is those?"

Marta glanced down reflexively, like she needed a reminder. "Converse," she said.

"What they run ya?"

"I don't know. Sixty, seventy bucks."

The woman nodded. "They look about my size. Comfortable. Casual. You got an interesting sense of style. Sneakers and silk pants. Like putting on a sweatshirt when you're wearing diamond earrings."

"Not a fan of heels," Marta said.

"If it was me, coming in here alone, looking for some company, I'd have some fuck-me pumps on."

Marta flashed a smile, said, "You have a nice evening," and headed for the door.

Once outside, she crossed the street, got into her car, and said aloud, "Shit shit shit."

Cherise's likely supplier, striking up a conversation like that? Had Marta been made? She should have changed into a pair of jeans. Had she sent off some kind of cop vibe? Was she getting sloppy? All these years in the department, and suddenly she felt like some kind of amateur.

Well, the night wasn't over yet. She'd hang in, wait for the woman to come out, see if she got into one of the other cars parked on the street. Check the plate, see where she went.

She waited.

And waited.

After half an hour, she wondered whether she could have missed her. If the woman had, in fact, suspected Marta was a cop, maybe she'd slipped out the back door.

She got out of the car, debating whether to go back into the bar, just take one step in, see if the woman was still there. If she was gone, there was no point sitting out here all night like an idiot.

Behind her, someone said:

"Bet you thought I'd never finish my drink."

Marta had spun around only halfway when something hit her across the side of the head. Everything went black and down she went.

"Thought something was off about you. And then that sad fucker next to me confirmed it. Don't mess with us, darlin'."

But the words were wasted on her. Marta was out cold.

TWENTY

Richard

After any social engagement, Bonnie and I would typically start our debrief once we were in the car and driving away. Maybe it would be a comment about how neither of us could eat the undercooked fish, or the kid who was a monster, or how the husband always cut off his wife before she could finish a single sentence. Not to give you the impression that we were the nastiest, most backstabbing couple in history—we would just as often talk about how that was the best chocolate mousse we'd ever tasted, or how she was the funniest person we'd met in a long time, or that we really clicked and should have them over to our place as soon as possible.

But we didn't do any of that because Rachel was in the car. It was Rachel, in fact, who was ready to start talking immediately once we were driving away from seeing Trent and Melanie.

"Can I get some bugs?" she asked.

"Say again?" I said, looking over my shoulder at her in the backseat.

"Bugs," Rachel said again. "Amanda has all kinds of them. Dead ones and live ones. She's going to be a lemontologist."

"An entomologist," Bonnie said.

"What?"

"You said lemontologist."

"That would be someone who studies citrus fruits," I offered.

Rachel carried on. "She used to have this glass thing full of dirt where ants lived but she had to get rid of it because of her dad. Can I get one of those?"

I glanced over at Bonnie, who was biting her bottom lip. I could guess what she was thinking. The last thing she'd want would be to discourage our daughter from pursuing a new interest, especially when she'd seemed at loose ends lately. And the second last thing Bonnie would want is a wide variety of insects, living and/or dead, taking up residence in our house.

"She has dead butterflies," Rachel continued. "With their wings spread out and they were under glass, held there with pins."

Bonnie asked, "How does Amanda's mom like having all those icky bugs in the house?"

Rachel adopted a lecturing tone. "Mom, bugs are not icky. They are part of the *envierment*. The world would die without bugs. And her *mom* is fine with it. It's her *dad* who hates them. That's why they're in the garage. Isn't that sexist, Mom? Thinking girls are all scared of bugs and boys aren't?"

The kid was on fire today. I had to admit that I was pleased and was betting Bonnie might be, too. This might be just what Rachel needed. A new focus.

Although, as Bonnie said after Rachel had bolted from the car when we got home, "Why couldn't Amanda have had a big fucking dollhouse?"

So later, as we got ready for bed, we debriefed. At least, up to a point. I did not share the details of my conversation with Trent.

"She was pretty shaken up, maybe even more than Trent," Bonnie said of Melanie. "She put on a good front for you guys, but when I was in the kitchen with her she was still having a hard time with it. She put dressing on the salad a second time, forgetting she'd already done it."

"It was a little on the wet side," I said.

"She's terrified that something like what happened Monday could happen again. If not a bomber, then a shooter. It's like a virus, a contagion, spreading through the country. Hardly a week goes by you don't hear about another one."

"Did she know Trent had a gun at school?"

"She not only knew about it, she'd encouraged it. And Melanie said some wonderful things about you. How if you hadn't done what you did, it could have been a much bigger tragedy. I think it hit her hard because she knew Mark LeDrew."

That was news to me, but it shouldn't have come as a surprise. He'd been a student at her husband's school. They lived in the same town.

"They hired him one summer to look after their place, the year she and Trent rented a house up in Maine for all of July and half of August."

"She say what he was like?"

"Seemed like a nice kid, but kind of sad. She got the impression maybe it had something to do with his father, who was pretty distant, not very involved." Bonnie paused before saying, "You and Trent seemed to have a lot to talk about."

I shrugged, like, after what we'd been through, what would you expect?

"It's just, when we came out, you both had this look."

I frowned. "We were talking about what happened, and when you came out, it felt like time to move on to something else."

I was in nothing but my boxers and Bonnie, who had herself just stripped down to her underwear, slipped her arms around me and said, "I know you did what you had to do, and I'm sorry if it seems like I've been punishing you for it. I just . . ."

She bit her lip and held back tears. "You're a better person than I am."

"That's not true."

"You put yourself out there. It's who you are."

She held me tighter, then moved her hands around to my butt cheeks, gave them a squeeze, then moved one hand around to the front and down into my boxers, where there was, to my surprise, a stirring. I'd been so stressed lately, I wasn't sure I had it in me.

"Give me one minute," I said, and mimed brushing my teeth. "Don't start without me."

As I headed for the bathroom, Bonnie took off what few clothes she still had on and threw back the covers. As I was putting toothpaste on my brush, I heard a ding.

Someone got a text.

"It's you," Bonnie said from the bedroom.

I brushed, spat, rinsed. I was drying my hands when Bonnie appeared in the doorway, my phone in her hand.

"What's this?" she asked.

She handed me my phone. It was a text from Jack, next door.

Thought it through. Weve got a deal. Will go to the bank Monday. Will provide funds as requested. Those fish wont know what hit em.

"What deal? What money?" She had one hand on her naked hip.

I licked my lips, trying to figure out what to say. The only thing I could think of was the truth.

"He's buying the boat," I said.

Bonnie blinked, looked at me like she wasn't sure she'd heard that right. "Your boat? *Our* boat?"

"He was interested, and I thought, we didn't use it all that much this summer, and it's just sitting in the driveway, so I—"

"How much did you sell him the boat for?"

"Ten thousand."

"Ten thousand? What did we pay for that—"

"It doesn't matter. It's a used boat, it's not in perfect con—"

"So you decided you would make a decision like that without discussing it? Rachel loves that boat. She loves it when we go up to the lake."

The only thing I could think of now was a lie. And I had what I thought was a good one.

"It's the lawsuit," I said. "I'm probably going to need a lawyer, and they're not cheap."

"That's crazy. The school board, the union, they'll have your back."

"Yeah, but if they don't, I need—"

"Even if they don't—Jesus, we could have found a way to pay for that without selling the boat. You're doing it again, making decisions without—" She was too angry to finish the sentence, but then started up again. "Have you actually *spoken* to a lawyer yet?"

"No."

"Picked one out?"

"No. I'll start Monday, get recommendations."

She looked angry, sympathetic, and flabbergasted, all at once. She took a moment to calm herself and said, "You have to talk to the union. Look, I'm not in it anymore but I know someone. I'll make a call, put him in touch with you."

Now that I'd committed myself to a lie about legal representation, I hoped she was right, that my legal costs would be covered, given that I needed the ten grand for something very different.

Bonnie looked at the text again. "What's he mean here? Getting funds as requested? What's that?"

"I asked . . . I asked Jack if he could do it in cash."

Bonnie was briefly speechless. Then, "You want him to take out ten thousand in *cash*?"

"I don't know. I guess I didn't want the money going into our account."

"Why?"

"Look, maybe I wasn't thinking straight. I thought, it goes into your account, it looks like income, I don't know. Anyway, he seems okay with it."

"So once you get it, you going to go into a lawyer's office and dump a pile of hundreds onto his desk? He'll think you're a drug dealer or a hit man or something."

That almost made me laugh. "A hit man."

"It's not funny. Christ, when it rains, it—"

Before she could finish, the phone was ringing. Not the one in my hand, but her own cell, on her side of the bed.

"Jesus. What *now?*"

She grabbed her phone, put it to her ear.

"Yes . . . Ginny, what's . . . oh my God . . . yes . . . okay. I'm coming."

Bonnie ended the call, looked at me, and said, "My sister's in the hospital."

TWENTY-ONE

Lucy Finster was up before her husband.

Billy liked to sleep in on Sunday. Well, truth be told, Billy would sleep in every day of the week if he could get away with it, but he didn't have an airport shift today, and Lucy was due at the hospital. She was among those who got the cafeteria prepped for the midday crowd. It wasn't as busy on the weekend. There were still plenty of nurses and support staff and doctors around, although the specialists usually weren't to be found on Saturday or Sunday unless there was a real emergency. The admin people were nowhere to be seen, either. But there were usually more visitors on the weekend, people coming to see their sick friends and relatives, and the gift shop did well selling cards and flowers and little pink teddy bears wearing shirts with GET WELL SOON! written on them.

Lucy didn't deal much with the public. She was in the back, making tasteless sandwiches by the hundreds, preparing huge vats of thin, bland soups, filling plastic cups with green cubes of Jell-O, pouring gravy from a can over reheated slices of meat loaf. Lucy sometimes thought that if you came to the hospital in perfect health to visit a relative, and then had lunch here, you'd be begging to see a doctor.

How she hated this job. And the pay was shit, too.

Billy didn't like his work any better, but at least lately it had afforded him the opportunity to make some money on the side. Billy's job unloading baggage from planes at one of the state's smaller regional airports had put him in a position to help out what Lucy liked to think of charitably as international businesspeople, although *thugs* was more apt, which had become abundantly clear after one of them had nearly ripped off Billy's nipple.

She hadn't had a face-to-face with them. Billy didn't want her around when they made their pickups, but Lucy had peeked through the curtains and seen the skanky-looking woman and heavyset guy showing up at the garage to retrieve the shit Billy'd taken off the plane.

Billy was picking up a few hundred here and there, sometimes even as much as a thousand. Cash. And it had been coming in on a pretty steady basis for a couple of months now.

And what did he do with it?

Blew it all for himself, that's what.

Bought premium beers to guzzle down with his sicko friend Stuart, who, get this, wanted to show her a video the other day of a guy losing his finger in a hedge trimmer. Billy had loaded up on new tools he supposedly needed to restore that old Camaro. It wasn't fancy tools Billy needed to get that car running. What he needed was expertise. A thousand years from now, after the polar ice caps had melted and much of the world was sitting underwater, that fucking car would still be up on blocks waiting to be fixed.

Every time she needed some extra cash, she had to *ask* for it. What happened to the notion that whatever funds each of them brought into the house were to be shared? Their paychecks went directly into their joint account, but the cash Billy made on the side? That was all his.

Lucy was more steamed than the limp, overcooked broccoli she was dumping into a large metal serving dish.

She'd brought the subject up more than once, the unfairness of it all, and Billy always had the same answer. He was taking all the risks with the airport thing, so he was the one who should reap the rewards. Made it sound like he was doing her a favor, that he was keeping her "hands clean."

"Want to make some extra money?" he said one day. "You're in a hospital. Get your hands on some morphine or something."

Like they should become a true husband-and-wife criminal enterprise.

At first she thought she'd simply help herself to some of the money. Find where he stashed it, peel off a few twenties and fifties. She'd hunted through every drawer in the house, atop closet shelves, even in his stash of old porn mags under the couch in the basement that he didn't think she knew about. She even searched the freezer, taking out a Tupperware of frozen spaghetti sauce and running it under hot water to see if maybe the cash had been wrapped in a baggie and secreted in the center of the frozen clump. (She'd seen that in a movie once.) No luck.

That left the garage. And that locker.

Billy'd been right about what she'd done, in part. She'd taken his ring of keys when he'd nodded off on the couch. They were sitting right there on the coffee table next to the Cheetos. She knew which key it was. He'd had seven of his high-end beers and was down for the count, so she had time to hit Home Depot and have a copy made before he woke up. Having her own key meant she could get into the locker whenever she wanted, like when she was off work and Billy was at the airport.

Which she did the very next day.

And it was a good thing she hadn't added it to her own key ring, which Billy checked when he found her in the garage. She'd kept the key tucked away in her underwear drawer.

She used the key on the oversized lock that kept the two locker doors together and opened it wide. This was not, she learned after a thorough search of every shelf, where Billy was keeping his cash, assuming of course that he had any of it left. It was, however, where he stashed even more porn, plus a few DVD players still in their original boxes. Some brand-new laptops. Half a dozen burner phones. That was an eye-opener. Billy was also selling stuff that had fallen off a truck somewhere.

What Lucy didn't find was any money. Maybe Billy was hiding it in his locker at the airport.

But she did find what he was holding for his associates. Not that anyone would have known at first glance what it was. Jammed in between two shelves was a small, wheeled dark blue carry-on bag, the kind a traveler could stow in the overhead compartment of an airplane.

She cleared a spot on the workbench and hauled it out for a closer examination. But when she went to open the bag, she found that the two zipper ends had been linked together with a small lock.

"Shit," she said to herself. "Shit shit shit."

Not that the case was impregnable. A good sharp box cutter from Billy's toolkit would open it up. She could saw her way through the canvas. But then it would be obvious the case had been broken into. And, while the lock was small—not much bigger than her thumb—it still needed a key.

The Internet, Lucy thought, *has a solution to everything.*

She opened a browser on her phone and typed "how to break into a carry-on bag." And within seconds, there was a two-minute YouTube video.

"Fuck me," Lucy said as she watched. "How could it be that easy?"

With the tip of a pen she found on the workbench, she separated the teeth on the zipper just to the left of the locked ends. The zipper parted as easily as walking through a bead curtain. She widened the opening, forcing the joined zippers to one end, and opened the case.

Candyland.

That was certainly what it looked like. Dozens and dozens of containers, all packed neatly, each one about the size of a box of Junior Mints. The packaging was fun and colorful. Under the word

FLIZZIES, a cartoon girl was pictured against a wall of round pink candies, popping one into her mouth. A slender, clear acetate window showed the delicious pink treats within.

Lucy understood what this shit was—that it was definitely *not* candy—and knew full well the power these little pills had to make pain go away. Lucy ran into people all the time who were suffering. She worked in a fucking hospital.

It could be so easy.

She wouldn't be dumb enough to swipe several boxes of Flizzies. That would be noticed, for sure. But if she were to take a few pills— sorry, *candies*—from, say, twenty of these packages, who'd notice? It was like taking home a few seashells from the beach.

So that's what she did.

She gathered close to two hundred pills, put them into a Glad freezer bag, put all the boxes back into the case just as she had found them, then followed the YouTube video's instructions on how to reclose the carry-on bag, reengaging the zipper teeth even as the two zipper ends remained locked together. No one would ever be the wiser.

You'd think, she thought, drug smugglers would be a little more careful. What were they teaching criminals these days, anyway? She blamed the schools.

Lucy knew pretty much everyone at the hospital, and had an idea of the right people to discreetly approach. The truth was, the ones who were really hurting were the overworked staff. They'd all been through so much these last few years, what with the pandemic and all. Everybody was burned out, and many had never snapped back when COVID started to fade away. She did some quick online research and decided twenty bucks a pill was fair. If she could sell them all, that would be a cool four grand right there.

So fuck you, Billy, and the Camaro you rode in on.

She sold out in a couple of weeks. Had a few who came back for more, like that orderly Digby. Short, stocky dude, with short black hair, a kind of walking-talking fire hydrant with a fox tattoo on his shoulder. Always licking his lips. Reminded her of Heath Ledger when he played Joker in that Batman movie.

When Billy discovered her in the garage, she'd been hoping to restock, see if there was a bag in the locker that hadn't been picked up. But when he found her it was game over. If more stuff went missing, he was going to know for sure it was her. Good thing that loose cupboard door gave her an excuse to be looking for a screwdriver.

Did Billy believe her? Lucy hoped so. It made sense to lay it on Stuart. He knew what Billy was doing. He knew where the shit was. Billy wasn't cutting him in, so Stuart had a reason. Lucy was sorry she hadn't saved a few Flizzies. She could have found a way to plant them on Stuart, someplace where Billy would find them.

The lunch rush was over, and Lucy was hosing down the huge serving dishes that, moments earlier, had held Salisbury steak and mashed potatoes, when Digby sidled up to her and whispered, "Is the store open?"

She whispered to him, "Store's closed."

Digby said, "When should I come back?"

"Never," she said, setting the tray in the sink. "We've got one of those supply chain problems. Already had a going-out-of-business sale."

"I didn't get the flyer," Digby said.

"Can't do it anymore. It's over. Done. Too much heat." Sounding like some girl in a movie.

"Not what I want to hear," he said, moving in close enough that his nose was nearly touching hers. She could feel his hot, fetid breath on her face. "I'm not interested in any supply chain bullshit. Your store needs to reopen."

And he reached down between her legs and gave her a quick, hard squeeze before flashing a smile and finding his way out, Lucy quivering like the green leftover Jell-O she'd pitched earlier.

TWENTY-TWO

Richard

Bonnie went alone to the hospital Saturday night. I would have accompanied her, but Rachel couldn't be left on her own, and it was, after all, Bonnie's sister. She promised to text updates on Marta's condition as they became available.

What I learned, over the next few hours, was that Marta had been doing a one-woman stakeout trying to get a lead on who might have sold fentanyl to the mother of Bonnie's student who had overdosed. Someone had hit her in the head as she stood by her car and she'd briefly lost consciousness. A couple coming out of Jim's, the bar Marta had been keeping an eye on, saw her and called 911. Marta was awake by the time the ambulance arrived, and tried without success to talk them out of taking her to the hospital.

Good thing, too.

She was diagnosed with a mild concussion. A doctor conducted several neurological tests and to be on the safe side Marta was kept until they could do a CT scan much later that evening. Bonnie had stayed at the hospital with Ginny, who was, according to Bonnie, a complete wreck, until the results of the scan were available, which was well after midnight. The scan did not show anything alarming, but the ER staff decided it would be best to keep Marta there at least until the morning.

I tried to stay awake until Bonnie got home, waiting up for her in the living room, but when she came through the door shortly before two, I was out cold in the recliner. The sound of her entry woke me. We had a brief chat, and then we both went to bed. If she was still angry about my selling the boat to Jack, she was too tired to show it.

Around nine Sunday morning, Bonnie texted Ginny for news. Marta was to be discharged around eleven, and had asked Ginny to bring her a pair of shoes. The ones she'd been wearing when she was assaulted had been stolen right off her feet.

Bonnie said she would drop by later. When she went, Rachel and I joined her, stopping along the way to buy flowers and pick up some chocolate croissants from Marta's favorite bakery.

She was sitting on their front porch, feet up, sipping on some lemonade and reading a Scott Turow novel when we pulled into the driveway. Marta didn't much want to talk about what had happened to her, at least not in front of all of us. Rachel and I spent some time in the kitchen with Ginny so that the sisters could talk privately. And when Rachel mentioned her newfound interest, Ginny offered to take her on a tour of their backyard garden to see what specimens they might be able to find.

That left me alone for a few minutes in the kitchen, affording me time to ponder my current predicament, not that I wasn't already thinking about it all the time. I got out my phone, considered searching "hit men for hire," but instead killed time looking at all the unused apps I had and deleting them. Did I really need to know the value of the Swedish krona against the U.S. dollar? Delete. When was the last time I turned on white noise when trying to get to sleep? Delete.

And then I saw Voice Memos.

I'd never used that recording app, wasn't even really aware it had been on my phone all this time, so there seemed little sense in hanging on to it. But in that moment, it struck me as worth hanging on to. That maybe it might come in handy.

Ginny came rushing in without Rachel, opened a cabinet door

below the sink, and was searching through a blue bin of recycled items. She came up with an empty glass jar with a spaghetti sauce label on it, metal lid still screwed on top. With a bottle opener, she made a couple of very small holes in the top, then looked at me and smirked.

"I'm not even going to ask," I said.

I went out to the front porch and found Bonnie and Marta wrapping up their chat. "If there's anything you need," Bonnie said, "you let me know."

Marta smiled. "I will, I promise. But I'm fine, really."

We headed home shortly after that. Rachel showed off what she had in the spaghetti jar: a stick-like green insect that was nearly three inches long. Ginny had told her it was a European praying mantis, the state insect of Connecticut. "He can stand on his back legs and he puts his hands together like he's praying."

I could think of a few things it could pray for.

If Bonnie was still angry with me about selling the boat, she was hiding it well. Her sister's situation had put everything else on the back burner. I gave an excellent performance of someone who had things under control, even if below the surface I was pretty much going out of my mind. And any time Bonnie observed that I seemed distracted, not quite there, she attributed it to a holdover from my LeDrew encounter.

And before we knew it, it was Monday.

Midday, when I had a free moment, I popped into the high school office. There was a counter at the entrance where you could usually find a student in crisis—couldn't get into their locker, lost a phone, thought they were going to throw up—but the teachers scooted around the end of it like they had special visas.

It wasn't often a staff member came in here looking for Trent. He was only the principal. If you really wanted some student's academic records, a contact for a parents' group, an on-call dentist who could help a kid who'd fallen and chipped a tooth, you went to Belinda.

Her title was "head secretary" but that did her a disservice. A better one would be "head honcho" or "field commander" or maybe just "chief executive officer." She'd been at the school for the better part of two decades, outlasted five principals, kind of the way the Queen of England had dealt with fifteen prime ministers during her reign before passing on. Belinda, as they like to say, knew where the bodies were buried.

Trent was smart enough to know his place. "I work for Belinda," he'd told me more than once. "If there's one person you don't want to cross, it's her. She will gut you like a fish." But he'd made the comment with a wry grin, and no shortage of respect and affection.

We all loved her. She was tough and firm and I'd even heard her use a few f-bombs under her breath when things became chaotic, but beneath that thick hide was a woman who would do anything for you.

When I came around the corner and caught her eye, she said, "Hey, Richard."

"Belinda."

"How you doing?"

It was only my second day back since the incident, so many on staff were still inquiring as to my state of mind, wondering whether I was on the verge of some kind of PTSD attack.

"I've been worse," I said.

"Good to hear. Trent's out."

"Looking for you. You keep all the old yearbooks around here someplace?"

"Sure," she said, nodding toward a shelf than ran along one wall. She got up from her desk. "What year do you want?"

"Maybe 2015 through '17?"

She went to the shelf, scanned the spines, pulled out the three books I was looking for and handed them to me. "Anything else I can do for you?"

She didn't ask what I wanted them for, nor had I expected her to. Belinda had enough on her plate without getting the details on matters that were none of her concern. But that didn't mean she didn't know just about everything.

"You have any recollection of a kid named Billy Finster?" I asked.

Belinda's brain had more memory than a MacBook. She took two seconds to retrieve the data, then said, "Yes. Bit of a jock, not a great student. Always looking for shortcuts, the easy way out. Suspended once for smoking pot in the boys' bathroom. Also some health issues. Missed several weeks one year with mononucleosis, as I recall. We had a wave of it that year. And another year, a sports injury. Shoulder dislocation playing football. Played basketball, was on the wrestling team. Parents were kind of ditzy, not in the picture all that much."

"What was his shoe size?"

Belinda's mouth opened, as if she expected she would know the answer to that question, then stopped, looked at me, and said, "Wise guy."

I smiled.

Even though she hadn't asked, I felt I needed a reason to be making inquiries about a former student.

"Ran into him the other day, he came up, said hello. I couldn't quite place him, but I knew the name." I held up the books. "Was going to look through these, see if I remember him."

Belinda had gone back to her desk and dismissed me with a wave of her hand. "Enjoy."

I took the books back to my room and started going through them, starting with 2017. Billy Finster wasn't in it anywhere, which led me to think that he'd graduated the previous year.

So I went through the 2016 book. I couldn't find a headshot of him as I looked through the graduating class, but spotted a list of those absent when the profile shots were taken. Finster was on it. But I still went through the book looking at pictures of the school's various athletic teams, and found him in a couple of those, a blurry face in a cluster of others. I even found a picture taken during one of our wrestling tournaments, at an away game, and there I was, standing in the background.

There was a second shot of the team, the Lodge High crest emblazoned on an overhead banner, so obviously it had been taken on home turf. This must also have been when the regular wrestling coach was still on leave, because he wasn't there and another Lodge teacher was in his place.

Herb Willow.

I had no memory that he'd also filled in around that time. Getting Herb to coach any sports activity would be like asking a caveman to oversee a computer studies class.

Finally, I went through the 2015 book. That year, Finster had been present when the class photos were taken. He'd changed since then, which was no surprise. The Billy Finster I'd met was fuller in the face, thicker in the neck, and his hair was much shorter than it was back then, when a lot of it was hanging over the left side of his face. A decade could do that to a person, especially after their school athletic career was over. I wished I looked as good today as I had ten years ago, as I did in that shot of the wrestling tournament. A little less weight, and definitely more hair, although even then I didn't have a lot.

I wasn't sure if there was a point to this. Maybe I was hoping refreshing my memory of who Finster was when he attended Lodge would provide some further insight into who he was now. I'd struck out there, but that picture of Herb with the wrestling team was something that stuck with me.

Trent appeared in my doorway.

"Belinda says you came by."

"Yeah, but I wasn't looking for you."

He held his spot.

"Something up?" I said.

"Just wondered how it was going, after our talk Saturday."

"I don't have any news. Just . . . figuring out what to do." I told him, briefly, about Bonnie's sister and how her injury had overtaken other events.

He shook his head sympathetically. "One thing after another."

"Yeah."

"And there might be one more."

Christ, what now?

"I had a call from a Violet Kanin," Trent said. "You've got Andrew in your class?"

I nodded.

"She, and a few other parents, it seems, are looking to have a meeting," he said.

"About?"

Trent sighed. "What you're teaching."

My mind raced as I tried to guess what this might be about. It didn't take long. "A literary tour through a post-apocalyptic world's not Andrew's idea of a good time."

"Go figure," Trent said, and left the room.

Slowly, I bent over and touched my forehead to my desk.

Kill me now.

TWENTY-THREE

"**N**ice shoes," Gerhard said.

"You think?" Andrea said, looking down at the Converse runners on her feet. "I was afraid they might pinch, but they're actually maybe a half size too big, but that just gives my toes room to wiggle."

They were leaning up against Gerhard's shiny black Audi, parked in a Home Depot lot, Andrea smoking a Marlboro, Gerhard with his hands in his pockets, looking up into the sun with his shades on. They were waiting to meet one of their local distributors. Once they'd picked up a shipment from Billy, they'd keep some to sell themselves, but also divvy it up among a dozen other area dealers.

"That *was* pretty dumb," he said.

She blew smoke out through her nostrils.

"Draws attention to us," he said.

She drew in some more smoke, then opened her mouth and let it drift out slowly. "Had to send a message."

"Message," he said dismissively. "Like we don't have enough problems. A dead junkie, Tijuana on our ass."

Andrea hadn't known that Cherise chick had died in the alley until after the cop had left the bar. That sad sack of shit sitting next to her said something about it, guessed that must be why that cop was sniffing around. Andrea thought there was something off about the woman, that she didn't fit in, but how did this guy know she was a cop? Came to our school, he said, after that kid blew himself up. And then he started moaning about how that was how he lost his janitorial job, like she gave a fuck.

Maybe, Andrea thought, that cop had been looking for her.

When Jim was busy with some customers on the other side of the room, Andrea slipped out the back. Didn't take long to spot the cop sitting in her car, watching the place. She didn't have Gerhard's Audi that night. She had her own Jeep Wrangler, legit plates on the bumper that could lead someone straight to her, parked a short ways up the street. Couldn't be seen getting into that.

So Andrea watched the watcher. Took cover behind a tree by the curb, a car length away. When the cop got out of her vehicle, Andrea did her thing. Got the bitch's shoes, too.

"You should thank me," Andrea said.

"Say again?"

"Now we know the cops are looking into this. We know now to be extra-careful. That calls for reassessment. Look at our risks, reevaluate."

Gerhard considered the comment. "Like?"

"Alter our routine. Make personnel changes."

"Like?" he said again.

"Billy's a liability. If he didn't steal from us, he was sloppy enough to let someone else do it. Either way, he's gone. Find someone else. Use a different airport. Start over."

"That'll set things back."

Andrea blew out more smoke. "Better a setback than have everything go to shit. What if that cop finds her way to him?"

"He does a retrieval today," Gerhard said. "We've got a pickup tonight."

"Last time," Andrea said, stubbing out her cigarette on the hood of the Audi.

"The fuck?" Gerhard said, taking a tissue from his pocket and rubbing the spot. "What's wrong with you?"

"Never call me dumb," Andrea said. "I'll put the next one out in your eye."

TWENTY-FOUR

Richard

Not long after Trent left, I had a text from someone named Arthur Crone, with the teachers union, saying he'd had a call from Bonnie and wondered if now was a good time to call. I texted back: Yes.

"I did some checking," he said moments later. "You don't have to worry about this lawsuit. It's flimsy to begin with anyway. But we've got your back on this. Won't cost you a penny."

"Did you already tell Bonnie?" I asked.

"No, she asked me to look into it and then I went directly to you. You want me to let her know?"

"Leave it with me. And thanks."

The moment I was done with Arthur, another text. This one was from Jack. He had been to the bank and had the ten thousand in cash for the boat. I replied with a thumbs-up emoji.

When I returned the yearbooks to the office, I asked Belinda if the school had addresses on file for former students.

"Name?" she asked.

"William Finster. Billy. The one I mentioned earlier, that I ran into."

She tapped away on her computer. "We've got one, but it's old."

"I'll take it anyway," I said, bringing out a pen and a small pad from my pocket.

Belinda gave me an address on Sycamore Drive. I scribbled it down. Uncharacteristically for her, she asked, "What are you looking for him for again?"

"I might engage his services," I said. "When I ran into him he mentioned something about doing renovation work. Should have got his number from him at the time."

That was enough to satisfy Belinda. I hoped.

Now that I had an address, what was I going to do with it? It was likely outdated, and even if it was current, what was the plan? Knock on his door and ask him to reconsider? Sneak Trent's gun out of his desk and shoot Billy through the head?

Yeah, *there* was an idea.

"Belinda," I said, "can I bug you for one other thing?" She looked at me expectantly. "Still have an address for Anson Reynolds?"

"There's a name I haven't thought of in a while," she said, turning to her computer and tapping away. "Not too long after he died, his wife sent us a change-of-address in case there were any benefits forms or anything to pass on. She sold their house and moved into an apartment. Here we go. On Golden Hill." She wrote an address and phone number on a notepad sheet and handed it to me.

"What's her name again?"

"Grace."

Before she could ask, I offered a reason. "This Billy and a couple of his buds were wondering what happened to their coach, didn't know he'd passed, and were thinking of sending his wife a note about, you know, how they had nice memories of him."

"Isn't that nice."

After the last bell went, and as I was heading for the door that would take me out to the parking lot, I passed Herb's room. The door was open and I glanced in as I walked by. He was sitting at his desk, scrolling through his phone.

I stopped, went back, and walked straight in without knocking.

I was at his desk, standing in front of him, before he raised his head. He reared back slightly, my presence clearly startling him.

"Richard," he said.

"We need to clear the air, you and I."

Herb moved his tongue inside his left cheek. "Okay," he said slowly.

"You're pissed I told Trent and the police what Mark LeDrew said about you. That somehow I impugned your professionalism. If you had any, that might be the case. Way I see it is, I did more than save your life. I gave you a heads-up. There might be more Mark LeDrews out there. If I were you, I'd be thinking about that, about all the kids I've mocked and humiliated and put down. I'd be looking over my shoulder. What goes around comes around. You might think I've got some score to settle with you, but I don't. I'm only a messenger. Deal with it."

I walked out.

I decided to pay a visit to Grace Reynolds before I did anything else.

If it was her late husband, Anson, who'd abused my blackmailer, that was something I would like to know, and not just to clear myself in his eyes. The truth needed to be exposed to the purifying power of sunlight if it helped those who'd been wronged.

I wasn't naïve enough to think a conversation with Anson's widow would provide me any real answers. It wasn't like I could flat out ask her if she'd ever suspected he had exploited his students sexually. What I wanted to know and what she was likely to divulge were two entirely different things. But I thought, maybe by talking to her, I could get a better sense of who he was and how she felt about him.

It didn't seem fair to drop in on her unannounced, so I called first. Told her who I was, that my course load at Lodge High was shifting, that I was going to be taking on some physical education classes for which I was not in the least qualified, and wondered whether it was possible she had saved any of her husband's lesson plans from when he taught.

If my story raised any suspicions on her part, it didn't come across on the phone. "Well, you're welcome to drop by, but I don't know what I might have," she said, and then told me where she lived, which of course I already knew.

She lived on the first floor of a three-story apartment building that would have been built in the first half of the last century. A plain red-brick structure that backed onto a commuter line. Grace buzzed me in right away and met me at the door to her place.

"I put on some coffee," she said. "I should have asked if you liked coffee. Do you like coffee? If you don't, I can make tea. I might even have some beer in the back of the fridge but it would be pretty old."

I said coffee was fine.

We sat in her very small and crowded living room. I had the sense that when she downsized from a house to this place, she hadn't wanted to part with much, so the space had enough furniture for two living rooms.

We engaged in some general small talk as we drank our coffee. The weather we'd been having, how the traffic seemed worse every year.

"I didn't have a chance to pull anything out for you," she said. "But I did save some of Anson's school stuff."

Considering my cover story, I should have been delighted, but I was also a little worried. I wondered how many boxes of material I'd have to lug out of here to maintain appearances.

"I'll show you," she said, putting aside her coffee and leading me down a short hallway. The unit had two small bedrooms. The first one we passed was clearly where she slept. A pink chenille bedspread, a dozen throw pillows, a painting of the ocean you might find in any hotel room in America.

The door to the second bedroom was closed.

"I have to put my shoulder into it," she said, turning the knob and pushing. Something on the other side kept her from opening it wide. Once there was a two-foot gap she stepped aside and let me look in.

Sweet mother of God.

The room was filled, almost to the ceiling, with dozens—more likely hundreds—of boxes. Banker boxes, liquor boxes, shoeboxes even. And other items randomly scattered about, like a small fake Christmas tree, a pair of ice skates, drapes rolled up in a heap, more throw pillows without covers. Somewhere in the back, I could see handlebars that I was guessing were attached to an exercise bike.

"His lessons would be in one of these boxes somewhere," she said. "I labeled some of them, but not all. But you're welcome to have a browse."

"Well," I said. "Looks like I've got my work cut out for me. Could take a while."

"I thought you might say that. I should have told you over the phone, but I guess I was just happy to have someone come see me."

I smiled. "Why don't we go back and finish our coffee before I get started."

When we were back in the living room, Grace said, "You might be the first person from Lodge I've seen since Anson passed."

I said, honestly, "I feel badly I never came by to see you. I don't even think I went to the funeral, and for that I apologize."

"Oh, don't feel bad about that. There was no funeral."

My eyebrows went up. "No?"

"Considering everything, I couldn't do it. Couldn't handle the questions."

I wondered what she meant by that. "I wasn't even aware that Anson had been sick. It seemed like one day he was there, and one day he wasn't."

She nodded slowly. "Everyone was pretty good about keeping their promise."

"I'm sorry. What do you mean?"

"About how Anson passed. It's been long enough that it's easier to talk about now." She sighed, got up, and as she headed for the kitchen asked, "Can I get you something stronger than coffee?"

"I'm okay."

I heard a refrigerator open, the sound of some ice cubes being scooped up and dropped into a glass, and when Grace returned she had a small tumbler filled to the top with something clear. She took a sip and sat back down.

"Anson killed himself," she said.

TWENTY-FIVE

I t had been one of those days that, when it was over, Bonnie couldn't remember what she'd actually done. She'd found it hard to focus. There were so many different things on her mind that she couldn't zero in on one.

She felt sad for Allison Fowler. She was not present at school today, nor would she be again. This morning her absence was explained to Allison's fourth-grade classmates, and her teacher had accepted Bonnie's offer to be present.

"We have sad news today," the teacher began, doing her best not to be too maudlin. "Allison has moved to a new school. She has gone to live with her aunt, who doesn't live near here." She paused. "Allison's mother died last week. I'm sure Allison would have liked a chance to say goodbye to all of you, but this all happened late on Friday."

"Her mom was a druggie," said a boy sitting near the back of the class.

Bonnie and the teacher both shot the boy a look. If their eyes had been laser-equipped, he'd have burst into flames. He got the message and said no more.

The teacher continued, "It's true that Allison's mother was going through some difficult times, but I know we all would want to wish her the very best and hope that she gets through this."

Bonnie stepped in. "If any of you wish to send a note to Allison, telling her you'll miss her, and telling her how sorry you are that her mother has passed on, I will make sure those get to her. Or maybe the class would like to make a large card that everyone could sign."

With that, she excused herself from the classroom. Back in her office, she found her thoughts constantly returning to Marta and Richard. She'd texted with her sister early that morning to see how her recovery was going, and Marta continued to assure her she was fine and likely returning to work later that day. Bonnie fired back a text urging her to take the week off, but knew trying to talk sense into Marta was a lost cause. She doubted Ginny would have any better luck.

And then there was Richard.

God, the week he'd been through. As if his encounter with Mark LeDrew weren't enough, now those parents were suing. As a principal, she wasn't in the union, but she had contacts there, and she got in touch with Arthur Crone. He promised to look into it and reach out to Richard.

Later, she called him back.

"Had a good chat with Richard," he said. "He said he'd fill you in."

She wanted an answer now. "Are you guys covering him or not?"

"I told him not to worry. We've got this."

She smiled when she ended the call. He didn't have to sell the boat. Good thing, too, because it was a *family* boat. Rachel might not have been a huge fishing fan—it was hard for a kid that age to sit still waiting for some dumb perch or pickerel to hit her line—but she loved exploring the lake and knifing her hand into the water as Richard cranked the throttle to full speed. There were good memories attached to that boat, and every reason to believe they would be making more.

Bonnie dealt with a few administrative matters through the afternoon, then told her vice principal she'd had enough and was heading home early. She'd get something organized for dinner, then head down and pick up Rachel from Mrs. Tibaldi.

As she arrived home, Jack was also pulling into the driveway next door. He waved. Bonnie waved back and approached him as he was getting out of his car.

"Hey, Jack," she said, but she couldn't be heard over the loaded dump truck rumbling past. She tried again. "Hey, Jack!"

"Bonnie."

"Got a second?"

"Sure."

"Richard was telling me he sold you the boat."

Jack nodded. He patted the chest of his suit jacket. "Have the money right here."

"The cash," Bonnie said.

Another nod. "Don't usually go to the bank asking for that much. I think the teller thought I was doing a drug deal or something." He grinned. "Do I give off that kind of vibe?"

Bonnie tried to smile but couldn't quite pull it off.

"I'm really sorry, Jack. I don't like doing this. I know you and Richard had a deal, but . . ."

He waited.

"This has been a pretty traumatic week for Richard," Bonnie said.

"Of course."

"He's not thinking as clearly about things as he should be."

"I can well imagine."

"He's making decisions he really hasn't thought through. And I think what motivated him to sell the boat is no longer an issue. Don't know if you'd heard, but he's being sued—it's a ridiculous thing—and he thought he'd have to pay the legal costs himself, but it turns out he doesn't have to. That was what he needed the money for."

"Oh my."

"So, in light of that, and I hate to ask, but I wonder if you'd be willing to cancel the deal."

"Of course. It's not a problem."

"I'm really, *really* sorry about this."

"I'm the one who should feel badly. That maybe I was taking advantage of him in a weak moment. That was never my intention. But it seemed like he'd already made up his mind to sell." He patted the cash again. "Maybe we'll go out for dinner."

That made Bonnie laugh. "I know a great little café on the Champs-Élysées."

"You have a wonderful evening," Jack said, and continued on into the house.

Bonnie gave him one last wave, waited until he was inside, then continued on to the sitter's.

It was the right thing to do, she told herself. And she was betting that once she told Richard what she'd done, that he didn't need the money for his legal defense, that he could keep his boat, he'd be happy.

TWENTY-SIX

Richard

O n my way to the Sycamore Drive address Belinda had given, I thought about what Grace Reynolds had revealed to me.

Her husband Anson had been depressed for some time. He'd been good, she said, at not showing it at work, but outside of school he was a man tormented by private demons. She'd urged him to seek help, to talk to someone, anyone, but he said he couldn't bring himself to do that.

"You've no idea what was troubling him?" I asked.

She had shaken her head sadly. "You read stories all the time about people, like these big celebrities who you think have everything, but they're miserable. There doesn't have to be a reason."

Unless there was.

When Grace wasn't home, he'd started up the car in the garage with the doors closed, and sat behind the wheel until he'd accomplished what he'd set out to do. Before dying, he'd paid off the monthly bills, changed the batteries in all the smoke detectors, and fixed a plugged drain in the kitchen that he'd been meaning to get to. He hadn't, Grace said, wanted her to have to deal with any of the everyday stuff in the days and weeks after his passing.

She hadn't wanted the world to know how he'd gone, and the various authorities acceded to her request to say he had passed of "heart failure." She didn't even think Trent knew how he had actually died.

I thanked her for her time and the coffee, told her I would think about whether I had the time to come back and search through those boxes in the second bedroom for Anson's lesson plans, and caught a glimpse of her knocking back that drink as I was showing myself out.

And now I was on Sycamore. The Finster house.

It was a modest bungalow with an attached garage. As I did a slow drive-by, I saw that all the drapes were drawn, the grass needed cutting, and there was a FOR SALE sign on the lawn. There were some flyers sticking out of a jammed mailbox by the front door.

The place did not look lived-in at all.

I went to the end of the street, turned around, drove past the house once more, then pulled over to the shoulder and parked. I got out and walked up to the house one door over from the Finster house and rang the bell.

A harried-looking woman in her twenties, balancing a baby on her hip, appeared after about thirty seconds. "Yes?" she said, opening the screen a foot.

"I was looking for the Finsters," I said. "Is that their place next door? Up for sale?"

"Yeah, well, it was," she said, shifting the baby to her other hip. "First Mr. Finster died about three years back, then Mrs. Finster. But they didn't own the house, they rented. Owner had it on the market awhile, hasn't rented it out to anyone else."

"I was looking for Billy," I said.

"Billy?" she said, and blushed. "Him and me actually went out for a while there, back in the day, but he got married to someone used to be a friend of mine." The emphasis on "used to be" suggested this friend might have had something to do with her breaking up with Billy.

"You know where they live now?"

"Yeah, sure."

Finster's house was a small one-story on Wooster, a few blocks from the Housatonic River. Gray siding, black shutters, a separate garage toward the back of the property at the end of the driveway. A small silver Kia was parked on the driveway, closer to the street. As I passed, I held up my phone and fired off a few shots. When I reached the top of the street I made a right onto Windy Hill Road, pulled over, and stopped. I wanted to check the pictures I'd taken, making sure I'd captured decent images of the house and the car and its license plate. I didn't know that I had a use for them, but if I came up with one, I was ahead of the game.

I made a loop around the block so I could drive by one more time. I was three houses away when I spotted a woman coming out the front door. I pulled over to the side. There were no sidewalks, so I rolled onto the edge of a front yard and stopped.

The woman was probably about the same age as Finster. Five-three, slender, blond hair down to her shoulders. She walked purposefully to the Kia, got in, and when she backed out of the drive she had the car pointed in my direction. I glanced down, as if dealing with my phone. I raised my head once she'd passed and caught a glimpse of the car in my rearview mirror.

Billy's wife, I presumed. Maybe the blackmail was all her idea. Anything was possible.

Someone rapped hard on the passenger window. A woman, mid-seventies, glasses, gray hair pulled back, looking very pissed.

I powered down the window.

"You're parked on my goddamn grass," she said.

I gave her a nod, edged the car's right side back onto the asphalt, and that must have satisfied her, because I glanced around and she had disappeared.

There didn't seem to be much point in hanging around any longer. I now knew where Billy Finster lived.

My phoned dinged. I took it out of my pocket and saw that it was from Bonnie.

Have some good news.

Well, I could use some of that. I was about to reply when I heard the back door on the passenger side open. The car listed slightly as someone dropped into the backseat. As I turned in my seat, the back door slammed shut.

It was him.

And if I hadn't been so caught off guard I might have had time to react more quickly to the fist heading straight toward my face. I had just enough time to turn so that I took the hit on my temple, immediately to the side of my right eye, instead of my nose.

I let out a yelp of pain and reared back.

"Stalking me?" he asked, and made a sniffing noise.

I put my hand on the side of my head. Christ, it hurt. I glanced in the mirror, its letterboxed shape acting like a mask for my attacker, giving me a view of his eyes and nose, which he wiped with a tissue.

"Billy, listen," I said, my temple throbbing.

"Our arrangement's changed," he said. "I was going to give you more time. But I want the money tonight."

"Fuck you."

"I get the money," he repeated, "or everybody knows. Get ready for some breaking news, asshole. Perv teacher! Film at eleven!"

"I didn't do it," I said. "I swear. It had to be somebody else."

Was it fair to the dead to ask if he remembered Anson Reynolds? I had no proof it was him, but a man who felt badly enough to take his own life might have been wanting to punish himself for something he shouldn't have done.

"Did you have a teacher named Mr. Reynolds?" I asked.

"What?"

"Anson Reynolds. Taught gym. Coached wrestling." I had another name in the back of my mind. "Or maybe Mr. Willow."

He leaned forward so his mouth was close to my ear. "Here's the thing, Mr. Teacher. It really doesn't matter whether it was you or not. Maybe it was, maybe it wasn't. All I care about right now is my ten grand."

"Christ, Billy, once you expose me with your bullshit," I said, "*you're* exposed. They'll look into your background. Maybe you've pulled this kind of shit before."

"Not if it's anonymous," he whispered.

"I'll say it was you," I said.

"And how will you explain that? Only way you could know it was me would be if you did it."

This wasn't happening. It *couldn't* be happening.

"So you better get my money," he said.

I recalled the text Jack had sent. He had the cash.

There had to be a way out of this. If I brought him the money, if I had someone with me, someone who could be a witness, someone—

"You hear me?" he said.

"I hear you."

"Give me your cell number. I'll be in touch about when and where."

I gave him the number, heard him enter it into his phone, then the opening of the back door.

"Later, asshole," he said, slamming it shut.

I was in free fall.

Panic welled up inside me. I didn't know what to do other than pay this man and hope to God that was the end of it. I'd been a fool to think knowing where he lived would afford me some advantage. He'd turned the tables on me. Caught me in the act.

I drove quickly out of the neighborhood, my tail between my legs. Moments later I wheeled into a McDonald's parking lot to pull myself together. A glance in the mirror revealed that my right temple was already turning black and blue. My vision was not affected, but my eyelid was slightly swollen.

How was I going to explain that when I got home?

After about five minutes, I pulled back out into traffic and aimed the car for home. Once on our street, I saw Jack's vehicle in his driveway. I'd be able to get the money from him before I went into the house and faced Bonnie and Rachel. I had my car parked and was heading for Jack's front door when Bonnie came striding out of the house.

"Hey," she said. "I'm glad you're—"

The second she saw my face, she stopped. "Oh my God, what happened to you?" she asked. She reached her hand up, as if she were going to touch the right side of my face, but held back.

"I need to get some ice on it," I said. "If it's not too late."

"What happened?" she asked again.

"Stupidest thing," I said. I'd been rehearsing this in the car. "I was making a shortcut through the gym, walked right into the path of a basketball. Got whomped good. Kid could really throw."

Bonnie looked unconvinced. "A ball did *that*?"

"He's got an arm on him."

She examined the bruising more carefully. "Looks more like someone took a swing at you."

I said, a little too brusquely, "It's nothing, okay?"

Bonnie took a step back. "What's going on? Talk to me."

"Nothing. Look, find me an ice pack, I'll be in in a minute."

"What are you going to do?"

"Just going to see Jack for a second."

Bonnie's face froze. "About that."

"What?"

"When I texted? When I said I had news?"

"Yeah?"

"You already know, but I talked to Arthur after he talked to you. They'll cover your legal bills. They'll get you a lawyer. The lawsuit's bullshit. And honestly, if they didn't support you, and it went public, the blowback would be significant." She made quote marks with her fingers, like she was reading a headline. "*Hero Teacher Screwed Over by Union.*"

"All good, I guess." *That fucking Arthur.* I was going to tell Bonnie I was on my own, that I still needed the money.

"So you don't need to sell the boat." She smiled. "Simple as that."

"Great, but I made a deal with Jack and I don't intend to break it."

"I already have," Bonnie said.

For a second there, the world was spinning.

"What?"

"I talked to him," she said. "I explained things."

"Explained things how?"

"I told him why you thought you needed the money and now you don't. That selling the boat was a hasty, impulsive decision at a time when you've been under so much stress. He totally understood. He was fine with it." She paused, and then, with a hint of attitude, said, "You're welcome."

I had put both hands atop my head. I turned away from her, pacing. "Shit," I said. "Shit shit shit."

I brought my hands down, turned and faced her, shaking my head from side to side. "You shouldn't have done that. You shouldn't have done that without talking to me first."

"Oh, so *you're* the one who has to be consulted, but not me."

"Fuck!" I said. "Did he have the cash?" Almost without even realizing it, I had put my hand on my chest, trying to slow my heart down. "Did he have it on him? He said he was going to have it."

"Yes, he had it! And I told him to keep it!"

I made a move in the direction of Jack's place and Bonnie grabbed my arm, stopping me. "No," she said.

I shook her arm off. "You don't know what you've done." I was starting to tremble. I could feel sweat bubbling up on my forehead.

"If I don't know, then maybe you'd better explain it to me. Maybe you better tell me what the fuck is really going on."

"I'm handling it," I told her. "I've got it under control!"

"Handling what, for God's sake? Are you gambling? You don't even buy scratch tickets. What the hell *is* it?" Suddenly her face fell, imagining the worst. "It's not a woman. Tell me it's got nothing to do with another woman."

"For fuck's sake, Bonnie," I said, exhausted.

"If you won't tell me what's going on, don't blame me for thinking the worst."

I had to get the money. I had to tell Jack that Bonnie didn't know what she was doing. He'd think we were both nuts, but so long as I got the cash, I was confident I could resolve this mess.

I didn't know what else to do.

"Trust me," I said, but the words barely came out. My breathing was quick and shallow. Something was wrong.

Bonnie shook her head. "No, I can't." She raised a finger, pointed it at me. "If you don't tell me why you need that ten thousand dollars, right now, right this second, I'm going in that house, packing two bags, and Rachel and I are going to a hotel. We're leaving. I'm dead serious. It's up to you. Make a choice. Tell me what's happening, or say goodbye to us."

I took three wavering steps toward my car, put a hand on the front fender to steady myself, and said, "I think I'm going to pass out."

TWENTY-SEVEN

For Lucy, it was becoming a question of who to fear most. Digby, the hospital orderly who wanted more fentanyl and was ready to hurt Lucy if he didn't get it? Billy, if he figured out she'd dipped into the shipment? The pair he was working for, whose idea of a good time was hooking battery clamps to a guy's tits? The cops?

So far, Billy appeared to buy her denials that she'd had anything to do with it, but that could change. If and when he knew the truth, would he give her up to the people he worked for? If she stole any more from Billy, it upped the odds he'd catch her. Maybe he'd set up some cameras in the garage. It was a wonder he hadn't done that from the get-go, if only to protect his precious automotive tools. And now, if Billy had even half a brain—and, to be honest, this was often in question—he'd have put a new lock on the cabinet where he kept the drugs, be more careful with the new key.

No way she was YouTubing her way into that carry-on bag again.

And even if she did dare to, Billy's associates kept pretty close tabs— no pun intended—on the inventory. If he came up short again, what would they do to him? Lucy wasn't sure just who these people fronted for, but it wasn't the Girl Scouts. The flights were coming from south of the border, so it wasn't hard to connect the dots. The cartels, baby. They controlled the drug trade down there, had their own labs making this stuff. So long as the money kept coming in, Billy didn't ask questions. He really didn't want to know.

If there was an easy way out of this, Lucy didn't know what it was. Could she chip away at her list of potential threats? Cross one off, move on to the next? Digby, for example. Could she make an anonymous tip to the hospital admin? Say he was stealing pharmaceuticals, helping himself to patients' personal belongings, fondling female patients while they slept? It was probably true, anyway.

She'd returned from a trip to the grocery store and was sitting at the kitchen table, staring into space as she nursed a beer, thinking about how she'd go about ratting out Digby, when she heard Billy's van pull up beside the house. She got up, left the beer on the table, and went outside to meet him.

He'd reversed the vehicle up to the garage, gotten out, raised the rear hatch, and was swinging open the garage door when Lucy approached.

"Hey," she said.

"Hey," he replied.

He was unloading boxes and carrying them to the rear of the garage. He had brand-new power tools, all in their original packaging. Belt sanders, jigsaws, drills, reciprocating saws.

"You gotta be kidding me," Lucy said. "I thought you were all tapped out. No money left."

"Didn't buy it," he said, puffing as he made another trip.

"Don't tell me. You know a guy."

It would go with the other goods she'd seen in the locker, she thought. Laptops, DVD players, phones.

"I'll pay them off one way or another," he said, more to himself than to Lucy. "I got merchandise. Makes up for the shortfall."

"Is this enough?" she asked. "And what makes you think they're even going to want this? What are they supposed to do? Put it up on eBay?"

He ignored her. Once he had placed the last load in the garage, he came outside and lowered the door, took three deep breaths, and said, "I need a drink."

She followed him into the house, where he went straight to the refrigerator and grabbed a beer. He took one long draw, set it on the counter, and then did something that made Lucy's jaw drop.

He reached under his jacket and pulled out a gun. He set it on the kitchen table and stared at it for several seconds, panting.

"Jesus fucking Christ, Billy. The hell is this?"

"That's a gun, Lucy. You should get out more."

"Why do you have it?"

He took another drink. When he put the bottle down, let go of it, his hand was slightly trembling.

"Insurance," he said. "Just . . . need to be ready."

He couldn't look her in the eye. He studied the gun on the table in front of him, turned it slowly with his index finger, the barrel briefly pointing at Lucy as it revolved.

"Is it loaded?" she asked.

"Wouldn't be much good if it wasn't."

"Where'd you get it?"

He rolled his eyes. "Lucy, this is America."

"What are they gonna think, they see you with a gun?"

"I'm not an idiot. I'll hide it. Someplace I can grab it fast. In case things go sideways."

Lucy pictured it. Billy shooting two people dead in the garage. Like *that* would be the end of their problems. What was he going to do with two bodies? What did Billy think would happen next? That their bosses wouldn't be wondering what happened to them, wouldn't send someone from Mexico to find them? That Billy wouldn't be the first person they'd want to have a word with? Would he shoot them, too?

The thing was, there'd been a moment there, when they'd first come into the house, when she was thinking she should just tell him. Come clean. Tell him it was her, that she dipped into the stash, that she was really, really sorry, but lay some of the blame on him, too, because he'd never been willing to share any of the proceeds, and if he had, maybe she wouldn't have done what she'd done.

But she'd tell him she'd find a way to make it right. She'd give him what money she hadn't already spent after selling the stuff to Digby and others. Maybe she could hit up her mom in Utah for some cash. Lucy hadn't talked to her in six months, but maybe if she told her she was pregnant, that she needed help setting up a nursery and buying a car seat and a stroller and all that other shit, her mother would be so excited she'd dip into her savings. (Even if it *did* mean that it was Billy who got her pregnant. Lucy's mother had tried to tell her the guy was a loser, but did she listen?) Later, when there was no baby, she'd come up with some sob story about losing the kid.

Or maybe she'd tell him they should disappear until things cooled down. Go stay with her mom. Couple of drug dealers really going to chase them all the way to Salt Lake City? They might not head off with a fortune, but they'd have enough to buy gas and junk food till they got there. After they arrived, they'd try to figure out a way to get out of this mess.

Those ideas, and others, had been running through her head, right up until the moment Billy set that gun on the kitchen table.

That gun changed everything.

You did not tell your significant other that you'd been stealing from him and putting his life in danger when he had a gun.

A *loaded* gun.

"You know," Lucy said, changing her tone, trying to be upbeat even if she didn't feel that way, "I think they'll love the tools, the laptops, all that stuff."

Billy slowly raised his head, fixing his eyes on her, as though he'd had some sudden realization.

"What did you say?"

"I said I think they'll go for it. You can buy some time this way."

"You said laptops."

"What?"

"Laptops. That's what you said. Laptops. I didn't bring in any laptops."

"You brought in all kinds of shit," she said. "I thought maybe there was some laptops in there."

"It was you," he said.

"What was me?" she said, reaching for her beer, her mouth going dry.

"How would you know I had laptops if you haven't been in my locker?"

"Come on," she said, smiling nervously. "That's crazy talk."

"Christ, what have you done?" he asked her, picking up the gun. "You're going to get us both killed."

TWENTY-EIGHT

Richard

I didn't pass out.

Bonnie helped me into the house and got me as far as the kitchen, where I sat. Rachel, thankfully, was in the backyard, and did not see me in distress. Bonnie had her phone out, her finger poised over the screen.

"What are you doing?" I asked.

"Calling an ambulance," she said matter-of-factly. "You're having a heart attack."

"No, no," I protested. "It's not a heart attack." I licked my lips. "I think it's a panic attack. I'm okay now."

She set the phone down, went to a cupboard, and brought out a small plastic container of aspirin. She shook one out into her hand and held it in front of me. "Chew this."

I did as I was told.

Bonnie picked her phone back up and, despite another protest from me, hit 911. Three seconds later she was telling a dispatcher our address and that she was worried her husband might be having a heart attack. "Yes," she said, "I just gave him one."

She ended the call.

"I'm not having a heart attack," I said again.

"I hope you're right, but we're not taking any chances."

I nodded, knowing it was pointless to argue now that the paramedics were on their way.

"You're going to tell me what's going on," Bonnie said, "but not now."

While we waited for the ambulance to arrive, Rachel came into the house and could tell immediately that something was wrong. I tried to persuade her it was nothing serious.

"I was feeling a little off for a minute," I told her, "and your mother called an ambulance just to be sure I'm okay."

Her face looked like it might break. "You can help," I said. "You can let us know when the ambulance gets here."

She nodded and ran. A couple of minutes later, she screamed, "They're here! They're here!"

She had the front door open before Bonnie could get there and lead them into the kitchen. It was a team of two, a man and a woman.

"I'm fine," I said before they'd even said hello.

They asked me a slew of questions, checked my blood pressure, conducted an electrocardiograph with some little gadget Rachel watched with a mixture of fear and fascination.

"What's with the bandages?" the female paramedic asked, noticing the ones on my neck and forehead.

"They're old."

"And what about this?" She was indicating the bruise on my temple and my puffy eyelid. "Did you fall when you had your episode?"

I'd forgotten I'd been hit. "No, I didn't fall." I needed a second to remember the lie I'd told Bonnie. "I got hit with a basketball. It's fine."

When they were finished with their speedy tests, they concluded it was unlikely I'd had a cardiac event. But they advised me to come to the hospital anyway.

"I'm okay," I insisted. "I've been under a lot of stress lately, that's all."

Rachel piped up, "Dad nearly got killed when the bomb went off."

Bonnie added more details. The paramedics nodded. They knew all about the LeDrew incident.

"We can't force you to come," the woman said. "*Something's* happened to you. Just how serious it is would take further tests."

I was adamant. And maybe stupid. But I sent them on their way.

Once the house was quiet again, and Rachel, still looking somewhat stricken, went to her room after being persuaded I was not going to drop dead, Bonnie went to the freezer for one of the soft ice packs we keep on hand.

"It may be late for this, but hold it on the side of your head." She handed me the pack, and a towel to hold it with so it didn't freeze my hand. I did as I was told while Bonnie made some tea, and then sat across the table from me.

"Let's hear it," she said.

And so I told her.

Pretty much all of it. Everything that had happened since Finster first approached me on the street Friday out front of our house. How I'd tried to find out more about him. Found his house. Him turning the tables on me, striking me. (At that point in my story, Bonnie's face flushed red with rage.) I explained the anguish I'd been going through about what was the best way to handle this. My fears of what an allegation like this could do not only to me, but to Bonnie and Rachel. How, given my history, it was just one more thing.

I'd asked Bonnie at the outset to let me get the story out before asking questions. I knew she'd have plenty.

I was afraid her first one would be whether the abuse allegation was true. So I decided to beat her to it.

"Are you going to ask if I did it?"

She shook her head without hesitation. "No," she said, and put her hand on mine and squeezed. "Somebody might have, but not you."

I'd included Anson Reynolds in my story, the newly revealed information that he had taken his own life.

"Thank you," I said weakly, taking a sip of the tea with my free hand. The right side of my head had gone numb from the ice pack.

"You should have told me right away."

"I've told you why I didn't."

"Not good enough."

I nodded. I took the ice pack away from my head and put it on the table. "How's it look?" I asked.

Bonnie examined me. "The swelling might have gone down a titch. Your eyelid looks less swollen." She pressed her lips together angrily. "That son of a bitch."

"Yeah."

Bonnie said, "Marta got it right. How what happened might affect you. This whole week you've been in shock. You're not thinking clearly. You're not making rational decisions. Look, this would throw anyone for a loop, but for someone who's just gone through what you have? It's over the top."

"Maybe it's not irrational to spare us from a scandal, even if it's bullshit."

"There's no proof. If he comes forward, we level the extortion accusation. And if he makes an anonymous allegation, no one's going to put any faith in that. Wouldn't be the first time some student tried to smear a teacher who'd given him a bad mark or suspended him, or just did it out of mischief."

"What about Lyall Temple?"

Again, she shook her head. "That boy himself said what you did was compassion, pure and simple. That you comforted him in a time of need. His father had died. You can ride this out. They might put you on a paid leave, but you'd get through it. We'd *all* get through it. I don't think you have any *choice* but to ride this out. If you pay him, you're saying you're guilty. And if you pay him once, he'll come back again and again."

I knew she was right, but it still felt like rolling the dice, doing it her way. I still had a backup plan in the back of my mind, one I didn't want to share.

"He wants the money tonight."

"If he shows up, we call the police," she said emphatically. "And we shouldn't wait for that to happen. We need to bring Marta into this. She needs to know. That's how we get ahead of this."

I was less sure about that. "You might believe I wouldn't molest some kid, but will she?"

"Yes," Bonnie said, but I thought it took her about half a second too long to answer. "She will. If she has any doubts, I'll make sure she comes around."

"The thing is," I said, and this was going to be difficult to admit, "I feel humiliated. I allowed myself to be bullied. I let this fucker intimidate me. It's as if I had only so much courage—or stupidity, depending on how you look at it—in reserve, and used it all up when I faced down Mark LeDrew, and I need time to build it back up."

In what was the only moment of levity that entire day, Bonnie grinned and said, "It's kind of like trying to have sex twice in half an hour."

"Thanks for not adding 'at your age.' But yeah, like that. So can you let me think of this till morning, about whether to bring Marta to the rescue?"

Bonnie thought about it. "Okay. And anyway, I need to find out how she's doing. I hope she wasn't foolish enough to go back to work today."

"I'll bet she did."

"I'd promised to drop by and then things got away from me." She glanced at the wall clock. "I'm going to order you guys a pizza. And pick one up on the way to Marta's."

That made me nervous.

"Promise me. Not a word about this to her. Not yet, anyway."

Bonnie considered my request, and nodded. "I promise."

She picked up her phone, opened an app that would take her to the place we always patronized, and with a couple of taps placed a repeat of a previous order. As she finished, my own cell rang. I took it out of my pocket and looked at the number. I didn't recognize it.

I said, "This might be it."

The phone rang a second time. A third.

Bonnie looked at me, said nothing. She didn't have to. I knew what she wanted me to do. And she was hoping she'd given me the strength to do it.

Fourth ring. Fifth.

I picked up. "Hello?"

"Bring the money to—"

I said, "Fuck you. I'm not paying. Do what you've gotta do, asshole."

As I ended the call and put the phone down on the table, Bonnie gave me a smile. She might even have looked proud of me.

"I'm going to go upstairs, check on Rach, and then I'm out of here," Bonnie said, and slipped out of the kitchen.

I sat there, taking deep breaths to keep myself on an even keel. I muted my phone so that if that asshole called back, I wouldn't have to listen to the ring. But a minute later, I saw the screen light up with a text.

You'll be sorry.

I turned the phone facedown, tried to pretend I hadn't even seen the message. Moments later, Bonnie reappeared long enough to grab her purse and keys. "Pizza's on its way," she said, kissed my forehead gently, and was gone.

It arrived ten minutes later. I got out two plates and placed a couple of slices on each.

"Rach!"

She came running into the kitchen. If she had been worried earlier about her dad being looked over by a pair of paramedics, she was over it now. There was great healing power in the aroma of cheese and pepperoni.

"Can we eat in front of the TV?" she asked. I had no objection.

Rachel went onto one of the streaming services and picked *How to Train Your Dragon*, a movie she'd watched at least ten times already. My mind was not on the screen. I couldn't stop thinking about that last text I'd received.

My blackmailer was half-right. He'd said I was going to be sorry. I was already sorry. Sorry that I'd allowed him to manipulate me. Sorry that I hadn't stood up to him. Sorry that I had allowed myself to become a victim.

No more.

Bonnie had led me to something of a breakthrough. I wasn't going to take this shit any longer. I had to find a way to take control of my situation, on my own. Tonight. And if I failed, then I'd have to accede to Bonnie's wishes and bring Marta into this in the morning.

But in the meantime, I felt I needed someone else—someone other than Bonnie, and not Marta—to hash this over with.

I wanted to talk to Trent, tell him the rest of the story, reveal my blackmailer's identity. I wanted to know if he was aware Anson had taken his own life and whether he thought there was anything to be read into that. I needed to know he'd have my back if and when this all became public. And I had a hell of a favor to ask.

I slipped out of the family room and phoned Mrs. Tibaldi.

"Hi, Richard," she said, obviously seeing my caller ID.

"Mrs. Tibaldi, hey, sorry to bother you. I know it's after hours, but would you be able to take Rachel if I brought her over in a few minutes? Couple of hours or so. Just add it into what we pay you at the end of the month. Bonnie had to go out, and now there's something I have to do."

"Bring her over."

I thanked her and went back into the family room to break the news to Rachel.

"Everything is crazy around here," she said.

Once I'd dropped Rachel off, I texted Bonnie to let her know I'd gone out and that Rachel was at the sitter's, just in case she returned home before I did and wondered where we were.

I drove straight to Trent's house. Parked out front, walked up to the door, and rang the bell. It was nearly dark. The curtain fell back an inch, and I saw a sliver of Melanie's face.

"Hello, Richard," she said, opening the door and admitting me.

"Melanie. Sorry for dropping by like this."

"You looking for Trent?"

"I am."

"He's not here. Is there something I can help you with?"

I sighed. "Where is he?"

"Something at the school. What did you do to your head?"

"It's nothing. Listen, I'll catch up with him later."

"I'll tell him you came by."

I exited the house, heard her close the door behind me, and got back into my car. And sat. Didn't turn on the engine. Stewed.

Maybe it was just as well Trent hadn't been home. I wasn't able to ask him that favor. It would have been a big ask, and he probably would have said no. I wanted him to come with me to Billy Finster's. I had this crazy idea Trent could stay out of sight while I got my blackmailer to admit that there was nothing to his allegations. That if he had been abused, I wasn't his abuser. He'd as much as admitted that in our last encounter when he'd said maybe it was me, and maybe it wasn't. Trent would be my witness.

It would have been wrong to put Trent in that position. It would have been too risky for him, personally and professionally.

I heard an incoming text. Probably Bonnie acknowledging my earlier message. I got out my phone and had a look.

Not Bonnie.

Don't fuck with me. Gonna tell everybody. Just you wait. Pay up asshole.

I exited the texting app and stared briefly at the phone's screen, at all those other apps, including the ones I'd briefly considered deleting.

Voice Memos.

Maybe I didn't need Trent after all.

TWENTY-NINE

Billy, wild-eyed, had snatched the gun up off the table and was pointing it straight at Lucy.

"What did you do?" he shouted. "What the fuck did you do?"

Still sitting, she had her hands partly raised, palms forward, like she was about to be arrested. "Billy, please, put down the gun. You're freaking me out."

The gun did not go down. He kept it trained on her forehead, his arm shaking. "Just tell me what you did," he said, trying to bring some calm to his voice. But he still looked ready to blow her head off.

"It was only a little," she said, slowly lowering her hands and placing them palms down on the table. "A few pills or candies or whatever. I didn't think anyone would notice. There was so much of it."

"How?"

"I took your key, copied it, put it back on your ring," she said, shrugging, like it was no big deal.

"The bag was locked," he said.

"I YouTubed it," she said. "How to open it, zip it back up like it never happened. You should tell your guys it's pretty easy, they might want to try something a little more secure. I got into it like it was nothing. If I could do it, anybody could do it."

Make him think she'd done them all a favor, a little demonstration that would prompt everyone to up their game. "I can show you, if you want."

"Goddamn it, Lucy. What'd you do with it?"

"Sold it. Billy, please, I'm begging you, put the gun down. If you're gonna shoot me, shoot me and be done with it. But I swear, I'm gonna piss myself if you don't put it down."

He considered the request a moment, then lowered the gun, pointing it more at the table, but hanging on to it just the same.

"Sold it to who?" he asked.

"Some patients. Current ones and former ones, and this one guy at work. He became my best customer pretty fast. Thing is, I only dipped into the stash once, and he's already leaning on me for more. I told him it was all over. I swear. I said I couldn't get any more. I'm done. I'm sorry."

"Sorry," he said, sneering, the word leaving a bad taste in his mouth. "Is that what I should tell them? That you're sorry?"

She pushed back her chair and stood. "I will, I'll do it. I'll take the blame. I'll tell them you had nothing to do with it. That it was me. That I'll find a way to make it right. I'll hit my mom up for it, make up a story."

"Don't you get it?" Billy said. "Doesn't matter if it was you. It's still my fault. They trusted me with their shit. I'm fucking *toast*."

He started waving the gun around in frustration, pointing it nowhere in particular. "Shit shit shit shit," he said under his breath. Then, "How many times?"

"I told you. Just the once." She was thinking. "Maybe . . . maybe there's some way we could make them think it was at their end. I'll show you how to get into that carry-on case, then you can show them. Tell them maybe someone on the plane got into it."

But Billy wasn't listening. His eyes had glazed over, like he was looking into his own future and didn't like what he saw.

And then Lucy said something she'd been holding back. "You should have shared," she said.

"I what?"

"Coming into all this cash, but still sending me off to my shit job every day. I mean, not like I would have quit, but it would've been nice if you spent some of that money on me instead of on yourself."

Slowly, he fixed his eyes on her. "Just like Stuart. Everyone wants a piece of my action. You both think you're entitled." He pointed the gun at her again. "Fuck you."

"Okay! Okay!" she said, hands in the air once more.

She moved slowly over to the counter, not sure whether Billy was going to pull the trigger or not. Grabbed her car keys and said, "I'm leaving, okay? I'm just going to get out of here for a while. When you've cooled down, text me or call me or whatever. But right now I'm out of here."

And she was gone. A moment later, Billy could hear her car start up and drive off.

He decided to head out to the garage and see for himself how easy it was to get into the carry-on bag.

Taking the gun with him, he unlocked the side door, put the gun on the worktable, and used his key to open the locker. Took out the carry-on bag, set it on the bench.

Billy found, if not the same video Lucy had watched, one very similar, which illustrated how easy it was to get into a locked bag. Working a pencil between the zipper teeth made a joke out of the small lock that held the two zipper ends together.

"Fuck me," he said to himself when he realized how simply it could be done.

Maybe Lucy was right. He'd demonstrate what he'd learned when Psycho Bitch and Butthead came to call. Not that this made him any less angry with her. She'd landed them in shit up to their eyeballs, and damned if he didn't nearly pull that trigger at one point.

Good thing he hadn't. First of all, what a mess it would have made. And what would he have done with her afterward? What would he say when the hospital called and asked why she hadn't shown up for her shift? Maybe he could've said she'd left him. He thought that was probably a tale he could sell, because even Billy had enough self-awareness to know he wasn't the Porsche in a lot full of Pintos.

And the thing was, he loved her. Sure, in the moment he could have put a bullet in her head, but he loved her.

So, yeah, maybe Andrea and Gerhard could be persuaded that it might, just might, not be his fault. Or at least raise some level of doubt in their minds. And if that kept them from killing him, fine and dandy. If they wanted to get someone else to do what he'd been doing, find another guy at another airport, fine by him.

Frankly, Billy'd be glad to see the ass end of them. Especially the woman. His nipple still hurt like a motherfucker.

He closed the case back up, again following the tips he'd learned from the video, the zipper ends still linked together with the tiny lock. He was about to return it to the locker when he heard a rapping at the side door.

Had Lucy come back? Had she forgiven him for waving a gun in her face? The real question was, had he forgiven her for getting them into this mess? He didn't think she'd be back this soon.

The pickup was set for tonight, so he shouldn't be surprised if Andrea and Gerhard were here, although it was a little early. They usually showed up after nine, sometimes closer to ten. So Billy didn't bother securing the carry-on bag behind a locked door.

He tucked the gun behind his back, under his belt. Didn't think his associates would respond well if he opened the door with a gun in his hand. He took a deep breath, wanting to look as relaxed and unruffled as possible.

He opened the door. The bulb in the lamp above it had burned out, but it wasn't so dark yet that he couldn't see who it was.

Stuart.

Billy invited him in with a nod of his head.

"You look pissed," Stuart said. "This a bad time?"

"Had a huge fight with Lucy. She took off."

"What's it this time?"

Billy shook his head tiredly. "You were right."

"Fuck, no."

"Yeah. It was Lucy. She dipped into the stash."

"Oh man. What're you gonna do?"

"Don't know. Not so sure they'll understand. Maybe take one last shot at trying to convince them there was a way someone else could have got into the case before it reached me. If Lucy could figure it out watching YouTube, anybody could."

Heading over to his workbench, he turned his back to Stuart, who noticed for the first time what was tucked under the belt at Billy's back.

"Uh, what's with the gun, man?"

"Oh," Billy said, like he'd forgotten it was there. He reached around for it, placed it sideways in his palm, and held it out for inspection. "Got it just in case. Wanna hold it?"

Stuart's eyes went wide with wonder. Tentatively, he took it from Billy's hand.

"Loaded?" he asked.

"Wouldn't be much good otherwise. Just don't fucking point it at me."

Stuart raised the weapon as though getting ready to fire it, squinting over the barrel. "*Pew, pew*," he said.

"It's not Luke Skywalker's blaster," Billy said. "Give it to me before you do something stupid."

Billy put the gun back on the workbench, turned around, leaned his butt up against it, crossed his arms, then placed his hand on his stomach. "So much shit going on, I forgot to eat. Stomach sounds like a cement mixer."

Stuart said, "I could get some wings. Be back super-fast."

Billy shrugged. "Sure." He pulled out his wallet, handed over a couple of twenties. "Sorry for the way I've treated you, man."

Stuart waved him off, slipped out the side door, and closed it behind him. Billy remained propped up against the workbench and gave the Camaro a long, defeated look.

"I really got no fuckin' idea," he said to himself.

Only a minute or two had passed before there was another rapping at the door. He opened it.

"Billy Finster," said his latest visitor.

"The hell do you want?"

"This shit is over."

THIRTY

Richard

I drove.

I drove through downtown Milford. I drove across the bridge into Stamford. I drove around aimlessly for maybe half an hour while I rehearsed in my head what I was going to say to my blackmailer.

Something along the lines of this:

Do what you want, Billy. I don't care. I won't be blackmailed. You know it's not true. I'll just have to roll with whatever happens. If someone really did do this to you, you have my sympathies. I was willing to help you, hold whoever did it to account, but I won't let you smear me with a lie.

Yeah, something like that.

What I needed from him was an acknowledgment that he was lying, that he knew I'd never assaulted him back when he was a Lodge student, that his only goal was getting some money out of me.

And I would record it all on my phone.

I'd pulled over at one point and done a practice run. Opened up the Voice Memos app and slipped the phone down into the front pocket of my sport jacket. Put on the car radio, said a few words of my own, then checked to see whether the phone had picked it all up.

Perfectly.

If he said the things I needed him to say, and if he went through with his threat, I'd have something to play for the police.

Sure, if I'd been smarter, I'd have brought in the police—or, more specifically, my sister-in-law—from the get-go. But now I was determined to solve this problem on my own. I needed to restore my honor and this was the only way I could think to do it.

The persistent throbbing on the side of my head was a reminder that maybe this confrontation warranted being armed with more than a recording app. I didn't own a gun and had never wanted to, and now was not the time to find one and learn how to use it. But that didn't mean I had to go into this empty-handed.

So when I spotted a Dick's Sporting Goods store, I pulled into the parking lot and went inside. Found my way to the aisle where they kept the baseball bats.

I hadn't owned a bat since I was a kid, and was taken aback by the selection, and the prices. Some of them were going for up to four hundred dollars. But I found a Rawlings made out of maple that went for about eighty bucks that I believed was up to the job.

Paid for it in cash and tossed it onto the front seat of the car.

It was time.

THIRTY-ONE

Billy stood there, gun in hand, stupefied, trying to make sense of what had happened. Just when you thought your problems could not get any worse, a new one came knocking at the door. He reviewed everything that had transpired over the last few days, looking for something that might explain this.

Could it have something to do with Stuart? Was he into some kind of shit he hadn't told Billy about? When he returned with the chicken wings, Billy would ask. Wasn't it kind of convenient Stuart decided to take off just before this latest person showed up?

Maybe he'd have learned more if he hadn't started waving the gun around. No one was going to be interested in sticking around one once they'd seen that. You think you're gonna get shot, you get back in your car and hit the fucking road.

But Billy had an idea what was behind the visit.

Lucy.

She'd probably been pretty careless when she'd sold the stuff she'd stolen from the locker. Wasn't discreet. Put the word out. Maybe one of her customers had overdosed, and now a loved one wanted to put the fear of God into both of them. Stop selling this shit or else.

That made as much sense as anything.

He didn't know what he was going to do about her. If she was waiting for a text from him saying he was sorry, that he shouldn't have waved that gun in her face, well, she was going to be waiting a long time.

But at the same time, he wanted to protect her from Andrea and Gerhard. Because God help her if they found out what she'd done.

I'm in what you might call a no-win situation, he thought.

He heard another car pulling up to the garage. The engine died, a door opened and closed. He hoped it was Stuart with the wings. Didn't think to tell him to get extra-spicy. Kind of had a lot on his mind at the time.

Billy went to the door, opened it, found someone standing there.

Not Stuart. Not that other nut who'd come earlier.

But Billy sure knew who it was.

This evening had no end of surprises. Way things were going, there'd be fucking Girl Scouts here selling cookies before the night was through.

THIRTY-TWO

Richard

I parked where I had before, although this time I didn't let the right side of the car rest on that woman's lawn. The last thing I needed was her coming out and giving me shit again.

I killed the engine and the lights, and made sure the Subaru's doors were locked so as to keep anyone from surprising me again with a backseat visit. I sat there in the dark, watching Billy Finster's house, listening to the engine tick as it cooled. The bat was on the seat next to me.

The street was quiet. The silver Kia I'd seen the woman get into and drive off in was not there. Nor was the rusted-out pickup truck Billy'd been driving when he'd first approached me at my home. But there was what looked to be a GMC mostly windowless van parked up close to the garage. Maybe Billy had two vehicles, and the pickup was tucked away.

It looked as though someone was home. There were lights on in the house, and slivers of light around the edges of the garage door.

"Showtime," I said to myself.

With my right hand I grabbed the bat, and with my left opened the door. When the car's interior light came on, I winced. *Idiot.* Nothing like announcing your arrival.

I got out and quickly closed the door to extinguish the light. I stood there a moment, holding my breath, then did a three-sixty, looking to see whether anyone had noticed my arrival.

So far, so good.

I switched the bat to my left hand and with my right opened the Voice Memos app on my phone, set it to start recording, and dropped it into the front pocket of my sport jacket. I took the bat back into my right hand and gave it a light swing at my side, getting the feel of it.

I am not going to beat this man to death. I only have this to defend myself.

I started walking toward the house and hadn't gone more than a car length when I heard a vehicle turn onto the street. Slight squeal of tires, the engine roaring.

I looked back and saw headlights coming my way. They hadn't caught me in their beam, and I certainly didn't want them to. I quickly stepped off the street and sought cover behind an oak tree broad enough to shield me.

The car, an Audi A4 or A6 in black, went speeding past my hiding spot. The brake lights came on, the car slowed and turned abruptly into the driveway of Billy Finster's house.

Hello.

The driver killed the headlights and the engine and got out. A woman. About five-five, skinny, scraggly hair down to her shoulders. A stocky guy got out on the passenger side. Together, they walked purposefully to the front door, the woman banging on it with her fist hard enough that I could hear from my hiding spot.

They waited maybe ten seconds for someone to answer before she banged on it again. When the second knock produced no response, they headed for the garage. This time the guy did the knocking, hitting the small door at the side with his fist.

No one came, so he turned the handle, found the place unlocked, and went inside, the woman following.

Billy must have been there, because I could hear indistinct conversation that soon turned to shouting. From my location, I couldn't make out much of what was said, but I did hear this:

"*Where is it? Where the fuck is it?*"

Banging and crashing followed. I heard what sounded like a metal door being slammed shut. Whatever was going on in there between Billy and his visitors, it wasn't going well. Who were these people? More blackmail victims? Was Billy into other shenanigans that hadn't made him any friends?

The man and the woman emerged about five minutes later, closing the door behind them. I couldn't tell for sure, but it looked like they were wearing gloves as they headed for the house. Although I couldn't see them going to the back door, I was able to hear them kicking it in.

It wasn't a big house. One story, with a basement, judging by the low-rise windows at ground level. I could make out hurried shadows moving behind blinds or curtains. They were searching the place. And, from the faint sounds I could hear, tearing it apart. At one point, through what was most likely a bedroom window, I thought I saw a mattress being overturned.

Ten minutes went past.

Finally, the two came out the back door. If they'd found what they were looking for, it wasn't evident. Neither of them was carrying anything.

They walked quickly and purposefully back to the Audi, like they wanted to run but didn't want to attract attention. They looked, as best I could tell from my position, grim-faced. The woman got back in behind the wheel. The man got in on the other side and slammed the door angrily.

The Audi kicked up dirt and gravel as it backed quickly out of the driveway. Once on the street, the car sped off in the direction it had come from.

Everything went very quiet.

I didn't move. The bat hung at my side from my right hand. My phone was still recording. I took it from my pocket, hit the stop button, and deleted the recording.

Things had become a little more complicated.

I'd come here to confront Billy, but someone had beaten me to the punch. The smartest thing would be for me to abort. Take my bat, get in the car, and go home.

And yet.

An overwhelming sense of curiosity had taken hold. No longer was I here to take a stand. I wanted to know what had happened in that garage.

I brought up the bat, holding it crossways in front of me, right hand at the base, the wide end to my left. I cut across grass, wanting to make less noise than I would walking down the gravel driveway. When I got to the door, I rapped on it lightly.

No response.

I tried the handle and, just as those two visitors before me had, found it unlocked.

I opened the door, let it swing wide.

The lights were on.

I went inside.

THIRTY-THREE

Mrs. Tibaldi came to the door within ten seconds of Bonnie ringing the bell.

Even before saying hello, she turned and shouted over her shoulder, "Rachel! Your mother is here!" Then she turned to Bonnie and said, "Hi."

"I'm so sorry," Bonnie said. "I had no idea Richard was going to do this."

"It's fine," Mrs. Tibaldi said. "Rachel's never any trouble."

Rachel came running to the door, shouting, "Can I watch the rest of *How to Train—*"

"Get in the car," Bonnie said.

"I'd only seen half of it when Daddy brought me—"

"*Get in the car.*"

Rachel knew the tone and said no more. She scooted around her mother and ran to the Mitsubishi crossover. Bonnie followed without saying another word. Mrs. Tibaldi, evidently expecting some token thank-you or nod of appreciation, looked taken aback.

"Good night!" she called out.

Bonnie, her back to the woman, waved a hand in the air and got into her car. Rachel was already in the back, seat belt buckled.

"Are you mad at me?" Rachel asked as Bonnie backed the car onto the street.

"I'm not mad at you," she said, the car now heading in the direction of home.

"You *seem* mad."

"I'm not mad," she said.

"Are you mad at Dad?"

"I'm not mad at anybody," Bonnie said. "Stop asking questions."

"But can I watch the rest of the movie when we get—"

"Rachel! *Enough!*"

Bonnie, too preoccupied to look in her mirror, oblivious to the headlights behind her, neglected to hit her turn signal as she cranked the wheel to the left to turn into their driveway. The car behind had pulled out to pass. The driver hit the horn and the brakes, nearly broadsiding Bonnie's vehicle.

"Oh God!" Bonnie screamed. "Sorry! Sorry!" she shouted, even though her window was up and there was no way the other driver could hear her.

She pulled into her driveway as the other driver laid on the horn some more before driving off.

Bonnie put the car in park, turned off the engine, put her hands and head atop the steering wheel, and began to weep.

"Mommy?" Rachel said.

"I'm so sorry," Bonnie said. "It's okay. Everything's fine. Mommy's just a little on edge."

Rachel said nothing as her mother leaned over to open the glove compartment and pulled out a packet of tissues. She used two to dab her eyes, then put the packet back and closed the door. It didn't latch and dropped down. Bonnie closed it a second time, and again it dropped down.

"Goddamn it!" she shouted, closing the glove box a third time with such force that it sounded like a shot going off inside the car. The third time proved a charm.

Bonnie collected herself before turning to look at Rachel. "I'm sorry, sweetheart. I just—I've got a lot on my mind."

Hesitantly, Rachel asked, "Is Aunt Marta worse?"

"What?" Bonnie said, dabbing her eyes.

"Is her head still hurting?"

Bonnie took a moment before answering. "She's fine, sweetheart. Much better." She gave her nose a quick wipe and asked, "Why did your father go out?"

"I don't know," Rachel said. "He just said he had to. Didn't he text you?"

Bonnie had seen the text, but Richard had offered no explanation. "I just thought he might have told you what he was up to."

Rachel shook her head.

"Let's go," Bonnie said.

Once they were in the house, Bonnie told Rachel to get ready for bed. "I'll be up in a minute."

Rachel did as she was told.

Bonnie went into the kitchen, found an open bottle of cheap white wine in the fridge, brought it out, and unscrewed the cap. She made no effort to bring down a wineglass from one of the upper cupboard shelves. She grabbed a coffee mug and filled it to the brim.

Drank it down.

She set the mug on the counter and held her right hand out. Watched it shake.

She filled her mug a second time, emptying the bottle. Took another drink, and held her hand out again.

Still shaking.

Where the hell was Richard?

She went back to the front hall, got her phone out of her purse, and texted him:

Where r u?

Bonnie waited for the dancing dots to indicate he had received the text and was in the process of writing back to her.

Nothing.

She was about to send a second text, asking the same question, this time tapping it out entirely in capital letters. Let him know she meant business.

But then she stopped.

Maybe she really didn't want to talk to him. Because once she started asking where he'd been and what he'd done, he'd want details about how her evening went. Like whether she'd told Marta about his situation.

Bonnie definitely did not want to tell him what she'd done.

THIRTY-FOUR

Lucy went to the mall.

She wasn't remotely interested in shopping, but had no idea where else to go. She thought maybe if she wandered around Macy's and Target and Boscov's and in and out of the countless smaller stores, it would take her mind off her troubles, and maybe while she was doing that Billy would text her and tell her to come home. She wasn't expecting him to say he'd forgiven her, but if he at least said she could come back, and promised he wouldn't hurt her, that would be a first step.

If and when he did get in touch, she would tell him again how sorry she was, that she would do anything she could to make things right, but he had to get rid of that gun. That gun had scared the living shit out of her. So long as it was in the house, she wasn't safe.

She went to the food court and bought a coffee and muffin and sat at one of the small tables for four, wondering where she would go if Billy didn't get in touch before the mall closed. She had friends from work, but none close enough that she could ask to stay over. Even if she did, she'd have to explain why she couldn't go home, and did she really want to get into all that?

One thing she wasn't going to do was call the police. Sure, she could tell them Billy'd threatened her with a gun and they'd go arrest his ass, but inevitable questions would follow. Why'd he have a gun in the first place? Who was he afraid of, and why? Why had he threatened her? What had she done?

Oh, well, I was skimming from this fentanyl shipment he was holding for these two dealers who bring the stuff in from Mexico.

Calling the police was what you might call a nonstarter.

Lucy sipped on her coffee, not really tasting it, and picked away at her muffin, eating some of the top crunchy part and destroying the rest of it, nervously breaking it down into little bits. She left the empty cup and crumbled muffin on the table and resumed her wandering.

The stores were starting to close. The metal-and-glass fronts were being slid into place, lights going off, so Lucy left the mall and went back to her car. Got behind the wheel but did not start the engine. She took out her phone and brought up her texts.

Stared at the screen, willing Billy to send her a message.

She'd take the first step. She typed:

I love you and I want to come home.

Hit send. The message, her phone said, had been delivered.

Come on, come on. Reply, you dumb asshole.

Nothing. No little dots. That didn't have to mean he was still too pissed to reply. He might not have seen the message.

She decided to give him another minute before sending a second message.

I understand if you don't forgive me but we can work this out.

She followed this with two heart emojis, waited another thirty seconds, and sent it.

Nothing.

The parking lot was thinning out. Lucy began to feel vulnerable, sitting here alone in a car as night fell. It was time, as they say, to face the music. She keyed the ignition.

Billy's van was still in the driveway. There were lights on in the house and the garage, so it was a toss-up where he was. She decided to go into the house first. If she saw that gun on the kitchen table before she found Billy, she'd hide it. But as soon as she walked through the door, all thoughts of the gun left her.

Holy shit.

The place looked like a tornado had swept through.

Chairs turned over, the sofa pulled away from the wall. The stereo cabinet open, CDs and DVDs scattered.

"Billy?" she called out, unable to keep the fear out of her voice.

All the kitchen cupboards were open, dishes scattered about, broken. Boxes of cereal emptied onto the floor. A canister of flour upended. The oven door wide open. The lower freezer compartment of the refrigerator pulled out.

"Billy!" she screamed again.

She ran toward the back of the house to their bedroom. Dresser drawers yanked out, dumped. The closet open, the top shelf emptied. The mattress on its side up against the wall.

Lucy went to the top of the stairs that led down to Billy's man cave. Her voice softer now, but still shaky. "Billy? You down there?"

Slowly, she descended the steps until she could take in the room. The tornado had been through here, too.

Still no Billy.

There was only the garage left to check out.

Lucy went out the back door, crossed the yard to the garage. Her hand still shaking, she turned the handle and entered.

Things were torn apart in here, too, but not to the same degree. The locker was wide open. What Lucy knew to be the most important item that should have been in there was gone.

"Billy?" she whispered.

There was a smell in the air. And not just one thing. There was a whiff of something unpleasant, almost . . . septic? But that was mixed with a more familiar aroma, something spicy. There was a closed take-out food box on the roof of the Camaro. Lucy lifted the lid an inch. Chicken wings slathered with orange hot sauce.

And then she spotted what had to be the source of the other smell.

Billy lay facedown, his head turned only slightly, his nose jammed into the concrete floor. His arms were splayed out at awkward angles, and a large puddle of blood spread out from under his torso.

Lucy screamed until she brought her own hand to her mouth to stifle it.

"Billy?" she said a few seconds later after taking her hand from her mouth and kneeling next to him. She touched his back lightly, gave him the slightest shove, as though trying to wake him from a nap.

"Billy?" she said again.

The toe of her shoe touched the slowly expanding blood pool. She stood, backed away, turned, and ran from the garage as though it were on fire.

THIRTY-FIVE

Richard

Bonnie's car was in the driveway when I got home, so I was betting she had already been to Mrs. Tibaldi's and picked up Rachel, having seen my text.

I took a couple of deep breaths before I got out of the car and slipped quietly into the house. I did not announce my arrival. It was nearly ten. Maybe Bonnie'd gone to bed. Rachel would surely be asleep by now.

I gently set my keys into the decorative bowl on the table by the front door, slipped off my jacket, and hung it over the bottom post on the stairs.

When I went into the kitchen, I found Bonnie sitting there.

Looking at me.

"Oh hey," I said. "I thought maybe you'd already gone up."

"No," she said flatly.

She had a coffee mug on the table in front of her, her finger looped into the handle. Bonnie didn't usually drink coffee this late at night. But then I saw the empty wine bottle on the counter by the sink.

"Where were you?" she asked. It wasn't a casual question. It carried an accusing tone.

"Out," I said.

"You hadn't said anything about going out when I left."

"It was a last-minute thing."

"It must have been important, if you had to get Mrs. Tibaldi to take Rachel on short notice."

"Went to see Trent," I said.

"Why?"

"I needed to talk to him. About . . . everything. I wanted to hear what he had to say."

"I thought I'd helped you with all that."

"You did. You helped a lot."

"But you still needed to talk to Trent."

I shrugged. "I guess."

"So what did he say?"

"He wasn't home," I said. "He was at some school meeting."

"Oh," she said. "Then why didn't you come back home if he wasn't there? Did you go to the school, find him there?"

"No."

"Then where were you?"

"I drove around. You know, sometimes you just need to wander to think things through. What's with the wine?"

"What?"

"There was the better part of a bottle there, last time I looked. You killed it off?"

She shrugged. "I felt like a drink."

"Looks like more than a drink."

"I was a little stressed when I got home," Bonnie said.

The truth was, I needed one, too. Badly. I went to the freezer, brought out a bottle of vodka, poured some into a glass, and added some soda.

"Why are you so stressed out?" I asked, then I remembered where she'd been. "Marta. Did something happen with Marta?"

She took a beat too long to answer. "She's fine."

"You told her," I said. "I asked you not to."

"I didn't tell her," she said, bristling.

"Then what's with this?" I asked, nodding at the empty wine bottle.

"Who wouldn't be stressed, after everything you told me? Christ, I thought you'd had a heart attack today. Of course I'm stressed. *You* look stressed."

She had that right.

The room went quiet. Something was going on here. With both of us. I knew what was going on with me, the tension I was holding in, how I was replaying in my mind what had happened in Billy Finster's garage. But Bonnie was holding back something, too.

She bit her lower lip and looked away. I knew that look. She was on the verge of tears and was determined to hold them back. She was deciding whether to tell me why she'd been sitting here alone in the kitchen, getting drunk.

She suddenly blurted out, "I almost had an accident on the way home."

"What?"

"I got your text, had picked up Rachel, and I was turning into the driveway when this asshole tried to pass me. Nearly T-boned me."

"Jesus. You're okay?"

"Yeah, I'm sitting here, aren't I? But it never would have happened if you hadn't gone out and I didn't have to get Rachel. We could've been killed."

So if they'd been hurt, it would have all been on me. Okay. I didn't believe this was what had her so preoccupied. She was channeling, getting angry with me about one thing to cover up something else.

I broke the silence that had lasted the better part of half a minute. "What's really going on, Bonnie?"

"I could ask you the same," she said. "Why'd you go out?"

I countered, "Did you even go to Marta's?"

Bonnie finished off whatever was left in her coffee mug. She set it down with a bang, stood up, and said, "I'm going to bed."

"Bonnie, please, *talk* to me."

"You talk to *me*," she said.

I knew what I needed to tell her, but I couldn't make the words come. I'd opened up to her earlier in the evening, told her everything, but things had changed. One problem had been replaced by another that was potentially far worse.

Exponentially far worse.

She walked straight past me on her way to the stairs. That was how our day ended. I was keeping something big from her, and she was clearly keeping something big from me.

We were in some deep kind of shit here.

THIRTY-SIX

Marta, as anyone who knew her could have predicted, did not take any extra time off despite spending Saturday night to Sunday morning in the hospital. Ginny, who'd catered to Marta all Sunday, ordering her to rest, making her linguini primavera for dinner, made a few vain attempts Monday morning to get Marta to take another day or two to make sure she was okay, but Marta would have none of it.

"I'm fine," she insisted. "Gonna find that bitch."

That part Ginny understood. She wanted that bitch found, too.

At least Marta had the morning and early afternoon of Monday to rest up before her shift started at four. While she waited to head in, Marta linked up to the department's computer system to look up possible suspects, or, as they liked to put it, "persons known to the police." She scrolled through hundreds of photos, pausing occasionally when she found someone who might be Cherise Fowler's supplier—and Marta's attacker—then moving on to the next batch of headshots.

She made herself a tuna sandwich at noon and continued scanning while she ate. Ginny texted three times to ask how she was doing, the first two times Marta responding with a simple Fine and then on the third FINE!!!!

As if that weren't enough, there had been the occasional text from her sister seeking detailed updates. How was she feeling? Could she bring her anything?

Enough already.

When she got to work at four, her boss wanted a word with her. Once Marta had persuaded him she was fit for duty, she went to it, finishing up a few reports, making some calls to a contact with the DEA to see what she could learn about fentanyl distribution in this part of the state.

When she had only an hour left in her shift, a call came in about a body.

Two uniformed cops in a black-and-white Milford police cruiser had been on a routine wander when they were passing the Finster house and noticed the side door to the garage was open, the light on inside.

People didn't generally leave doors open and lights on late in the evening. The cops decided it was worth a quick look-see. Maybe the homeowners had gone to bed, forgotten to lock up the garage, leaving themselves vulnerable to theft.

Then they found Billy Finster.

Not twenty minutes later, Marta was in that garage, slip-ons over her shoes, latex gloves over her hands, taking in the scene. The victim was white, mid-twenties, about two hundred pounds. Given the amount of blood on the floor, she was guessing gunshot or knife wound, but she'd know more once the body was turned over and the medical examiner had done her work.

Marta took note of the open locker filled with electronics and tools still in their original packaging. There was a spot on one of the upper shelves, about three feet wide, that was conspicuously empty. There was a box of untouched chicken wings from a place called Paulie's. Marta wondered whether someone, possibly the dead man, had picked the wings up, or had them delivered. Maybe someone from Uber Eats or DoorDash had seen what had happened here.

Marta, continuing to step carefully, walked around the car and knelt down to get a peek under it. The front end was raised, the wheels on blocks. She spent another five minutes in there, studying the scene, before stepping outside.

The night was a kaleidoscope of flashing lights. Four police cars, an ambulance, all lit up like Christmas trees. A couple of uniformed officers—the ones who'd responded to the original call—had strung yellow police tape around the property's perimeter. They'd been talking to neighbors, learned that the deceased was married, but there was no sign of the wife. Was she their killer? Was she on the run from whoever had murdered her spouse? Was she dead, too?

Marta put on a new pair of slip-on booties and went into the house. What a mess. Someone had been hunting frantically for something. Living room, kitchen, bedrooms, the basement, all in total disarray. The frenzied way in which items had been thrown about suggested to Marta the search was rushed, not meticulous.

When she went back outside, she noticed a woman intently watching the proceedings from the other side of the police tape. Mid-seventies, wearing a housecoat to protect her from the cool night air. Looked to Marta like she was wearing pajamas under her robe. She approached.

"Ma'am?" she said, displaying the badge clipped to her belt.

"Yes?"

"What's your name?"

"Dorothy. Dorothy Envers."

"Which house is yours?"

The woman pointed to the closest one.

"You know the people who live here?"

She nodded. "Lucy and Billy. What's happened? They're saying something happened to Billy."

"Lucy would be Billy's wife?"

"That's right."

"You seen her around lately?"

"Her car was here earlier today. She could be at work, although she doesn't usually have shifts this late."

Dorothy told Marta that Lucy worked in the cafeteria at a hospital in Bridgeport. Marta asked which hospital, got a description of Lucy's car.

"You see anything out of the ordinary tonight? Cars you didn't recognize coming by?"

The woman shook her head, but then thought of something. "Someone was watching the house at one point, in the afternoon. Parked right on my lawn."

"Tell me about that," Marta said.

THIRTY-SEVEN

Richard

I should have called in sick Tuesday.

Sleep had eluded me. I tossed and turned all night, spent much of the time staring at the ceiling. I wasn't the only one. Bonnie, beside me, was awake, too, but neither of us would acknowledge that we weren't sound asleep.

We barely spoke at breakfast. Moved around each other in the kitchen like well-choreographed but silent dancers who could execute their moves without tripping over each other. Rachel looked dismayed. For a day or two there, she'd had reason to believe her parents were working through their differences. Attentive to one another. Chatting. But now a frost had settled in again. Mom and Dad not saying any more to each other than they absolutely had to. Rachel had kept her nose to her iPad through breakfast, reading about some disgusting bug or other, disappearing into her new interest.

I was in a brain fog. I couldn't focus on the lessons I had to teach, and when any of my students asked me anything, I often didn't register hearing my own name. Like I said, I should have called in sick, but was worried that doing so had the potential, later, to make me look suspicious.

I did have to field a few questions, from students as well as colleagues, about how I'd earned that bruise on my right temple and cheek. I was sticking with the story about getting hit with a basketball, and more than a few looked skeptical, some pressing to know who'd thrown the ball. I sidestepped, said I didn't want to get anyone into trouble.

Despite that, I tried to act as though nothing unusual had happened to me in the last twenty-four hours. But all day I kept looking out that same window where I had spotted Mark LeDrew, expecting to see a Milford police car pull into the lot. Sooner or later, I feared, something was going to connect me to my visit to Billy Finster's the night before.

All they had to do was look at the call history on his phone. They'd see he'd called me not long after I'd told Bonnie everything, even texted me when I'd told him I wasn't going to give in to his demands.

How would I explain that? What reason could I come up with for his *You'll be sorry* text?

I hoped he'd used another phone for that, a burner, that maybe he'd gotten rid of. Why hadn't I looked for it when I was there? Too shocked, that's why.

During a free hour in my schedule, Trent came to my room.

"You came by the house last night?" he said.

"Yeah," I said, my back to him as I wiped down my blackboard, erasing a lesson on symbolism.

"Everything okay?" he asked.

"Everything's fine. I was just . . . just going to talk to you some more about my circumstances."

"Well, I'm here now."

"It's okay," I said. "I've burdened you enough with all this. I appreciate it, I do. I'm sure things will find a way of working out."

"So . . . what are you saying?" He closed the door. "You paid him? It's over?"

"I didn't—I think my blackmailer's had a change of heart." More like his heart stopped working.

"You heard from him?"

I put down the eraser and raised my palms, signaling I really didn't want to talk about this anymore. "Trent, really, forget I ever mentioned any of this. Put it out of your head."

He stood there, studying me. "What aren't you telling me?"

"Nothing. Just . . . let it go."

Trent nodded slowly, mulling over my request. "Okay, then," he said. "If you change your mind, if you want to talk, you know where to find me."

"Thank you." I expected him to withdraw, but he was still standing there. "What?"

"I know you need this like a hole in the head, but—"

God, what now?

"Another lawsuit?" I said. "I already got served by the LeDrews, forwarded the paperwork to the union."

"Not that," he said. "Remember me telling you about some parents being concerned about the books in your class?"

I needed a second. Andrew Kanin. *The Road.*

"Yeah," I said.

"They'd like a meeting. How do you decide what book is worth studying? What are the criteria?"

"Really? There's not a book out there someone wouldn't find objectionable. Maybe we should abandon the teaching of ideas, Trent. Just teach them the times table and the state capitals and send them on their merry fucking way."

"I'm on your side here."

I sighed. "I'm sorry. I'm at the end of my tether."

"I get it, but let me tell you the spot I'm in. I can't dismiss their concerns even if I have problems with them. I have to listen, and we have to make our case. They'd like to meet tonight. The best person— Why do you keep looking out the window?"

"What? Sorry, I was—it's nothing. Go on."

"The best person to talk to them, to explain why *The Road*, or any number of other books, might engage students, get them thinking, get them talking, would be you. But at the same time, you've been to hell and back and don't need this. I can handle it if you want to be excused."

In my head, I was screaming. But I managed to say, calmly, "No, it's okay."

Maybe, with any luck, I'd be arrested sometime today and would have a good excuse for not showing up.

"If you can handle it, great, but you should think about a leave of absence," Trent said. "A week, a month, whatever you think you need. I know I can get it approved."

Now Trent looked out the window. He'd spotted what had caught my eye a moment earlier out on the school's field. Wandering it aimlessly was Ronny Grant, our former caretaker.

"Oh shit," Trent said. "He won't stay away."

He looked woefully at me, as though expecting a question. "I didn't have any choice. He'd been told about the door, that it wouldn't latch. I had a list of things he was supposed to do and he hadn't gotten to any of them. Even without the LeDrew incident, I'd been thinking I was going to have to do something about him. He's been in to see me three times begging to get his job back. I've told him there's nothing I can do. The board wanted his head on a platter. Now he's moping about like Charlie Brown, making a nuisance of himself. The second time he came in to see me, he'd been drinking."

I felt a certain kinship with Ronny in that moment. A twist of fate had left its mark on both of us. He'd fucked up and lost his job. I'd played the hero and drawn the attention of an extortionist. Neither of us could have predicted where our actions, or inactions, would lead.

"Maybe I should have a word with him," I said. Sometimes I couldn't stop being me. I just had to help.

"Hey, Ronny," I said, crossing the field, hands in my pockets, like maybe I was out here for a stroll, too.

Ronny was a thin stick of a guy, slightly stooped over, his chest slightly caved in, all of which made him look shorter than his six feet. He was dressed in his work attire, olive-colored shirt and pants. He always had a day's growth of whiskers, but now it looked like he hadn't shaved in a week.

"Mr. Boyle," he said. Ronny, like one of the students, always addressed staff members by their surnames. I'd told him more than once to call me Richard, but it wouldn't take.

I offered a hand and he shook it. When I was that close to him, I could smell alcohol on his breath.

"I don't think I ever properly thanked you," he said. "I mean, if that LeDrew kid had got in and blown us all up, it all would have been on me. They'd have done more than fired me. The townspeople'd probably have got together and strung me up."

He laughed weakly.

"I'm sorry," I said. "I don't know that what happened to you is fair. You fighting it?"

Ronny shrugged. "They say I should. But I don't know. If they transferred me to another school, that'd be okay."

"You married, Ronny?" I asked. I realized that I knew very little about this man I'd seen every day in the hallways of the school.

He nodded. "Yup. Just me and Trace. When I'm not here—well, that would be all the time now—but when I wasn't here, I'd be looking after her. Trace lost her sight about two years ago. First one eye, about five years back, and then the other one. She's okay through the day, but I do most everything around the house. Laundry and cooking and cleaning. Sometimes I sneak out late when she's asleep and go to Jim's for a drink or two."

"Kids?"

"Got a daughter comes to visit once in a while. She's a dental assistant, lives and works in New Haven. Got a husband and two kids. She says I should get a lawyer."

"Lot of that going around," I said.

He looked at me through narrowed eyes. "Yeah, I heard something about them coming after you. The parents. Fuckers."

I had no response for that. We stood there, not talking for a moment.

"You know I been here nineteen years?" Ronny said to me.

"I did not."

"Lasted through five principals. Seen them come and go. I thought this latest one, I thought me and him had a good working relationship, you know. Just goes to show that things are never what they seem. I was going to fix the door that very day. I swear to you. It was the top of my list." He shook his head regretfully. "Only one been here as long as me is Belinda." He grinned. "She knows where the bodies are buried."

Exactly the phrase that had occurred to me on several occasions.

Finally, Ronny said, "I miss the kids."

"Sure."

"It made me feel younger, surrounded by young people, you know? You get really close to them while they're here, and then they're gone, making lives for themselves, and a new crop of them comes in."

"I know," I said.

"A lot of them, they called me Willie," he said. "You know, for the Simpsons character? Groundskeeper Willie? That was actually the part I liked best. Keeping the grounds."

His gaze wandered over to the back of the school and a set of doors that led to his former domain. Behind them were the guts of the school. His office, the school's boiler and electrical system, a backup generator, cleaning supplies, a small garden tractor he used to maintain the grounds. In winter, he attached a snowblower to it to clear the sidewalks.

"I liked riding the lawnmower, cutting the grass," he said. "Gives you lots of time to think, doing that. And it's one of those jobs where you can immediately see what you accomplished. Every time you make a loop, it's right there for everyone to see." He smiled. "I'd ride that lawn tractor all day if you let me."

Something Mark LeDrew had said to me eight days ago suddenly popped into my head.

"You're a real lawnmower man, Ronny," I said.

"Yeah," he said, grinning. "I guess I am."

THIRTY-EIGHT

T his was the third hospital where Andrea was running her game, holding a bouquet of flowers, telling the woman at the reception desk that she wanted to deliver them personally to Lucy Finster for taking such nice care of her mother.

"Lucy Finster?" the woman said, tapping away at her computer. "What department does she work in?"

Andrea recalled that just before she put the clamp on Billy's tit, he'd said something about his wife Lucy working in a hospital cafeteria. Would have been nice if he'd said which fucking hospital. There was one in Milford, a couple in Bridgeport, two up New Haven way, one in Westport. If Andrea had thought to ask, she and Gerhard wouldn't be driving from facility to facility trying to find the elusive little bitch.

Because that was exactly what she was. Elusive.

They'd doubled back to the Finster place, after the police had arrived, mingled with the gawkers lined up along the yellow police tape. Listened to the gossip, how no one had seen Billy's wife.

Which got Andrea and Gerhard thinking that there might be a very good reason for that. She'd run off with their Flizzies. The carry-on bag was not there. Billy sure didn't have it, and he wasn't exactly in a state to tell them where it might have gone. But with Lucy in the wind, well, you didn't have to be fucking Sherlock Holmes to connect the dots.

They realized, of course, that if Lucy had their stuff and had gone on the run, she might not be showing up for work the next day. But if they could figure out which hospital she worked at, then they might be able to find some of her friends. Maybe one of them would lead them to her.

So here she was, at a hospital in New Haven, her second stop, holding a cheap bouquet she'd bought from someone on a street corner, asking for Lucy.

To the receptionist, she said, "I know it sounds funny, her being able to help my mom when she worked in the cafeteria, not being a doctor or a nurse, but Mom, bless her, in her last days, she'd come down to the cafeteria and Lucy always made time for her and she didn't have to do that. It just shows that everyone who works here, in whatever capacity, really cares about the patients."

The receptionist looked up from her screen. "I'm sorry, but we don't have anyone here by that—"

"Thanks for nuthin', bitch," Andrea said, heading for the door and hoping these shit flowers wouldn't completely wilt before she got to the next hospital.

By Tuesday afternoon, Marta was reviewing everything she had, so far, on the death of one William "Billy" Finster. He had died of a gunshot wound, at close range, to his upper abdomen. The bullet had gone right though his heart. It would have been quick.

A check of footage from neighbors' surveillance video turned up little. Only a couple of homeowners had tricked their places up with security cameras that captured street traffic, and what video that had been recovered had not proved useful. They did have a partial license plate and the make and model of a car that had been seen near the Finster house, and Marta had been waiting to hear back on that.

No cell phone had been found at the scene. Not on Billy, not in the garage, not in the house. If Billy'd been in the habit of carrying a phone, someone, presumably whoever had shot him, had taken it.

Before packing it in the night before, she had gone to Paulie's, the chicken wing place. She'd found a receipt tucked into the folds of the box and showed it to the manager. He said it hadn't been a delivery. The customer had come to the shop, placed the order, and waited outside in his pickup truck until it was ready.

"You get his name?" Marta asked. She already knew, from looking at the receipt, that it had been a cash transaction. No credit card to help with an ID.

The manager shook his head. "Nope. When it was ready I just waved and he came in and got it."

"He a regular? Seen him before?"

"Once or twice, maybe? I'm not sure."

When asked for a description, the manager was beyond vague. Height? "Kind of average." Weight? "Sort of average, I would say." Hair color? "Kind of average."

The best Marta could get out of him was that the guy was white, in his twenties, and, after Marta showed him a picture of the deceased she'd taken from his driver's license, definitely not Billy Finster.

"The truck?"

"An old Ford, I think. Look, I'm deep-frying wings all night. Don't have time to take notice of anybody."

Her next stop was the hospital in Bridgeport where Billy Finster's wife worked. The Finsters' neighbor had come up with that information. No one had seen Lucy since the discovery of her husband's body, so Marta wasn't counting on her being at her job, but it was a place to start in trying to find her.

As a courtesy, Marta went directly to the administrator's office to explain why she was there. She wanted to speak to Lucy Finster's coworkers. She was taken to a woman named Svetlana, who oversaw the cafeteria operation. Lucy, she said, had not shown up for her shift that morning.

"I called her but her phone went straight to message," Svetlana said.

"She ever just not show up for work before?" Marta asked.

"Never."

"How's she seemed lately? Anything different? Anxious about anything?"

"Not that I have noticed. What's going on? Does this have anything to do with Billy?"

"What makes you think that?"

"She talks about him all the time. Like, nothing specific, just, if she is acting like she is having a bad day, I will ask, and she just shakes her head and says, 'Billy.' Have you talked to him?"

Clearly, Svetlana had not gotten the memo, Marta thought.

"Who are Lucy's friends here?"

Svetlana shrugged. "She does not have many. You could try Digby. I see her talking to him sometimes."

"Digby?"

She lowered her voice to a conspiratorial whisper. "She might have something going on with him, but I don't like to start rumors."

"Where would I find Digby?"

Digby, it turned out, was an orderly, and Marta tracked him down on the third floor, wheeling a patient back to her room from the X-ray department. When he had her settled back into her bed and was coming out of the room, Marta held up her badge and introduced herself.

"I gotta help a guy take a dump," he said. "This important?"

"Digby's an unusual name. First or last?"

"First name," he said. "My parents are from Nova Scotia."

Marta looked at him blankly, not making the connection.

"It's a place there," he said. "That's where they, like, you know, conceived me, when they were on a vacation. So they named me Digby. My last name's Wentworth."

"You seen Lucy Finster today, Digby?"

"Who?"

"Digby, some days I have lots of time for bullshit, but I'm on a tight schedule today."

"Oh yeah, *Lucy*," Digby said. "Didn't hear you right the first time. Haven't seen her, no. Not sure she's on today. You should talk to the Russian chick runs the caf."

"She a friend?"

Digby pursed his lips. "We talk once in a while, but other than that, not really. She's got a husband. Billy."

"When you *do* talk to her, what do you talk *about*?"

Digby shrugged. "Like, how are you today? What shows you watching? Shit like that."

"If you hear from her, I'd like you to give me a call right away," Marta said, handing him a card.

He gave it the quickest of glances and tucked it into the front pocket of his white pants. "Anything else?" he asked.

Marta shook her head slowly.

She took the elevator back down to the first floor and was twenty feet from the reception desk, on her way to the front doors, when she stopped dead.

That woman asking questions at the desk. Holding a bouquet of flowers.

If it wasn't the woman from the bar Saturday night who'd knocked her out, it was her twin sister.

And then Marta looked down at her shoes.

Converse sneakers.

Marta placed a reassuring hand on the weapon attached to her belt. She held her ground another moment, waiting to see whether the woman would turn this way, give Marta a better look at her face.

She could hear some of the conversation.

"So she *does* work here?" the woman said.

"Yes," said the receptionist, tapping away at her computer. "If you'd like to leave those with me I can make sure she gets them."

"I'd really prefer to give them to her in person."

"Why don't I call down to the cafeteria and see if she's on today. No sense sending you all the way down there if she hasn't come in for her shift yet."

"Thanks, I appreciate—"

The woman must have noticed someone was standing off to her left. She glanced that way and saw Marta.

The glint of recognition didn't take longer than a millisecond.

Marta said, "Nice shoes."

The woman dropped the flowers and bolted.

"Stop!" Marta shouted. "Police!"

Others in the reception area froze, looked around, watched as the woman was forced to wait half a second for a set of sliding glass doors to retract, only to encounter an elderly man on crutches in her path. She shoved him out of her way and he went down, collapsing on the floor in front of Marta, who was torn between helping him and continuing her pursuit.

It's a fucking hospital, she thought. *Someone will tend to him.*

In the moment it took to make that decision, the glass doors had slid shut. They began to retract again as Marta took a step toward them, but goddamn, they were slow. Marta squeezed through before they'd fully reopened, and came tearing out of the building at a gallop.

Would have really helped Marta if those Converse sneakers had been on her own feet.

She lost sight of the woman as she reached the bottom of a set of concrete steps and turned right onto the sidewalk.

"Stop!" Marta shouted again. She didn't know whether the fleeing woman was armed, but Marta had her gun at the ready. Not that she was likely to be able to use it. She couldn't shoot a suspect in the back. She couldn't risk hitting someone else on the street.

The woman was sixty feet ahead of her, arms and legs pumping hard. She was a scrawny thing, Marta thought, and fast. But Marta was no slouch herself. She ran three mornings a week, usually four miles, and believed she could keep up this pace for as long as it took.

But then the game changed.

A black Audi had barreled up the street and was riding along right beside her. Then, with a squeal and a large thump, it jumped the curb, aiming for Marta.

"Shit!" she cried, and moved sharply to the right. She'd been running so quickly she lost her balance and fell, thinking, in the two seconds it took to hit the sidewalk: *Not your head. Don't hit your fucking head.*

The car kept going until it reached the woman, screeched to a stop long enough for the woman to leap in, then sped off, burning rubber.

Before Marta slowly got to her feet, she looked at the car, hoping she'd be able to get a glimpse of the plate, but it was already too far away.

She limped her way back to the hospital and went straight for the reception desk.

"What did that woman want?" she asked, struggling to catch her breath.

The woman at the desk said, "She wanted to deliver some flowers."

"To who?"

"A woman who works in the cafete—"

"*Who?*"

"Lucy Finster."

Marta was continuing to catch her breath, trying to absorb the significance of what she'd just been told. The woman who'd sold Cherise Fowler fentanyl, who'd knocked Marta out, who had stolen her goddamn shoes, was looking for the wife of the guy who'd been murdered the night before.

Her cell phone rang. Marta got it out, tapped the screen, and managed to say, "Harper."

"Got a hit back on that plate and car description," a man at the other end of the line said.

Still shaken from nearly being hit by the car, it took a moment for Marta to figure out what this was about. That plate number one of the officers had come up with after talking to the Finsters' neighbors. "Right," she said finally. "Hang on a second."

She snapped her fingers at the receptionist. "Pen. Paper."

The woman quickly handed her something to write with and a pad.

"Shoot," Marta said into her phone.

The caller read her the information. Marta looked at what she'd scribbled, and blinked. She said, "That can't be right."

"That's what came back."

"Check it again. I'll wait."

Marta heard the clicking of keys in the background. The man came back on a few seconds later and said, "Yep, that's it."

Marta ended the call without so much as a thank-you, stared at the notepad, and said, "Fuck me."

THIRTY-NINE

Richard

I'd been struggling to compose some notes for what I would say that evening to the parents concerned about what I was having the kids read, but was having a difficult time pulling my thoughts together.

I'd opened up the laptop on my desk intending to see what others in the trenches fighting book banning and censorship had said, but instead of entering that subject into the search field, I typed in "Billy Finster" and then refined that to "William Finster" and right away my screen was filled with stories from the last twelve hours.

There was a short news item in the New Haven paper.

Milford Police homicide detectives are investigating the suspicious death of a man whose body was found late last night.

Police said the deceased, William Finster, 25, of Wooster St., was discovered after officers in a passing patrol car investigated a garage door that had been left open. The garage, a separate building behind the Finster residence, was where Mr. Finster had been restoring an old Camaro.

Sources say Finster, an airport baggage handler, was shot at close range. Police are currently looking for his wife, Lucy Finster, 27, who is, police stressed, not a suspect, but someone they wish to speak to in a bid to gather more information. She hasn't been seen since Monday afternoon.

I would like to say that the story came as a total shock to me, but it did not.

There was also a video clip from one of the local TV news stations. The item was shot earlier today out front of the Finster residence, which was still roped off with police tape. The woman standing with the microphone in her hand didn't have much information beyond what was in the newspaper, but she did have an interview with a woman I recognized as the one who'd asked me to move my car off her lawn. At the bottom of the screen was her name: *Dorothy Envers*.

Christ, I had more to worry about than Billy's texts to me. Would she tell police she'd seen someone watching the Finster house earlier in the day? And did she, or anyone else, see me when I returned several hours later?

I was hopeful I'd left no trace of my presence there. Recently, I'd read something about "touch DNA," where a sample can be obtained if someone does nothing more than touch a surface. The good news there was, I hadn't touched a thing except for the handle of the door into the garage, and I'd wiped that down with the sleeve of my jacket when I'd left. And that would mean I was in the clear with finger-prints, too. I'd seen no surveillance cameras, and if there had been any, chances were the police would have been at my door by now.

But there was the issue of footprints.

When I'd run across the yard to the garage, I'd passed through grass damp with evening dew, and I supposed it was possible my shoes could have left an imprint on the garage floor. So this morning I'd taken those shoes—an old pair of Asics I'd been wearing for about four years—and dropped them into a trash bin out back of a fast-food joint out on Boston Post Road.

I knew how that looked.

But I didn't want anyone knowing I'd been there last night. How would I persuade anyone I wasn't a suspect if they knew the game he'd been trying to run on me?

Well, he wasn't going to be running it anymore.

I'd heard nothing from Bonnie all day. No call, no text. But then again, I hadn't been in touch with her, either. Maybe tonight we could sit down. Clear the air.

I might even find the strength to tell her what I'd done.

As I was heading to my car at the end of the school day, I nearly bumped into Herb Willow as he was coming out of his classroom.

"Excuse me," I said.

We hadn't spoken since I'd let him have it the other day. If he was still holding a grudge, it wasn't evident by the smile on his face when he saw me.

"Richard," he said amiably. "How are you today?"

"Fine, Herb," I said, and would have continued on my way but he wasn't done.

"I hear the townsfolk are gathering their pitchforks and torches for a meeting with you tonight."

So that hadn't been an amiable smile. More like a devilish one.

"Once these book-banners are convinced something's unacceptable, it's hard to win them over," Herb said. "They just zero in on the objectionable part and won't consider it in a larger context."

"There some kind of point you're trying to make here?"

"I should think it would be obvious. You don't see the parallels?"

"Enlighten me."

"You got parents judging what you give their kids to read based on one small excerpt, and you've got the whole goddamn school judging me based on one small thing said by a crazy person who wanted to kill us all."

I couldn't see what was to be gained, debating a worm.

"I wonder why I see your hand in this meeting," I said.

Herb feigned offense. "How could you say that? How unprofessional would it be to cause problems for a colleague?"

I turned and walked away.

When I got home, I walked over to Mrs. Tibaldi's to pick up Rachel. I figured the trip back to the house would give us a chance to get caught up. I'd been so consumed with my own problems that it was easy to forget that it wasn't all about me.

"How's Mrs. Tibaldi?" I asked.

"Are you going to make me go there again tonight?" Rachel asked.

"Don't have any plans to, sweetheart. Last night, it was something unexpected." She had nothing to say to that. "How's the bug collection coming?"

Rachel shrugged.

"It's nice you have a new interest."

Another shrug. Then, "Amanda said she might give me all her bugs because her dad hates them, but I don't think I want them."

"Why's that?"

"It's like zoos. It's mean to keep things locked up, even if they're dead. They should all be set free."

"When I was a kid, I collected stamps for a while."

"Stamps? What are stamps?"

That stopped me cold. I shouldn't have been surprised. Why *would* a kid who'd been raised in an age of emails and texts, whose parents paid all their bills online, know anything about sticking a little square of paper onto an envelope and dropping it into a box down the street?

I laughed. "Never mind. It was pretty boring, anyway."

"Did you sell the boat?" Rachel asked.

"You heard about that?"

That shouldn't have surprised me, either. She could have overhead Bonnie and me talking about it, or Bonnie might have mentioned to her that I'd been thinking of it.

The truth was, there was no need to sell it now.

She nodded and I said, "No, I didn't sell the boat."

"Okay," she said. "For sure?"

"For sure."

"And you won't change your mind?"

I shook my head. "You seem pretty worried about it," I said, patting the back of her head. "How come?"

"The boat's a family thing, and if we didn't have the boat maybe we weren't going to be a family anymore."

I stopped, knelt down, took her two hands in mine, and looked her in the eye. "That would never happen." I took her into my arms for a quick squeeze, and we continued on our way home.

In the freezer, I found some meatballs we'd made up a month ago and sealed in a plastic container, let them simmer in a tomato sauce, put on a pot of water to boil for spaghetti, and then scrolled through my phone looking for more stories about Billy Finster's death.

Then I thought, if someone checked my phone's search history, they'd have to wonder why I was so interested in Finster's murder. And then I realized my laptop at school would be equally incriminating. Someone might get around to talking to Belinda, who'd be able to report I'd asked her if we had a current address for him. Just how many clues had I left behind?

Stupid stupid stupid.

Bonnie arrived home shortly before six. When she found me in the kitchen I put the phone aside and smiled weakly at her. I didn't know where things stood between us at that moment. I decided to make the first move, walked over, and put my arms around her.

"Hey," I said.

She started to cry. Then she started to shake.

"It's okay," I said, holding on to her more tightly. "It's okay."

She wiped a tear from her eye and pulled back far enough to ask, "Where's Rach?"

"Watching her movie."

Bonnie nodded, like that was a good thing. "I have something I have to tell you," she said.

"Okay," I said, leading her to the table so she could take a seat.

"I need a drink of water."

I ran the tap and filled two glasses. Bonnie drank half of hers and stared down at the table.

"I did a very dumb thing," she whispered.

"Just tell me," I said. "Whatever it is, we'll sort it out."

She opened her mouth, then closed it, like she wanted the words to come out but something was holding her back.

"You were right," she said.

I knew it. She'd told Marta.

"I didn't go see my sister," she said. "She went back to work."

That threw me. "Okay. So where *did* you go, then?"

"I went—"

The doorbell rang.

We both sighed. "Shit," I said.

Rachel, in the family room nearby, shouted, "Someone's at the door!"

"I'll get it," Bonnie said, and got up.

I heard her open the front door and say with surprise, "Oh, hi!" Some murmuring followed by Bonnie saying, "Yeah, sure, come on in."

Seconds later she returned to the kitchen with her sister, Marta, in tow. I stood.

"Hi, Marta," I said, and felt a worm turning around inside my gut. What had Bonnie said a second ago? "*She went back to work.*" *This is it. It's over.*

"Richard," she said, nodding. Marta wasn't the cheeriest person in the world, but you could usually find some trace of a smile on her face. But not today.

Bonnie said, "Can I get you something? A beer? Some coffee?"

"I'm good," Marta said. "A beer's tempting, but I'm on duty and all that." She took a good look at me, at the bruise still visible on my right cheek and temple.

"What happened to you?" she asked.

"Stupid basketball thing," I said. "So, you're back on the job." She nodded. "What's up?"

"I'm investigating something that happened last night," she said, leading into this slowly. "And it may be that I shouldn't even be here, asking you anything about it. I should probably recuse myself from this. But then again, there might be a pretty simple explanation and handing this off to someone else wouldn't even be necessary."

"I don't understand," Bonnie said to her sister.

Marta let out a long breath. "I'm investigating a homicide. Someone by the name of William Finster—Billy, everyone called him."

I could barely hear Bonnie's sharp intake of breath. Surprise, no doubt. I thought it unlikely she'd also been googling stories about his demise today. I could sense her wanting to look at me, to exchange glances, to try to read into my expression whether this was news to me, but she could not. I could only imagine what she might be thinking, where her mind was going.

When we didn't respond, Marta pressed. "That name mean anything to either of you?"

Bonnie and I remained stone-faced. I slowly shook my head, but then said, "I think there was a Lodge student by that name a few years ago."

"Yes," Marta said. "He did go to Lodge."

"And he's dead?" I said. "Somebody killed him?"

Marta nodded solemnly. "That's right. We're in the early stages of the investigation. But we do have some leads, as it turns out."

I hoped Marta did not notice me swallowing. My mouth had turned into the Sahara. I reached back to the table for the glass of water and had some. I'd no sooner done it when I wondered how guilty that made me look.

And then I thought of something.

Pictures.

There were pictures on my phone of Billy Finster's place. Shots I'd taken when I went by there in the afternoon. I should just stick out my wrists and tell Marta to put on the cuffs.

"What sort of leads?" Bonnie asked.

I slipped my hand down into the front pocket of my jeans, got my hand on my phone.

"A car was spotted parked near the Finster property," Marta said. "Like maybe someone had been watching the place."

"Okay," I said as I brought the phone out of my pocket.

"One of the neighbors thought it looked kind of suspicious, so they made a note of the plate, the make and model of the car."

I tried to look down at my phone discreetly, brought it to life by pressing my thumb to the button at the bottom.

"Am I boring you?" Marta asked.

"Sorry," I said, glancing up half a second after I opened the photos app. "I muted my phone and thought I felt a text coming in."

I quickly glanced down. The most recent photos were those I'd taken of Billy's place. I tapped the garbage can icon. Once. Twice. Three times.

"Did you?" Marta asked.

"Did I what?" I asked, slipping the phone back into my pocket.

"Get a text?"

"No. Sorry. Go on."

Marta said, "So I had them run the plate, and when I got the result back I had them run it again, because it didn't make any sense to me."

Should I get ahead of this? I wondered. Admit it was me? But what kind of excuse could I come up with that didn't mention the blackmail scheme?

"And so here I am," Marta said. "The plate's attached to a dark blue 2020 Mitsubishi, just like the one out front in your driveway."

Marta looked squarely at her sister and said, "That's your car, isn't it, Bonnie?"

FORTY

S tuart Betz couldn't stop thinking about the box of chicken wings he'd left behind. That was pretty damn stupid.

Not just because it was a terrible thing to waste good food that way. Paulie's made good wings. Stuart had actually considered going back for them, although not so much because he was hungry. He had, to be honest, kind of lost his appetite there for a while. The reason he thought about going back was because the box of wings was a *clue*.

When the police found it sitting on the roof of the Camaro, they'd figure no one leaves food behind unless something happened, something that scared a person shitless. What you'd have then was a potential *witness*. And then their next stop would be the wing joint, and pretty soon they'd have a description of him, maybe even a description of his pickup truck. At least he'd paid in cash, so they wouldn't have a credit card to track. *That* was smart. The other thing that gave Stuart hope was that the guy making the wings barely looked at him. He was running the place on his own and didn't even want to make small talk when Stuart said, "Busy night, huh?"

So he'd been going to the window of his motel room every few minutes to see whether there were any cop cars in the parking lot. It had been nearly twenty-four hours, and if they hadn't figured out yet that he'd been there, maybe they were never going to.

Of course, it wasn't just cops that had Stuart worried.

When there had been a knock at his door early that morning, before the sun was even up, he figured it was game over. Wasn't that when police conducted raids? When you were still asleep in your PJs or wearing nothing at all?

He'd sat up in bed suddenly, his heart jackhammering in his chest. "Who is it?" he'd shouted.

He was expecting to hear: *Open up! It's the police!*

But instead, it was a woman's voice. Whispering loudly, "It's me!"

Who the fuck was *me*?

Stuart got out of bed, wearing nothing but a pair of boxers, and padded over on the threadbare wall-to-wall carpet in his bare feet. He peered through the peephole. The motel manager hadn't been very attentive to the number of lights that had burned out, but there was enough illumination to make out who was out there.

Lucy.

"Shit," Stuart said under his breath. He unlocked the door, undid the chain, and opened the door six inches. "Lucy?"

While he was not expecting her, he wasn't surprised she knew where he lived. She'd come by more than once to scoop up Billy when he'd been too drunk to drive himself home.

She looked bad. Her eye makeup was smeared under her cheek like she'd been crying or hadn't had any sleep and she was hunched over, like she was trying to make herself invisible.

"Let me in," she whispered. Stuart widened the gap, pulled her inside, and quickly closed the door. "He's dead," she said. "Billy's dead."

Stuart's jaw dropped. He figured that's what you were supposed to do when you wanted people to think you were shocked by something they said.

"What?" he said. "What do you mean, Billy's dead? The car finally fall on him?" He wanted to pat himself on the back for that one. Coming up with something he knew wasn't true but was entirely plausible.

"No!" she said, dropping her butt onto the end of the unmade bed. "They killed him! There was blood everywhere!"

"God, no," he said. He was about to sit beside her, but was starting to feel a little self-conscious about being in nothing but a pair of boxers. He was afraid that if he sat down next to her, put his arm around her shoulders to console her, he might, in spite of everything, get a woody, and that would definitely be wrong in these circumstances. So he grabbed his jeans off the floor and pulled them on as Lucy kept talking.

"The dealers," she said. "Those people he's been dealing with. It had to be them." She started to cry. "It's all my fault. All of it. I got him killed."

"How? What do you mean?"

She shot him a look. "You already know. Billy thought it was you at first. But it was me, skimming off the shipment."

Jeans now on, it was safe to sit next to her and offer some comfort. He slipped an arm around her shoulder and squeezed. She seemed to resist a bit, but it felt good to him.

"Oh, Lucy, I don't know what to say."

"It was such a dumb thing to do. If I'd ever thought they'd notice, I never would have done it. But . . . but they did some kind of count, knew they'd been ripped off. I've been driving around all night. I don't know what to do. I don't know where to go. And you're the only other one who knew what Billy was involved in. So . . . I came to see you."

"Sure, okay. You can always count on good ol' Stuart, you know that." He gave her a warm smile, then thought about his morning breath, how he should go brush his teeth. "You don't know how happy I am you came here, that you trust me. Because I want you to know I'm here for you one hundred percent."

"I can't go to the police. I'd have to tell them what Billy was doing, that I stole some of the stuff and sold it. And those people, they've got to be looking for me. If they'd kill Billy over what happened, what do you think they'll do to me?"

"Okay, I hear ya. We need to think about this. You got any money?"

She shook her head. "I've got like forty bucks, cash. I can't use my cards. They trace ATM withdrawals, right?"

"Yeah, yeah, they can do that for sure. Where's your car?"

Lucy told him she had parked her Kia around the back of the motel, hidden mostly by a Dumpster.

"They might find it," Stuart said. "I can try to get rid of it later, leave it at the mall or something. What about your phone?"

"I turned it right off," she said. "They can trace those, too, right?"

"Oh yeah, big-time. That was smart." He gave her another smile. "You're a smart girl."

Stuart suggested she stay there with him until they could come up with a plan. He went out for take-out through the day and brought it back for her. Burgers for lunch, some Chinese food for dinner.

"I'm gonna need clothes," Lucy said to him after they'd finished off the Chinese. "All I have is what's on me. I can't go home for more. The cops, or the dealers, they're probably watching the house, waiting for me to turn up."

"I saw something on the news," Stuart said, waving his phone in the air. "They're looking for you. You're like, a person of interest." He smiled. "You are that."

"I didn't kill him," she said. "How could they think I killed him?"

"You're not listening. That's not what they said."

"Can you get me some clothes?" she asked.

"I don't know anything about getting women's clothes."

"I can write it all out for you. The sizes and stuff. You could go to Walmart. Get everything there."

"Okay, you write it out. But we're a little short on cash right now and I'm kind of maxed out on my cards. But that's all gonna change soon."

"What do you mean?"

"All in good time, sweetheart," he said.

He didn't like the look on her face when he called her that. And here he was, trying to help her.

"But before I get into explaining all that, there's something else I got to do tonight."

"What?"

"A business thing."

Lucy was pacing the room, and given how small it was, she was going back and forth pretty furiously. She happened to glance, at one point, at something that was poking out from under the corner of one of the take-out boxes. She picked it up. It was a phone, with a photo of a Camaro on the protective case.

She looked at Stuart accusingly. "This is Billy's phone."

"Uh, yeah, it is."

"Why do you have Billy's phone?"

"I grabbed it when I was there. But don't worry, it's turned off, too, just like yours. Can't be traced right now."

"When were *you* there?"

"Okay, you need to sit down for this."

"Why do you have his phone?"

"Just sit the fuck down and let me tell you." She sat in one of the chairs at the small dining nook table. "So, I already knew Billy was dead when you came here."

"How did you know? Jesus, Stuart, did you—"

He was already shaking his head. "Went to get some food and they must have shown up and done it then, because he was dead when I got back. I went to check, like, to see if there was any chance he was alive, and I felt his phone in his pocket and I took it."

Her face said, *Why?*

"I was formulating a plan."

"What kind of plan?"

"Something that could help us both out. I know the code to get into his phone. If he got a text or something and the phone was closer to me, he'd ask me to check it. He told me the password. So I can see what his calls are, all his history. Turned it on for a bit, saw all your texts to him that you wanted to come home and be forgiven and shit. Guess you guys had a fight?"

Lucy just looked at him.

"Anyway, so I got a number for the people he was dealing with. Who killed him."

"Stuart, why would you want to get in touch with them?"

He sighed. "Go have a look in the shower."

She was frozen for a second, then got up out of the chair and went into the bathroom. Stuart waited, heard her slide back the shower curtain.

Lucy let out a short scream, then said, "Holy mother of fuck."

She came out of the bathroom with a carry-on bag in her hand.

"So you want to get us both killed."

FORTY-ONE

Richard

I was trying to put it together. You can do a lot of thinking in a millisecond.

Last night, at some point before or after I'd been there, Bonnie had also been to Billy Finster's place. And whatever had happened, it had left her rattled, so rattled that when she'd gotten home she'd downed better than half a bottle of wine in less time than it takes to open a can of Bud Light.

She'd been on the verge of telling me what had happened. She hadn't been to see Marta. That much I knew. When she'd left the house, she'd clearly intended to go to the Finster place, and, having gone there, had done something that was, in her own words, *very dumb*. I wish there'd been time for her to spill the rest of it, because then I would have had a better idea what to say to Marta in this moment.

I had no idea why Bonnie had gone there or what had happened in that garage that left her totally freaked out.

Marta had a witness that put Bonnie's car at the scene. I couldn't think of any possible excuse Bonnie could provide that would be exculpatory. What could she say, other than possibly the truth? But how damning would the truth be, to her or to me?

I felt a need to protect Bonnie, to cover for her, even though I didn't know what act I might be covering for. My mind was racing, but not quickly enough. I needed another moment to come up with something.

Rachel, God bless her, bought me some time.

She strolled into the kitchen and her face went wide with a smile. "Aunt Marta!" she said, and threw her arms around her legs.

"Hey, kiddo," Marta said, leaning over to return the hug.

"Is your head all better?" she asked.

That made Marta smile, too. "Yeah, I'm all better in the head."

"Are you gonna have dinner with us?"

"No, honey. I just needed to talk to your mom and dad about something. But it's good to see you, sweetie."

Rachel seemed to understand that amounted to a dismissal. She gave Marta another squeeze to the thighs and went back to the family room as a familiar rumble from outside made the wineglasses tinkle in the cupboard. Marta seemed about to ask Bonnie what that was, but I had a statement to make.

"It was me," I said.

Marta cocked her head to one side. "What's that, Richard?"

"I was out last night, took Bonnie's car."

I know Bonnie wanted to ask me what the hell I was doing, but there was no way she could. Not now. I'd crossed that line and there was no going back now. And I was already second-guessing myself. What if Marta's witness had seen who was behind the wheel? If she had, Marta would catch me in a lie any second now.

"What were you doing in that neighborhood last night?" Marta asked.

"Following a car," I said.

Marta waited.

"I was coming along West Ave when this asshole in a Corvette cut me off. I try to be cool about these things, but, I don't know, it just pissed me off so much that I went after him. We were both heading east, and then he—I'm assuming it was a guy—made a hard right onto Utica and took off like a bat out of hell. I was going after him, but Bonnie's car's not exactly a sports car, and I lost him. I made a turn onto Wooster and pulled over for a second to decompress, you know?"

"Did you catch the license plate on the 'Vette?"

"No," I said. "But it was white. An older one, from the seventies or eighties, I'd guess."

"Why were you driving Bonnie's car instead of your own?" she asked.

"Come on, sis, he answered your question," Bonnie said.

"No, it's okay," I said. "We switch cars lots of times. And I couldn't find my keys right away and saw Bonnie's, so I grabbed them instead. It didn't really matter which car I took."

"What were you doing, going out at that hour?" Marta asked. "And in that part of town? It's nowhere near here."

I sighed and looked downward. "I didn't really want to get into this, but . . ."

Bonnie touched my arm. "You don't have to—"

"Might as well tell her," I said. A dramatic pause. "We'd had a fight."

"A fight?" Marta asked.

"About the boat."

Another cock of the head. "Go on."

"So, you know about the LeDrews suing me. As frivolous as the suit might seem, you have to take these things seriously, and I hadn't had it confirmed until today that the union would cover any legal costs."

I had to hope Marta wouldn't follow up on this, wouldn't learn that I'd been given this news yesterday.

"So I was going to sell the boat to our neighbor."

"Jack," Bonnie said, helping out.

"Right, Jack. He wanted to buy it and we'd agreed on ten thousand, but before we could make the deal final Bonnie went behind my back and canceled it."

"I didn't think it was right, or fair," Bonnie said. "And we all love the boat. But I shouldn't have canceled the arrangement they had. Not without talking to Richard about it first."

Go ahead and let Marta check *that* part of the story, I thought. Jack would confirm it.

"Anyway, I said a few things I shouldn't have. I know you understand better than most what I've been going through. The trauma, the, you know, aftereffects of what happened to me at the school. So I just walked out, went for a drive. I wandered all over Milford, and I don't even know if I realized where I was when that jerk cut me off. I was already so tense about everything that had happened, I snapped. I went after the car. It's a good thing I couldn't catch him. Not for his sake, but for mine. He'd probably have beat the crap out of me or, worse, shot me. You know how these road rage things can spiral out of control. So I guess I pulled over, calmed down, and then I came home."

"And pulled over by the Finster house," Marta said.

"I guess," I said. "I had no idea whose house it was."

"Did you get out of the car?" she asked.

I had a feeling this was a trick question. Had the witness seen anyone in the car or not? But Marta had only said that Bonnie's car had been spotted. Nothing about anyone being behind the wheel.

"Yes," I said. "At one point. Just to kind of walk things off."

"You see a guy walking his dog?"

"No," I said. "Is that who saw the car?"

Marta nodded. "Thought it seemed odd, the car sitting there. Made a note of the plate. And some lady next door saw a man watching the house earlier in the day."

I felt my chest tighten.

"But she didn't note the plate, wasn't good at identifying cars, and has cataracts. So she wasn't much help."

I relaxed only slightly. There was still the matter of Finster's call to me. If Marta knew about that, all these other lies would be for nothing.

I glanced at the wall clock.

"Have to be somewhere?" Marta asked.

"An event at the school later. It's okay, go on."

"When you stopped, did you see anything?" Marta asked.

"Like?"

"Any other cars speeding off? Did you hear a shot? People running? Anything at all out of the ordinary?"

I shook my head. "No."

Another pause, and then a quick nod. "Okay, then," Marta said. "I guess that explains it. When the report came back on that license plate, I have to tell you, it threw me for a loop. It's a hell of a coincidence."

"Coincidences happen," I said.

"I guess they do. Sorry for barging in here and causing you all this trouble. You mind saying goodbye to Rachel for me?"

"No problem," Bonnie said. "Let me see you out."

"Take care," I said, and watched as the two of them walked out of the kitchen.

I dropped into a chair. I'd broken out in a cold sweat. Had Marta bought it? And if she had, for how long?

A minute later, Bonnie came back into the kitchen, crossed her arms, leaned into the doorway, and looked at me.

"Why did you do that?" she asked.

I had a question for her.

"What were you doing at Billy Finster's place?"

FORTY-TWO

ullshit, Marta thought.

She'd been at this long enough to know when people were lying to her. What made this worse, and far more complicated, was that this was her sister and brother-in-law trying to put something over on her. Okay, maybe there was some kernel of truth somewhere in what they'd told her, but something was off with those two. The way they were trying to send subtle signals to one another, trying to get their story straight without a word between them, Richard going onto his phone and deleting something, thinking she wouldn't notice.

She wanted to believe them. She didn't want to think her sister and her brother-in-law could, in any way, be involved in the death of Billy Finster. What possible connection could there be between them and the dead man, beyond the fact that he was once a student at the school where Richard taught? And yes, coincidences *did* happen. He and Bonnie could have had an argument, he could have gone off in her car, he could have been cut off by a dickhead in a Corvette and pulled over to the side of the road to cool off not far from where a homicide had been committed.

But it still sounded like bullshit to her.

The right thing to do, the *professional* thing to do, would be to withdraw from this investigation. Talk to her superiors, tell them that her sister and her husband might have some tangential connection to this case—that maybe they were witnesses who were, for whatever reason, reluctant to come forward—and, to ensure everything was aboveboard, another detective could take over.

That was certainly what she *should* do.

But Marta wasn't prepared to do that. Not yet, anyway. Just suppose Marta's instincts were wrong, that her sister and brother-in-law were being straight with her, imagine the fallout if Marta turned the case over to a colleague who turned their lives upside down. Good luck at the next Thanksgiving dinner.

Shit.

Heading for her car, she stopped halfway down the driveway and decided part of the story she'd been told could be verified right now. She went to the neighbor's house and rang the bell.

She had met Jack and his wife, Jill, a few times. They'd all been invited to a barbecue for Bonnie's birthday one time. Jack had asked her a few questions about her work, and Jill had seemed nice enough.

It was Jill who answered the door. It took her a second to place Marta, but once she recognized her, she smiled and invited her in.

"That's okay," Marta said. "Sorry to bother you, but—"

Jack appeared. "Hey," he said amiably. "Detective Harper. How are you today?"

She smiled. "*Marta.*"

He smiled. "Nice to see you, Marta."

"What's up?" Jill asked.

"I wondered if I could ask a favor of you."

"Sure, yes, how can we help?" Jack asked.

"You know, of course, the kind of stress Richard and Bonnie have been under lately. The pressures they've been dealing with."

"No kidding," Jack said. "A terrible thing. But Richard really saved the day."

"He did," Marta said, and thought, *Yes, he did.* Which didn't make her feel any better about checking to see whether he had lied to her. "But not everyone sees it that way. You probably heard about the lawsuit."

"Ridiculous," Jill said.

"There's always people out there who can find a way of turning a positive into a negative."

"There's so many nuts," Jill said, nodding agreeably.

"So all I wanted to ask is, if you should see anything suspicious, anyone driving by too often, something that doesn't look right, don't be afraid to get in touch." As she was saying this, she was taking a card from her pocket and handing it to Jack. "That number, the second one, you can always reach me at that."

"Absolutely," Jack said, tucking the card into his shirt pocket.

"Of course," Jill said.

"That was really all I wanted to say. And to say hello." She smiled at both of them, then focused on Jack. "Did I hear right, that you're buying Jack's boat?"

Jack grimaced. "Oh, well, that kind of didn't happen."

"Oh," she said, feigning surprise. "Richard sold it to someone else?"

He looked uncomfortable. "I think there were some crossed signals. Richard offered to sell it to me, I said yes, and then Bonnie explained that the deal was off." He paused, then added, "She said Richard had made some impulsive decisions since what happened at the school, that he hadn't been thinking everything through. So that was okay by me. I didn't want to get into the middle of anything."

Marta nodded.

"That's too bad," she said, "but maybe it's for the best. They get a lot of use out of that boat in the summer. Listen, you folks have a pleasant evening."

Goodbyes were said, and the door was about to be closed, then Jill said, "There was something."

Marta stopped, turned around. "Something?"

"The other day. I think it was Friday? Although I could be wrong about that."

"What happened on Friday?"

"I was looking outside, from the living room window, watching for Jack to get home, and saw this man talking to Richard. I didn't really think about it at the time, but now that you say there might be people wanting to give him a hard time, well, that brought back the memory."

"What did you see?"

"He'd parked a pickup or something just down the street, and when Richard got home he came over and talked to him. Kind of pointing his finger at him a couple of times, and it didn't look like a very friendly conversation."

"What did this man look like? White? Black? Age?"

Jill tried to think back. "He was white, and in his twenties, I guess. A little overweight, dark hair. I wasn't close enough to get a very good look at him."

A vague description, Marta thought, that could fit any number of young men, including Billy Finster.

"How long did they talk for?"

"Five minutes? I had to go answer the phone at one point, and when I came back the man had driven off and Richard had gone inside."

"What about the truck? Did you get a look at that? A license plate number, maybe?"

"It was a pickup truck. White. With some rust on it. It never would have occurred to me to write down the plate number."

"Of course. Why would it?" Marta smiled. "Thanks very much, and you have a nice evening."

She went to her car, got settled in behind the wheel, and thought about how to proceed. After hearing about the boat transaction with Jack, Marta was ready to think she'd overreacted, that her sister and brother-in-law had leveled with her.

But that follow-up story changed things. Something was going on that Bonnie and Richard were not prepared to discuss with her.

She needed to talk to her sister again.

Alone.

FORTY-THREE

Andrea and Gerhard opted to keep a low profile after their run-in with the cop. No more hospital visits for now. And just when they were so close to finding Billy Finster's wife.

Andrea had wanted to ditch the Audi. What if the cop had spotted the license plate? Failing that, what if she checked CCTV footage from along that route and got it that way? Gerhard didn't want to ditch his car, and besides, he reminded her, the car already had stolen plates on it. Anyone who ran a check would be led to some guy in New Haven with a 2018 Malibu. He'd swipe another set of plates, slap them on.

Which was what he did, unscrewing the plates off a blue Golf GTI and bolting them onto the Audi.

"Anyway," he said, "there's only about a thousand black Audis in this part of Connecticut." He shot her a look. "But just one with a cigarette burn in the hood."

"You should have run her down," Andrea said. "If it'd been me driving, that's what I'd've done."

"Then we would have to ditch the car, her brains all over the windshield."

Andrea, sitting in the passenger seat, shrugged. "Good thing I had her shoes. Speedy."

It was about the only positive spin she could put on the situation.

Tracking down Billy's wife, Lucy, was now much more difficult. Not only were the cops looking for her, that detective knew *they* were looking for her. But they needed to find her. It made sense that she was the one who'd helped herself to the carry-on bag. This was no longer a case of someone skimming a little off the top. This was the entire weekly shipment. It was their asses on the line here. If they didn't recover that case, there was going to be a little delegation flying up from south of the border to have a word. Followed, perhaps, by a bullet to the head.

Gerhard turned the car into a strip mall parking lot, killed the engine, turned to look at Andrea.

"Let me run something by ya," he said.

Andrea waited.

"You got anything put aside? If you do, you might want to consider your options. I have some stashed away. We don't find that case in the next twenty-four hours, it's gonna get ugly. I know a guy, can fix us up with new IDs, shit like that. Passports, whatever. I'm thinking, Germany. I got people there."

"You go where you got people, they'll find you," she said.

"I could regroup when I got there, go someplace else."

"Don't worry about me," Andrea said.

"You need a plan."

"Maybe I have one. What makes you think I'm dumb enough to share it with you?"

Gerhard made a clicking noise with this tongue. "Fine."

"I don't need your protection."

"Fine, okay. Forget I mentioned it."

"Maybe I'll just tell them it was you took the shit." She smiled slyly.

"You got a fucked-up idea of what's funny."

"You think I'm being funny? Maybe a better idea would be for you to put on your big boy pants and find that fucking bag."

"And what would you suggest we—"

Gerhard's phone rang. He got it out of his pocket and raised his eyebrows when he saw the name on the screen.

BILLY.

He turned the phone so Andrea could see it before she even asked.

"Don't answer it," she said.

"Gotta."

"Could be the cops. They'd have his phone. They're going through the numbers."

Gerhard's cell continued to ring.

"If it is, they've already got my fucking number because they're *calling* it. What if it's the wife? What if she took his phone?"

Andrea let that sink in. "She wants to make a deal. She wants to sell it back to us. Answer the fucking thing."

Gerhard tapped the screen, put it on speaker. "Yeah?"

"Hey," said a male voice on the other end. "This who I think it is?"

Gerhard and Andrea exchanged glances. Definitely not the wife.

"I don't know," said Gerhard. "Who the fuck do you think it is?"

"You're one of the ones Billy dealt with. That he held the stuff for."

"Who is this?"

"Not important. What's important is what I can do for you."

"And what would that be?"

"I'm guessing you're missing something."

"What about it?"

"Wondered if you'd like it back."

"How would we go about making that happen?"

"We set something up," the man at the other end said. "A handoff."

"That . . . would be greatly appreciated."

"I'm guessing what's in this is worth a lot of money."

Andrea made a face, like she'd been waiting for this.

"What are you proposing?" Gerhard asked.

"I'll sell it back to you. Got to be worth, what? A million? Two million?"

"I'm afraid that's a little out of our price range."

"I'm not looking for that. Just, like, a finder's fee."

"I see. What were you thinking?"

"A hundred."

Gerhard looked ready to laugh, but Andrea raised a cautious finger. For the first time, she spoke. "We can offer you fifty."

"Who's this?"

Andrea ignored the question. "Fifty. You've got five seconds to decide. One . . . two—"

"Okay," the caller said. "Fifty."

Andrea said, "Done."

Gerhard gave her a look, as if to say, *Are you kidding me?*

"I'll get back to you on when and where," the caller said. And then he was gone.

Gerhard said, "You got fifty grand up your ass?"

"I don't have fifty fucking cents," she said.

She'd already figured out how this would have to be handled. They'd get the bag back from this guy and kill him. But what was really on her mind was Gerhard's backup plan, that the two of them would run off together to Germany and start new lives.

That was never gonna happen.

FORTY-FOUR

Richard

"I went there," Bonnie said.

"To Billy Finster's," I said.

Bonnie nodded.

"It was stupid, I know. I was so angry, so . . . enraged by this shit he was pulling, what he was doing to you after you'd already been through so much. You didn't deserve that. So I . . . I went there to confront him."

She sighed. "Even while you were telling me what happened, I knew I was going to do it. Threaten him. Tell him who my sister was. That if he didn't stop this, I'd see that he got arrested."

We were sitting in the kitchen. Marta had left about ten minutes earlier. In another ninety minutes I was supposed to be at my school to talk to parents about the books I had assigned their kids to read.

I said, "Let me guess what happened. When you got there, he was dead."

Bonnie slowly shook her head no. "I went to the house and no one answered. I saw a light in the garage and went out there. That's where I found him."

She took a breath.

"He was alone. I told him who I was, that I was your wife, that I knew what he was doing, and it had to stop. He pretended to have no idea what I was talking about."

"He denied it?"

She nodded. "He told me to get out, but I wasn't having it. I guess I raised my voice, kind of lost it. Told him you were a good man and would never have done what he was accusing you of, and he said something like, 'I don't know who the fuck you're talking about.' And that's when he started waving a gun around."

I shuddered. "Jesus."

"He pointed it at me, and . . ."

Bonnie's hands were starting to shake. ". . . and I wondered at that moment whether he was going to kill me. I'd never in my life had anyone point a gun at me, and it changes you, you know?"

Like facing down someone with a bomb, I thought.

"And I thought about you and Rachel and what a huge mistake it had been, to go there. So I said I was leaving. And the second I was out of that garage I ran back to my car, didn't look back, was scared that he might be chasing me, that he'd take a shot before I could get out of there."

I put my hands over hers to calm them. "But you're okay. Nothing happened."

Or hadn't happened *yet*. Because at some point, things came to an end for Billy.

She nodded and wiped a tear from her cheek. "I guess, for a moment, I was thinking I was back learning how to be a cop, before I decided to do something different. Thinking I could handle this. What I should have done, what *we* should have done from the beginning, was bring Marta into it, tell her everything. I'd been thinking all day that when I got home, I'd talk to you about it, insist we call her, because this wasn't something we could handle. But then she shows up here, and says he's dead . . . I had no idea. Somebody killed him, and my car was spotted, and even then I thought I could find a way to explain it, but then you—"

"Jumped in and covered for you."

"*Why?* Why would you—" Bonnie cut herself off. She was trying to put it together. "Because you thought maybe I'd done it."

"I never seriously considered that as a possibility."

"Not seriously," she repeated. "But you hadn't ruled it out. Oh my God, Richard."

"I didn't think it was good for anyone to think you might have been anywhere near Billy Finster's place."

"So you came up with that story because . . . you knew he was dead. You knew he was dead before Marta came here."

"I did."

The kitchen suddenly seemed very quiet. The only sound was the faint noise of Rachel's movie.

"How . . . how would you have known he was dead?" she asked tentatively.

"I was there last night, too," I said. "Clearly, after you were. I wanted to confront him, get real evidence he was lying in case he went public. So I asked Mrs. Tibaldi to look after Rachel. I was thinking I shouldn't face him alone, so I dropped by Trent's place to see whether I could talk him into going with me. But he was out. By then I was hyped up, had to see it through. I had this idea I could record him on my phone, get him to admit there was nothing to his accusations, that he just wanted money. So I went there."

"You shouldn't have."

"Look who's talking."

"Richard, tell me you didn't . . ."

"Let me finish," I said. "I get there, but then this other car came along. A man and a woman get out, go to the house first, and then the garage, and I hear shouting and all this banging about. And then these two came back out, went into the house, and I could kind of make out through the blinds and curtains that they were tearing the place apart. Finally, they left."

Bonnie waited.

"So that's when I went to the garage and found him. Facedown, not moving. There was blood all over the place and I didn't have to feel for a pulse to know. He was dead. I hadn't touched a thing except the door handle and I wiped that down and I threw out the shoes I was wearing because I was worried I might have left footprints in the garage."

"They killed him," she said. "Did you hear a shot or anything?"

I shook my head. "There'd been so much banging around I thought maybe they'd beat him to death. A story online said he'd been shot. So maybe they used a silencer or something."

"Who could they have been?" Bonnie asked. "Why would they kill him?"

I shrugged. "I don't know. But they were looking for something, that's for sure."

Bonnie put her head in her hands for a moment. "We have to tell Marta."

"If we do," I said, "and she doesn't believe me, I've put myself at the scene. I had a motive, I was there."

"Yeah, but there's those two that came to the house."

"There's just my word that that happened. I could be making that part up, for all she knows."

"Oh come on. She *knows* you. She knows you wouldn't do anything like that."

I was not convinced. "Does she? Who knows what someone in my situation might do? Accused of something like that."

Bonnie was thinking. "Do you think it happened at *all*? Do you think someone—someone from your school—*did* abuse him? I mean, why come up with something like that if there's absolutely no basis for it?"

"I think someone did do it to him. Someone from the school. But how does that become a case of mistaken identity? Someone messes with you, forces you to do things to them, how do you not remember who that was?"

"None of this makes any sense," Bonnie said.

"No shit." I glanced at the digital display on the microwave, noticed the time. "You won't believe this, but I have to go to this thing at the school." I quickly filled her in.

She shook her head in exasperation. "Cancel."

"If I don't go, and Marta finds out, it would look like her visit freaked me out. I have to see these parents."

"I don't know how much more the two of us can take."

We got up from the table and held each other. "I know," I said.

"What now?" Bonnie asked. "I don't know, what with that man being killed, whether our problems are over or just beginning."

I was at the school forty-five minutes later, a good fifteen minutes before the meeting was supposed to start. Trent had arranged for it to be held in the library. Not only was that a good place to set up chairs, but we'd be surrounded by books. Seemed appropriate.

I was out of the car and heading into the school when I heard a woman call out my name. She was getting out of a blue SUV parked over on the far side of the lot. She looked familiar to me, but I couldn't quite place her. I stopped and waited for her to close the distance between us. I assumed she was part of the delegation tonight and wanted a few words with me ahead of time.

"Mr. Boyle," she said once she had reached me. She was in her early fifties, thin and wan-looking, in a shapeless pale green dress that hung on her like it was still on the hanger.

"Yes?"

"I'm Fiona LeDrew."

Now I knew where I'd seen her. On the news. Christ, it wasn't enough the LeDrews were suing me? They didn't like the books on my curriculum, either?

"I came by late this afternoon and you'd already left, but they said you'd be at some meeting tonight and I wanted to catch you before it started."

She extended a hand hesitantly, unsure I would take it. I did.

"Ms. LeDrew." I wasn't sure what to say. "I don't believe we've ever spoken, certainly not recently."

"No, I don't think we've met. Not even when Mark attended here."

"I'm very sorry for your loss."

She nodded. "I'm going to make my husband drop the lawsuit."

I let that sink in a moment. Jumping up and down didn't seem right in the circumstances, but it was nice to have some tidbit of good news. "I see," I said.

"It's the only way he knows how to deal with the situation," she said. "To lash out at everybody else, like he—like *we*—didn't have anything to do with it. And I think . . . I think he's trying to make up for things even if it's too late."

She took a breath.

"He's . . . he's a cold man, my husband," she said. "I love him, and I know he loves me, and that he loved Mark, but he wasn't very good at showing it. After Mark died, Angus . . . he's been doing a lot of soul-searching. But not enough that he hasn't wanted to shift the blame to others. Good people like you."

I said nothing.

"We shouldn't be going after you. It's wrong. We should be thanking you. I hope you can find it in your heart to forgive."

I didn't know what else to say but "Of course."

"I can't imagine what might have happened if you hadn't talked to Mark. He was a very, very unhappy young man, an angry young man. He was blaming so many others for how his life had turned out. But we have to be responsible for our actions, don't we, no matter what has happened to us?"

I nodded.

"Nothing would justify coming here and . . . and doing what we all know he planned to do. But he was hurting. *Someone* hurt him here."

"Hurt him how?" I asked.

Fiona pressed her lips together hard and looked away briefly. "There were things he never told my husband, things he only told me, that he made me swear never to tell his father. He was too ashamed."

"What kinds of things?" I asked.

She looked like she was about to tell me, stopped herself, and then tried again. "Abusive things," she said finally. She reached out and

248

touched my arm. "And I know it couldn't have been you. If it had been . . . he'd have taken you with him when that bomb went off."

"Are we talking some kind of sexual abuse?" I asked.

She nodded. "Mark said it . . . made him doubt who he was. He felt . . . like he went along with it to get things in return."

"Did he say what?"

"No."

"Ms. LeDrew, did your son say who did this to him? Was there a name?"

She shook her head. "I tried to get him to tell me. He only talked to me about this a couple of times, and when I tried to bring it up later, he shut me down."

A thought occurred to me.

"Did your son wrestle? Was he on the team?"

"No, I mean, he might have done wrestling in his gym class, but he wasn't on a team."

"What about Herb Willow? Mark mentioned his name when we talked."

"Mark hated him, for sure, but not because of . . . you know. Mr. Willow just put him down all the time, made him stop believing in himself. And, you know, that's pretty bad, too, crushing a young man's spirit."

"Was there *anyone* you suspected?"

"No. The closest Mark ever came to telling me was that he called him the lawnmower man. He would never give me a name. There'd be too much trouble, he said."

FORTY-FIVE

When Stuart finished making his call on Billy's phone, he was close to giddy.

"This is great!" he said to Lucy, who was sitting on the end of the motel room bed. "Fifty grand! Fifty grand they're gonna give me for it." He was shaking his head with wonder. "I started higher, and we bargained a little, and I'd have settled for twenty. But fifty? That's fantastic."

"You're crazy," Lucy said.

"No, no, this is brilliant," Stuart said. He suddenly became serious, pulled over a chair to the foot of the bed, turned it around, and sat on it backward, facing Lucy. "I need to talk to you about something."

She waited.

"I know you've always kind of thought of me as an asshole."

"I never said that."

"It's okay, I get it, you don't have to admit anything. But there's more to me than what you've seen. I've got dreams, too. All sorts of potential. Billy didn't see it and you didn't see it, but it's there. I can do big things. And this, what's happening now, this is my big chance to get started. To show everybody that Stuart Betz isn't some dipshit do-nothing. Hear what I'm saying?"

"I guess," Lucy whispered.

"You and I have something in common. Guess what it is?"

"I can't."

"We were both treated like shit by Billy. He ever share any of his riches with you?" He didn't need an answer. He could read her face. "Exactly. Kept it all to himself, spent it all on his stupid fucking car. Same with me, and I was his friend. He was selfish. It was all about him. You get what I'm saying?"

"I suppose," Lucy said.

"But I'm not like that. When I give them the goods and get my money, I'm sharing it. I'm sharing it with you, Lucy."

"I don't want any of that money."

"No, listen." He took a deep breath, getting ready to bare his soul, checked his watch, then said, "The thing is, Lucy, I've always really liked you."

The look on her face did not suggest this was welcome news.

"Don't freak out. I'm not going to get all stalker-like on you. I'm just saying I always liked you, and admired you. The kind of work you do, helping people in the hospital, and—"

"I work in a cafeteria. I make Jell-O."

"Yeah, but that's helping. People have to eat, right? And I always admired how you stood by Billy even when he was treating you like shit. That says something about your character. Now that he's gone, you need someone to look after you."

"Look after me?"

He nodded. "I mean, why are you here? Why were you wandering around all night? Because you were scared, right? You're scared of the cops. You're scared of those people who killed Billy. But you can't go to the police because you were selling stuff from the shipment. You knew what Billy was up to. That would kind of make you an accomplice, right?"

"I'm no accomplice."

"Well, I guess that would be for a lawyer to argue, and my law degree is still in the mail. But you're kind of in limbo, right?"

She listened.

"So you'll have to go on the run, at least for a while, till things cool down. And that's not easy. Because you've got no money, and you can't go to an ATM or use your Visa. But, see, that's where I'm going to help you out. When I get that fifty grand from those assholes, we're golden. That money, that's for both of us, you understand? I'm not going to pull a Billy on you and keep it all to myself. I'm going to share it with you. And when we get it, we're going to get out of town and hide out someplace nice. You with me?"

Lucy hadn't said anything for a long time. Finally, she said, "You're totally batshit."

"No, no, I've got it all worked out." He looked at his watch again.

"They'll kill you. Just like they killed Billy."

He shook his head vigorously and smiled. "I got a plan for that." He went over to the motel desk, opened the drawer, and brought out a gun.

"Oh Jesus," Lucy said. When she was over the initial shock, she said, "Is that Billy's?"

Stuart nodded. "It was on the floor. I grabbed it." He smiled. "Pretty smart, huh?"

"What if that's the gun they killed him with? And the cops find you with it? How do you think that's gonna go?"

Stuart's smile vanished. "I hadn't thought— No, it doesn't matter, because once we have the money and we're out of here, I'll get rid of it. Won't need it anymore. I just need it for when we do the swap. Need this to make sure nothing goes wrong."

"They'll shoot you the second they see you," she said.

"That's where you're wrong. I'm not going to be the one doing the handover."

Lucy's eyes narrowed. "No way," she said. "I'm not going face-to-face with the fuckers who killed Billy."

"Don't worry," Stuart said, looking at his watch yet again. "It's not going to be like that. You don't have to do anything but stay here and hold down the fort and wait for me to come back. When I do, everything's going to be okay."

"I don't want any part of this."

Stuart couldn't hide the hurt on his face. "Okay," he said, a sudden brusqueness in his voice. He set the gun on top of the desk. "There's the door."

"What?"

"Just go. You don't want my help, you don't want to be a part of this, then go. I'm sure you'll be fine. I'll keep the fifty grand all to myself. Just keep your eye out, that's all. The police are looking for you, and those drug dealers are looking for you. But, sure, handle it on your own."

Lucy looked at the door, back to Stuart, and back to the door.

"You decide," he said, and tapped his watch. "I gotta go see somebody."

FORTY-SIX

Richard

Trent was waiting for me when I walked into the school.

"Hey," he said, greeting me with a handshake. "Was thinking you could use some moral support."

That was true, and probably not a bad idea, given that I was going into this meeting more than a little distracted.

I told him about running into Fiona LeDrew, finding out that she was going to get her husband to drop the lawsuit. Trent beamed. "Excellent," he said.

I wasn't smiling. "But we got talking about Mark, and how messed up he was." A few parents were entering the school, finding their way to the library. I lowered my voice to a whisper. "What do you know about Ronny Grant?"

"That he didn't fix the latch on that door. Which is why he lost his job."

"I'm not talking about that. This whole blackmail thing, I don't think it comes out of nothing. I think there *was* someone abusing students, and I'm wondering whether it was Ronny."

"Why Ronny?"

"It goes back to something Mark said, and now something his mother told me. This lawnmower man thing."

Trent slowly shook his head. "Ronny had his problems. He's borderline alcoholic. But an abuser? I never got a hint of that. I mean, he *liked* the kids, yeah. But we all *like* the kids. Why else would we work here?"

"Herb doesn't like the kids."

"Don't get me started on him. He's here, by the way. I saw him come in about five minutes ago."

"I think he stirred the pot on this," I said.

"Fuck Herb," Trent said. He took a long look at me. "Don't take this the wrong way, but you look like shit."

I had no reason to doubt him. Marta's visit, Bonnie's revelations. It had left me frazzled. And the right side of my face was still swollen, bandages still on my neck and forehead.

"I gotta go do this thing," I said.

There were two doors to the library: a main one and a secondary entrance that was by the librarian's office. I used that one to enter unnoticed while the parents started filing in through the main entrance. Chairs had been set out by whatever caretaker Trent had brought in to take over from Ronny.

I found a library cart, the kind that gets loaded up with books when they are being reshelved, and wheeled it down the fiction aisle. I started loading it up with hardcovers and paperbacks. *Star Trek* novelizations and Stephen King tales of horror. The Twilight series and Harry Potter. *The Hunger Games* and all of Tolkien. The Anne of Green Gables books and the His Dark Materials series by Philip Pullman. Judy Blume and The Maze Runner books. Toni Morrison and Margaret Atwood. Classics the parents would know, like *To Kill a Mockingbird*, *Lord of the Flies*, Ray Bradbury's *The Martian Chronicles*, *The Call of the Wild*, and one of my own personal favorites, *The Princess Bride* by William Goldman.

I stacked the cart with these books and others. Our librarian, who was not here this evening, would have a fit when he found out what I'd done, or was planning to do. I could hear murmurings at the other end of the room. People taking their seats.

Trent found me loading the cart.

"They're here," he said. "Fifteen, maybe twenty, tops. Not exactly the biggest mob in the world." He paused. "And Herb."

"Okay," I said.

"Why don't I say a few words, and then this group's spokesperson will do some kind of opening statement."

Sounded like a plan. He worked his way to the other end of the room and I followed, pushing the cart ahead of me. Fewer than half of the chairs that had been set out were filled, and Trent was right in his estimate. I did a quick count and came up with sixteen, eleven women and five men. But to get sixteen parents out to an event was still something of an achievement when everyone's lives were so busy, so I wasn't about to discount it.

At the back of the room, seated alone, was Herb.

I stood behind and to the side as Trent introduced himself to the room.

"Thanks for coming," he said. "It's always gratifying to me, and I know I'm speaking for Mr. Boyle here, too, when parents take a keen interest in what their children are studying. So we appreciate you taking the time to be here this evening to talk about this important issue. What I'm going to do is turn the meeting over to Mrs. Kanin, who's going to explain why she asked for this opportunity to have some matters clarified, and then I'll invite Mr. Boyle here to say a few words and take your questions."

No wonder Trent had worked his way up the administrative ladder. What a politician. Not once did he use words like *concern* or *complaint* or *censorship* or *ban*. Trent, who was going to head back to the office, whispered to me as he slipped away, "Let me know how it goes, and text me if they look like they're getting ready to string you up."

Wasn't it nice that one of us still had a sense of humor.

Violet Kanin stood up from her chair, but did not come to the front of the room. I recognized her, of course, as Andrew's mother, who had for several years schooled him at home and, as I've probably already pointed out, did a pretty good job of it, at least where math and writing skills were concerned. She always attended parent-teacher events, and gave me a quick smile before speaking.

"Hi," she said. "Forgive me if I seem a bit nervous, I'm not much of a public speaker." She forced a laugh. "I want to say from the outset how grateful we all are for Mr. Boyle's recent actions, and know that any of the issues we bring up tonight aren't in any way meant to be critical of you."

I nodded.

"But tonight we're here to get some insight, we hope, into how you go about choosing what books our children will read, and whether they are really the best of the best, and just how appropriate they are. And it's not about just the one book, this *Road* thing, but other books, too. Anyway, that's all I have to say. I didn't write anything down."

Violet looked at me, sat down, and I took that as my cue. I took a step forward, hands in my pockets, trying to adopt a casual air, and said, "Thanks very much. I'm glad to have the chance to talk about—"

One of the men blurted, "Why would you be teaching books celebrating cannibalism? What on earth is the point of that?"

I guess we weren't going to waste any time getting into it.

"Okay," I said calmly. "Let's start there. I'm sure many of you, at some point, may have read your children the story 'Hansel and Gretel,' or had it read to you as a child, and will recall that it's about a witch who is trying to fatten up a couple of children on sweets before she cooks them and eats them, and that the children escape after pushing her into the oven and killing her. If I were teaching fourth grade, say, instead of high school English, and you learned the children had read 'Hansel and Gretel,' I doubt many of you would have been in touch. Cannibalism and murder are themes in 'Hansel and Gretel,' just as they are in the novel *The Road*, which, admittedly, is a much darker and more realistic tale, but in neither case are they things to be celebrated, although I don't think we mind when the witch gets hers."

Hoped for a laugh there, and didn't get it.

"Most novels, most good novels, involve conflict and what human beings do to resolve it. *The Road* is a story about survival in the wake of a global catastrophe, and for kids who have grown up on stuff like *The Walking Dead* and *28 Days Later*, it's a way to engage them, to get them past the gore and the sensationalism and guide them toward a discussion of complicated moral issues."

Violet said, "But this kind of material can be upsetting to some. Like my Andrew."

I nodded. "It's true. And if your son is troubled to the point that he does not want to continue reading the book, or participate in discussions about it, then I would find him an alternate. I think, if you were to ask him, he'd want to continue. Andrew has some pretty interesting insights into things that I'd be sorry if the rest of the class missed. But, and this is a question for all of you, don't you think I would be doing your children a disservice if I made every effort to protect them from things that might challenge or upset them? I could cocoon them, avoid anything that might spark debate, that would raise questions of right and wrong. Of course, that would mean not reading any works of fiction at all, because that's what we hope good fiction will do. Get the kids talking, thinking. Good fiction provokes and bridges gaps, can bring people together by exposing them to all sides of an issue."

I stopped. I wasn't foolish enough to think my little speech would win them all over, but at least a few of them appeared to be considering what I'd had to say.

I decided to go on, and wheeled out the cartload of books.

"Here's a sampling of reading material from our library. We have a wide variety of things for kids to read here. Classics, more modern stuff. Everything from Huck Finn to vampires. I'm inviting you to take two or three books with you when you leave here tonight, read them, make notes about what you liked about the book, what troubled you about it, whether you think it's right for your child. And if it's a book you do like, that you think your child would get something out of, how would you feel if another parent decided your child shouldn't be allowed to read it? And then—"

One of the men had his hand up, but didn't wait to be called on. "Hang on. You want us to *read* these books?"

"The best way to understand what the kids are studying—not just in my class or any other teacher's class, but on their own—is to have a read of it yourselves. It might change your opinion, and then again, it might reinforce the opinion you already hold. But once you've read some of these—"

"I don't have time for that," said the same guy.

"I do," said one of the women.

I smiled. "Some of you may have noticed Mr. Willow sitting at the back of the room this evening." A few heads turned around as Herb sat up a little straighter in his chair. "I want to thank him for coming tonight and showing an interest in this subject, and I'm delighted that he has volunteered to be part of all this. When you've read your books and written your assessment of it, Mr. Willow will be happy to look at what you've done and put together a report."

Herb's face flushed. *Fuck you, Herb.*

"But there's one other point I would like to make," I said. "And what I don't want is to come across like I'm lecturing any of you. I know your concerns are sincere. You care about what happens here, in this building. So do I."

I paused.

"Mrs. Kanin started off by mentioning what happened here last week, and thank you for the kind words." I was looking right at her. "I see the world a little differently now than I did just ten days ago. A young man came into this school intending to do harm. Your kids were here for that. You received frantic phone calls while they were in lockdown. You raced to the school. It's something you and your kids will never forget. The longest couple of hours of your lives. What made this person want to hurt us? What's happening to our young people?"

I waved my hand toward the cart full of books. "Maybe the answers are here. Somewhere in these thousands of pages. The inspirations and motivations for these works are varied. Some writers set out to simply entertain, and that's great. Others seek to understand who we are, to promote understanding, to bring people together. I don't believe keeping our kids from reading them will make them safer. I believe shielding them from ideas will make them less tolerant, less understanding, less willing to engage, and that, ultimately, will make them less safe."

Violet Kanin slowly stood.

"I don't think you understand," she said. "I know what you're probably thinking. That we're a bunch of ignorant book banners, that—"

"I didn't say that. I didn't accuse—"

"Please allow me to finish," she said quietly. "I don't need reminding about how terrified we all were that day. We all remember it very well. I could have lost my son that day. Any one of us here could have lost a child when that man came here with a bomb. We see the news. The shootings. We see what's happening at one school after another. At malls and churches. We know our kids are exposed to drugs and awful things online and under all kinds of pressure from their friends. And here's the thing: we don't know what to do about it."

I listened.

"We feel helpless and scared and overwhelmed. And then one day our kids are assigned a book to read. A book with all sorts of ugliness in it. It may be a wonderful book, and maybe you should keep teaching it. I don't even know anymore. But we think, we can't control any of these threats our children face, but maybe we can fool ourselves into thinking we're making a difference in one small area if we ask, will this book make our kids' lives better?"

Her eyes were wet. "I guess that's all I have to say." She forced herself to smile and said, "Andrew's liking *Hoot*, so I thank you for that."

She sat down.

The room was quiet for a moment. I nodded slowly, looked at Violet Kanin, and said, "I hear you. Believe me, I do. This, right here, these are the kinds of discussions I want to have not just with parents, but with my students, so we can come to a better understanding of how we feel. I think we all really want the same—"

I stopped. Someone new had entered the room. A latecomer.

And I suddenly felt light-headed.

Billy Finster had arrived.

FORTY-SEVEN

Back in her teens, Bonnie smoked. Not for all that long. Couple of years when she was in high school. Gave up cigarettes when she went on to college—mostly she couldn't afford them, and only smoked when she could bum one off a friend—but she remembered the pleasures of drawing smoke into her lungs and blowing it out slowly, how soothing it was. She used to hide them in the garage when she still lived with her parents.

God, how she wished she had a pack stashed away someplace in the house right now.

Richard should have bailed on that school meeting tonight. They needed to talk more, figure out what their next steps could be. There had to be *something* that would allow them to put all this behind them.

Bonnie stood there in the kitchen a moment longer, imagining a Camel between her index and middle fingers.

Enough of this.

"Rachel!" she called out.

"Yes?" she shouted back from the family room.

"Bed!"

"But it's only—"

"*Bed!*"

Bonnie could hear her daughter scrambling up the stairs. Bonnie would go up in a few minutes, make sure she was actually getting ready. Brushing her teeth, putting on her pajamas.

The doorbell rang.

"God, what fresh hell is this?" Bonnie asked of no one in particular. She went to the front door and found her sister, Marta, standing there.

"You're back."

"I'm back," Marta said, stepping in without being invited. Bonnie stepped out of the way, and closed the door once her sister was inside. "Richard off to his school thing?"

"Yes."

"Where's Rach?" Marta asked.

Bonnie pointed to the ceiling. "Getting ready for bed."

"Let's go to the kitchen."

Where, it occurred to Bonnie, all important discussions are held. She didn't feel good about where this one might be going.

"Can you make us some coffee?" Marta asked when they got there. "Decaf, if you prefer, given it's kind of late in the day. But I'm good with either."

Bonnie decided to make the real stuff. She wasn't going to get any sleep tonight, anyway.

Marta made a show of unclipping her badge from her belt and setting it on the counter. "Don't let me forget that."

"I don't understand," Bonnie said.

"Right now, I'm not a cop. I'm just your sister, and it's just us. I'm going to do something right now that could very likely get me fired, because I should really turn this over to someone else, shouldn't even be talking to you at all right now, but I don't care, because I love you, and fuck it."

Bonnie fumbled the sugar bowl, spilling some onto the counter.

"Let me do that," Marta said, directing Bonnie to a chair.

Bonnie didn't fight her, took a seat, and watched as Marta took off her jacket, hung it over the back of a chair, and waited for the water to drip down through the coffee filter. She filled the two cups, adding a touch of cream to her own, and half a teaspoon of sugar to her sister's.

"You remember," Bonnie said.

Marta brought the two cups to the table and said, "You got any cookies or anything?" Bonnie pointed to a cupboard. Marta found a bag of biscotti. "Ooh, fancy." She brought them to the table and sat down at an angle from Bonnie. She pulled out a biscotti, smiled when she saw that the end was dipped in chocolate. "I love these."

Bonnie hadn't said a word.

"I was thinking about when we lived in the house on Breakneck," Marta said. "I was eighteen, and you were sixteen, and Mom and Dad had to drive up to Boston when Dad's best friend from college died. You remember that?"

"Yes," Bonnie said, taking a sip of her coffee. "His name was Lenny. They were on the football team."

"They were worried, leaving the two of us on our own. The arguments we were famous for. Borrowing each other's clothes without asking. Fighting over that one computer that was connected to the Internet, how you even yanked my hair so you could have a turn. Plus all the stories about teenagers throwing crazy parties when their parents were out of town, and they were worried that even if we didn't intend to throw a party, all the neighborhood kids might descend on our place, anyway. I think you were going out with Roy somebody at that time."

"Roy Knightley," Bonnie offered.

"Right. Not a bad-looking guy."

Bonnie smiled. "You always remember your first."

"That you do," Marta said, taking a bite out of the chocolate end of the biscotti. "You tried to set me up with his older brother, Fletcher. He was, if I recall correctly, even better-looking than Roy. And I wasn't the slightest bit interested. I think you must have seen him as a kind of test. That if Fletcher didn't get my motor running, no boy could."

"Busted."

"I hadn't come out. I couldn't. Mom and Dad, I was sure they'd never be able to handle it. Anyway, while Mom and Dad were off in Boston, you were going out with Roy, and I'd told you I was going to the movies with some friends or something, so you figured the house was empty and you came home. You and Roy were going to get it on."

"But the house wasn't empty," Bonnie said. "I heard noises in the TV room."

"Where you found me and Sandra Jane Wiler. Kind of making out."

"Kinda?"

"Okay, maybe even more than that. Gettin' into it."

"Why are you telling me this story?" Bonnie asked.

"Just wait. So we pulled ourselves together, and it was all pretty awkward, and I took you aside and tried to explain. That we weren't really making out, but Sandra Jane's brother had this VHS porn tape with two women fucking around with each other and it was just the dumbest thing she'd ever seen and we were just reenacting it and killing ourselves laughing because it was so ridiculous, that we weren't really doing anything, and that what you'd seen wasn't what you *thought* you'd seen. And do you remember what you said?"

Bonnie slowly shook her head.

"You said, 'Bullshit. You think I'm an idiot?' That was what you said."

Bonnie said nothing.

"And so I told you what you pretty much already knew, but confirmed it for you. That I was gay, that I didn't know how long I could keep it from Mom and Dad, and you put your arms around me and said you loved me and that you would support me in whatever way I wanted to handle it. And I felt this great weight lift off my shoulders, that whatever happened, you had my back. I've never forgotten that, to this very day."

A tear welled up in Bonnie's eye.

"So now, after all these years, it's my turn," Marta said. "This is what I have to say after talking to you and Richard. Bullshit. You think I'm an idiot?"

Bonnie's mouth moved, as though she were trying to say something, but the words would not come out. Marta put her hand atop Bonnie's and said, "Something's going on, and you're going to tell me what it is. Because I'm your sister, and I love you, and if you don't, I'm gonna yank your hair out by the roots."

FORTY-EIGHT

Richard

"I have a question," another woman in the library said, "about this whole trigger warning thing people have been talking about. Like, you're supposed to warn people ahead of time if there's something in what they're about to read or see that they might find upsetting, but how are you supposed to know what might upset a person? I mean, everybody's bothered by *something*. I don't like to read anything where animals are hurt, but I'm not expecting something on the title page that says, oh, watch out, *this* is coming. What do you think?"

I said, "What?"

I was ever so slightly distracted.

Billy Finster was standing at the back of the room. Except it couldn't be Billy Finster, because Billy Finster was dead. So either Marta was investigating the death of someone she *thought* to be Billy Finster, or this guy grinning at me was not, and never had been, Billy Finster.

He made a small come-hither gesture with his index finger. Like, *Hey, buddy, we need to talk.*

"Mr. Boyle? Do you want me to repeat the question?"

I looked at the woman who'd been talking.

"I'm sorry," I said. "I have to go."

I walked slowly toward the back of the library, catching curious reactions from the crowd as I passed. Like, I was just going to walk out on them? Yes, that's exactly what I was going to do.

As I walked past Herb, he said under his breath, "I want to talk to you."

I ignored him and went face-to-face with my blackmailer and whispered heatedly, "Who the fuck *are* you?"

He reared back slightly. Quietly, he said, "We should take this outside. Betting you have questions."

We exited the room and started walking down the hall toward the main entrance. Behind us, I heard Herb, who had stepped out of the library, call out: "Boyle. *Boyle!*"

My blackmailer and I rounded a corner and as we passed an open classroom I steered him inside. I closed the door behind us. We were in a chemistry class. Raised desks with stools, a chart of the periodic table on the wall.

"What the fuck is going on?" I asked.

He smiled. "Okay, so you've figured out I'm not Billy." He extended a hand. "I'm Stuart. Pleased to meet you."

I didn't take his hand.

He took in the room, shook his head. "I fuckin' hated chemistry class. Flunked it." He took a breath. "Flunked pretty much everything, you wanna know the truth. Hate schools. Didn't want to do this here. Was heading for your place, saw you leave, followed you. What was that meeting all about?"

"Who are you, Stuart?" I asked, wanting to bring him back on track.

"Billy's friend. Well, I *was* Billy's friend, until what happened to him. That was fucking wild, right? Listen, don't look so pissed. I'm here with good news. Well, good news and bad news."

I was simmering. "Why don't you give me the bad news first."

Stuart thought about that and shook his head. "No, it makes more sense to start with the good news, which is that I'm no longer interested in getting your ten grand. Consider it forgotten. Wiping the slate clean. No hard feelings, okay?"

"What's the rest of it?" I asked.

"You're not quite off the hook. I know you killed Billy."

"I did not kill Billy."

"Sure looks that way to me. Way I see it, you're the most likely suspect. I mean, come on, didn't it ever cross your mind to kill me? So you went to see Billy and offed him before you realized you'd made a mistake, that you got the wrong guy. You shoot him in the back? Did you even get a look at him? Anyway, when I tell the police what I know, that *he* was blackmailing you, they'll put it together."

"If you think I did do it, you should be more scared of me right now."

"What are you gonna do?" He looked around. "Hit me with a beaker?"

"I didn't kill Billy," I said. "But I have a pretty good idea who did."

Stuart's eyebrows popped. "Oh?"

"Two people—a man and a woman—went into his garage. There was a whole lot of shouting. They took off. I went in after, and he was dead."

"Oh, so you were watching the place *again*? Didn't learn your lesson from the first time? That looks very bad for you. Very, what's the word, incriminating. The police'll be interested to know you were there."

He was wrong thinking I'd murdered Billy, but he was right that he could do me a world of harm if he told the police I'd had a reason to want him dead. One anonymous call would do it. And who would believe my story? About this mysterious Stuart who'd pretended to be Billy who'd been putting the squeeze on me for something I hadn't done. How crazy was all that going to sound?

But even before I could contemplate what fate might be awaiting me, I wanted to know why Stuart had gone after me in the first place.

"Why me?" I said. "Why pretend to be Billy? Why threaten to expose me for something I didn't do to you?"

"Not to me," he said. "To Billy."

"I never did anything to *him*."

Stuart nodded thoughtfully, then looked chagrined. "I might have gotten it wrong."

"Gotten *what* wrong?"

"There was this thing on the news," he said. "About that guy who was going to blow up the school. Billy's watching, and he goes, oh, that's *my* school, and he's looking at the TV and he's like, there's that perv who liked to touch my dick when I was on the wrestling team. I look and I see you, and then I found your picture with the team in Billy's yearbook and put it together."

"Who else was on the TV?" I said.

Stuart's brow wrinkled as he tried to recall. "Bunch of people standing around outside the school after the police got there. But I got a better look at you than anyone else." He shrugged. "Billy might have meant one of the others."

I tried to think back to what had been going on after the police arrived. It was all something of a blur. I was in shock. I remembered that at one point we moved outside, all of us, and that there was a TV news crew out on the street beyond the yellow police tape. I did remember one thing for sure. I remember Ronny was out there, being more or less interrogated by Trent about that goddamn door not shutting properly.

"Yeah, so, whatever," Stuart said. "That's why they put erasers on pencils, right? And, you know, you killing Billy, makes me think it all works out in the end."

"I told you. I didn't do it. It was those two people who came earlier." And even though I probably knew the answer, I had to ask: "Why'd you do it in the first place? Blackmail me?"

Stuart looked at me like I was an idiot. "Uh, the money? Fucking

Billy was making out like a bandit doing his thing. I had to find some action of my own."

"I could have known it wasn't you. Remembered Billy from school."

"Thought about that," Stuart said. "But it had been a few years, and we both kind of looked alike, you know. Lucy, Billy's wife? She called us two peas in a pod."

"*Boyle!*"

Herb, out in the hall, calling my name. He must have missed seeing us duck into this classroom and was hunting me down.

"Look," I said, trying to sound reasonable, "we're done, okay? I didn't do it, you had the wrong guy."

"I didn't get to the bad news yet," Stuart said. "Although, depending on how you look at it, it's good news, too."

I waited.

"I'm willing to, like you say, be done with all this. I just have one favor I'd like you to do for me before we go our separate ways."

"A favor."

He nodded.

"Nothing big. I need you to deliver something for me. Do an exchange. Not a big deal. A few minutes and you're done."

"You got something to return at Walmart?"

Stuart smiled. "That's funny. You're a funny guy, Mr. Boyle. No, what I need you to do is just a little more complicated."

My stomach began turning over. I had an inkling where this was going. That man and woman who came to Billy's. They'd been looking for something, and they appeared to have left empty-handed. Why did I have a feeling Stuart had it? And, given that he didn't care about my ten thousand dollars anymore, was willing to exchange it for a significant amount of money?

Why didn't he want to do the deal himself? I had a pretty good idea. He could end up dead.

"I don't want any part of this," I said. "Get yourself somebody else. Make your anonymous call to the police. I'll take my chances."

"I was afraid you might see it that way," Stuart said. He reached behind his back for something tucked under his jacket.

A gun.

"This change your mind?"

He took a step back so there was room to point it right at me.

"Christ, put that away," I said. Would he shoot me right here in the school? Maybe. I couldn't make a run for it. I'd have a bullet in my back before I got to the door.

"So. Willing to do a guy a solid?"

"Okay," I said. "Whatever you want."

"That's good, that's good. So we're going to walk out of here and head out the main door. My truck's out there. I'm gonna give you the keys"—and he dug into his pocket and handed them to me—"so you can do the driving."

I took them.

"And don't do anything crazy on the way, because I might just lose it and start firing, you know."

"Understood."

"Take out your phone and power it off."

Slowly, I reached into my jacket, took out the phone, and did as he asked. He motioned for me to hand it over, and I did.

"Okay," Stuart said. "Let's go."

He held the gun down at his side, tight to his leg, where it was not immediately visible. When we came out of the room, farther up the hallway people were starting to drift out of the library meeting.

"Quickly," Stuart whispered, nudging me toward the main entrance.

We both walked briskly. As we passed a trash bin, Stuart tossed my phone into it. We were outside in no time. It was fully dark now, the school parking lot illuminated by towering lampposts.

"That way," he said, giving me a shove, making a sniffing noise.

I saw his truck on the far side of the lot, the same one he'd been driving when he showed up at the end of my driveway . . . how many days ago? Time seemed to have lost all meaning lately.

Someone shouted, "There you are, you son of a bitch."

I glanced over my shoulder and saw Herb running across the parking lot. I stopped, turned around, and raised a hand.

"Go back, Herb."

He stopped about ten feet from me. He gave Stuart one quizzical glance, then looked back at me and said, "I guess you feel pretty clever, dumping that shit on me."

"Herb," I said calmly, "this is not the time. We can talk about this tomorrow."

"No, we can talk about this *now*," he said. "Okay, so maybe I poked the bear here, put an idea into that woman's head. But you had it coming. You screwed me over, and I warned you, I warned you I wouldn't take it."

"Man, you need to back off and get the fuck out of here," Stuart said, the gun still at his side.

"Who the hell are you?" Herb asked.

"Herb," I said one more time, "for your own good, I'm telling you to walk away now, and if you want to ream me out tomorrow, then by all means."

Now it was Stuart who was looking at Herb quizzically, as though he had seen him before.

"I know you?" Stuart asked.

And I thought: *He saw him on the news.*

"I never met you in my life," Herb snapped. "And I'm not talking to you."

"Yeah, well, we're not talking to you anymore, either," Stuart said. Then he raised his weapon and shot Herb in the neck.

FORTY-NINE

"**R**ichard's in trouble," Bonnie told her sister. "Or, at least, he was while Billy Finster was still alive. Now, honestly, we don't know what to think."

"What kind of trouble?"

Bonnie told Marta about the blackmail scheme. How Billy must have seen Richard on the news following the LeDrew incident and decided to victimize him.

"And before you ask, it's not true," Bonnie said. "Richard never molested anyone. Not Billy, not anybody else."

"But he was prepared to pay him off anyway," Marta said evenly.

"I know. Let's say someone said you took money under the table to look the other way when some robbery or something was going down. There wouldn't have to be anything to it, but there'd still be an internal affairs investigation. They'd turn your whole life upside down, wouldn't they?"

Marta slowly nodded. "Maybe."

"You don't look convinced."

Marta took a long breath. "I know a teacher can be the victim of a bogus accusation just as easily as a police officer can, I'll grant you that. But, Bonnie, I've seen so many cases where the wife had no

274

idea. I'm not saying I believe he did it. I'm saying that your certainty isn't enough for me."

Bonnie leaned back in her chair, putting some distance between herself and her sister, and hugged herself, putting up a shield. "The only way this is going to work, the only way I tell you any more of this, is if you believe what I'm saying about Richard." She paused. "I know. That's it. End of story."

Marta nodded slowly. After a few seconds, she said, "Okay. I believe."

Bonnie unwrapped her arms from around herself and told Marta as much as she could remember of what Richard had told her. About the initial approach, attempting to sell the boat to the neighbor, scoping out where Billy lived and getting hit in the head for his trouble. And how Richard must have thought, at least briefly, that Bonnie herself had had something to do with the man's death, which was why he'd covered for her, said he'd been in her car the night before, parked near the Finster house.

"But it was you," Marta said.

Then Bonnie told her what had happened when she'd confronted Billy, how he had pointed a gun at her and left her shaken.

"Jesus," Marta said. She looked stunned, and more than a little angry with her sister. "Just how stupid are you? The fuck were you thinking?"

"You want to hear the story or chew me out?"

Marta went quiet.

"Anyway, when I told him to back off, that Richard wasn't paying up, that we weren't going to be blackmailed, he acted like he didn't have any idea what I was talking about." Bonnie paused. "He was pretty convincing. If I hadn't known better, I'd have believed him."

Marta was looking into her cup of now-cold coffee, trying to make sense of it. She had eaten one biscotti and was thinking of reaching for another.

"Why deny it?" she asked.

"I don't know," Bonnie said. "There's something else."

Marta raised her head, a look on her face that said nothing would surprise her now.

"Richard did lie, saying it was him watching the house and not me. But the truth is, he *was* there earlier that evening, in addition to being there in the afternoon. And he thinks he saw who killed Billy Finster."

"This just gets better and better."

She told Marta about the man and woman showing up in the black car. The shouting in the garage. The searching of the house.

Marta perked up. "A man and a woman? In a black car?" Bonnie nodded. "What kind of car? An Audi, by any chance?"

"I don't know," Bonnie said. "I don't know if Richard noticed that or not."

"A couple in a black car have been looking for Billy's wife," Marta said. "The woman's the one who got the drop on me Saturday night." She thought for another moment and said, "It's time."

"Time?"

"I have to talk to him."

Bonnie nodded resignedly. "He didn't want me to tell you anything. But . . . but we can't handle this alone. It's out of control." She wiped a tear from her cheek and put a hand on Marta's and squeezed. "Promise me you won't do anything to Richard for not telling you all about this from the beginning. Promise me that."

"I'll do my best," Marta said. "From everything you've told me, if this all checks out, I think the only thing we can accuse Richard of is being an idiot."

Bonnie almost laughed. "Thank you."

"Get him on the phone. I don't care if he's still in some meeting. I have to talk to him right now. If he's on the way back, I'll wait for him here."

"Okay, okay," Bonnie said.

While she got up and went to the front hall to get her cell phone from her purse, Marta retrieved her badge from the counter and clipped it back onto her belt. She was taking the coffee cups to the sink when Bonnie returned.

"He's not answering," she said, holding up the phone, her face grim. "It went straight to message."

Before Marta could respond, her own cell phone started to squawk. She snatched it from her jacket pocket and put it to her ear.

"Harper," she said. Her face turned dark. "Jesus Christ. On my way."

She ended the call and looked at her sister. "Someone's been shot. At Richard's school."

FIFTY

Before he'd left the motel, Stuart had made it very clear to Lucy what he wanted her to do.

Stay put.

Don't open the door, don't turn on your phone, don't make any calls from the motel line, don't talk to anybody, don't go out to get food. Watch TV and chill out.

Lucy got where he was coming from, but she felt like a prisoner. And this motel room of Stuart's was a shithole. The house she shared with Billy was no villa on the French Riviera, but it was a damn sight better than this place. There was a mousetrap under the desk and some roach bait in the corner. Lucy was used to a spotlessly clean workplace. The hospital cafeteria was checked for vermin and bugs on a weekly basis. They needed to send someone over here.

Stuart had said he had one important errand to run before doing the trade. Said something about having someone help him, someone to make the exchange less risky. Once he had that done, and had been back in touch with the dealers, he'd return for the case.

And when he came back after *that*, they'd be all set. They'd have their money and they could hit the road. Well, that was all just fine, Lucy thought, except for one small detail:

Stuart made her sick to her stomach.

If Stuart had always had a thing for her, she hadn't been mindful of the signs. He'd always been this dumbass friend of Billy's who hung around in the basement drinking beer and eating Cheetos and wiping his dusty orange fingers on the furniture. Looking back, maybe he liked to stand a little too close to her at times. Once or twice he'd dropped by when Billy wasn't there and, rather than take off, had hung around a little too long. A lot of times he'd be real quiet, just looking at her, which was almost creepier than if he'd tried to cop a feel or kiss her. He knew if he tried something like that she'd tell Billy, and God knows what Billy would have done to him.

But with Billy out of the picture, Stuart was changing.

How stupid had she been, coming here in the first place? She hadn't been thinking straight in the hours after finding Billy dead in the garage. She'd been in shock, wandering around without a plan.

Then she thought of Stuart.

He'd been pretty welcoming when she showed up. That seemed like a good thing initially, but now? Not so much.

Even if Stuart didn't make her skin crawl, fifty grand wouldn't last forever. What happened when the money ran out? How were they supposed to get jobs and support themselves if they couldn't use their real IDs? Were they supposed to get new identities? And how did one go about that, anyway?

Stuart was not someone who took the long view. He could only see as far as getting the money.

Lucy, on the other hand, while admitting to herself she was no criminal mastermind, either, could see the bigger picture. Okay, she did something wrong. She did something *illegal*. But she hadn't been working with a pair of drug dealers or taking payoffs. She hadn't cooked the stuff up herself in her own lab. She hadn't *killed* anybody. And she'd never been in any trouble with the police beyond a few parking tickets and a grass bust when she was sixteen, but no one was going to hold that against her.

Maybe she should walk out that door, turn herself in to the cops, and tell them everything she knew.

As bad as that sounded, it beat going on the run with Stuart Betz. Even if they actually *did* get away, there were certain benefits Stuart was going to expect. Here he was, fashioning himself as her knight in shining armor. He'd rescued her from the bad guys. What was his idea of a thank-you going to be? A handshake? A hand *something*, that was for sure. And a whole lot more.

Lucy felt a little queasy.

Maybe she was looking at this wrong. This was not an either/or situation. It wasn't a choice between running off with Stuart or turning herself in. What if there was a third option?

One where she walked out that door and went back to her life? And where Stuart was removed as a problem?

She was already working out a story for the police as to why she'd disappeared, and it had the added benefit of being true. She knew her husband was bringing fentanyl into the country and holding it for pickup. When he got killed, she was terrified she might be next, that she might be murdered because she knew too much.

Yeah, that had a nice ring to it.

She went back into the bathroom, pulled back the shower curtain, and looked at the carry-on bag. When Stuart returned, he'd grab the bag and head off to make his deal.

She grabbed the bag by the handle, wheeled it out of the bathroom, and hoisted it up onto the small dining table.

Looked at it.

And thought, *I already figured out how to open this once before.*

FIFTY-ONE

Richard

I was stunned. I could not believe what I was seeing.

Herb Willow dropped to the pavement like a bag of wet leaves. No protestations, no wild gyrations, no screams. Herb simply hit the ground after Stuart shot him.

My mouth hung open. I might have said something. Probably "Holy shit" or "Oh my God." Could have been any number of things. I honestly don't know. I said something, and I said it reflexively. I probably should have run. I probably should have tried to tackle Stuart, wrested the gun away from him.

Something.

But my feet were rooted to the asphalt. I was frozen in shock.

"We gotta go," Stuart said.

I blinked a couple of times, turned, and looked at him as if the words he'd spoken were in some language I didn't understand. I managed, at this point, to form a sentence.

"You fucking shot him," I said.

"You're driving, remember? Can you drive?"

I looked down at my right hand. There was a set of keys in them. Stuart grabbed me roughly by the arm, steered me over to the door of his truck, opened it, and shoved me in behind the wheel. If I'd been more familiar with the vehicle and known immediately where to insert the key, I'd have tried to start it and slam it into drive before Stuart had a chance to run around to the other side and open the passenger door. But I was disoriented. I looked at the keys in my hand, trying to figure out which was for the ignition, and once Stuart was sitting next to me he grabbed the keys from my hand and slid the correct one into the slot on the steering column.

"You think you can turn it, dick bag?" he asked.

I turned it. The engine rumbled to life.

"Don't forget your seat belt," Stuart said. "Can't be too careful."

I reached around for the belt and buckled up. I figured Stuart cared less about my safety and more about slowing me down if I tried to make a run for it.

The truck had a column-mounted shifter, a type I hadn't seen since I'd learned to drive on my father's Ford Galaxie. I pulled it back and down into drive and hit the gas. The truck had been left parked in such a way that I could pull out straight ahead. The windows were down, and as I headed to the street, Stuart pointing his gun at me, I could hear shouting in the background. Someone screaming that a teacher had been shot. Another calling out for 911.

Stuart hadn't told me which way to go once we hit the street, so I simply went right and kept on going.

"Hang a left at the light," he said, and wiped his nose with his sleeve. I didn't know whether he had a coke problem or just a runny nose.

I considered driving erratically, that doing so might catch the attention of a police car should we happen to encounter one. But Stuart had that gun aimed right at me, and it wouldn't take much for him to pull that trigger, so I steered that truck down the road like I was taking my driver's test.

"Yeah, here," he said as I moved into the left lane, put on the blinker, and made the turn. "You know where the Eastway Motel is?"

I did not, and shook my head in answer.

"So, you keep going this way, then a right at the third light, and it's up that way." He moved the gun to his left hand and went into his pocket with his right for a phone. He brought it up, tapped the screen, and put the phone to his ear. When someone answered, he said, "Yeah, hi, can you put me through to room two-nineteen?"

He waited. And waited. "Come on, pick up. *Pick up.* Pick up the fucking phone. Shit." He ended the call, lowered the cell, and said, more to himself than to me, "I guess I *did* tell her not to answer the phone." Stuart sighed. "Okay, not a problem." He put the phone back into his pocket and transferred the gun to his right hand.

We were almost to the third light. I slowed, put on the blinker again, made the turn. I could see the motel up ahead, on the right. I recognized it, had driven past it a thousand times here in Milford, one of those places that's always there that you never notice. The neon sign said EA TWAY MOT L, and as I turned into the lot, I quickly sized it up as a place where you might rent a room for an hour, or by the month, but nothing much in between. It was a two-story building, the second-floor units accessed by an exterior set of stairs and a long balcony-type walkway.

"Stop right here," Stuart said, indicating the middle of the lot. I could have pulled up closer to the building, between an old Volkswagen Beetle and a panel van, but then we wouldn't have had a view of the second-story units. "Keep the engine running and hit the horn a few times." He was looking up at the window to a specific unit, Room 219, I guessed.

I tapped the horn a couple of times while Stuart kept an eye on the drape-covered window of the room.

"Come on, come on," he said. "Come to the window. Hit the horn again."

I did. Someone pulled the drape back a few inches for a quick peek. Stuart waved his right hand wildly out his window and shouted: "Lucy!"

The drape was pulled open several more inches, then fell back into place. About ten seconds later, the door opened far enough for a woman to stick her head out. The lighting was dim and I couldn't be sure, but it looked like the woman who had left Billy Finster's house the first time I'd been watching it. What was she doing with Stuart?

"Lucy!" Stuart shouted again. He waved her toward him.

Lucy came outside, closed the door behind her, walked to the stairway and descended it, then crossed the parking lot until she was at the open passenger-door window.

"Hey," Stuart said to her.

Lucy looked small and afraid. "What's going on?" she asked. She saw me behind the wheel and said, "Who's this?"

"My new assistant," Stuart said.

"Why are you pointing a gun at him?"

"He's kind of a reluctant assistant. Look, everything's ready to go down. Get the case."

"I have to lug it down?" she asked. "You can't go up and get it?"

"I'm kinda busy, unless you want to stay here and keep a gun on this guy while I get the bag. But you have to be prepared to shoot him."

She looked at the gun and said, "I'm not touching that thing." She turned and walked away. She went up the stairs like someone climbing the scaffolding to be hanged.

"Billy's wife," I said.

"Yeah," Stuart said. "She's in kind of a rough patch right now. I'm helping her through it."

"How, exactly?"

"By providing for her future," Stuart snapped. "It's all good. And you get to be part of it."

I waited.

"I have something I have to deliver to these people, and in return they're going to give me enough money so Lucy and I can start this new life together." He smiled. "I've always really liked her. It's going to take her some time to warm up to me, I understand that, because she's just suffered a loss. So I'm going to give her a week or two. But by then we'll be on the beach in Boca Raton, or maybe we'll go out to L.A. or someplace like that." He nodded confidently. "It's all gonna be fine."

"You're giving the bag to those people who came to see Billy last night."

"I'm not an idiot. I don't trust them. I give them the bag, they're supposed to give me the money. But I'm thinking, what if they don't? What if they pull some kind of double cross? If it was just me with the bag, on my own, I couldn't do a very good job of defending myself. So you'll handle the bag, do the delivery, and I'll be ready with this"—he waved the gun around—"in case they try something."

There were a hundred ways this could go wrong. And I couldn't think of a single way I was going to get out of this alive.

Run. Just run.

As if reading my mind, Stuart said, "I know where you live. You bail on me, I go to your house. You've got a wife, and a kid, too, right? You take off, and I'm heading straight there. You get me?"

"I get you," I said.

Lucy had gone back into the motel room. Seconds later she emerged with a wheeled carry-on bag, dragging it behind her to the stairs.

"What's in the bag?" I asked.

"I guess you'd call it pain medication," Stuart said. "From south of the border. Got themselves a little lab down there. Probably more like a fucking factory. They ship finished product up by plane. Billy would take it off, hold it for pickup."

"You took the bag from Billy?"

"He didn't have much say in the matter," Stuart said. "I go out for food, come back, the fucker's dead on the floor. Was pretty shook up, didn't stay long, but I have a nose for an opportunity, you know? The bag was there and I knew what was in it and that it was worth a fortune, so, you know."

"You took it."

"I took it, yeah. Wasn't like Billy was going to care, and I knew his associates would pay to get it back."

Lucy had the bag halfway down the stairs. Unable to wheel it, she was moving it one step at a time, holding it by the top handle.

"Billy was already dead, and the bag was there," I said, more to myself than to Stuart. "And you left with it."

"Could she *be* any slower?" Stuart said, watching Lucy descend the stairs.

Something wasn't tracking. When I was watching the house, and those two showed up, the bag wasn't there, so Billy had to already be dead. Shouts of "Where is it?" had been between themselves, not between them and Billy.

If Stuart was to be believed, someone else had visited the garage before either he or the couple in the black car had gotten there, and that person—or persons—had killed Billy. I could think of only one other person who'd been there that evening.

Bonnie.

No, couldn't be Bonnie. She'd told me what had happened, and I believed her.

Maybe the answer was coming our way. Lucy had reached the bottom of the stairs and went back to wheeling, instead of carrying, the bag. She pulled it as far as the truck's passenger door.

"Here you go," she said. "I don't think I can lift it into the back." She tilted her head toward the pickup's empty bed.

"Can't go back there," he said derisively. "Go over some railroad tracks and it'll fly out." He opened the door and slid out, keeping the gun on me. There was some space between the seat and the back of the cab. Stuart tipped the seat forward, grabbed the bag, and stowed it.

He moved in to give Lucy a quick kiss, but she pulled back, like you might if someone with the Ebola virus tried to embrace you.

"Okay, not pushin' it," Stuart said. "All in good time."

He got into the truck and slammed the door shut. He smiled at Lucy and said, "See ya later, babe."

"Goodbye, Stuart," she said.

FIFTY-TWO

Marta didn't want to have to wait for Bonnie, but there was no way she could hop into her unmarked car and go racing off down the street, siren wailing and lights flashing, without her. She waited while Bonnie ran next door to the neighbors' house and told a startled Jill at the door that she needed her to watch Rachel.

"There's been a shooting at the school!" she said breathlessly, and as she ran to get into the front seat of Marta's cruiser, Jill beelining it for Bonnie's house, she added, "Don't tell Rachel!"

Marta had the car in gear before Bonnie had the door closed.

"It's him, oh God, I know it's him," Bonnie said.

Marta, keeping her voice as calm as possible, said, "We don't know, Bonnie. We don't know anything yet."

"He didn't answer his phone!"

"He might not be able to get to it," Bonnie said. "He could have muted it."

A block away from Lodge High School they saw the kaleidoscope of flashing lights. Several marked cruisers and ambulances had swarmed the area. Marta had taken the call only eight minutes earlier, but the shooting itself must have occurred sometime within the last half hour. There would have been initial calls—probably several—to 911, then cars would have been dispatched to the scene, and as soon as word got back that someone had been shot, the call had gone out to Marta.

She could think of nothing comforting to say to her sister. The truth was, she expected the worst. She didn't quite have a handle on the extent of the mess in which Richard was entangled, but these kinds of things often got worse before they got better.

The cruiser screeched to a halt by one of the marked cruisers. As Marta got out she said to Bonnie, "Stay here!"

She ran to the center of the school parking lot, illuminated by tall fixtures overhead, where the attention was focused. She pushed her way through a small crowd of civilians, yelling at them to "Get back!" as she did so, until the scene opened up for her. There were three uniformed officers there, two men and one woman, holding out their arms so no one would get too close to the body on the ground.

Marta hadn't even had a second to take a close look at who it was when she heard a scream behind her.

It was Bonnie.

"Oh God, no!" she said, and before she could get any closer, Marta threw her arms around her to hold her back. Bonnie was able to look over her shoulder, see the dead man splayed out on his back on the pavement.

"It's not him," Bonnie whispered into her sister's ear. "It's not Richard."

But that revelation did nothing to stop Bonnie from shaking. Marta released her hold on her and took a closer look at the dead man. She could see that Bonnie was right, that it was obvious that this man, even with his neck blown away and his head and chest covered in blood, was not her brother-in-law. This was an older man, heavier set. And Marta was even thinking she knew who he was, that she'd spoken with him the day Mark LeDrew came to the school.

"Where is he?" Bonnie asked. "Where's Richard?"

It was a good question. He certainly wasn't among the people who had gathered here.

"Richard!" Bonnie cried out. "Richard!"

She worked her way back through the crowd and started running for the school, no doubt hoping she'd find her husband there, Marta thought. *God, what a clusterfuck.*

She turned to the woman wearing a Milford police uniform. "What happened here?"

The cop said, "People heard a shot about twenty-five minutes ago."

"One shot?"

The cop nodded. "A meeting had just ended and some of the people were coming out to their cars. This lady"—and she pointed to one woman standing over by a van—"saw something."

Marta broke away and approached the woman, who was standing with her back to the van, wringing a tissue in her hand, her fingers shaking.

"Ma'am?" Marta said. "I'm Detective Harper. What's your name?"

"Violet. Violet Kanin."

"What did you see, Mrs. Kanin?"

"I was . . . I was coming out the main door over there, and I . . . this man came into the meeting at the end, and Mr. Boyle seemed very upset by it."

"What man was this?"

"The one who shot Mr. Willow."

"Herb Willow. A teacher."

The woman nodded. "He was in the meeting tonight."

"Meeting?"

"About the book."

"Book? What book?"

"*The Road.* It's by Cormac Mc—"

"Let's go back. This man who came into the meeting late. Mr. Boyle wasn't happy to see him?"

"No."

"Did Mr. Boyle say his name?"

"No, I don't think so. He didn't say anything. He looked stunned."

"Describe the man."

"He was . . . he was in his twenties or thirties. He was a white man, a little heavy. Kind of a round face. He had on a sweatshirt, I think, with some writing on it or a picture."

"Do you remember what that was?"

"There were *B*s."

"Bees? Like bumblebees?"

"No, the letter. Two of them. Boston something."

"Boston Bruins?"

"I think so."

"Okay. Tell me what happened after he came into the room."

"They went out into the hall together to talk. I thought maybe Mr. Boyle would come back, but after a few minutes when he didn't we figured the meeting was over, like, it was a funny way to end it, just walking out. And so I was going out to my car and Mr. Willow was talking or arguing with Mr. Boyle and this man and then the other man . . . he . . ."

Marta wanted to be patient, to help this woman get her story out her own way, but she needed to know things. *Right now.*

"Mrs. Kanin, what did the man do?"

"He pointed the gun at Mr. Willow and he shot him. Just like that. Like it was nothing. And Mr. Willow fell and, oh my God, I can't believe what is happening here. First that boy who was going to blow up the school, and now—"

"What happened then? After Mr. Willow was shot."

"They got in the truck."

"This man and Mr. Boyle?"

"That's right."

"They just got in the truck and drove off? Who was driving?"

"Mr. Boyle, I think. The other man, he was pointing his gun at him."

"Describe the truck."

"It . . . it was a pickup truck."

"Color?"

"Uh, white, I think. But I guess it could have been gray. But I think it was white. And it had rust on it."

"Was there a cover on the back?"

"A what?"

"Was there a cover on the bed part of the pickup? Or was it open, uncovered?"

"The last thing. There was no cover."

"Did you notice a license plate?"

The woman shook her head. "I'm sorry."

"No, that's fine, you did good," Marta said, and placed her hand briefly on the woman's arm. "You stay right here, okay? Because we're going to need to talk to you some more."

Marta ran back to the closest police car and got on the radio to call in descriptions of the car, Herb Willow's shooter, and last but not least, her brother-in-law.

FIFTY-THREE

Lucy went back up to the motel room, glancing back only once to see Stuart and his so-called "new assistant" drive out of the parking lot in Stuart's pickup. Once she was in the room, she closed the door behind her, leaned up against it, and let out a long sigh of relief.

There were ways it could have gone wrong. Stuart might have wanted to open up the bag before they left, but as far as she knew, he didn't have a key to the small lock that joined the zippers together. And when he lifted it into the back of the truck, he hadn't noticed that it weighed any different. She'd tried to get it as close as possible.

Now she needed to get out of here. There was one more errand to run, and then she'd lie low for a while. A few hours at the most. Then she'd go to the police. She had her story all worked out. Might need some tweaking, depending on how things went. A bit of improvising.

The way Lucy saw it, she had four big problems that were, in no particular order, these: the drug dealers, Stuart, Digby, and the police.

The first two she was hoping would be resolved shortly, one way or another.

Then Digby.

Then the police.

While Stuart was out, she'd opened the bag using the technique she'd learned from YouTube, dumped out the contents, and stuffed all but two of the little packages into two pillowcases. She knotted the tops of them and tossed both into the closet, where they would be easy enough to find later for anyone who went looking.

Lucy didn't have anything of her own to pack. She'd arrived with nothing. But she was going to take something of Stuart's with her. In the cheap dresser across from the bed, in one of the warped drawers that she had struggled to open, she had found a dark green hoodie. She gave it a sniff when she pulled it out, but it hardly mattered that he'd probably never washed it. She pulled it on, brought the hood up over her head, and had a look at herself in the mirror. Adjusted it so that it covered up more of her face.

"That'll have to do," she said to herself.

She stuffed into the right pocket of the hoodie the two packages she had set aside, then grabbed her car keys and left the room, pulling the door tight as she left. Her Kia was tucked away behind the motel and she didn't see that she had any choice but to drive it. She didn't have enough cash for a cab and she couldn't use her phone to order an Uber. All Lucy could do was cross her fingers that no one would spot the car on her way to the hospital in nearby Bridgeport.

She didn't worry about pulling the hood up over her head while she drove. If she got stopped, it would be because someone spotted the car. But once she was close to the hospital, she parked several blocks away, and shrouded her head and face the moment she was out of the vehicle.

She had to be in and out fast.

Lucy walked in through the main entrance at a steady pace, like one of hundreds of people who came through those doors every day for appointments or to visit sick relatives. Strolled past the main desk, hoodie up, limiting her own field of vision to what was right in front of her.

Instead of heading to the bank of elevators that serviced the upper floors and patient rooms, she pushed open a door to a stairwell that led down to the bowels of the building. Utility rooms, generators, furnace and air-conditioning units, the laundry.

Locker room.

Digby worked a lot of nights, so there was a good chance he was in the building somewhere. She hoped he was midway through a shift. He'd normally hit the locker room at the beginning or end. Employee lockers lined all four walls of the room and two further banks of them were in the center. She knew where Digby's was. And she had a key, because Digby was dumber than a jar of tongue depressors and had given her a copy. The few times she'd sold him some fentanyl, he had paid her and asked her to slip the stuff into his locker later.

Which was just what she was going to do now.

A freebie.

She glanced furtively about the room to make sure she was alone and opened the locker. A pair of shoes at the bottom, a jacket on the hook, as well as a full change of clothes, including socks, a pair of jeans, and a polo shirt, on the top shelf. Some toiletry items. Soap, shampoo, a shaving kit.

Lucy took the two packages from her pocket, went on her tiptoes, and tucked them at the back of the top shelf, beyond the clothes. High enough, she believed, that even if Digby were to remove everything that was up there, the packages would go unnoticed.

She closed the door and was about to lock it when a thought occurred to her. She opened the door and dug through the pockets of the jacket. First the side ones, where she found his car keys. She had no use for them. Then she tried the inside pocket, felt something crinkly, and smiled.

Money.

She pulled out a twenty, a five, and three ones.

Lucy was fucking starving. Once she got the hell out of here, she was going to get herself something to eat.

And wait to see what happened.

FIFTY-FOUR

Richard

"The meet's all set up," Stuart said. "Called them before I went looking for you. Drove by your house earlier, and when I didn't see your car I was hoping I'd find you there."

I said nothing. He'd tell me what I needed to know sooner or later. I was still at the wheel of this shitbox truck.

"You know Walnut Beach?" he asked.

"Yeah."

"Down by a senior citizens residence on Viscount," he said. "Had an aunt who used to live there. There's a parking lot, kind of wide-open, but it won't be busy late at night. You can see who's coming and going."

"Right."

"I set it up for"—and he stopped to look at his watch—"twenty minutes from now. We get there, like, ten minutes before them, we'll be ready."

"And what are they giving you again, in return for the bag?"

"Fifty."

"Fifty thousand," I said. "Nice jump up from the ten you wanted from me."

Stuart smiled. "You're a fucking teacher. I'm a reasonable man."

Since I knew where we were going, I didn't need any more directions from him. There wasn't a second that went by when I wasn't thinking about some way out of this. I glanced over regularly to see whether the gun was trained on me, and Stuart was very attentive in this regard. I thought about hitting the brakes suddenly, throwing him forward, grabbing his head, and smashing it into the dash, knocking him out, the kind of stunt you'd see a Jack Ryan or a Jack Reacher—one of those Jacks—do in a movie. But this was no movie. I could end up with a bullet in my gut if I tried something like that.

I still wondered about jumping from the truck while it was moving. But, again, that was the kind of thing you could do in the movies and not get a scratch. I figured I'd end up run over by the back wheels. And with the seat belt on, the moment I went to unfasten it, Stuart could pull that trigger.

I kept waiting for an opportunity that might never come.

What worried me less was his threat to go after my family. If I could get away, the first thing I'd do is notify the police, give them my address and tell them to get there ASAP.

We were heading south on Viscount Drive, Long Island Sound shimmering in the moonlight ahead of us. I slowed as I reached the end of the street and made a right into a parking lot that, on a summer day, would be filled with cars as people hit the nearby beach.

Bonnie and Rachel and I had been down here many times. We'd bring towels and an umbrella and some sand toys for Rachel and pretend we were in Florida. Not quite as tropical, and not a palm tree in sight, but there wasn't a twelve-hour drive to get here, either. Sometimes we'd walk out to the end of the Albert Munroe Pier, which extended some three hundred feet out into the Sound and afforded a view of Charles Island, a small state-owned bird sanctuary that was only a few hundred yards out there, and could be walked out to on a sandbar during low tide. None of that, of course, was visible at this time of night.

"Okay, okay, let's just drive around, make sure they haven't tried to pull a fast one and get here ahead of us," he said.

"I know the car," I told him. "That is, unless they've ditched it and are in a different one. Last I saw them they were in a black Audi."

"Don't see anything like that," Stuart said.

He was right. There were maybe five cars scattered across a lot that would hold one hundred or two hundred vehicles. Stuart pointed.

"Let's settle in up at the far end there. At the edge. Back into a spot."

I did as I was told. Once the truck was in position and we had a good view of anyone who might arrive, I had a question.

"What's to keep these people from taking your bag, giving you nothing in return, and shooting you in the head?"

Stuart smiled, like he had all the angles covered. "Thought we went over that. That's why you're here. You deliver the bag and I hang back by the truck. They try something dumb, I start shooting."

And I'd get caught in the cross fire. "Have you even met these people before? I mean, when I walk out there and hand over the bag, are they going to think I'm you?"

Stuart thought on that. "They might. I never met them. Billy didn't want me around when Psycho Bitch and Butthead did their pickups."

Their nicknames did nothing to allay my fears, especially that first one.

"You don't really think I killed Billy," I said.

He shrugged. "I don't think you've got it in you."

"So you think it's these drug dealers."

"Would make sense," Stuart said.

"Then why didn't they take the stuff with them?"

"Huh?"

"You say you came back with food and Billy was dead. If they did it, why'd they leave the bag there? Why'd they leave it for you to take?"

Stuart went very quiet for a moment.

"Maybe . . . maybe they killed him, and figured the shit wasn't going anywhere, and they were going to come back later and get it."

"Why?" I asked, pressing him. "What would they be thinking? Okay, we just killed this guy, let's grab a drink, and then we'll come back? Who'd be that stupid?"

Stuart was looking annoyed. "What fucking difference does it make?"

"I don't know. Maybe it might be kind of important to you, being Billy's friend and all."

It was possible Stuart was right. What fucking difference did it make? Still, something seemed wrong.

"Headlights," Stuart said.

There was a car coming down Viscount. It slowed as it reached the end of the street, then turned into the lot.

A black four-door Audi.

"That's them," I said.

FIFTY-FIVE

Bonnie was running through the halls of Lodge High, calling out her husband's name. She'd been to his homeroom and the library and was heading to the office when she encountered Trent running toward her from the other direction.

"Have you seen him?" she asked, nearly collapsing into his arms. "He's not in his room, he's not anywhere."

He put a hand on each of her shoulders to steady her. "I was just outside, talking to the police, to your sister. She said he's gone."

"Oh God, tell me they don't think Richard had anything—"

"No, no, he's with some man who's—it sounds like this man has taken him hostage or something, and that he's the one who shot Herb."

"Hostage?"

"They left in the man's truck. Richard driving."

"What is happening? Why would someone—I don't understand."

"Neither do I. I hung in for part of the parents' meeting and it seemed to be going well. No shouting, no crazy accusations. Something must have happened after I slipped out. I came back to my office and I heard the shot."

Trent swallowed hard, looking almost as shaken as Bonnie. "I couldn't believe it was happening again. Another school attack."

Bonnie noticed Trent was holding his hand over the pocket of his jacket. There was something large and bulky there that he didn't want falling out.

"What's that?" Bonnie asked.

"It's nothing," he said.

"Trent."

He lowered his eyes, looking as though he'd been caught stealing from a candy jar. He pulled the butt end of a gun from the pocket, just enough so Bonnie could see what it was. It was, he told her, the one he admitted, after the LeDrew incident, to keeping locked up in the bottom drawer of his office desk.

Bonnie recoiled when she saw it, as though the weapon's very presence signaled the gravity of the situation.

"Only if there's an emergency," Trent said. "I'd really rather not use it at all, but when I heard the shot—"

"Fine, whatever. We have to find Richard, we have to figure out where—"

"Okay, okay," Trent said. "Let's go see if they know anything more."

Together they went back outside, where Marta and officers in uniform were busily asking people for details of anything they might have seen. When Marta saw Bonnie, she ran over to her.

"We've got everyone looking for the truck," she said. "We're going to find him."

"Why would someone take him?"

Marta shook her head. "I don't know any more than you right now. Go home. The second I know anything, I'll call you. I can find an officer to take you back—"

"I can take her," Trent said.

"Great," Marta said. She brought her sister in for a fast hug, then looked her in the eye and said, "I'm on this."

Bonnie nodded tearfully, then accompanied Trent to his car. He opened the door for her, ran around and got behind the wheel.

"Your sister's got everyone working this," he told her, trying to find something reassuring to say.

"We're not going home," Bonnie said.

"Where—"

"We're going to drive around. We might see them. We might see the truck."

"Bonnie, we don't even know what kind of truck it is, or the plate number, or—"

"Then take me home and I'll drive around myself."

Trent waited a moment, sighed, and said, "Okay." He keyed the ignition and drove out of the school lot. "Where do you want to go first?"

"I have no idea. Just drive."

"Got it."

Trent said he'd already called his wife to let her know he was okay. News spread quickly and he needed to let her know right away that nothing had happened to him. But now that he was going to be roaming Milford with Bonnie for an undetermined amount of time, he wanted to give her another heads-up.

"Of course," Melanie said, her voice coming out of the car's speaker through the Bluetooth feature. "Bonnie, you're there?"

"I'm here, Melanie."

"I'm so sorry. This is so awful. Let me know when you find Richard."

"Sure," Bonnie said, her voice close to breaking.

Trent, glancing at Bonnie, said, "Gotta go, Mel. We'll be in touch."

They drove in silence for a moment, Bonnie's eyes searching for pickup trucks, trying to make out who was behind the wheel when one passed. "Why don't we take a spin through the downtown," Trent said.

They explored Milford's business district, then drove along Bridgeport Avenue, past the various car dealerships and the Taco Bell and the McDonald's.

301

Neither of them had spoken for at least five minutes when Bonnie said, "I know what you're thinking."

Trent waited.

"You're thinking this is a waste of time. They could be anywhere."

"I wasn't thinking that," he said. "I'm prepared to keep driving around as long as you want, Bonnie. And if you hear from Marta, we're already on the road, we can be wherever we have to be even sooner."

Bonnie's chin quivered. "Thank you." She paused, then said, "Rachel."

"Sorry?"

"What must she be thinking? I ran out of the house, got the neighbors to watch her. If they're watching the news, if they see something online—"

"Why don't you call?"

"I don't even know their number."

"Call your house. You still have a landline?"

Bonnie nodded, thought about what to do, got out her phone, and tapped the screen. Seconds later, someone picked up.

"Mom?" said Rachel.

Just one word, but Bonnie could hear the anxiety in the little girl's voice.

"Hey, sweetie. Who's there with you?"

"The next-door lady."

"Can you put her on, please?"

There was the sound of the receiver being fumbled, then a woman's voice. "Bonnie?"

"Jill, yes, it's me. Does Rachel know what's happened? Do *you* know what's happened?"

"I don't. I've just been trying to get Rachel to go to bed."

"Okay, well, don't let her look at the news on TV or a phone or anything. Something bad happened at the school and we can't find Richard."

"Oh, Bonnie, what's—"

"I can't explain now. Can you stay?"

"As long as necessary. I can sleep over. Jack can bring me what I need."

"Thank you, Jill. Say goodbye to Rachel for me."

She got off the phone hurriedly, fearing Rachel might grab the phone from Jill before she could hang up.

"I can't talk to her," Bonnie whispered. "I wouldn't know what to say."

FIFTY-SIX

Richard

"Flash your lights," Stuart said.

I turned the pickup's headlights on for one second, then off. The driver of the black Audi popped his high beams for a moment in return. The car drove slowly into the lot, coming to a stop, angling across two spots, about three car lengths away from us. The light from a phone dimly lit the interior of the Audi by the steering wheel, as if the driver was making a call or sending a text.

"Oh shit," Stuart said. "That's probably for me."

He got out a phone and powered it on. I was guessing it was a phone he was afraid could be tracked, so he'd been leaving it off whenever he wasn't using it.

"Come on come on come on," he said to the phone, waiting for it to be active. Once it was, he waved it in the window, a signal to the other driver.

The phone rang.

"Yeah," Stuart said, hitting the speaker icon immediately.

"We're ready," a woman said.

"Same here. You got the money?"

"Do you have what's ours?"

"Of course, what the fuck? Yes. So I'm gonna send someone over with it."

"We want to deal with you. Who's this other person?"

"Just a friend," Stuart said, and gave me a smile, like we were pals. "He's not a cop or anything, if that's what you're thinking. I'm not stupid."

"No, of course not," the woman said.

"Show me the money," Stuart said.

"Can't very well show it to you from here."

"Hold it up or whatever."

"A moment."

We could see some movement in the car. Then the passenger door opened and a man stepped out.

"That'd be Gerhard," Stuart said. "And the woman is Andrea. Billy told me their names."

Gerhard was holding a backpack by one of the shoulder straps. He held it up high so we could see it.

"Okay, that's good. He can just stay there," Stuart said. "Give us a minute on this end. Sending him over shortly."

Stuart ended the call, dropped the phone onto the seat between us. It was still glowing.

"I don't trust those two," he said. "I'll get the bag. Don't try running off. If I don't shoot you, they probably will."

I said nothing. My eyes kept going to the phone.

"Give me the key," Stuart said. I removed the key from the ignition and put it into his hand. He got out of the truck. Once he had his feet on the pavement, he folded the seat forward so he could drag out the carry-on bag.

I had been waiting for an opportunity. This was as good as it was going to get. I picked up the phone with my right hand and immediately moved the small switch on the side down, muting it. I opened up the messages app.

"Fucking thing is really jammed in here," Stuart said.

I tapped the icon in the upper right corner to send a text. Where it said "To" I quickly tapped in Bonnie's phone number.

Stuart hauled out the bag, set it on the pavement, and pushed the seat back into position. I was about to type out a message, but stopped, rested my hand casually over the phone. Stuart closed the passenger door, extended the handle on the top of the bag, and started to wheel it around to my side. While he was passing the truck's front end, I moved my thumb across the miniature keyboard as quickly as I could. Hit send. Took one fast glance at what I had texted.

WALNT BEAHC.

Two typos, but clear enough. I turned the phone over onto the seat as Stuart reached my side of the truck and opened the door.

"You're on," he said, the gun in his left hand, the suitcase handle gripped by his right.

I undid my seat belt and slid out of the truck. I took the case from him and took a step away from the vehicle. Stuart moved the gun to his right hand, positioned himself behind the door, using it like a shield, and rested his right arm on the sill of the lowered window.

"Away you go," he said.

I walked slowly toward the Audi. The driver's door opened and Andrea got out. She and her partner, still holding the backpack, met at the front of the car and waited for me to get there.

When I was no more than six feet away, I stopped, wheeled the bag around to stand in front of me, and said, "Hey."

"Hey," Andrea said.

"So here it is." I let go of the handle and held out my hand, expecting Gerhard to give me the backpack.

"Not so fast," the woman said.

"It's here," I said. "It's all here. Look, I'm not a part of this. That asshole basically kidnapped me to help him do this. Just give me the backpack and let us get the hell out of here."

Gerhard handed the backpack to Andrea, grabbed the case by the handle, and set it on its side on the pavement. He got down on his haunches, took a key from his pocket to undo the lock that held the two zippers together.

Fine, I thought. *See that it's all there, give us the backpack, and let's get the hell out of here.*

He undid the lock, pocketed it and the key, and then slowly drew back the two zippers so he could flip open the top of the bag. I had a view of the contents that was almost as good as his, lit by one of the parking lot lamps.

Gerhard froze.

I didn't know what was supposed to be in there or how it was supposed to be packaged, but it seemed obvious from his reaction that this was not what he was expecting to find.

"What the fuck?" he said under his breath.

He started pulling things out of the bag. A bottle of shampoo, a pair of shoes, some wadded-up clothes. The more items he pulled out, the farther he tossed them, getting angrier and angrier, shouting, "Fuck!" and "Cocksucker!"

I took one quick look back at Stuart to see whether he was aware that something was amiss. He had stepped out from behind the driver's door, had a puzzled look on his face.

"Is there a problem?" he called out.

Andrea was looking over her partner's shoulder to see what had so upset him. She was grim-faced as he stood and gave the bag a good kick with his right foot.

I'm not sure when she got her hand on a gun, or what pocket she pulled it from. But it was there now, and it was pointed straight at me.

This was not good. This was not good at all.

FIFTY-SEVEN

Trent and Bonnie continued to drive aimlessly around Milford.

"I'm sorry," Bonnie said. "This is starting to seem pointless."

"It's okay. I don't mind. You never know. We might get lucky, see something."

Bonnie slowly shook her head in dismay. "I just don't—"

The sound of an incoming text stopped her midsentence. Bonnie looked down, the phone already in her hand in case she received a call or message from her sister.

"What is it?" Trent asked.

"What the . . ."

"What?" Trent asked.

She raised the phone up briefly so he could see the screen. There was a number at the top, and then a text of just two words.

"Who's it from?" he said.

"I don't know."

"What's it say?" He hadn't been able to make out the message when Bonnie had flashed the screen at him.

She said, "There's typos, but I think it's meant to say Walnut Beach."

"Walnut Beach?"

Bonnie looked at him and nodded. "I know where that is."

"Me, too," he said, taking his foot off the gas and letting the car slow.

"It's him," she said. "It has to be Richard. He's sending a message. Has to be. *Has* to be Richard."

Trent nodded furiously. "That'd be my bet, too."

He brought the car to a stop, glanced in his side mirror, saw no car coming, and did a U-turn, tires squealing. Once the car was pointed in the right direction, he floored it.

"Call your sister," he said.

Bonnie was already on it. Marta answered on the second ring.

"Walnut Beach!" she shouted.

"What?" Marta said.

"We think we know where he is! Walnut Beach!"

Marta said, "How do you—"

"A text! I got a text!"

"From Richard?"

"Not his phone. But I bet it's him!"

"Okay, wherever you are, stay put and—"

"We're going there now."

"No, Bonnie, no, let us—"

"I'll text him back, tell him we're coming!"

"No!" Marta shouted. "If it's Richard, he must have done it secretly. If you send a text back—"

"Okay, okay, I won't," Bonnie said. "Trent and I are on our way!"

"Do *not* go—"

Bonnie ended the call.

FIFTY-EIGHT

Richard

"**I** do not know *anything* about this," I said, raising my hands to shoulder level, trying to appear nonthreatening with that gun being pointed at me by Andrea.

"What the fuck is this?" Gerhard asked.

"I'm telling you, I don't know." I pointed a thumb behind me. "Ask him. Ask Stuart. This is his deal. I'm just a bag boy."

"Hey, dipshit!" the woman shouted at Stuart. "The hell is this?"

"What are you talking about?" Stuart said.

"Come and see for yourself," Gerhard said.

Stuart slowly approached, the gun at his side. He scanned the items that had been tossed from the bag.

"Those are my shoes," he said disbelievingly. "That's my shampoo. That's . . . that's all my stuff. It's all stuff from my place." He looked at me, as if somehow I would have the answer, then at the woman. "I don't understand."

"I understand," Andrea said. "You tried to fuck us over."

"No, no, that's not true," Stuart said. "Someone's playing a trick here."

"Yup," Gerhard said. "I'm looking right at the trickster."

Stuart shook his head. "No, it's— Shit. It's *Lucy*. It's got to be Lucy. Goddamn it. I don't know how . . . she wouldn't have a key. I don't have a key. Maybe she switched bags." He took a moment, trying to puzzle it out, licked his lips. "Billy said something . . . something about how she could open a bag and—"

"Where is she?" Gerhard asked.

"She's . . . she's at my place," Stuart said, bewildered. "Look, I'll go back. This is a minor hiccup. I'll find her. I'll find her and get your stuff. All of it." He forced a laugh. "Just a bump in the road, is all. I can get this all sorted out fast."

I had my own doubts. If Lucy had helped herself to the contents of that carry-on bag, what were the odds she was still hanging around, waiting for Stuart to return? I could tell from Andrea's dubious expression she was thinking the same.

"But first," Stuart said, "I want to make sure you guys are keeping your end of the bargain, so I want to see the money."

The man laughed. "You bring us Reeboks and Head & Shoulders and you want to know whether we're ripping *you* off?"

Stuart forced a chuckled. "Just being thorough."

"Yeah, thorough," Andrea said. "It might be better if *we* had a word with Lucy. Where would we find her, if she hasn't already taken a flight to Bolivia?"

"I got a place at the Eastway. The Eastway Motel. Room two-nineteen. It's on the second floor. There's stairs up and—"

"I know the Eastway," Gerhard said. He glanced at his partner. "How do you want to handle this?"

"Like this," she said as she raised the gun that had been in her hand all this time and shot Stuart in the chest. The gun, even though it appeared to be equipped with one of those silencer attachments, still made a hell of a racket, and I jumped.

Stuart staggered backward a couple of feet and looked down at the blossoming red spot on his chest. "The fuck," he said. This was followed by some coughing and gagging noises.

And then he started to wobble, knees buckling, and then he was on the pavement, moaning. "Shit shit shit," he said, becoming quieter with each utterance. The gun he'd been holding slipped from his fingers and settled on the pavement next to his thigh with a dull metallic clatter.

Gerhard must have caught me noticing the gun, as he immediately bent over, picked it up, looked at me, and said, "I don't think so." He went over to the Audi and tossed it through an open window onto the passenger seat.

"And now you," Andrea said, looking at me.

"I had *nothing* to do with this," I said.

In my head, I was reciting a mantra. *Hold it together. Hold it together. Hold it together.* I'd seen two people shot to death this evening. I wasn't sure a mantra was going to cut it.

"You know where we can find this Lucy?" Andrea asked.

Not at the motel, I was betting. And if not there, I had absolutely no fucking idea where she would have gone. I'd set eyes on her only twice. Once when she was leaving her house, and once more when she brought the suitcase down to Stuart.

But what I said was "Maybe."

"Maybe?"

"I know what she drives. She's got a Kia. A little silver one. I'd know it if I saw it."

"I guess now that you've told us that, we'd know it if we saw it, too."

I wasn't very good at this.

"She might go back to her house," I said.

"We know where that is, too. And dumbass Stuart here just told us where he lived."

Gerhard said, "We don't need him."

I took a look at Stuart. No more moaning, no more breathing. The pavement was black with his blood.

"There's nothing in that backpack, is there?" I said. They said nothing. "You were always going to kill him."

"We don't like people holding our stuff for ransom."

"Sure, I get that. He was a piece of shit. He was blackmailing me for something I didn't do. For something bad that didn't even happen to him, but had happened to someone else, and—"

"Did I ask?" Andrea said. "Do I strike you as someone with an inquisitive nature?" She gave her partner a quick look. "Let's try the Eastway in case she's still there."

Then she looked my way and raised her gun. "Sorry, pal," she said.

So here I was again. Staring death in the face, just like eight days ago with Mark LeDrew. I'd been able to talk my way out of that one, but I didn't see that happening this time.

I thought of Bonnie and Rachel. That I wished I'd told Bonnie it was time to change all the smoke detector batteries, a task I always took on. That the property tax bill was due this week, that I'd meant to do it but I'd been so stressed it had fallen through the cracks. Thought about Rachel's upcoming birthday, how she'd been begging us to take her to the Mystic Aquarium so that she could see a beluga whale, and that I hoped Bonnie would still take her even if I couldn't be part of it.

You can think of a lot of things in the split second before you're going to die.

And then we heard the car.

A squeal of tires first, like someone taking a corner too fast, followed by the gunning of an engine. Not a throaty, sports car kind of sound, but a regular car being driven beyond its normal limits.

It was coming south on Viscount at probably fifty or sixty miles per hour in what had to be no more than a thirty zone. Headlights on, heading straight for the Sound.

Andrea lowered her gun and turned to look.

"Shit," she said.

The car—it looked to be an SUV, actually, probably a Lexus—was soon going to run out of road, and the driver knew it, because suddenly the SUV braked hard, the tires screaming, no doubt leaving long rubber streaks on the road. It had slowed to make the turn into the

Walnut Beach parking lot, but was still going too fast, looking like it might topple over as it made a sharp right in our direction.

I recognized the vehicle. It was Trent's Lexus. And if it was him behind the wheel, I was betting Bonnie was with him. She'd have received the text, figured out it had to be me.

The driver did some quick correcting to keep the vehicle from going into a roll, and once the SUV was back on a straight path, it headed our way.

Far off in the distance, I heard a siren. Maybe more than one.

In the intermittent light that was cast across the windshield of the Lexus, I made out Bonnie in the passenger seat next to Trent. The car slowed to a stop, the headlights aimed straight at the three of us, the Audi and the pickup.

"Who the fuck is that?" Gerhard asked.

Andrea wasn't going to wait for introductions. She'd turned the gun away from me and was aiming it at the Lexus.

FIFTY-NINE

"Faster!" Bonnie said.

Trent was hunched over the wheel like an octogenarian driving through fog. "This isn't a Ferrari."

They were almost to Walnut Beach. But that text Bonnie believed to be from Richard didn't exactly go into detail. Was he out on the pier? Was he on the beach itself? They could already be too late.

Don't let your mind go there.

"Over there!" Trent shouted, pointing.

She looked. At the far end of the parking lot she saw what looked to be a pickup truck and a black car and at least three people standing around.

"That must be them!" Bonnie said. "Has to be!"

Trent hit the brakes. If he didn't slow way down, he'd roll the car making the turn into the parking lot. He still ended up taking it too quickly, and the steering wheel whipped back and forth in his hands once he'd made the turn, and it took a moment for him to regain control. If Bonnie was at all worried that he was going to get them killed, she showed no sign.

"It's Richard!" she cried.

Trent saw him, too, standing there by the black car with a man and a woman. Trent had been crossing the lot at a good clip when he thought better of it and slowed to a crawl.

"What are you doing?" Bonnie said.

"We don't know what we're getting into here. We've found them, we know where they are. We should wait for Marta and—"

Bonnie shouted. "She's pointing a gun at—"

The windshield shattered. Bonnie screamed as shards of glass littered the dash and fell into their laps.

Trent cranked the wheel hard and hit the gas.

"Goddamn you, sis," Marta said under her breath as she ran for her car.

Bonnie had never listened to her when they were kids, so why, Marta asked herself, should things be any different now? But this was a life-or-death situation, and Bonnie had no idea what she might be getting herself into. Marta hoped, if she put on the siren and broke every Milford speed limit, she could get to Walnut Beach before Bonnie and the principal.

She got in her car and tore out of the Lodge High parking lot without telling anyone where she was going, but once she was on the way she got on the radio to tell the dispatcher that the suspect in the school shooting might be at Walnut Beach, but that any cars responding would need to exercise extreme caution.

Once she'd made her call, she wondered whose phone Richard—if it even was Richard—had used to text Bonnie. They'd never found Billy Finster's, nor had they been able to track it. Marta was also thinking about those chicken wings that had been left at the scene, how the manager at the wing joint said a guy driving a pickup truck had waited for them at the shop.

Maybe, Marta mused, Billy Finster's killer was Herb Willow's killer.

She was on Viscount now, heading south. Once she had passed the seniors residence on the right, she was able to get her first view of the Walnut Beach parking lot. Something was going on. At that far end sat a dark car and a pickup, and midway in the lot, heading in that direction, was the Lexus she'd seen Trent and Bonnie driving away in.

She heard what sounded like a muffled gunshot.

The Lexus veered wildly.

SIXTY

Richard

I t all happened very fast.

Andrea fired at Trent's car, shattering the windshield.

Bonnie. Please, God, don't let it have hit Bonnie.

Trent cranked the wheel hard to his left, steering toward the water. The car did a complete turnaround and zoomed off in the opposite direction, but came to a stop a few seconds later. Did that mean Trent had been shot? Had Bonnie been shot and he'd stopped to see how she was?

Gerhard's attention was on Andrea and the Lexus, which gave me an opportunity to do something I'd been wanting to do for some time:

Run.

Lanes of parking in that lot were divided with mini-boulevards adorned with tall trees, so I had intermittent cover as I ran, moving right and left, thinking, bizarrely, of that old Peter Falk–Alan Arkin movie *The In-Laws*, where Falk offers advice on dodging gunfire: "Serpentine!"

While my route might have looked haphazard, I was heading for Trent's car to see whether, and how badly, he and Bonnie had been hurt. I glanced back over my shoulder a couple of times to see whether the drug dealers were in pursuit.

They weren't coming after me. They were jumping into the Audi.

Gerhard was getting in on the driver's side, Andrea hopping in next to him. She barely had the door closed before the car started to move.

Someone else was coming to the party.

A dark unmarked Dodge Charger police cruiser—the kind Marta drove—was wailing its way down Viscount, lights flashing.

I was still running for Trent's car, and was relieved to see Bonnie bailing from the passenger side.

"Bonnie!" I shouted.

She turned and looked my way as the Audi went screaming past me, heading for the exit.

Trent was out of the car now, too. Worried Andrea might try shooting at them again, I yelled as loud as I could, "Get down!"

Bonnie dropped. Trent ran to her side of the Lexus and threw himself over her. But Andrea wasn't worried about them and took no shots in their direction as the car continued heading for the exit.

There was a problem there.

The Charger had screeched to a stop and was positioned sideways, blocking the Audi's path. Someone was leaping out. It was, as I'd suspected, Marta. She was running toward the Lexus.

The Audi altered course and started gunning straight for her, engine roaring.

Marta had drawn her weapon, grasping it in both hands, arms raised.

She fired off three shots before she had to dive out of the car's path. She went flying off to the right, landing on one of the grassy medians, the gun slipping from her hand. The Audi kept going and smashed hard into the side of the unmarked police car with a thunderous shriek of metal on metal.

I was still running.

Trent had crawled off Bonnie and was on his feet, and by the time I got there Bonnie was upright, too. Neither of them appeared to be injured. Bonnie threw her arms around me, but there wasn't time, not yet, for any kind of joyous reunion.

The Audi passenger door swung open and a dazed Andrea staggered out, gun still in hand. She took a moment to get her bearings and fired a shot at Marta, who was scrambling across the grass, looking for something.

Her gun. She'd lost her gun. When it flew from her hand, she hadn't seen where it landed. She managed one quick look at Andrea, and there was a microsecond of recognition.

I could barely read Marta's lips. "You bitch," they seemed to say.

Andrea was running from the parking lot and toward the beach. More sirens became audible. A cruiser was speeding down Viscount.

Bonnie, Trent, and I ran to Marta. I helped her to her feet, but her eyes were on the ground, scanning it.

"My gun!" she said. "It flew out of my hand!"

She turned her head, caught a glimpse of Andrea running off into the darkness.

"Trent," Bonnie said.

"Huh?" he replied.

"Give her yours!"

Trent must have brought the gun he was known to have kept locked in his office desk. He looked hesitant about handing it over.

"Trent!" Bonnie shouted.

He dug into his jacket pocket, brought out the firearm, and held it out to Marta. She gave it a quick look, appraising it, snatched it out of his hand, and ran.

"Keep looking for the gun!" I said to Bonnie and Trent, and then I ran to the Audi. I knew there was another gun in there, and if Gerhard was still alive, he might be looking for it.

I reached the open passenger door. The airbags had deployed, and partially deflated. The windshield was a spiderwebbed mess, and there were glass shards throughout the front of the car. Gerhard's head was resting on the steering wheel. I wasn't about to touch him to get a better look, but he appeared to have taken a bullet in the right cheek.

There was no reason to worry about him. But the gun Stuart

had used to shoot Herb was down in the passenger footwell, and I grabbed it.

And did something I knew even then was very stupid. I went after Marta. She didn't have any backup, not yet, and I didn't want my sister-in-law out there alone.

Marta was shouting over the sound of the waves breaking against the shore. "Stop!" she cried. "Stop!"

At the other end of the beach, flashing lights. There were more police coming from the opposite direction. If Andrea kept running that way, she'd be handing herself to them.

My eyes having adjusted to the darkness some time ago, and with the help of a half-moon and a clear sky, I could make her out, pumping her legs about fifty feet ahead of Marta. She'd reached the base of the pier and, clearly having run out of alternatives, started running toward the end of it.

What did she think she could do? Swim to freedom?

I could hear her footsteps on the wood decking, then Marta's in pursuit. I'd reached the point where the pier met the beach, but was hesitant to go any farther. Just as well.

There were more shots.

Marta went down. At first I was worried she'd been shot, but she was taking a defensive posture. She flattened herself onto the deck, arms outstretched in front of her, and aimed at the silhouetted figure that was almost to the end of the pier.

And fired.

Andrea went down.

It was over.

Or so we thought.

SIXTY-ONE

Three days had passed since the shoot-out at Walnut Beach, and Detective Marta Harper was still mired in paperwork and loose ends and plenty of departmental oversight and second-guessing. That was what you could expect when you shot and killed two people and got your cruiser totaled in the process.

She'd been taken off regular duty and put on the desk while all the circumstances surrounding that night of mayhem were scrutinized. A bunch of armchair quarterbacks, the lot of them, she thought, but she'd been around long enough to know this was the way things always played out.

Even more upset than Marta was her wife, Ginny, who was outraged at how much bullshit Marta had to endure for doing her job. She was also a total wreck about how close she'd come to losing Marta, and not for the first time in the last week, either. It was all Ginny could do not to talk Marta into taking up a less dangerous line of work. Lion-taming, for example.

Even though she was off the street this week, Marta had learned a great deal about what had led to Walnut Beach.

What was known: Gerhard Waldheim and Andrea Falluci, who worked for a fentanyl-producing operation in Mexico, distributed product to various dealers in the Connecticut area, and even sold some of it to line their own pockets, were dead.

Gerhard died behind the wheel when Marta fired at the Audi as he tried to run her down. Moments later, Marta had brought down Andrea during the pier shoot-out. Andrea, Marta already knew but had since confirmed, had sold that deadly dose of fentanyl to Cherise Fowler, and was the one who'd assaulted Marta outside of Jim's. And the bitch was still wearing her Converse sneakers when she'd shot her.

Stuart Betz, a somewhat dim-witted, but dangerous nonetheless, friend of Billy Finster's, was fatally shot by Andrea while attempting to sell back a carry-on bag full of drugs he'd swiped from Finster's garage. He'd been blackmailing Richard over something that had allegedly actually happened to Finster, although there was no evidence to suggest Richard had done anything to anyone. (This was from Richard's account, of course. Marta could not question Finster or Betz for further clarification.)

Betz shot and killed Herb Willow when he'd interfered with Betz's plan to force Richard to do the exchange with Gerhard and Andrea.

Oh, and Marta found her gun. It had landed in the grass near the base of a tree.

Finster's wife, Lucy, whom the police had been searching for, walked into the station voluntarily the day after the Walnut Beach event and asked for the detective in charge of the investigation into her husband's death. She had quite a story to tell, and was able to fill in some of the blanks.

After she'd found Billy's body, she'd gone on the run, fearing she might be next. She hadn't seen Billy murdered, but assumed Gerhard and Andrea had done it.

Lucy sought out Stuart, thinking she could hide out with him until things cooled down. She told Marta that Stuart had always planned to double-cross Gerhard and Andrea—to keep the money and sell the drugs himself and shoot the two with the gun Billy had recently acquired—and that she believed the drugs were still someplace in his apartment.

That checked out. Marta found the drugs in pillowcases stashed in the closet at Stuart's place.

Lucy admitted knowing Billy was helping smuggle drugs into the country through his airport job, and added that an orderly at the Bridgeport hospital where she worked, a man named Digby, also knew. He'd been threatening her—he'd already sexually accosted her—with violence if she did not steal from the cache and give it to him. She did.

That part checked out, too. The candy-like fentanyl was found in the top of his locker. Digby was arrested. The hospital fired him.

The local district attorney didn't think there was a solid enough case to charge Lucy, and there was a host of mitigating factors, like Digby's threats of violence and fears of retaliation from her husband had she gone to the police about his role in the drug operation. Lucy said she was going to move back to Utah to live with her mother and look for work in some other cafeteria. A school, a hospital, didn't matter. Cubed Jell-O was pretty much the same everywhere.

Despite the DA's decision, there were parts of Lucy's story that never sat well with Marta. Digby, for example, had said she was lying, that he'd been framed, that she had a key to his locker and had planted the stuff. And when Marta got back to Lucy about that, she'd said, "Yeah, well, what would you expect him to say?"

She was a crafty one, this Lucy, Marta thought. But she didn't think she'd killed Billy, which was the big, outstanding riddle. Not that she'd written off Lucy as a suspect completely, but her gut said it was someone else.

It made the most sense that Gerhard and Andrea had killed him, but a ballistics test of the bullet that killed Billy did not match the weapon Andrea used to kill Stuart, or shoot at Marta. Nor, after a test was conducted, did it match the weapon Richard took from the crashed Audi.

Marta theorized that it could have been Stuart. He was, according to Lucy, mightily pissed off his friend hadn't cut him in on his profits from helping the drug smugglers. He'd been at the garage that night, and the gun he'd used to kill Herb Willow was one Billy had bought. He could have shot Billy with his own gun, except there was a problem there. That damn ballistics report again. Billy was not shot with his own gun.

Which brought Marta back to Richard and Bonnie.

They both had a motive. They had both been to the Finster property that night.

Marta didn't want to think it could be either one of them. And where the hell would her sister or brother-in-law get a gun? Okay, admittedly, getting your hands on one was not exactly like trying to find the Holy Grail. It was easy enough, but seemed so out of Richard and Bonnie's wheelhouse.

But Billy's death sure helped Richard. There was no getting around that. Could he have killed Billy before realizing he had the wrong guy? And once Bonnie'd been brought up to speed by her husband, she had a motive, too. She'd never been face-to-face with Billy. She wouldn't know she had the wrong person.

Shit.

Marta wondered how much trouble she was facing for not immediately disclosing that her sister and brother-in-law were, at the very least, persons of interest in this case. She should have withdrawn from it. She knew that. The best excuse she could come up with was that things were happening so quickly, she hadn't had time.

Maybe Ginny would get her wish. Maybe Marta wouldn't be a cop all that much longer.

And this morning, when Chief Constance Barnes wouldn't look her in the eye when she entered the building, she had a feeling things were about to come crashing down around her.

Shortly before ten, Barnes came over to her desk and asked her to accompany her to one of the interrogation rooms. When she got there, she saw a man from the Internal Affairs Department was already in a chair. She'd met this guy before. Stanley Dinkins was his name.

"Have a seat," Barnes said.

Marta sat.

The chief had a sorrowful expression on her face as Dinkins opened a folder that sat on the desk in front of him.

"Look, before this gets underway, I can pretty much guess what you're going to say, so there are some things I'd like to clear the air about," Marta said.

Barnes and Dinkins waited.

"When I learned my brother-in-law was being blackmailed by someone claiming to be Billy Finster, whose murder, as you know, I was investigating, I should have immediately stepped back and let someone else handle the investigation. I didn't. That was wrong. My only excuse is developments were happening at such a rate I felt turning it over to someone else could have hampered things. It's entirely possible my personal connection compromised my judgment. If that means I'm subject to some sort of disciplinary procedure, I accept that. If you want to fire me, well, that's also your prerogative. My wife would be delighted. So, anyway, that's my statement. I'll answer any questions you have about that."

The room was quiet for a moment.

Finally, Dinkins spoke. "That's not what we're here to talk about, Detective. What we want to talk about is Billy Finster."

Marta blinked. "Okay."

"What previous encounters have you had with Mr. Finster?"

"Previous encounters?"

"That's correct."

"None."

"You'd never met Mr. Finster? Never had any interactions with him at all?"

"No. I mean, none that I know of. Maybe, when I was still in uniform, I pulled him over for speeding or something, but no, I have no recollection of any dealings with Mr. Finster."

"You're sure."

"That's what I'm saying. The only time I ever got near him was when he was dead."

The chief and the Internal Affairs guy were quiet.

"What's this about? What's going on?"

Chief Barnes stepped in. "Detective," she said, "we've read your report, we've been through your statement about everything that happened Tuesday night, but there's something that leaves us somewhat puzzled. You're sure there's nothing you've already told us that you'd like to amend?"

"Nothing."

"Because we've been doing our due diligence," the chief said. "Checking everything, going over every aspect of what happened." She sighed and said to Dinkins, "Can you pass me that ballistics report?"

Dinkins slid a sheet of paper across the desk to her.

"Which ballistics report is this?" Marta asked.

Barnes looked at her and asked, "We're wondering if you might find it curious that the bullet taken from the woman you shot at Walnut Beach is a match for the bullet taken from Billy Finster."

SIXTY-TWO

Richard

"Another beer?" Trent asked.

I'd already had two and was okay for now. I was feeling, more or less, pretty good. The swelling on the right side of my face had shrunk and the bandages on my neck and forehead were gone. Bonnie was on her second white wine spritzer. Trent's wife, Melanie, had just brought it out to her on their backyard deck. Bonnie took a sip and proclaimed it to be perfect.

So here we were again, gathered together early on a Friday evening in the wake of another catastrophic week. There had been a funeral that afternoon for Herb Willow. We'd all attended. His elderly mother was there, but it wasn't clear that she had any real sense of what was going on, or even understood her son was dead. It was all very sad. Fortunately, she had a sister in Vermont who was going to either take her in, or arrange for her to be moved to a seniors' residence up her way.

Trent had invited Bonnie and me over to talk about the future. Neither Bonnie nor I had been back to work all week, and Trent believed we both qualified for stress leave. At first I was inclined to fight him on this, but Bonnie had urged me to reconsider. I knew she wanted some time off. While she hadn't been abducted at gunpoint, she'd been through a hell of a lot that night.

We all could have died.

This time, we'd offered to bring some steaks for Trent to throw on the grill, and Rachel had been left with Mrs. Tibaldi, once again, for the evening. Trent and Melanie's daughter was at a friend's house for a sleepover, so it was just the four of us.

"I'm feeling a little tipsy," Bonnie said.

"I've been there for a while," Melanie said. I wasn't keeping track, exactly, but I had a feeling she was on her fourth spritzer.

"Maybe you should go away," Trent suggested, firing up the barbecue. "Paris or someplace." The steaks were sitting on the plate to the side.

"Yeah, well, that's kind of costly," I said. "Maybe something this side of the Atlantic. San Francisco or L.A. or San Diego. We could take Rachel to Disneyland. We've never been to the West Coast."

Bonnie nodded. "We couldn't go for long. Two weeks is about the max I'd ever want to take Rachel out of school. She can't afford to miss any more time than that."

Trent was scraping down the grill with a barbecue brush.

"You could get some lessons in advance," Melanie said.

Bonnie shook her head. "What kind of trip would that be for her, and us, if we have to spend time doing homework? No, I'm not crazy about that. I don't know. Maybe we just need some time at home, do things locally, go into Manhattan. See some shows, go to museums. Rachel would love that. Anything to make us forget, even for a while." She looked at me. "If you can even do that."

"Won't be easy," I said. "And there's still things we don't know, that we're never going to know. Like, who really molested two—or maybe even more—Lodge students? Mark LeDrew's mother said someone assaulted him, and Billy Finster was evidently victimized by somebody. He'd told Stuart Betz about it, and Betz used that story to go after me. Hate to speak ill of the dead, but I've wondered about Herb. Or maybe Anson. And there's still Ronny, although I don't have anything more than a feeling about him."

"Ronny," Trent said, shaking his head. "He'll drink himself to death before the truth's ever known."

He had stopped scraping the grills and was now examining the barbecue brush. "The bristles are coming off this thing," he said. "Last thing we want is little bits of metal in our steak."

"Didn't you buy a new brush?" Melanie asked him.

"In the shed," Trent said. "I got half a dozen of them."

Melanie looked at Bonnie and smirked. "Trent never fixes anything. He won't even let things wear out. Battery dies in his watch, he buys a new one. Gets a hole in his sock and he throws it out."

"Well, hang on," Bonnie said. "Who darns socks anymore?"

Melanie turned to me. "Richard, are you sure you wouldn't like another beer?"

"You talked me into it," I said.

Trent said, "Back in a sec."

He stepped off the deck and headed for a metal garden shed located in the back corner of the yard. I decided to accompany him. As we walked across the yard, I said, "I'm worried that if I take a leave of absence, in about a week I'll be bored anyway and want to come back."

"Maybe," he said. "So ask for three weeks or something like that. Honestly, I think you should take the rest of the semester."

We'd reached the shed. He slid a metal door to one side and we stepped in. It was crammed full of gardening and other implements. Various rakes and shovels hung from hooks on the wall. Two battery-operated weed trimmers. I was guessing one had conked out and Trent bought a backup. There was yet another barbecue in here, the lid and supporting structure rusted with age. Bags of fertilizer and topsoil. A wheeled spreader for distributing grass seed or weed killer.

And three lawnmowers.

There were two gas-powered ones tucked toward the back that didn't look to have been used lately, and an electric one within reach. A coiled extension cord lay on the floor next to it.

My eyes were on the lawnmowers. I couldn't stop looking at them.

"You know me," Trent said. "Like Melanie said. Something breaks down, I just buy a new one. Gotta admit, I'm a bit of a hoarder. I never get rid of the old stuff. I have this delusion that one day I'll get around to fixing it. Oh, here we go."

He'd found the new barbecue brush, still in its cardboard packaging, the price tag still dangling from it, hanging from a nail tapped into the wall.

I wasn't aware Melanie had followed us out.

"Here you are, Richard," she said, and I turned around to see her standing there with a beer in her hand, beads of moisture bubbled on the cold bottle.

I guess she must have seen what had caught my attention and laughed.

"I guess it's no wonder that sad boy was always calling Trent the lawnmower man."

SIXTY-THREE

"You're right, I've explained this," Marta said. "That wasn't my gun I was holding when I shot at the woman. The car was coming at me. I dived. My gun fell out of my hand. I couldn't find it. It was dark. This Andrea woman was running away, was armed, had already tried to shoot me, she was a risk to anyone she might encounter, and I needed to pursue her. Bonnie—my sister—told Mr. Wakely to give me his weapon."

"Tell us about Mr. Wakely," Barnes said.

"He's the principal at Lodge High. He was at the school when Stuart Betz shot the teacher, Mr. Willow. I'd been at Bonnie's house when the call came in that there'd been a shooting there. And of course my sister was worried it was her husband who'd been shot, so we raced to the school. Once we all knew more, Mr. Wakely offered to drive Bonnie home."

"Go on." Dinkins, the Internal Affairs guy, this time.

"This is all in my report on—"

"Go on," he said again.

"On their way, Bonnie received a text she believed was from her husband, saying he was at Walnut Beach. We converged on the site. The rest you know."

The chief was nodding slowly. "I know you've been waiting for a ballistics report on the Finster shooting, whether it was a match to anything else. That happened this morning. It landed on my desk before it went to you, and when I saw it, I thought, what the hell is going on?"

Marta didn't say anything for a moment. Then: "The day Mark LeDrew came to the blow up the school, Wakely acknowledged he kept a gun locked in his desk, in case a shooter ever came through the doors. He had it out, was ready to use it on LeDrew, but didn't when he saw the dynamite, the guy's thumb on that button." She paused. "Jesus Christ."

"What?" asked the chief.

"He didn't want to hand it over," she said.

"What do you mean?"

"When Bonnie was telling him to give me the gun, he didn't want to," Marta said. "He had to be thinking, if it got fired, there'd be a ballistics test . . ."

She stood.

"Are we done here?" she asked Barnes and Dinkins.

They nodded.

Marta left.

SIXTY-FOUR

Richard

I had to force myself to look away from the lawnmowers and give Melanie a smile. I held out a hand and took the beer from her.

"Thank you so much," I said.

I couldn't look at Trent. I didn't *want* to look at Trent. All I could think about was how, when I first told him how Mark LeDrew had gone on about the "lawnmower man," Trent acted as baffled as I'd been. He pretended to have absolutely no idea who LeDrew might have been referring to.

And then there was what LeDrew's mother had told me, earlier on that evening when all hell broke loose. How Mark had been abused by someone at the school, someone he would only refer to as the "lawnmower man."

It was Melanie who'd mentioned that there was a summer when they'd hired Mark LeDrew to maintain their property while they were away. He'd been here. He'd been in this utility shed.

I exited the structure and started walking back toward the deck, getting ahead of Melanie. I took one sip from the beer and set it on the patio table. Bonnie could read my expression and see that something was wrong.

"What is it?" she asked quietly.

"We're leaving," I said.

"Why? What—"

"Richard!" Trent shouted. I glanced back, saw him coming out of the shed with the new barbecue brush in his hand. "Wait up!"

When Melanie reached the deck, I turned to her and with a look of apology on my face said, "I'm so sorry, but we have to go. Bonnie just got a text that Rachel isn't feeling well, so we're going to have to pick her up."

"Oh no, that's terrible," Melanie said. Trent was at her side now, an excessively jovial smile on his face.

"You're leaving?" he said. "I won't hear of it."

Melanie said, "Rachel's sick."

Bonnie, reading the signals, tried not to look confused, stood up from her chair, and played along. "That's right. We're so sorry."

"You must take the steaks home with you," Melanie said. "Let me wrap them up."

"It's okay, really," I said. "Enjoy. You can make it up to us next time."

I didn't think there would be a next time.

Bonnie and I made our way through the house, heading for the front door, Melanie and Trent trailing us.

"Why don't you bring Rachel back here," Trent suggested, his voice on the verge of pleading.

"I think she'll want to go home," I said.

We were out front now, by the car. Melanie, all smiles, giving Bonnie a hug as she got into the passenger side, expressing hope that Rachel would feel better soon, you know how kids are, they can be sick to their stomach and an hour later devour a hot dog, and while that was happening Trent was following me to the driver's side, trying to engage with me.

"Richard," he said with quiet urgency. "I think you may have gotten some idea into your head that's wrong."

I shook my head. "I have to sort some things out." I was behind the wheel now, turning on the engine. My window was down and Trent wouldn't give up.

"Please, come on, we should talk," he said. He leaned his head in so only I could hear him. "I know Rachel's not sick." And then, "What I did, I did for you."

Whatever the hell that meant, I wasn't waiting around to find out. The car was in reverse. As soon as Bonnie got in, I took my foot off the brake, backed out onto the street, and sped off.

Bonnie was clearly waiting for me to explain myself, and when I didn't say anything, she said, "Talk to me."

I focused on the road ahead. "Something's not right," I said. "I haven't quite put it together, but something's not right."

"What? Tell me?"

"When I get home, there's something I have to check." My mind was racing. "Something Stuart said." I paused. "If I find it, if I can clear this up in my head, I'll explain."

"And just for the record, you didn't hear from Rachel? She's not sick."

"She's fine, far as I know," I said.

"We could pick her up on the way home anyway."

"No, I have to do this thing. When we get back, you can go get her."

Bonnie decided she'd pushed hard enough. We were home a few minutes later, and once I had the front door unlocked, I gave the set of keys back to Bonnie and she drove off to Mrs. Tibaldi's.

I went straight to the kitchen, where we had a laptop on the counter, plugged in and fully charged. I disconnected it, brought it to the table, flipped it open, and brought up Chrome. I entered some key words into the search field to find local news video reports about what had happened at Lodge High School the day Mark LeDrew blew himself up.

Stuart's entire blackmail scheme was based on a false premise. He thought I was the one who had sexually abused Billy Finster. They'd been watching TV. The news item had come up, a shot taken from the street at a moment when I and other members of the staff had been out front, talking to the police.

Only one station had sent a video team to the school in time to catch a shot of us in person, in real time. It was aired by a Fox affiliate in Hartford. When I found the segment on the station's archived news items, I clicked play.

A woman was standing in front of the school, mike in hand. Across the bottom of the screen were the words SCHOOL BOMB-ING AVERTED. Captured in the footage were Marta and some uniformed officers. There was me, bandaged, a quick glimpse of Herb Willow. Ronny Grant was there, too, but they were all quick, almost impossible to recognize unless you already knew who you were looking at.

"*It could have been much worse,*" the reporter said. "*The would-be bomber, a former student whose motivations remain unclear at this time, ended up taking his own life, perhaps accidentally, but not before threatening to come into the school and kill an undetermined number of people. Police said . . .*"

More general footage. A broad shot of the school. The woman talking into the camera.

"*. . . from here we can see teachers and administrators from Lodge High, including some of the staff we believe stood up to the bomber and persuaded him not to come into the school. Much credit goes to this teacher here.*"

There was already a close-up on the screen of Trent, without any identifying information, like his name, at the bottom of the screen, but the second she said "this teacher" there was another close-up, again unidentified, of me.

That was how it must have happened.

Billy said something like "That's the guy," when Trent was on, but by the time Stuart looked, I was the one on-screen. And then he'd gone to Billy's high school yearbook and picked me out like someone in a police station's catalogue of suspects.

Trent was Billy's abuser. And Mark's, too. Maybe Billy had sloughed it off in a way that Mark couldn't. Billy hadn't shown up at the school with a bomb, and Billy hadn't blackmailed me. But Trent had done Mark a more serious emotional injury.

Shit.

I heard the front door open. I called out: "Bonnie! In here! I found it!"

When she didn't respond, when Rachel didn't come running into the kitchen, I knew something was wrong. I was getting up from the table when I saw Trent standing in the doorway. He was red-faced and out of breath. He must have hopped in his car seconds after we'd left.

"Trent," I said.

"I should have just said something at the beginning," he said. "When you told me Mark had been going on about a lawnmower man, I should have said, yeah, that was his nickname for me, and come up with a reason for why he had it in for me. But covering it up, that was my mistake, wasn't it?"

I stood there.

"It wasn't my only one," he said. "I should have gotten rid of the gun. I shouldn't have had it with me. Bonnie and her big mouth, telling me to give it to her sister. I'm worried that might be a problem. I haven't been able to sleep since that night, like waiting for the other shoe to drop. You have to understand, Richard, that what I did, part of it was for you. It wasn't fair, you being victimized that way by that Stuart Betz guy."

I didn't quite understand, but the tumblers were slowly falling into place.

"It made no sense to me," he said. "Why would Billy be going after you when you never did anything to him? Yeah, I believed you when you told me you were blameless, because it was me." He looked down to the floor briefly, sorrowfully. "After you told me you were being blackmailed, you came to the office looking for those yearbooks. I asked Belinda about it, she said you were trying to track down Billy Finster."

"You went to see him," I said slowly. "That night."

"I never meant . . . he had a gun. I found him in the garage and asked him what the hell he was doing, putting you through that ordeal, what was he thinking? He said he had no idea what I was talking about, and we know now he really didn't, but at the time . . . He grabbed the gun and started waving it around, threatening me, and what he didn't know was, I had my own. Ever since Mark came to the school, I'd been pretty freaked out, was carrying it with me everywhere I went."

"You killed Billy Finster," I said.

"I ended up doing you a favor," Trent said, and managed a wry smile. "I'm not expecting a thank-you or anything, but once he was dead, your problems kind of went away."

That prompted a laugh from me. "Oh yeah, they just vanished. Everything's been fucking great since then."

"I'm sorry," Trent said. "I'm sorry about all of it."

"How many boys were there?" I asked. "How many did you take advantage of? How many did you assault?"

He couldn't look me in the eye. "Not . . . that many. I tried to keep it under control."

I thought back to that fateful Monday, how Trent had tried to get into position to shoot Mark LeDrew.

"You wanted to shoot Mark," I said. "When you saw him, you had to have a pretty good idea what his grievance was. He had his list, but you had to rate pretty high on it."

"No," he said vehemently. "He could have killed all of us, if he'd had the chance. It wasn't just about me."

I thought I noticed some tiny movement, something out of the corner of my eye, on the floor behind Trent. It was there, and then it was gone.

"I don't recall you ever filling in to oversee the wrestling team," I said, taking a step closer to him.

"A few times," he admitted. "When you, or Herb, weren't available."

"That was when you assaulted Billy. Was that a one-off? But with Mark there was more, wasn't there?"

"He was kind of a lost kid," Trent said. "I tried to help him. I tried to boost his confidence. Took him under my wing. His father didn't give a shit about him. Had high expectations Mark couldn't begin to meet. The boy was looking for a father figure and I wanted to be that for him."

"You exploited that need."

"I know . . . I know what I did was wrong, but I was good to him. I . . . I gave him work. Paid him well for looking after our place that summer. I . . . I came back a few weekends, alone, when I knew he would be there. So I could spend time with him. Mentor him."

He said it like he almost believed it. I could guess other ways he boosted that boy's confidence. With free beer, maybe, video games, companionship. All to get what Trent actually wanted. I took another step in his direction. We were no more than four feet apart now.

"Does Melanie know?" I asked, "About your extracurricular interests?"

I saw that movement again. I saw what it was.

He shook his head. "I've been a good husband to her. I'm a good father."

"You're a parasite," I said. "You used your position of authority to exploit a student. Everything that's happened, all of it, finds its way back to you. Your abuse of Mark, how it tormented him and drove him to consider something horrific. The subsequent mix-up that led to my blackmail, to Finster's death, to Herb's. All of it has its seeds in your sickness."

Trent reached into his pocket and brought out a small handgun and pointed it at me. I was surprised to think the police had returned to him the weapon he'd let Marta use.

"It's not the same one," he said, as though reading my mind. "You know I like to have backups of pretty much everything."

"What's the plan, Trent? Kill me? Then Bonnie when she gets home? You going to kill Rachel? Will that cover your tracks? I doubt it. Like you said, you've been waiting for the other shoe to drop. When they connect your gun to Finster's death, it'll be all over."

Trent's hand was shaking, but the gun was still leveled at me.

The thing that I'd seen was now crawling up his pant leg. A weird-looking bug. A three-inch-long stick with long, slender legs. Some kind of praying mantis, I thought. Its long legs were taking it higher and higher. I remembered Ginny putting it into a jar for Rachel when we went to visit.

"*It's mean to keep things locked up,*" she'd said. "*They should all be set free.*"

"I could disappear," Trent said.

"If you're going to do that, you hardly need to kill me."

"I'd need a head start. A few hours."

"They'll find you," I said. "It's time to pay for your sins."

I stopped looking him in the eye, and instead focused on the creature that was nearly up to his belt. Eventually Trent would have to look, would have to know what had caught my attention.

"You were always a good friend," he said. "I don't want to have to do this."

I said nothing. Instead, I stayed focused on the praying mantis.

Trent finally had to follow my gaze. He glanced down at his side, saw the creature, and acted as I had hoped, and expected, he would. Rachel had told us how freaked out he was about bugs.

"Fuck!" he said, and swept his left hand down, swatting the bug, knocking it from his belt and to the floor.

I only had a second.

I charged him, grabbing him around the waist and bringing him down to the floor. I reached for his right arm, got both hands around it between wrist and elbow, and slammed it onto the floor once, twice, three times, before the gun shook loose from his hand.

I scrambled over him to grab it, landing on it as though it were a live grenade I was trying to save the rest of my unit from.

Trent scrambled to his feet, and instead of attacking me to get the gun back, he bolted, heading for the front door.

I didn't want to chase him with the gun. He was unarmed now, there was no need to shoot him as he fled. But I didn't want to leave it lying on the floor, either. I picked it up and quickly placed it on a high cupboard shelf, atop a stack of plates.

And then I ran out after him.

He was standing in the front yard, hands in the air. Marta's unmarked cruiser was at the curb. She was out of the car, standing by the front bumper, hands clasped around a gun she had pointed at Trent.

"Don't move, Mr. Wakely," she said.

Driving up the street and coming to a stop behind the cruiser was Bonnie. She got out of the car and was about to open the back door for Rachel when she saw her sister training a weapon on my boss.

We all heard a rumbling.

One of those huge dump trucks was making its way up the street, the driver taking a shortcut once again through our neighborhood between the construction site and wherever he was taking all that landfill.

Trent saw it, too, and when the truck was only two houses away he dropped his arms and darted into the road. His timing could not have been better.

The driver hit the bullhorn not a millisecond before Trent ran in front of the beast, the bumper knocking him down like he was made of straw. The truck didn't come to a full stop until the right front tire had rolled over Trent and ended whatever life might have been left in him after being hit by the bumper.

I ran to Bonnie, who was standing there, hand to mouth, eyes wide.

I scooped up Rachel from the back of the car, pressing her head down onto my shoulder so she wouldn't be able to see what had happened, and then the three of us went into the house where we would start the hard work of getting our lives back to normal.

I was thinking, Trent was right. We needed a break. Maybe a trip up to the lake. We'd take the boat.

ACKNOWLEDGMENTS

I would definitely be ruined without help from a great many people.

First, as always, a thank-you to readers and booksellers. I would be nothing without your support.

In the UK, I am in debt to the team at HQ: Charlie Redmayne, Lisa Milton, Kate Mills, Claire Brett, Sarah Lundy, Emily Burns, Alvar Jover, Georgina Green, and Anna Derkacz.

At HarperCollins Canada, a big shout-out to Leo McDonald, Lauren Morocco, Cory Beatty, Neil Wadhwa, Brenann Francis, Shamin Alli, and Melissa Brooks.

At William Morrow in the US, thanks go out to Liate Stehlik, Tessa James, Jennifer Hart, Emily Krump, Lisa McAuliffe, Kelly Cronin, Rachel Weinick, Andrew DiCecco, Kerry Rubenstein, and Dave Cole.

For representing my interests, I am grateful to Steve Fisher at APA, The Marsh Agency, and especially Helen Heller, who has been with me from the get-go.

Finally, a nod to a group of professionals who are historically underappreciated, underpaid, and far too often under attack: Teachers. Bless you. I don't know how you do it.

ONE PLACE. MANY STORIES

Bold, innovative and
empowering publishing.

FOLLOW US ON:

@HQStories